DUSKLIGHT FALLING

DUSKLIGHT FALLING

OTHER WORKS BY PATCH KOLAN

Ghosts of Dreaming (Screenplay)
Age of Darkness: Final Stand (Game by PlaySide Studios)
Various Print and Online Publications

For Mikaela.

PRAISE FOR DUSKLIGHT FALLING

"Dusklight Falling, Patch Kolan's assured literary debut, is a pulpy delight, brimming with striking imagery, engaging characters and spectacular set pieces. It immerses you completely like a detail rich RPG but with a surprisingly robust sense of emotional connection and pathos. Frankly, it's a little bit obnoxious that any first time author's novel is this good but there you have it."
  ~ Anthony O'Connor (*Straya, Emma After*)

"Dusklight Falling is a thrilling fantasy story full of horrific beasts, and honourable heroes. It's clear that the author has a deep love and appreciation of the genre and has built a world worthy of readers to adventure in."
  ~ Steven "Bajo" O'Donnell

"A strong debut from a bold new voice in Australian fantasy."
  ~ Christian D. Read (Lark Case Files, Nil-Pray)

HAVROHD
MINOVARH
ATHERON RANGES
YRKANH
DORMANSTAR
REEDSRUSH
RIVER MARSHTIDE
WESTERLING TRAIL
SOLUMBRYA
CAPITAL CITADEL
COUNTY KEEP
DAWNPORT
SOLSETTER ISLES
ELSTEMER

Contents

~ ACT I ~

CHAPTER 1

OUTSET

When Tyel Branson was eleven, he broke his left leg in two places.

He knew the fault was his. He carelessly careened down the steep slope of loose shale and pebble and into the winding dry ravine. His horse, Fellstar, a mellow black gelding, caught his ankle and momentum rolled him sideways. Tyel rolled with him, of course, then fell beneath. It happened slowly, and then all at once: a disorienting sensation of upended gravity. In a dizzy panic, carried downward, his feet caught in the stirrups his family bound and wrought, the leather straps holding his short legs close.

The pain of impact exploded down his side as his ankle snapped like dry timber and his thigh bone was driven against worn river stones. His head followed course with a rattling, dry smack that blinded him momentarily. He could feel warm blood in his scalp, running down his ear, matting his brown hair. The sting did nothing to distract from the excruciating pain unlike anything he'd ever experienced.

In protest as much as pain, he screamed bloody agony at the sky, far enough from home as to be too far from anywhere at all. He pulled himself out from beneath his horse, feeling every tiny movement unbearably magnified.

Poor Fellstar lay sideways, thrashing, his long skull obtuse and crying—his own ankle bleeding and broken. Branson knew they were both in a very bad situation. His hot tears matched the intense burn of Sol; the Solum God laughed at his foolish child-ways. Fellstar would surely be put down. His father, Dain Branson, had warned him Fellstar was a workhorse – bred for toiling down roads and passages, not hills and ravines. Tyel had assured him he'd stick to paths. He'd known this was a lie as he'd agreed.

As soon as the cobblestone roads of County Keep transitioned to unsurfaced, compacted dirt, he'd spurred Fellstar on, and his energetic but sensitive companion had dutifully complied. He'd passed the small farmsteads and watermills, until the land gave way to vacant, untilled fields, feeling chaff and long grass whip against his cloth pants.

He would make for the dry ravine and ride through it like in the tales of great adventurers charting the unknown. Great adventurers always leap ravines and forded rivers, he'd thought. They forged their own paths. They certainly didn't let their fathers tell them what to do.

Now, his own path had led him here, and down.

He crawled in until-now unthinkable levels of pain, under a hot and indiscriminate sun, until the thin fabric of his pants stole away in strips and snags on greedy root and stone and bramble.

He crawled so long that the pain took on a familiar kind of pulsing rhythm to the extreme bursts of ache. His head reeling, he had a funny clarity that came with this exertion: Tyel realised that, even in the most crippling of situations, any fear of punishment his father might administer was still preferable to a slow, lingering death. He wanted to live. To survive was like the thirst he felt: a natural ache that needed to be satisfied above all else. He would not let himself die in a ditch. He would fight for himself.

Day turned to afternoon. He did not know how far he had crawled, only that Fellstar was far from him now; the squealing braying had long since subsided.

When he finally slipped from consciousness, he was grateful.

It was full-dark and bitingly cold when he awoke to the sound of dogs barking. His first thought was of wolves, but even in delirious pain, he knew they were rare this far south. Branson's dry throat elicited a croaking yell, which was just enough to bring attention his way. When he'd not returned that evening, his father and brother of just seven, Dilain, had picked up his scent and come to save his life that night. He would not have lasted much longer.

Tyel slipped in and out of conscious awareness on that ride back to the homestead. Time passed by in blinks and smeary, dragging runs. Every clop of hooves sent a new jolt of pain ricocheting through him on the return.

Laid out on one of his family's workbenches, later he would recall a small man with funny eyes forcing him to imbibe something caustic and bitter that took his agony and smudged it away. He slept there, on that hard surface, for weeks.

He lost weight. He lost track of time.

He lost his horse.

And in amongst all of this, he lost his sister, Carille Branson, to the Red Flux.

It was a terrible time for his family; it was a brutally unforgiving season of injury and death and the lingering pain and loss that come from both.

He could not attend his sister's burning, and for this he felt guilt and profound relief. He had been to the ceremonies before and they were grim and solemn things. She was so little; so little to burn, bound to the the golden ring of the circuitris – the symbol of the dominant faith of the land.

Work took place around him; his family's forge kept him warm and he watched with great fascination the creation of ingots and the hammering and manipulation of iron and steel into tools and attachments and weapons of war.

Through an open window high above him, the Lunum in the night sky shrank away and grew again. Days became months.

He would study the sturdy ceiling beams of their forge, counting iron nails and knots in the dark wood, reading the occasional book that was brought his way.

Tyel slowly regained his strength. It took many more months before he could put his full weight on that leg.

His friends visited for a time, then lost interest as the weeks carried on. Eventually, they stopped coming altogether. Tyel didn't mind; it was almost harder to know he couldn't join them in their days. Part of him wished time would stop altogether until he could rejoin his family, his community. By season's end, the days were cooler and the nights longer; work in the forge – the distraction that had become his whole world – had slowed, as illness ran through the towns and trade diminished.

Looking back, Tyel noted this year as the end of his childhood; he knew it. His family would need him to work – to ride again (a thought that tightened his chest), to begin to make deliveries and carry his own burdens. And in his heart, he knew he must be something of a burden to them. His father and brother, even at the height of their misery over the loss of little Carille, brought him food and drink and changed and washed him. They carried off his waste and loved him. He loved them all. His mother, Calisto, turned morbid. He missed his mother's smile. He could not blame her. That darkest year had left a mark on all of them.

Tyel carried his mark within for years to come; a permanent dull pain in his ankle and hip were solemn reminders of poor choices and odd fortune.

And here he was. Back on a horse – one he refused to name, his cart loaded with goods to be delivered and, crucially, food and water to keep him alive.

He took no risks now; he had responsibility. Six years of making amends will change a person's outlook, he supposed. He had his friends and his health – the pox had thankfully long since diminished in the lands.

Now, at seventeen, Tyel felt happy again. He felt pride. Many seasons had passed, and things were turning around for his kin. Dilain was riding now, occasionally by himself, though sticking to the path. His father, Dain, had regular work smithing essential items for the Capital and regional territories – a blessed order from the councils beneath the High Inquisitor himself. It was a tremendous honour to craft weapons of war for the Blessed Legionary Guard.

The sun shone down between clouds, warming his shoulders as the steady tock-tock-tock of his cart's iron-banded wheels rolled along. It was here, on the road north toward Reedsrush, that he found himself thinking back on the end of his youth and the start of his own tale.

His horse plodded along the path. There would be no fording of rivers today.

It was, however, a good and fine morning to be alive and out in the world. Tyel took a deep breath of sweet, clean air and looked to the cloud-banded horizon and the pale sky above.

On this cheerful morning he would discover that the residents of Reedsrush were missing.

~ ~ ~

This far north, the weather tended towards hazy, but in high-summer, the Sol would break through the mountainous peaks surrounding the lands of Solumbrya from early in the morning. Warm, dappled light speckled the southern farming lands with orange and gold, as the small hamlets and villages, some of thatch, some of clay and stone, woke to start their day. It was a peaceful life and an honest one: tilling soil, harvesting crops, raising chickens and sheep and cattle. Fishing, logging, brewing and trading. Raising families and keeping the spokes of the wheels of their carts in fine order.

Then, like that, the peaceful routine was over and gone – with the disappearance of every person in Reedsrush, an unremarkable village nestled in along the river Marshtide. Man, woman, child – vanished, seemingly instantaneously. Woven baskets dropped to the cobblestone, bowls of stewed barley and oats half-eaten, scythes left to rust in fields only partially hewn.

~ ~ ~

Tyel was tasked with delivering two anvils. He'd left County Keep, to the south, on a horse-drawn carriage the evening before. He'd slept well enough, piled beneath blankets and sheepskin in the cart itself.

Though he knew the ins-and-outs of running the family forge, he was still merely an assistant in his family's trade, in truth. It fell to Tyel to fetch the barrels of unrefined ore, to break down the components that would be smelted in the forge's flame-belching guts. That was fine by him, mostly. His younger brother, Dil, helped him, which he appreciated – but not today.

He generally did the deliveries unaccompanied – mostly farming implements like backhoes, horse shoes, tongs, shovels, mallets. Occasionally, his mother would tan leather and inlay the soft, oiled hide with patterns and symbols, using a hammer and metal stencils that his father had carefully crafted. The leather sold well enough and had innumerable uses, but even if they didn't, he could tell his mother loved the practice.

This was trade in peacetime; there was little demand for arms and armour when the lands were at rest. Still, sometimes, he'd get to handle the special orders. Those were the pride of his family; the intricately formed, carefully hammered plates of fine armour, and the worked and reworked edged weapons stamped with the Branson Smithing emblem: a curvaceous 'B' over simple crossed daggers, tips pointed downward and away.

These two anvils, as simple as they were, carried a high price. By weight alone, such items would be as prized by their new owners as a fine set of armour. In essence, these anvils enabled them to create their own. It had taken many turns of the Lunum to fire, hammer, form and finish each one. They would outlast the town that received them – they were damned near indestructible. The Branson "B" would live ever more, inlaid on each anvil's base for countless unknowable generations to come.

As Tyel rounded the familiar hill-bend into Reedsrush, he spied a woven bushel of red apples strewn carelessly in the path. There was an uncomfortable stillness in the cool morning air.

The ride had been sun-soaked, but now the clouds were rolling in; the beams were struggling – and failing – to break through the heavy rolling sheet of cumulous. It was quiet, too. No grey finches chirping, no rustling of green leaves. Only the gentle, repetitive clack of his horse's hooves, the creaking axle and the clapping spokes of his cart.

Tyel gently pulled the reins and slowed his cart to a standstill, before hopping off. He picked up an apple and examined it for a moment before allowing himself to absorb the situation. Nothing and no one stirred.

His stomach, however, growled. Tyel drew a bone-handled dagger, one forged, folded and hammered by his father, barely longer than a paring knife, and sliced a wedge from the apple. His pack horse, a brown and white colt with a docile temperament, eagerly ate the wedge from his hand. Branson cut another thick slice, ate it, and fed the remaining half to his hooved companion.

He thought of Fellstar for a moment. He had long since stopped naming the work-horses. Fellstar had been the last.

He returned to his cart. He didn't like the feeling in the air; it would be best to make his delivery quickly and return home, he considered. He picked up the remaining apples and returned the basket to the side of the cobbled path – figuring it a sort of payment-in-kind for the apple he'd taken – and continued down the road.

The drop-off location was a small workshop owned by a family he'd never met, but one his father had worked with in seasons past. Tyel rolled slowly down the road. He was relieved to see the orange glow of a hearth through glass windows; the flickering of candles on a table. And yet, no people. Perhaps they were in worship? The village would not have an elaborate Solum Temple – rather, likely a humble shrine with enough space for handfuls of villagers to gather and pray. Perhaps they even had a Lunum shrine tucked away somewhere.

The main road through the village forked as he passed a small waystation and signpost. He knew from instructions to veer left and head toward the far end of the town. The broad, occasionally hilly grassland was sparsely wooded out this way – cleared to feed the town's own construction needs, fuel their workshop furnaces and heat their homes. It made a perfect spot to set up their own blacksmith's forge; the clang of hammers would be far enough from sensitive ears to avoid incurring the wrath of grey-hairs and young parents.

A small wooden lean-to sat next to the makeshift blacksmith's workshop – itself a sturdy construction of brown and grey stone. It too showed no sign of life.

"Hello?" Tyel called out, breaking the off-putting silence. Nothing.

He turned to his horse. "How am I going to unload these? I better find *someone*, horse." His hoofed companion snuffled softly, and Tyel gave his muzzle an affectionate stroke, before uncoupling the horse from the cart. It might be a while before he found someone at this point; might as well rest his mighty steed. He led his horse to a thick mound of long, green grass alongside the lean-to and looped the leather rein over a crooked wooden post.

The cart sat, sagging slightly under the weight of the anvils. Tyel frowned. He would have to muscle them off somehow. Would that even be possible? Perhaps – very slowly. He sighed and started toward the rear of the cart. *And then what?* he pondered. *I can't very well spend all day trying to wiggle these into the workshop.*

He rapped on the door of the workshop and listened for any sound within.

What he heard came from far off, but loud enough that it rang in his ears for a moment. Tyel's blood turned frost-cold. He looked around, his vision narrowing as fear pumped through him.

A screech. Something akin to the squealing of a hound, but higher in pitch.

The sky had begun to turn dark now; the cloud line had snuck up like a pickpocket, stealing the sun's warmth. Now the edges of the grey sky were skirted in a purple veil, creeping up from the northern mountains, above the far-off pines and twisted treetops. Blue and hazy sky had become sackcloth.

The stillness of the air put Tyel's nerves on edge. Even the slightest movements pulled at his attention.

There came another screech – shrill and inhuman. Closer. The yellowing fields beyond the town rippled as a gust of cold wind blew through the expanse.

His horse whinnied and began to tug at the leather, and Tyel knew at once he no longer wished to remain in this village even a moment longer. His father would tan him, but he was going to have to leave the cart – unpaid and unreceived. He would have to work for a month unpaid, maybe two, in order to repay the iron – and then there was the cart to consider.

He sighed, weighed his options and shook his head. *The day had started off so well, too,* he mused.

Tyel unhooked the horse's bridle from the wooden post and guided her away from the lean-to. He took one last look at the cart and, with a pit in his stomach, pulled himself into the saddle. He was going to catch hell for this.

The thought crossed his mind to break into the small homestead and search for coin, but he shook the notion away as he gently spurred his horse back onto the road. Maybe he could come back with Dilain and retrieve the cart and payment tomorrow.

The sky was ringed with inky purple now; cloud cover seemed to swirl above the village. *Not a soul in sight, even now,* Tyel thought.

The wind picked up as Tyel began to gallop back through the village. Tree limbs swayed and shutters slapped against the sides of simple homesteads. Everything seemed in motion, but lifeless just the same. The wind tugged at the world around him, creating ripples of distracting movement in all directions.

As he turned to look over his shoulder at the empty stretch of village one more time, the attack came from above and in front.

Tyel's horse squealed in shock as it took the inertial weight of something fast and skeletal, like a malformed human with too many eyes and far too many teeth. It moved with the speed and viciousness of a rabid hound, diving upon them. Tyel shouted as he fell from his saddle, his right leg caught in the stirrup, causing him to swing down painfully onto his side.

It all happened so quickly, but that deeply buried sense-memory of falling off and beneath Fellstar in the ravine came reeling back. So too did the curious, nauseous sensation of his world quickly flipping upside down. Then, as the pain of his impact set in, Tyel wiped grit from his face and opened his eyes – though he could not believe what he was seeing. *A corpse? No. A boneskin, a shade? A beast of some kind—what was this?*

Tyel's steed had fled by now–some ways further down the road.

Gasping through the pain, he struggled to right himself. His old injury flared angrily – but this time, his leg held true. He raised his eyes and his stomach dropped away.

There, in front of him, wide-set jaws opened. Within, rows of thorn-like teeth, washed in crimson film, like oil splashed in lamplight. The stench of decay and coppery blood filled his nostrils.

He scrambled backwards on his backside, hands scraping against the rough surface of the road. Images of creatures flooded his mind's eye, nightmares from his youth told to him by his nan at bedtime – and by his friends playing by the riverside. It had terrified him then – but he knew the days of the old horrors were gone; driven from this land by the power of the Solum God, or so some believed. Nothing of the kind could exist anymore–so the Inquisitors and Priests had assured them. And yet—

And yet, there were horrors, still – and this one was in front of him, as real as the sharp, stinging cut he could feel on his cheek.

Strega.

The too-many ember-red eyes of this strega, focused and faintly glowing, locked on Tyel's as it shrieked the mocking cry of a predator who knows it has already won. Wolf-like, it scurried toward him on bony arms like dried branches, closing in on the young man.

Tyel grasped at his waist – *the dagger!* – and pulled it from its leather sheath.

The strega dove, slick as ice, on top of him, moving to pin his limbs.

Exposed as he was on his back, Tyel moved to strike at the horror. Any cut would do, anywhere – a moment of space between them to gather himself and get off the ground – a deep cut was all he needed to afford him time. A moment.

The strega slapped his hand aside as if it were no more than an irritating fly. The dagger flew from his grasp and landed somewhere off behind him. Gone.

The stench of decay was overwhelming, but Tyel's free hand instinctively pushed the strega's chest away, as its open jaws snapped at him. He could feel the slick, rotten thin skin under his palms, bony ribs portruding through the torn linen that it wore, barely draped.

With a grunting cry, Tyel lifted his leg and arched his knee up between them, trying desperately to keep the strega's clawed fingers away from him. He could feel them digging into the flesh of his upper arms. He screamed, and, with a sudden thrashing kick, sent the strega backwards and off him, tumbling in surprise by its prey's sudden burst of fight.

He had been gifted a moment of respite, by the gods perhaps, and he would not squander it.

Heart pounding and breathing raggedly, Branson scrambled to his feet. His side seared and shrieked – surely a broken rib, remembering the agony from a childhood fall from a tall bluewood tree. That kind of pain leaves an unmistakable and indelible mark in a person's mind.

Tyel's hazel eyes darted across the ground behind him, scanning for his dagger. He could not see it – and he was running out of time. He dared not take his eyes off the strega a moment more. It was back on all fours and angry as a cut serpent.

The road was littered with fallen tree limbs.

Tyel limped across the road and dove upon a long, straight branch, about as thick as thrice-corded rope, and pivoted towards the strega. He had his moment and made his choice. He prayed it was the right one.

The strega leapt at him.

Tyel braced, hands tight around the twist of wood. This time, on his guard, he readied himself for the impact, leaning forward on his front foot. He let out a cry.

The strega was on him again, sending him backwards and onto his side. The branch snapped like a dry bone.

He was left holding a broken jag of wood and nothing more. But that was all he needed. Instinct brought his hands back up, and, this time, his thrust found a pocket of unprotected flesh – deep in the strega's neck. It shrieked in surprise and pain; black blood poured from the wound as Tyel pulled the makeshift stake from the strega's throat.

The strega pulled back slightly, one hand clutching at the gushing wound. Tyel stabbed again, deep into the creature's recessed eye socket, as the gore-coated jag found new purchase. As hard as he could muster, Branson drove the stake deeper, a second hand joining in, leaning his weight into it with a gasping shout.

And the strega toppled backward with a spasming, choking garble and a dusty thud.

For a moment, there was nothing but Tyel's heaving chest and pounding, relentless heartbeat in his temples. Icy wind blew, but the rush of cold air barely registered on his skin. His chest was thudding like a war drum. He scrambled back, waiting for another dance with the undead horror.

Blood from his cut was running down his cheek; the sting of air against it cut through the adrenaline surge.

There was only stillness now. Tyel lay on his back, propped up on his elbows in the dirt, looking at the beast over his heaving chest, still not quite believing, but there it was. A blackened slick of blood was pooling around the head of the monster.

He let himself look upon this monstrosity that had nearly taken him off this plane of existence. A horror indeed – a deformed being, roughly Branson's own height, but half the weight. A corpse transformed into a thing of pure mayhem. A *strega*. No one would believe this. Surely.

He needed proof. He needed his dagger – and his horse.

The wind had begun to subside now. The sky, hazy though it was, had begun to lighten, it seemed to him. But the town remained as still as a crypt – and now Tyel began to suspect why.

He brushed his palms, dirtied from the scrambling onslaught, and examined his arms. His riding gloves, with their long leather cuffs, had prevented the worst of the injuries, but the strega had pierced his upper arms with its claws. His ribcage made each breath agony. Something felt very wrong with his ribs.

He was alive, however, and wounds would heal in time. The strega was dead. It was very much time to leave.

Tyel's dagger had slid under brambles, down into a ditch by the roadside. He retrieved it and kept it raised. Were there other strega watching? Waiting for him to lower his guard? He shuddered to think. He'd barely survived one encounter – a second one would surely be his end. If there were others, he dared not stay to chance fate.

He winced as he crouched down by the stinking corpse of the strega. At first, he considered removing the head. But the idea of riding with it back into town turned his stomach. No. he needed something small, but unmistakable.

A hand. He could stow it. And a tooth. He could pry one. The dagger sliced into the beast's wrist.

As carefully as his tired muscles could afford, Branson removed a few pieces of the strega; he could stow the hand in his satchel for now, though the blood reeked like death – and it would certainly ruin the leather. He slipped two fangs into his breast pocket for safe keeping.

He thought of the cart and anvils – and then of the strega hand. Perhaps his father would understand now; perhaps he would even reward him somehow. He would know by sundown – if he could get there by then. The ride was long and riding would be painful now, which meant slow-going.

Farther down the road, his senses caught the movement of his horse. The creature was far smarter than he, he smiled darkly – it had run when it had first-chance. But at least it hadn't fled far. He thought of whistling to it, then cursed his dull mind. He needed to keep low and get out of there without attracting any further attention. His steed shied from him as he approached, but relented to his reassuring touch.

The farther he wandered from town, the clearer his head became; it seemed as if the warmth had drained from his skin when the strega had pinned him. But the sun, though mostly obscured behind the din of cloud, was beginning to shine through.

When he began to ride, galloping fast, only the sharp, stabbing pain of his rib and the wafting smell of the strega's decaying hand kept his mind alert. All he craved was home and safety and sleep – but he couldn't let his guard down. Not even for a moment.

He sensed dark eyes falling on his movements from afar, like a stain on his soul.

There are more of them here, he thought, and tightened his grip on the rein. With that, he spurred his ride and turned south once more, following the beaten path of the Westerling Trail.

His horse knew this route by now; they'd ridden it countless times. As a main trade route, it accompanied other trade vessels up and down the River Marshtide in a slow and winding run toward the southernmost lands of Solumbrya. The wide river waters, at times as wide and calm as an enormous lake, were dotted with ships here and there. Logs, and loggers with them, floated south from the foot of the Atheron Ranges, ready to be milled into timber for the capital.

In the distance, he passed fisherfolk on their shallow netting vessels, their canvas flapping, lit gold in the reflected sunlight. On the Westerling, he nodded to bearded farmers in carriages and carts not unlike the one he had abandoned back north.

As the day wore on, he endured long stretches of nothing much at all, aside from the chirping of insects in fields of grass and thickets of twisted trees. If anything, there seemed to be fewer traders on the road today than usual.

Though the sky remained hazy, the sun was already beginning its descent by the time he reached the forked valley pass that marked his half-way point.

He had packed enough water in his skin for the day, but not enough to see him through much more than that. The pain in his side had slowed him; part of him sensed that even his horse had grown impatient with the lax pace. He uncorked his drinking bladder and took a long swig. He poured a little into his grazed palm, then, carefully so as not to spring another crimson leak, wiped the dried blood from the side of his cheek. The cut sang out in response. Tyel looked down at the rivulet of pinky-brown as it ran down his shoulder.

The valley fork was a low-slung intersection wide enough for three carts side-by-side. The road split around a natural sandy cliff face topped by a squat stone tower, topped with red clay tile shingles around a central raised lamplight, much like a lighthouse, that would burn from sundown to sun-up. Within, it housed a rotating posting of Citadel guards.

Branson took a painful breath and pulled on the reins once more. His horse complied and snuffled as it slowed to a stop.

The missing villagers. What did this mean? A strega – maybe many more.

He was holding proof of this creature, this horrible wretch – if indeed it was a strega, for there were many kinds of abominations in the Eld Age, it was said. Whatever it was, it had tried to kill him and, be it through sheer dumb luck, or maybe a tiny shred of survival instinct, he'd managed to dispatch it.

Going home seemed irresponsible now. He needed to tell – someone. Anyone. He needed to do something productive with this information. He looked up at the guard outpost, with its winding stone steps carved in a thin spiral. Hemmed by tufts of olivine and yellow-leafed trees, the barbican surely housed Citadel guards. Even those on what had to be a lowly assignment at this intersection north of the Capital, seemed better than no one.

Tyel wiped his brow. He didn't relish climbing those steps.

He climbed those steps anyway.

CHAPTER 2

INQUISITOR

High Inquisitor Boff Fendrigar felt the sting of the day's repentance as it bled into his finery. It had been a prayerful day. His backside was raw, and his cravings were much sated. Tonight, he supped with a clean conscience.

He dabbed at the corners of his downturned mouth with the edge of the table cloth and pushed his over-large bowl away. The evening's sup was fine, he supposed, but surely the right hand of the Solum God deserved more than the same bland boiled beef stew three nights going. He sat back in his ornate oak chair, which groaned under his weight as he shifted, feeling his skin stick to the fabric. *If only my Solumbryans knew how I bleed for them; how I suffer for Solum God's graces and good fortune,* he mused. He drummed the end of his engraved soup spoon a few times against the table top.

"Servant. Servant! The next course."

A spindly robed figure emerged from his perch at the side of the darkened room. The air was heavy with woodsmoke and sweet incense, which parted as the servant approached the High Inquisitor.

"Your Grace," came her small voice. "The kitchen sends its apologies. There will be no sweet course this evening."

The Inquisitor looked aghast. "What? How can that be?"

"Well, Your— Your Grace," she stammered, "It seems there's a resupply issue. Our cane sugar has run out."

"Outrageous!" The Inquisitor slammed his bulbous, ringed fist on the table, sending fine silvered cutlery scattering. "We have provisions for months!"

"I, I apologise, High Inquisitor. We are experiencing something of a shortage. Several of our suppliers – their farms – have gone quiet."

"Gone quiet? What are you blathering about, girl?"

A cold streak ran up the servant's spine, which had nothing to do with the chill of the stone-walled room. "Shall I see if the kitchen can prepare a fruit course?"

The Inquisitor "Tsk. Such fools, your kind. Fruit is a blasphemy after dark. One should never consume the sweet seed of the land after the sun has set. You know this."

"Yes, your Worship," The servant uttered meekly.

"See yourself to the Central Command. You will tell them you are to receive ten lashes, that the lesson is learned and the sin repaid in blood."

The girl's blue eyes widened. Their soft luminance hid threatening tears.

"Y— Your Grace! Please! I merely—" She stepped backward, sleeved arms raised in protest, exposing a delicately-featured face, pale in the dull light of the supper room's candles and hearthflame.

The Inquisitor shifted forward and rose to his feet with some difficulty. His fine crimson and white silk robes, lined with gold detail, were dotted with remnants of this evening's meal. A splash of red wine ran down the centre of his chest like an open cut.

"Go!" he bellowed. "*Now.*"

She turned to walk towards her punishment. Reaching the tall double doors, the girl turned and looked behind her at the formidable mass of the High Inquisitor, his round, red-robed body backlit by the fire light. Perhaps it would be possible to lay low this evening – or tomorrow, and perhaps His

Grace would forget. It was *possible*. His Worship was decidedly reactionary, but his follow-through was decidedly lacking at times.

Just as she reached out for the golden handles, the heavy double-doors flew open. She stepped back just in time to avoid being struck as three Holy Guards pressed into the room. The middlemost guard she knew to be Ser Bolfred Filip, Knight Commander of His Grace's Anointed Protectorate. His ageing, lined face looked grim.

The Inquisitor flinched at the sudden entrance. "Ser *Filip*." He practically spat his name back at the Knight Commander. "Your intrusion is most unwelcome. I am beset by the tribulations of fools. And now another approaches during my resting hours."

"Your Grace, my apologies. Please know, I do not wish to add to your pressures," he frowned. "However, we come bearing ill-word." Ser Filip swallowed hard. He had learned to ignore the High Inquisitor's barbs over the many long years of his rule.

The Inquisitor shifted uneasily. Food shortages, dark tidings – he did not like this. Not one jot. And no sweet course? This he took as a personal affront. He did so like his sweets before turning in. '*Sweets afore sweet dreams*', as it was said. Why would the Solum God punish him further after today's vigorous repentance?

"Your Worship, you may wish to be seated." Ser Filip offered a hand as he approached the Inquisitor, who brushed it aside.

His eyes narrowed to slits and his thick nostrils flared in opposition. "*Don't* invite me to sit in my own residence, Ser," he growled. But, after a moment, he took the opportunity and sat back down with a heaving grunt and folded his arms.

"Go on, then."

"Your Worship, we have received disturbing words from the Northerling and Westerling communes." Ser Filip stepped forward, his plate steel pauldrons catching the firelight, the filigreed sun emblems of his faith gracing each shoulder shining like two cat's eyes. "It appears a threat is emerging; we believe, from within the forests north of Dormanstar."

"You say it appears. *Appears*. Appearance and truth are seldom sameways." He drummed his fingers on the table cloth. "So too are beliefs."

Ser Filip nodded, unphased by the Inquisitor's dismissal. "*Strega* have been sighted, your Grace. And worse, we believe. If this is true, and we have reason to think so, then this is of grave concern to the realm."

The Inquisitor stroked his round, dimpled chin for a moment, eyeing the men in front of him.

A clap of laughter burst from deep in his prodigious chest. "You bring me nonsense and superstition, Ser!" He relaxed his posture slightly, leaning back. "Our holy army obliterated the last known strega four generations ago! The shining Grace of the Solum God has protected these lands unabated for many years! I refuse to believe this – this *impossibility*."

Ser Filip shifted uncomfortably, carefully weighing up his next words. The Inquisitor was not a fool – just arrogant in ways that grew from being sheltered and extremely hard-headed. He would have to make him see reason.

"Your Grace, while I respect your faith and reason, we bring you proof."

At this Ser Filip turned to his two guardsmen and nodded. At once, they parted the double doors. Standing just beyond the threshold, illuminated by torchlight sconces in the waiting hall, was a thin figure.

"Enter, boy," Ser Filip called out. Dutifully, Tyel Branson entered the room, head slightly bowed as if pulled down by the sheer gravity of the evening's events, but his eyes were levelled ahead.

Tyel took in his surroundings for a moment, shocked at the opulence. The Sept of the High Inquisitor was a holy space – safe from darkness, and certainly the innermost rooms were a mystery to all but the most central figures of the land. Tyel had never seen such stark wealth. Even the carpet beneath his boots felt plush enough to sleep upon. The smell of food wafted in the air, and rich spices he'd never encountered before. Why they had allowed him to enter these chambers he could only speculate. Perhaps they did not wish to handle the strega's hand themselves, he guessed.

Ser Filip walked to Tyel and pulled him through the chamber by his upper arm, towards the long table. The Inquisitor made no acknowledgement of him at first, then, looked him up and down, with a sour expression.

"Ser Filip, who do you bring before me now? This is most inappropriate."

The Knight Commander stiffened. "This is Tyel Branson. He hails from a smithing family from County Keep, by the river northeast. They used to supply our arms and armour in years past. Little more than workshop toolmakers in these times, but times are what they are."

Tyel felt that jab; what did Ser Filip know of it? His family – his father – needed income. Hammers and tongs paid for fishes and bread. There was no shame in that.

"Yes, yes. I don't need his life story." The Inquisitor squinted and leaned forward. "How old are you, boy?"

"Seventeen, Your..." He searched for the word. "Highness?"

Ser Filip corrected him. "You shall address him as your Grace or your Worship." Tyel nodded.

"Seventeen, Your *Grace*." Tyel observed the rotund figure seated before him. 'Grace' was not a term that particularly suited this man, he thought, suppressing the urge to smile.

"You look thin. Do they feed you in – where was it? County Keep?"

Tyel was taken aback. "Yes, your Grace." He supposed he would look underfed by comparison. Most would.

"Hm. Fine, fine. Ser Filip, why is the son of a Blacksmith in my private hall at this hour?" The Inquisitor was rapidly losing interest.

Ser Filip prodded Tyel's side with a crooked elbow. "Show him."

Carefully, Tyel tucked his hand into his breast pocket, pulling out two long, white fangs. The Inquisitor leaned forward, squinting down at two yellowed slivers, like dried bramble thorns.

"Bone needles. Or thorns." The inquisitor appeared almost amused. "Is this supposed to rattle me? A trifle. Someone is planting stories out there, Ser Filip, and you are jumping at them."

"They're *teeth*, your Grace." Tyel let them fall from his hand onto the lace tabletop. "I pulled them myself."

"Your… fangs… could be from any beast. A large hound, perhaps."

"The boy speaks true, your Grace." Ser Filip interjected. "We believe these are strega fangs. Observe the central hollow and the small cavity at the root. These mutations are unique to strega. It is how they draw up lifeblood, like a reed siphon. It's quite extraordinary."

"Your Grace," Tyel continued. "There's more." He looked down at the hard-won teeth for a moment and, with more composure, opened his side satchel, a simple tanned leather fold-over.

He upended the satchel. Out came the severed grey hand of the fallen strega, landing on the table with a rounded thud. Blackened blood had run down the long, knurled fingers, drying here and there in painterly streaks.

At once, the Inquisitor's disinterested eyes became like saucers on his Lunum face. He gasped and recoiled, throwing himself into the straining seat, and nearly toppling over backwards.

"How *dare* you! How dare you befoul this sacred space with this… this… darkness!" He turned his thick neck, as best he could manage, and held the backside of his hand over his eyes. 'Unclean! Most *unclean*!"

Tyel and Ser Filip exchanged looks as The Grand High Inquisitor's over-dramatic response seemed to break whatever air of tension had existed. "Branson, best you stow these," Ser Filip suggested. Quickly, Tyel scooped the two teeth and the curled hand, dropping them back into his soiled leather satchel.

Ser Filip motioned him to step away with a sweeping hand, before turning to the Inquisitor. The Inquisitor's displeasure, though explosive, subsided immediately. He dropped his hand from his face, peeking his eyes back towards the table before gingerly returning to a semblance of composure.

"Servant! Servant!" The hooded girl, who had been watching this whole, baffling affair from the corner nearest the entryway, hurried over, head low.

"Yes, Your Worship?"

"See that young… Brandon——-"

"Tyel Branson, your Grace——-" he corrected, before Ser Filip elbowed him roughly.

"Yes. *Branson* – see that young Branson is also lashed for his… utter befoulment… of this sacred space." He took a strained breath and closed his eyes, as if performing a complex calculation. Let's see. Twenty lashes. Yes, that should suffice."

Tyel's mouth opened to object, but Ser Filip held his hand up and shooed him back again. "Don't disobey. Go."

"And boy," The High Inquisitor called across the table in a low tone, "You will put this right. This is not over." Once more, he banged his fist upon the table.

Ser Filip pressed the issue. "Can we not send for the Battleblessed, your Grace? Surely a potential threat such as this warrants summoning a specialist party to venture forth and surmise the situation."

"Those withered relics? Don't be preposterous!" The High Inquisitor laughed at his own wit. "No. The Battleblessed are decaying in their posts and best forgotten to the ages."

Ser Filip's already thin lips pursed even further. He disagreed of course, but he knew better than to argue when Boff Fendrigar's blood was up. He also knew, as Knight Commander, the onus would then fall to him. It was not a thought he relished.

The conversation continued, but Tyel felt the rush of blood in his ears as his resentment grew. He looked at the girl in the robes–apparently also ordered by her master to receive a flogging.

The servant's large marine-blue eyes glowed faintly in the dim light. "Come. Follow me," she whispered. "We best not stay."

The sight of those luminous irises caught him off-guard. He'd never seen eyes quite like this before. There was little time to dwell though.

Earlier, Tyel had informed the guards at the watchtower of his encounter; he'd shown them the fangs and the severed hand, his various wounds and cuts – the measure of his exchange with the beast. If it had not been for this Ser Filip, the other stationed guards might have laughed him away – or worse, beaten him further for wasting their time.

The old man, this apparent Knight Commander, had intercepted the conversation and ferried him back to the Capital Citadel, riding alongside him. They spoke little, but Ser Filip assured Tyel he had done the right thing. If it was a strega, and it appeared so, then the spread must be stemmed as quickly as possible, with the full force of the Anointed Knights at the fore.

In his heart, Tyel didn't come seeking glory or fortune or to curry favour; if anything, he felt a sense of civic duty that surprised even himself. He thought of his father, on that long road back south, of his mother and brother. They had worked so hard to keep their business alive; to keep their family together. The idea of something disrupting their lives–something he could have helped prevent–made the choice an easy one.

Now the High Inquisitor wanted to punish him? The notion was appalling. Tyel wanted to run away, there and then – he was not going to take a beating tonight for his deeds. Backwards, this was – just senseless.

The room's energy seemed to darken slightly as he turned quickly and pushed past the servant and the two guardsmen, out into the entryway. He could take a hiding if he deserved it – but he would scrap until his fists bled if someone tried to beat him for trying to warn his people of a genuine threat. He could fight if he needed to, he knew. It hadn't happened often in his youth, but he had thrown fists from time to time.

"Wait!" The girl called – and started after Tyel, who had no intention of slowing down. His hands were balled tightly.

"Fresh hells to you. And hells to this city. You're all mad as muckmen." The servant caught Tyel's arm. He wrenched it free. "I came here to help – and now your master wants to beat me."

"Wait. It's not as bad as all that. Come with me." Tyel turned to look at the veiled voice. Her hood had now slipped back, gathering at the shoulders like a tall collar. He stifled surprise.

Elfkind – and strikingly beautiful. Her overly-large brilliant blue eyes swam with the latent magical energy of her people, iridescent in low light. Elfkind were uncommon across the Elstemer seas; their people were notoriously private by nature and rarely left the southern desert. In truth, he'd never spoken to one before.

"I'm sorry," she said. "He's a… cruel man. But forgetful, I assure you. Come. I'll show you the way out."

Tyel shook his head "I *know* the way out. I only just came in. I need to find my horse in the stables."

He continued down the hall, itself as longer and wider than the most stately homes Tyel had ever seen. The length ran with the same plush and ornate carpet, and the walls were lined with oil portraits of figures Tyel assumed were of great import, but he knew nothing of them. In that moment, the whole place could burn to ashes for all he cared.

"You have your own horse?" the girl asked gently.

"It's my family's horse. And I've already lost our payload today. If I leave the horse as well, my father will flay me worse than your guards ever could."

Double-doors, all of them white as purest alabaster and lined with golden sols, ran at even intervals down the hall—each leading who knew where. Tyel thought for a moment of opening one, just for the sake of it, and taking his pick of untold riches. Even a handful would change his family's fortune.

"I wouldn't do that, if I were you." The elfkind girl followed at a short distance.

Tyel stopped. "What?" Something just happened – an indefinite feeling in his head, like a tiny burst of static in his mind.

The girl stopped mid-step.

"Oh! I'm sorry, I— I didn't mean to intrude. It's just – well, your emotions are spilling over."

"You read my *thoughts*?" Tyel blinked and took a better look at her. Her too-large blue eyes seemed to pull at his mind, like a siphon gently drawing up water. "Stop that! You're still doing it! I can feel it. I can feel you in there."

"Ah! I'm so sorry! I'm still learning!"

He looked at her, at first feeling violated, like an invisible hand reaching through a hole in the wall of his essence. But something about her intrigued him. He found himself staring at her. Her pale skin held a shade of colour that sat somewhere between sunrise pink and summertime blue. Her hair was thick, straight and straw-gold – tucked behind her long, tapered ears. He thought her quite pretty – though Branson now wondered if she could read that thought too, and he flushed and turned away. She said nothing.

"Listen, Tyel, right?" Her voice lowered to a whisper. "I'm Alyse." She bowed her head slightly.

Tyel nodded. "Tyel Branson. But you probably knew that long before I said it back there." He turned back to her. He didn't need to read her mind to know a look of concern.

"I observe many things in the Sept," she replied. "It's sort of my job. It's hard to explain. But I didn't read you when you entered."

Tyel looked again at her, choosing not to respond. "Why are you here? Why do you stay? If he's so cruel, I mean."

"I— I have to stay. This is my home now."

Her eyes met his again. *Slave.* The word shot into his mind like a dart. He felt sick. He knew of slavers from far off lands, but the practice was outlawed by the church. So why would the highest seat of power keep a slave?

"Tyel, if what you say is true—"

"It *is* true." Tyel insisted. "You saw the hand. And look at my face. I didn't do this to myself."

She was studying his face. Young in human years; brown eyes underlined with dark rings. The young man looked exhausted and beaten down, and she felt a pang of pity for him. She had read more than just impulsiveness in his mind. She had felt a deep pit of pain – and of concern.

"I believe you. And what you've shown us – it frightens me, Tyel. These are unnatural things. They were a scourge for so long – so the stories go. If the strega have returned, they carry fresh disaster – for all of us." Alyse's words were like spider silk. They clung to Tyel far longer than he liked.

Before he could finish his thought, the doors to the Inquisitor's chamber at the far end of the hall opened once again – and with the same vigour with which he entered, Ser Filip spilled back out.

"Branson. Stop."

Ah hells, what now? he thought. Was Ser Filip to administer his lashings? Surely not – he had believed him enough to bring him here.

Alyse raised her hood once again and retreated to a sconce, next to a portrait of a large man with dark eyes and an equally dark beard.

Ser Filip trundled down the hallway, his long sword's leather sheath clanging against his side with every stride. Within moments, he was alongside Branson.

"Boy."

"Stop calling me 'boy'." Tyel turned and looked at Ser Filip.

"That's what you are, aren't you? Now close your trap before I close it for you. And open your ears."

He glanced at Alyse. She was watching him, unblinking.

The Knight Commander grasped his forearm.

"You're not leaving here tonight. The High Inquisitor has made certain demands of you."

CHAPTER 3

COMMAND

S er Filip considered himself a reasonable person. As Knight Commander of the Inquisitor's Anointed Protectorate, a lofty posting to be sure, he had certain discretionary freedoms. He could determine guilt and he could determine compensation. He was a mouthpiece for the judicial rulings of his Inquisitor, but he would also hold sway over those judgments. His sword was as sharp as his council – and both could be utterly deadly.

When he joined the Protectorate, he had a full head of black hair. Now it was thin, pulled back high on his scalp and clipped uniformly short until only white roots like dry grass peeked through. *Yes, a reasonable person with discretion.* The thought lingered. *But will that be enough in the face of what is coming?* He closed his eyes and sighed heavily before opening them again and looking at the young band across from him.

He removed a gloved hand and ran it back over his forehead and onto open skin where the hair of his youth was now only a touch-memory. "Branson." He looked across the mess room table at the young man, eagerly filling himself on a bowl of chunky rootstew. Dots of pale broth decorated the wooden table top.

Tyel looked up, forcing himself to swallow too large a mouthful. "Ser?"

The High Inquisitor's Anointed Protectorate was stationed in the largest of the Solumbryan capital's defensive outposts; one of eight round barbicans that lined the city walls. Within, units of young men did their best to look busy between meals in the mess and training in the inner courtyards. In peacetime, the standing army was merely a fraction of what it could swell to be, should needs arise.

"Branson, I have discussed your punishment with our Inquisitor." He spoke flatly, over the quiet murmuring of chewing mouths and clinking earthenware. "The Inquisitor believes you befouled his chambers with harrowed material. He would be right – except, these materials would not have, ah, *survived* entry into these hallowed spaces intact."

Tyel swallowed and set his spoon aside. He studied the face of the anointed Knight before him. He looked hard and tired – his eyes were sunken slightly with age and experience. He did not look unkindly upon Tyel, however.

"That is to say," Ser Filip continued, "If this creature was still materially present, body and soul, it would've been reduced to smouldering tinder. The sanctity of this space is far too powerful to be breached by tainted beings. A hand, teeth, drippings of dried blood – they present no real harm in and of themselves. Do you understand?"

"I think so, Ser." Tyel knew of the magical protections placed upon certain spaces in this realm; it was said that offices of high power, churches and blessed altars – and the Solumbryan capital, of course – were under some kind of protection from the Solum God.

"So then, by my reasonable logic, the hand you delivered was surely not a befoulment of the Inquisitor's chambers."

"Stands to reason, Ser." Tyel's remark elicited a smile from the Knight.

"It does at that, aye," Ser Filip laughed dryly. "You'd know if you were carrying powerful unholy objects. You'd be afire as much as they, by the time you crossed the threshold into the Inquisitor's Keep."

Ser Filip took a long gulp from a ceramic cup of wine.

"Of course, the High Inquisitor commanded you to be beaten – and that servant girl, too."

Alyse. The servant – the slave? Tyel pictured her large, luminous eyes again. She disappeared shortly after Ser Filip held him in the hallway earlier. She seemed to melt into the shadows – and by the time Tyel turned to look for her, as he and Ser Filip left the Inquisitor's residence, she had fully vanished.

"But you're eating now, as our guest," he continued, "And not currently being flogged with a barbed flail. So I imagine you've worked out I've spared you this outcome."

"I'm grateful, Ser. I truly only wanted to serve the realm – give warning, I suppose." And he did, in his heart, want that. But then, he also felt it fair that he receive some kind of credit for his deed – acknowledgement at least. He wanted to feel his scrape with death meant something. That it might make him *into* something – more than two working arms and a hammer on an anvil.

"*Tyel* is your given name, boy?"

"Yes, Ser. Tyel." He bristled at the boy-remark, but stifled it back down.

"Ah. Tyel. A strong name – Old Empire. Southern I believe. And your family's name is, of course, 'Branson'. A derivation. Do you know what that means?"

"Yes Ser. It refers to *'Sons of the Brand'*. We have been metal workers for many ages."

"Can you read, Tyel? And write in the Common?"

"Yes Ser, well enough."

"Good. An educated lad. The Branson name is a proud one, then?" Ser Filip asked, with a hint of underlying testing.

"I don't know about all that." He replied quietly. Tyel could feel a game being played out. He took a step to the side. "Just old."

"Sure – but are you proud of your line's accomplishments? Your family once provided fine armour to the capital. And they were paid handsomely to do so, if I know my history. You have a small landholding."

"Those days are long over." And it was true. "Those times were back before my father was born and before his father – maybe longer than that."

"Back in the days of open warfare on many fronts. Long over, thank the Solum God. Our families survived. Be proud of that family name, Branson. Perhaps you can bring to it fresh repute." Ser Filip's eyes held a sudden spark. "And do it great honour."

Tyel swallowed another bite, then set down his spoon. "What do you mean?"

The Knight Commander smiled. "Boy, I have stayed your punishment tonight. I have personally vouched for your good nature – I do hope you have a good nature. In lieu of a blood payment, you are now in service to the realm. In service to *me*, actually."

Tyel's eyes widened; he felt his pulse quicken.

"Service? What do you mean?"

This was not what he expected at all. Indeed, he knew breaking bread in the mess was perhaps some comfort to him before a whipping. He was bracing for that, but this?

Ser Filip rose to his feet. The mess hall fell into a respectful hush as dozens of eyes turned to them.

"The High Inquisitor has asked me to take on a squire. Tyel Branson, you are forthwith a squire of the Anointed Protectorate of the realm—until such a time as I have deemed your service to the realm is fulfilled."

"Wait! I— I can't be your squire! I— I have my own duties!"

"Boy, your *duty* is to your realm and to your Knight Commander now." Ser Filip teetered between authority and annoyance. "Sit. Be seated and be quiet."

Tyel ignored this. Was he to be made prisoner? He shoved his bowl away and tore from the wooden bench he was seated at. It was time to get home. This was all rapidly spiralling out of his control. The mess hall's entry was perhaps thirty feet from him. But there were also ten other soldiers between himself and the doorway. Blood was pounding in his skull.

"Guards. Hold him!" Immediately, two soldiers were on Tyel's sides. "Branson, if I must make you heel like a dog, I will do it." He held an index finger in his face. *Don't doubt it even for a second.* His voice was low and hard now. "I have put my name up for yours. I have covered for your debt to the realm in the eyes of the High Inquisitor."

"Covered my debt?" Tyel protested. "I did nothing wrong! I—" A large, leather hand slapped his right cheek. He could feel the sting of a cut lip immediately as heat rushed to the swelling spot. Tyel could feel the shame of tears working hard to pry to the surface. He fought them back.

The guard on Tyel's right side withdrew his hand. "When the Knight Commander commands you, y'listen and do. That's your place."

Ser Filip softened slightly. "Royne. That was *excessive*."

Tyel shot a look at Royne. A bald, melon-shaped head cursed with a crooked nose and teeth like old fence posts on a thick neck: to Tyel, he looked more like a tavern thug than an anointed soldier.

"Yes, Knight Commander." Royne's features only hardened further as he responded through gritted teeth.

"But why me? I'm no knight. I'm…" he stopped himself short.

"I believe anyone that can take down a strega is a man worth enlisting. You did it with a tree branch."

Royne scoffed. "Lies. You're a liar."

Ser Filip brushed him aside. "The High Inquisitor doesn't care if you live or die – but as my squire, you come under my protection. You want to help the realm? Then help me. Don't make me regret this mercy."

Tyel wanted so badly to be holding another jag of wood right then and there. He shook himself free from Royne's hold. The other guard stood silent. Tyel considered his options at that moment. There were none, really. None that didn't involve open hostilities with large, well-armed men.

"Now. Branson. Come sit and perhaps we can discuss your position. As for the rest of you, eat your fill and leave. That's my command." Ser Filip finished and the stillness of the hall began to fill once again with the sounds of laughter and consumption. Tyel made his way back to the bench, holding a hand to his cheek.

"Here." Ser Filip tossed him a dish rag. "For your lip. I think you've shed enough blood for one day. Many more cuts and bruises to look forward to, I'm sure."

Tyel said nothing; he felt ashamed for letting this lug, Royne, catch him off his guard. His lip throbbed, joining in the chorus of the rest of his pains.

"As I was saying – you are to serve as my squire. You may write your family and I will see that your letter is delivered. They will be compensated for the loss of your services—for as long as you are under my command. I cannot be more fair than this – and if you have any sense, you will see this as a generous situation. A situation very much in your favour."

He leaned in. "You are *not* high-born. You have a station, and that is all you would ever be, if not for this."

Tyel bit his tongue. Who was this old man to say that? Why should he determine what Tyel might amount to? He looked down at the table coldly.

"Don't be like that, now," Ser Filip tutted. "Stow your pride and look at me. I do not suffer from lack of choice – a squire is an enviable role. I have turned away the soft sons of many houses – fine houses. No squire has ever served under me in the many years I have held this title. But, until today, I've never met a man who has slain a strega. None in our generation have that I know of."

Ser Filip poured himself another cup of blackberry wine and, after a moment, reached for a second cup for Tyel. "That's a remarkable thing, lad."

The Knight Commander took a generous swig of wine. "Call it convenience – call it necessity… I am getting on in years. I don't feel the bite of age yet – but I will. It comes for all of us – first the bite of age, then the bite of death. If we're lucky, we experience the former then the latter." Ser Filip leaned in closer now.

"A squire – *you* – will help stave off that bite. You'll attend to my needs, whatever those might be. And in return, your own needs will be met, and your debt to the realm, at least in the eyes of our High Inquisitor, shall be repaid. The only blood that need be spilled should be from abominable beasts," he said. "Not from your backside. That helps no one."

"And that is our task most immediately; hunt these abominations, the blood-horrors. Tomorrow, we will take the saddle and ride north. Let us find this blighted town and determine the severity of the situation. If there are more strega out there, then we will bring the full force of the Anointed Protectorate down upon their kind. You will join me in escort of this company."

Tyel looked down at the baked earthen mug and swirled the contents. It looked thick and dark, like the vital fluid that spilled from the throat of the strega. His stomach churned. He didn't like this feeling of not being in control of his destiny. His sudden thrust into the lowly ranks of the Protectorate was a sharp detour from the relative simplicity of the life he had known. How could a letter to his family express his feelings? Would they think him brave or shameful if they knew his charge was forced upon him because of his deed?

"Ser," Tyel placed his cup back down. "Don't think me ungrateful—"

"Well, don't give me any reason to think it. *Drink.*" The Knight Commander indicated the cup. "It's customary to share a mug with your Commander after your appointment. Doubly so, if I'm your Commander."

Wordlessly, Branson took the cup and swallowed the sweet, strong wine. He had little taste for wine – his father would keep a barrel in the homestead cellar, but only for special occasions. Honeyed mead or oatmilk were commonplace at their table however. As a child, a mug of the mead would make his head swim. As a man, he could keep pace with his father, nearly.

He pictured his father's thick brown beard and ruddy cheeks; his broad smile that lit his face when he was full of joy – or full of ale, which was more often the case.

Ser Filip brought him back to the moment. "Tonight, you'll rest in the infantry bunkhouse. The housemothers will provide you with your linen – you best find them soon or you'll be cold and wishing you had. Tomorrow, I'll find you some slightly more suitable garb. And then your duty begins." And with that, the Knight Commander stood, looked around the room once, and departed.

In that moment, Tyel felt very much like a child lost in dark woods, surrounded by indifferent eyes. One set appeared in front of the bench. Royne craned over him, casting a shadow over the tabletop and across Tyel.

"You're gonna wish you stayed where'r it is you come from, squirt. This place is for 'ard men, not pouting piss-babies like you." He reached across the table and picked up Tyel's bowl of leftover stew, and the broad wooden spoon next to it. Without missing a beat, he scooped a clump of potato and flicked it at Tyel. It hit him mid-chest and tumbled back down into his lap.

Tyel said nothing; he merely stared back as the gap-toothed Royne revealed his dirty, yellow teeth in a crooked smile and stood back up, tossing the bowl casually back onto the tabletop.

At once, Tyel broke his stare and smiled warmly, picked up the chunk of potato from his lap and popped it in his mouth. "Mm. Thanks. I was still hungry." And with that, he stood up, nodded to the room – a collection of amused and bemused faces, some chuckling to themselves now – and left.

It was rapidly becoming clear to Tyel that this Royne figure might need to be dealt with – but contending with oafish bullies was something he was more than capable of doing. In good time, he supposed. No need to wage war with near-about the largest person he'd ever seen – especially if he would be serving alongside him. Tonight, he needed rest; his rib still ached unrelentingly, and he needed a wash.

The halls that ran between the outposts were quiet now; the hour was late and, by the time he found the dormitory, deep in the guts of the keep, the housemothers were nowhere to be found. Their small stowage was locked up tight and no one answered when Tyel rapped on the heavy wooden door.

With a sigh, Tyel started back toward the dormitory. He could live without fresh clothing for another night, and at this point, as long as he had space to lay, he didn't care about bedding.

Just as he rounded the corner into the long, curved main hallway that connected the outposts, a small voice called to him.

"Tyel."

"Alyse?" he replied, genuinely surprised by her sudden appearance.

He had walked straight past Alyse – or so it seemed; she appeared as if from nowhere. Perhaps her kind had a knack at making themselves as discreet as possible. In this place, that might be a very wise thing, Tyel figured.

"I hear you'll be staying with us for some time," she said, softly. He nodded. "The Knight Commander asked me to prepare a bath and some clothes for you. If you'll follow me?"

"Ah, sure," was all Tyel could manage. A bath? He could already imagine the warmth, and it reflexively made his muscles contract. Endless rooms, some labelled, some not, passed by. A person could get lost in here for moons, Tyel thought. He stole a glance at Alyse as they walked. She was very slightly taller than he; though he was certainly not short. She glanced back and Tyel's cheeks flushed as they walked wordlessly side-by-side down the curved corridor.

"I'll leave you here," Alyse said, as they came upon the door to the bathhouse. Beside the entry, Alyse opened a small cabinet. From within she retrieved a small parcel, bound by twine. "These are some… underclothes," she blinked rapidly for second, as if stumbling over the word. "And the Knight Commander will find you in the morning with some requisitioned attire.”

"Thank you, Alyse"

She nodded, a small smile forming across her pale lips. There was a protracted moment of silence.

"Well—" Tyel began. "I—" Alyse started. The stop-start interjections unleashed a ripple of simultaneous giggles.

"I probably would've been lost wandering in the halls until I passed out," Tyel smiled, fidgeting with the hem of his shirt. "This place is enormous."

"I know it wasn't what you were expecting, but I'm glad you're staying," Alyse replied, meekly. "Thank you. For being kind." Her large irises swirled. "Goodnight, Tyel. I hope you rest well."

And with a small bow, she backed away, turned and, smooth as fine silk, hastened back toward the dormitories. Tyel caught himself staring at her as she departed, but shook his head clear. She was so at-odds with this place – like a spark in a dark room. Alyse was far above her station, Tyel felt. The notion filled him with a curious kind of sadness.

He palmed the handle of the door. The room was pleasantly humid; rows of copper tubs, deep soaking basins, lined the room. The room was empty, those aside – and Tyel was at once grateful for the privacy. One basin was steaming-hot; a stool of scrubbing salts sat beside it, along with a horsehair brush. Tyel let the scent of salts and soap fill his lungs until the unpleasantness of the day, the high strangeness of it, faded into the far distance.

FAVOURS & GRACE

That night, once her rounds of the Sept had been performed, Alyse slept little. She spent most of her late evenings, when she had them to herself, in her small quarters – barely an oversized pantry off the staff kitchens, haphazardly converted with a bedrest against the back wall and some small wooden shelves on each side. Above her bed was a narrow slit of a recessed window with shutters that could be latched to keep out the cold and a sash of lavender fabric that served as a curtain, tied mid-wise with a length of ribbon she sometimes used in her hair.

On some nights, she would pilfer a book from the city library – the kindly librarians never seemed to pay her much mind – and return to her quarters to pore over stories of great conquerors and the lowly conquered, the rise and fall of whole clans and cities. Most books in the capital were written in the Common, but occasionally she would find tracts in Elfkind.

She missed conversing in her own tongue. She missed her family more.

When she could, she would experiment with simple spellcraft, in which she had little formal training. Her abilities had appeared years before, but had begun to blossom more lately, the way seeds that fall between stones in a path eventually bloom to life in bursts of surprising, unplanned hues.

She felt the innate power within her, but struggled to adequately harness it. It frustrated her. Alyse was young when she was taken, so she had precious little in the way of exposure to her culture – and even less of what magic could do, or create, or conjure. Or unmake.

On this night however, while she hardly slept, she could rest her mind, which was exhaustingly overactive. But even in sleep, her resting mind thought only of her own yearnings and needs. Of things and places she had seen during her time beyond these captive walls. Of new faces, too. Of an odd young man, just earlier tonight. She entered him accidentally, and felt the physical pain in his side.

Just as quickly, she forced herself to withdraw – but not before he noticed. How embarrassed she felt! How exposed! Alyse rolled onto her side and tried to push the thought away.

Of all her abilities, the strongest one was also her biggest frustration – and the reason for her… *vassalage*, as the High Inquisitor called it.

When she allowed it, her mind could run unfettered around the different lanes of the city, through the slums, the mid-markets, all the way to the city's peak, where the High Inquisitor's fine accommodation was located. Images and sounds swirled in her mind's eye – voices came most clearly, but when she focused on one sound – a bird's call, say, or a child's voice – her mind could slip inside theirs, like smoke gently puffed through a keyhole. It was not an entirely pleasant experience for her or the other party. Both experienced the sensation of being stretched and pulled at points inside themselves – not quite physical, but not intangible either.

She believed she connected with the core of a person; like a fine silver filament that might break so easily if she pushed her way in too forcefully. It was frightening, but she'd done it since she was very little and, even now, had great difficulty containing her mind's wandering.

The pillow's softness reminded her of her mother's lap. In her mind, she recalled her mother's long fingers gently combing through her hair. She felt the tenderness – and craved comforting.

Her eyes remained closed, even as tears crept to the surface and ran down her cheek, onto the pillow.

She slept briefly.

The too-brief night turned to dappled morning light; Alyse awoke to the sounds of the stock-hands drawing or depositing goods from the larder on the other side of her wall. Somewhere far off, cutlery clattered. The air smelled of toasted bread. The day would soon be underway and Alyse would dutifully serve her High Inquisitor, and his family, their substantial meals, cleaning their palatial bedrooms and keeping a free ear for His Worship's demands.

Just inside her quarters, a brass bell at the top of a twist of golden chord chimed vigorously.

~ ~ ~

The High Inquisitor woke up feeling clammy and stiff. His stomach lurched. Night terrors were common after courses of aged cheese, but these dreams struck him as somehow different; vivid and more tangible; the distinctive smells of loamy earth, fresh blood and ancient decay seemed to hang in the chamber air above his enormous canopied bed in the moments after he awoke. Now, rubbing his eyes and yawning, he could not remember what it was that upset him so. It was just beyond his grasp and then gone.

It was then that he noticed his lap was wet.

"Damn and blast it!" he shouted at no one. He rolled across his plump mattress and yanked down hard on the service bell chord a few times.

He needed to wash now; it wasn't his preferred activity and usually he would spend as little time in the bathing pool as possible. Ordinary river-borne water was beneath him, but his private bathing pool afforded him sanctified, cleansing waters, blessed by the Solum God. They were cold pools, however. Chilled water did not flatter his body parts, which were ample in some regards but less so in others. Today, he would forego the bathing and get the elf girl to cleanse him. There were far more important things to do than waste his hours in a ritual soaking; he was due to commune with the Oracular Magisterium of Nine – another task he did not relish.

The Nine were the only beings in the realm above his seat of power; all High Inquisitors served their gods – be it Sol, Lunum or Void, but only the Oracles could commune with them. Orders from the Oracles were sacred and, as he knew, rarely carried pleasant outcomes.

Where was that girl?

"Servant!" the High Inquisitor bellowed. "Bring my towels."

Silent as a shadow, Alyse crept into the room. Immediately she was hit with the overpowering stench of sweat and urine. She nodded at the Inquisitor and threw open the heavy, cream-coloured curtains, spilling beams of morning light onto the bedspread. She then opened a large ornate trunk at the foot of the bed. From within, she fetched an enormous folded towel, nearly as large as the quilt that the Inquisitor lay beneath.

"Your Grace, a towel for you."

"Blessings, girl. Now present it and turn away."

With a heaving movement, the Inquisitor rolled himself off the plush mattress, pulling off his thin cotton sleeping gown and sharply yanking the towel from Alyse.

He wrapped himself as best he could manage. Alyse stared at the doorway, desperately wishing she was on the other side of it. "Bring me water from the pools. I wish to take my cleaning in my chamber this morning."

Alyse bowed respectfully, knowing she would have to scrub him. Inside, she wanted to scream. She turned to leave.

"And fetch my children on your way through. Go."

Alyse turned back to him for the briefest bow and hurried out of the room with great relief. As soon as the door was closed, she took a deep breath and tried her best to clear the wretched smell of foulness from her lungs.

She did not have to travel far to convey the Inquisitor Fendrigar's other request; Gehard and Melodis Fendrigar both resided in the tower, a floor below their father and mother.

Gehard was twenty-eight; first-born and a stark physical contrast to the High Inquisitor. Stocky, but muscular and proportional, with only the round cheeks and thick, broad nose of his father. In all, however, Gehard was all a father could want in a Sol-chosen heir – and the High Inquisitor was known to lavish praises on him. Of course, Gehard was keenly aware of his place in society – born into his position as Luminary beneath the High Inquisitor. He certainly made no efforts to practise diplomacy or modesty in the course of his mostly ceremonial duties.

The High Inquisitor's daughter, Melodis, the youngest, was around nineteen years of age, and unfortunately born in the image of her father. It wasn't her fault, of course, but she shared many of the attributes of the livestock that appeared on the butcher's block in her kitchen. Her disposition was akin to a person force-fed sour milk before any interaction. Where Gehard was solid and straight, Melodis was soft and squat. Her underdeveloped chin sank into her great neck, which in turn melted into her round shoulders.

She looked almost entirely different from her mother, Lyssy Fendrigar.

Alyse rarely saw the Inquisitor's spouse; Lyssy was a slender woman with a long face and small mouth; she knew not her name, or her background – though Alyse suspected she was from far south beyond the seas, where skins tended toward olive or bronze and hair ran thick, dark and wild.

Never did she see The High Inquisitor bestow affection on his wife – not at a shared table during meals, nor in the rare times when they would appear together in bed, on the mornings she would be summoned to clean the chambers. Lyssy kept to her chamber, when she was even in the tower at all – and then, Alyse suspected she was often abroad to avoid her husband.

Certainly, the few times Alyse chanced to read her, all she felt was Lyssy's resentment toward her husband and a general longing to be elsewhere. There was more, but it confused her. She could certainly relate to Lyssy's feelings, however.

This morning, Gehard stood at a viewing window in the shared sitting room outside the private quarters. He was in full regalia, as if for show, which struck Alyse as odd. His mail had been scaled, his regal white cape ironed carefully and draped down behind him, revealing two gleaming steel pauldrons, shining like the surface of a still lake. In the crux of his arm he pinned a silvered helm, also polished to a fine sheen, glinted with accents of gold and rubies. The Solum God's emblem crested the front.

"The High Inquisitor has requested your presence, Luminary," Alyse said, as Gehard turned, his round cheeks raised in a smile.

"Will you wave to me, dear Alyse, as we leave the gates today?"

Alyse studied his face for a moment. "I beg your pardon, Your Grace, but I'm… not sure what you mean?"

"My father has decreed a riding company shall head north and I shall lead it. This is my first as point-rider, you know."

"I did not know, Your Highness."

"Well now you do. And would you grace me with your favour? A kiss would do nicely." His smile was small and sharp, but his eyes were cold.

"I—" Alyse of course wanted to refuse. She'd sooner give her 'favour' to a pig's backside. "As you request, Luminary." She bowed, face cold.

Dutifully, perfunctorily, she approached the large man in ridiculous attire. He leaned towards her, his eyes closing and a smarmy smile transforming into a pouting pucker. She avoided it and pecked him softly and quickly on his stubbled cheek. He was taken aback and turned to connect with her lips, but she withdrew and withdrew again, just as Melodis' shrill voice interrupted them.

"Aye there – a forbidden romance between a lord and a lowly washerwoman! Shame on you, Gehard! And shame on you, elf! You are not fit to touch his face!" She squealed, clearly delighted to have something to fixate on and scandalise. Her laugh carried on like a rusty hinge.

Alyse's large eyes turned to Melodis – who immediately went very quiet.

Alyse felt inside her – but instead of drawing out Melodis' feelings, she planted a seed of small horrors – of fear and despicableness and blackness. Then she left Melodis who, no wiser, certainly looked very pale.

"Melodis, your father has requested you and Gehard join him in his chamber," Alyse said, coolly.

"No need." The doors to the High Inquisitor's room were open and the largeness of his form filled the doorway. "Ah! Son! Daughter! You are blessed indeed, most blessed – on this glorious morning," he grinned.

"Melodis, your brother is to ride at the head of a company today to carry The Solum God's holy might to the north and smite all that sully this land."

Melodis clasped her stubby fingers together, her round torso wiggling slightly beneath her fine golden gown, mock-praisingly. "Oh good! The bold hero! The seasoned battlemaster! The people's champ—"

"That is *enough*, Melodis," Gehard snapped.

"Am I embarrassing you in front of your lady-love, sweet brother?" she replied, bitterly.

"Oh, bite your tongue, sow," Gehard snapped. Melodis' face contorted from a splash of cold reality.

"Quiet, both of you. You know how your bickering displeases me. Gehard will lead an assault – but also liberate food stores – as much as can be carried, and the rest to be directed back down south to the capital on any cart or carriage you can procure. Any *and* all!" It was clear to Alyse, Solum-brya's fate rested on the hunger of a large and glutinous man. His appetite served more motivation than any undead horror's threat.

"Oh, and keep your eyes open. There have been strange sightings of late up north."

"Sightings? Of what exactly?" Gehard raised an eyebrow.

"Probably nothing. Villagers jumping at shadows, most likely. Yes, yes." He cast his eyes down, pondering for a moment. "Gehard, use your best judgment and serve your realm. There's no need to concern yourself, I'm quite sure."

His face said otherwise, Alyse could feel his differing emotions quite plainly – and of course, she knew much differently, since Tyel had delivered his gruesome parcel. Why was High Inquisitor Fendrigar choosing to hide the truth of the strega attack? If she reached out and read him now and he sensed the intrusion, he might cut her in half – or rather, have someone do it for him. She turned away, but the troubling thoughts did not leave her.

The High Inquisitor coughed slightly and gently fanned his reddening face. "Servant, escort me to the dining room. And there had better be more food than last eve, or so help me."

Alyse nodded and The High Inquisitor raised a heavy arm for her to take. As she slid her small hands beneath his arm, she noticed how sickeningly damp he already was – and she'd only just changed him. She felt her meagre morning meal rising.

"Father, wait," Gehard interjected. "One more thing."

"Hmm?" The High Inquisitor's mind had clearly already moved on to other things – probably food, Alyse felt.

Gehard motioned to Alyse. "I want to bring the girl."

"Why, whatever for? His worship replied with disinterest, barely stopping.

"I have a need for a cupbearer."

"Well, you cannot have this cup girl. She is mine. My vassal. She stays with me." The Inquisitor took no notice of Melodis' feigned shock – but the moment was not lost on Gehard, who threw her a look of daggers.

"Father, I *must*. I— I have had *visions*, you see. From the Solum God." Gehard's voice rose in valorant triumph.

"The Solum God told *you* that a cupbearer – *my* cupbearer and house servant specifically – was to join your excursion? Am I to believe this?" The Inquisitor began to laugh, which served to prompt Melodis in a chorus of squealing, creaking laugher. "Come now, Gehard."

Gehard's cheeks rose. "Father! Oh please, won't you let her come?"

His father's guffawing ceased and he narrowed his eyes. "I don't need to remind you that invoking holy command on false grounds is a serious sin. Most heinous. Most *unholy*." There was venom in the Inquisitor's barb. His son balked. "Unholy actions carry grievous penance."

He stopped, levelling an upturned finger at the Luminary.

"You should know I am to commune with the Oracular Magisterium of Nine today. It would be wise to keep your sins few and to yourself." His voice lowered to a hush. "They see too much as it is."

"I— was only *joking*, father! Truly. You know my wit. You do *love* it, don't you?"

The High Inquisitor eyed him with a flat expression. "Quite."

The Inquisitor looked at Alyse, his eyes calculating. He sighed. "I suppose you *might* have a need for a cupbearer."

"More like a bed-warmer," Melodis jibed under her breath.

Gehard ignored her. "The ride is long, father. And she is surprisingly… experienced and well-travelled. She may prove useful beyond simple servitude."

The Inquisitor again looked at Alyse, the way an owner might look at his favourite hound or most prized trophy. "I don't know," he breathed heavily. "You must keep her from harm. If anything happens to her, our…. *Elstemeri friends* from far afield will take your head."

Gehard's round face lit up. "Oh thank you, father. She will be most cared for."

"Indeed." The High Inquisitor moved his arm away, Alyse still attached. She released her hold. Gehard's eyes were greedy, like a child stealing from a shopkeep.

Melodis looked agonized. "I'm hungry – and this silly verbal dancing bores me. Dip your wick in any girl you like, brother. Why you'd opt for a dirty elf over a high-born Solumbryan is beyond me."

"Most things are beyond you, sister," he replied, raising his nose at her and barking a laugh at his own magnificent wit.

"Leave, if you're leaving, Gehard. See you on your return. *Should* you return." Melodis waved him away dismissively and pushed past her father and out the door. The High Inquisitor turned his rotund body towards his first-born.

"Solum God preserve you and keep you in the light of the cleansing sun." He bowed, as much as he could. "Return with my vassal. And bring resupplies with you. Sugar cane. Barley. Huskcorn and such. You know." He gesticulated, on and on, then stopped, looked once more at Alyse, a tiny flash of remorse on his face – and left the room. That was that.

Alyse felt a sudden flush of emotions – but predominantly confusion and caution. Her eyes, swimming with aqua-blue energy, glanced at Gehard. He looked most amused with this outcome.

"What a splendid turn of events! Come. Gather your things, girl – whatever it is you have, aside from these drab smocks and robes and such," he remarked. "You will find me down at the gathering square near the gatehouse at high-sun. Oh, we will have fun together, won't we?"

~ ~ ~

Downstairs, in a small, quiet chamber off the central foyer, rested a single chair. The High Inquisitor stood in front of it, regarding it with unease.

This chair was nothing fancy – drab, too narrow for his sides and uncomfortable. Really, the High Inquisitor liked to spend as little time as possible in this seat, as this was the Oracular chamber, and Oracular dealings were generally unpleasant; often they involved a verbal undressing, a mental finger probing. Shadowed words and vague threats awaited him.

He couldn't change the seat however, as it connected in one continuous sweep of wood to an altar a few feet in front of it. Atop the altar, a golden ring sat atop a simple golden stand. The band of gold was wreathed in flared licks of hammered metal sun beams. This was the Circuitris: the sacred symbol of Solumbrya's religious creed beneath the watchful gaze of the Solum God. Solum Temples in each town were graced with the same carefully crafted adornment, smelted and wrought in a blend of gold and orichalcum ores.

This one, however, was special – infused with an ancient power he barely understood. He knew only that he did not like it; it penetrated him as the elf girl sometimes did; deeper than any physical object, tapping his most vulnerable points.

As the High Inquisitor wedged himself into the creaking, straining chair, his folds spilling over the arms of the seat, his essence connected with the altar. His body's energy fed the Circuitris by some magical means, and the chair and altar were conduits.

He experienced the familiar sensation of being outside of himself – disconnected from his body. If he could see his face, he'd notice how his eyes had rolled back in their sockets and his jaw now hung limp. Instead, all his mind's vision could perceive was the golden ring in front of him, enveloping his senses. The Circuitris' open heart burst into flames; a pool of pure, gently undulating blue and orange. In his mind's eye, the Inquisitor received the Oracle's words from shadowed faces on the other side of the flames.

When he came to, he felt dizzy and disoriented. He drew a fine silk cloth from his side pocket and dabbed at his brow. Beads of blood soaked the fabric. He wiped his eyes and saw yet more blood.

The words had been ill ones. They were most displeased with him today. Most displeased – with his dealings and decisions and company.

Talk of famine and conscription. A man from the south, now north, raising threats from the past. It would flow south and spread across the land, they said. Around him, blood and gold; fire and dark portends.

The words lingered long after the visions passed.

Perhaps he would take that bath after all.

CHAPTER 5

OMANON

The morning came too soon, and in the thin light of the dawn, Tyel read and re-read his hastily composed letter. The words felt thin; he couldn't encapsulate everything that had happened with the speed and intensity that they occurred. It just felt like a rolling list of ridiculous things, one after the other. Empty towns; strega; severed hands. The High Inquisitor's punishment and the Knight Commander's demands. Who would believe this? He scarcely did.

He dared not promise returning to the family forge – he had no timeline to work to – which worried him. What worried him more was leaving his brother to pick up his chores and deliveries. He breathed out heavily and looked up at the sky through the window behind him. Pale blue, peaceful. Completely at odds with the turmoil in his heart.

He signed the note with his love and asked to pass this on to his brother, Dilain. It all seemed so inadequate – but it was all he could do right now. Maybe, if things turned dark, he could break for County Keep and lay low for a time. The fantasy brought him a little comfort.

Tyel creased the parchment and folded it over twice, then inscribed his father's name upon a face "Dain Branson, Blacksmith". And below, he added "County Keep, care of Feldstone Inlet". He hoped it would reach him, but there was little assurance once it left his hands. From a tallowed candlestick, He poured a few drops of oily yellowed candle wax along an edge. The seal would keep the contents as private as they could be, what little there was to read anyway.

The bunkhouse was near-full when he awoke, but most of the soldiers paid him no mind at all. He did not see Royne, which was something of a small relief. Perhaps he slept in different quarters, he wondered. Regardless, by the time he finished his letter, it was near-empty. He dressed quickly in dark brown pants and a cotton shirt Alyse had brought him the night before and set out of the dormitory to find his new master, such as he was. His life had been rerouted in the space of a day – but he supposed that was sometimes how it could be. It was a peculiar situation.

The central curved hall between the outposts spilled into an expansive outer gateyard that separated the capital from the wider world. It was here, under a sky of mottled cloud and infinite, optimistic blue, that Tyel saw the small company he would be joining. Twenty mounts were being readied on able steeds. At the head of the line, Ser Filip stood with another broad-set man he did not recognise, who was struggling to steady his enormous white horse.

Ser Filip noticed Tyel's approach from across the yard, appearing immediately grateful for a sudden reason to leave this conversation.

"Tyel. You look more alive today," Ser Filip said.

"Yes Ser," Tyel replied. And it was true. Even his rib, which ached incessantly – and would for some time – felt somehow less burdensome. The scented soak in the copper tub was perhaps curative, restorative. He didn't know; he'd never really had a bath of such luxury before. He'd lain in that basin until his fingers and toes had shrivelled, which always amused him, and only raised himself out once the water had turned cool. He could still faintly smell traces of oil on his skin.

"Good. You'll need your wits. We have a long and winding ride ahead of us. Girl! Bring Branson his uniform."

And there she was again, this Alyse – seemingly omnipresent but rarely focused on by anyone at any given time—except, Tyel noted, this large and opulently adorned soldier at the head of the company. He'd now brought his white stallion under some semblance of harness and was presently staring at Alyse from across the yard. The look made Tyel's skin crawl.

Alyse took small but swift steps to Ser Filip's side and presented another bundle of clothes; these were far more elaborate than Tyel had expected. He received them with thanks, and, unblinking, Alyse nodded her response before retreating back toward the rider at the head of the company.

"Any squire in the service of the realm shall be trained in the short sword and shield," Ser Filip began. "You cannot perform your duties to me and to your High Inquisitor if you end up a bloated corpse lying in a ditch somewhere."

He couldn't disagree. It was much more pleasant and fruitful being alive. "Aye, Ser," Tyel replied. That was a morbid thought; would he really be seeing combat? He supposed he already had – but he did not relish the idea of another encounter with a strega.

"Good. Put those on – do you know how? If not, the elf will help you." He pointed to the neatly folded livery; a white and gold tunic, embroidered with a golden sun across the chest. Beneath it, a boiled leather jerkin, thick cotton pants, two bracers and a sturdy leather belt with several small, buttoned compartments. Compared to the mounted knights around him, in mail and plate, the leather protection seemed a far more comfortable option.

"Yes Ser, I'm sure I can manage." The notion made the blood bloom in his cheeks.

"Good, fine. Then find Quartermaster Omanon," Ser Filip continued. "Tell him who you are and he will find some suitable arms. He's expecting you. And be quick about it; we set out at full-sun. Which, by shadow-fall, is not long from now. Go."

~ ~ ~

Quartermaster Omanon was situated in a large storehouse next to the inner gate that led back into the city proper. His stockhouse was full to brimming with all manner of arms and armaments; on one wall, three-score types of blades–from throwing knives of oiled bluesteel and double-edged bastard swords to curved scimitars from the southern isles and a broad, long einhander of a red hue and a length that bordered on absurd.

The far wall, behind Omanon, was stocked with bucklers, heaters and kite shields; some were notched and arched, some were concave and looked more like a scooped bowl fit for a giant. They hung on walls, rested on the floors and covered the wall in an assortment of patterns–but most were gilt with the ring of the Solum God and its ring of flames. Barrels and cloth livery were neatly stacked along the third wall. In all, it looked much like his family's storehouse: a fortune of folded steel and worked leather.

At the centre of all of this sat the Quartermaster himself, perched on a stool behind a long, wooden workbench. Omanon's white beard covered a broad chest and round belly, but his arms looked like the limbs of an oak. A large crease of scar tissue ran from high on his brow down his left cheek. He wore a brown eye patch over the socket. He did not look up as Tyel approached.

"Uh, Quartermaster?" Tyel asked clumsily, feeling very out of place – despite being exactly where he'd been asked to be. "I'm Tyel Branson. Knight Commander Filip sent me."

Omanon said nothing; his attention was fixed on a thick ledger, lined and crossed with names and item numbers and scratchings that looked incomprehensible from Tyel's upside down view. Suddenly, Omanon looked up with his one functioning eye, brown as mud, and slammed the ledger shut.

Tyel half expected him to grab his shirt, yell, curse him for the interruption – such as he'd come to expect so far. However, Omanon's face immediately softened – and he brushed his voluminous white beard to the side and raised his arms in greeting.

"I *know* who ye'are, lad! Tyel, aye. I've known y'r father for many years now. I even held ya as a wee babe!"

He spoke jovially through a broad smile, barely visible underneath the thick moustache that peeked through. His Southern accent caught Branson by surprise and he spoke with a higher pitch than a man of his size ought. It was disarming in some ways – but his friendly greeting came as a relief, no question.

"'Hold on and lemme get the measure of ya'." Omanon lifted himself off the small round stool and trundled around the workbench to face Tyel dead-on.

"You–know my father?" Tyel stammered.

"Aye. Y'father used to run trips back and fro'–and he'd bring you along oft as not. You wouldn't remember that, I'd wager. Back then, y'r no bigger than my hand!" He freed a bellyful laugh and raised his large palm to Tyel's chest, giving it a solid thump. Tyel did his best not to recoil, but he staggered slightly.

"Y'r a wee bit bigger now." Omanon looked Tyel up and down. "Houl' your arms out. Like this." And Omanon raised his arms out from his side, forming a bulbous "T". Tyel did so.

"Hm. Aye. Bring your favoured arm fore—like this." And Tyel did– swinging his right arm across to his front.

"Aye. Right side. I see." Omanon. "Now raise your right arm up." And as he began, Tyel winced. His rib.

"What, lad?"

"I—can't." I broke my rib, I think," Tyel lowered his arms with a wince.

"That so? The men say you took on a strega."

Branson smiled. "I *killed* a strega."

"If that's a tall tale, yer likely to get a beating from some of the soldiers in 'ere. They hate braggards. Y'might wanna keep that to y'rself for now."

After his run-in with Royne, he knew Omanon had the right of it.

"Either way, yer lucky to be alive, lad. Raise, y'shirt. Let me see the damage." Omanon clearly knew what he was looking for; Tyel's mobility would be limited, which would hinder just about anything he'd need to do in the field. He must've seen his movements and read his condition immediately, Tyel figured.

With a heavy breath, Tyel painfully lifted his cotton shirt over himself and off. His body was lean – his shoulders were developed, but he felt stick-thin – and he carried a kind of confusing shame with him around his body. His father was broad and tough, as was his younger brother Dilain. Branson took more after his mother's build.

"That's a nasty bruise – I don' think it's broken, but I see the problem. Tyel, I can fix it – but it'll hurt like bloody murder fer a moment. You ready?"

Omanon started for him; Tyel took a reflexive step back. "Don't worry. I've done this 'fore. Now–hold onta the benchtop. Left arm. There." He slid a stack of books and paper away with his enormous, calloused hand.

Tyel, with abject fear in his eyes, reached over and leaned to the left, causing his right side to stretch. As he did so, fast and gentle for a large man, Omanon placed a cool hand on Tyel's side, just below the rib that was giving him agony. Tyel shuddered.

"Ready?" And without waiting for a response, Omanon issued a short, sharp push upwards and in. Tyel screamed. He felt a sickening, sliding *pop* – and it made his bowels clench; his stomach lurched. He fell against the table and to the floor with a groan.

Omanon leaned over him. "There! You'd managed to pop it out of place."

Tyel lay on the cold stone floor, breathing hard and heavy. A cold rush of sweat covered him now; and he instinctively felt his side. It felt… different now. It still hurt – but somehow less so.

"You'll bruise up nicely now – but y'rib is back in line. Aye." Omanon extended a hand and gingerly, Tyel raised his right arm. He could feel the ache – but he could also feel the relief of full movement; of being able to breathe again without the straining pain. "C'mon. Up," Omanon commanded, lifting Tyel to his feet again. "Better, aye?"

"Better, I think." Tyel raised his arm slowly above him and rotated his shoulder. He had his range of motion back. "Thank you, Ser."

"What's this 'Ser' business about? I'm no Knight, lad." And Omanon laughed. "Just a rusted ol' bookkeeper, more or less." Tyel suspected more. "Now – I'd tell you to rest and let y'rself heal – but then, that's not on the scryer's cards. No. But I need to keep you alive just the same." Tyel wondered how he'd received his scar – and lost an eye – if not in battle. But he held his tongue.

Omanon returned to behind his long workbench and continued to the back wall. Tyel took the opportunity to pull on his leather jerkin and don his colours. The material was of refined quality; the leather was thick and carefully worked; it smelled of rich oil and pleasingly earthy notes of tanned hide. The jerkin's neck was raised to just below the sides of his jaw, which at first felt odd – but then he recalled the strega; it's long fangs. He pictured them inching towards his neck, while he fought against it. He shook off the bleak vision.

"I think I know the implements you need. A squire, you're to be, right, lad?"

"Yes–for Ser Filip." Omanon appeared to ignored this; his back turned.

"Aye. And you're a decent enough rider, I hear."

"I think so, Quartermaster."

"It's *Omanon*. You can drop the title. No high and mighty folk in 'ere, that's for sure." Omanon laughed and shook his head as he parted hilts and pommels in an upturned barrel. Tyel watched with eagerness as Omanon moved from one barrel to another, evidently not finding what he was looking for in the first.

"And you're, let's see, pushing six measures tall? A decent reach, I'd say. And have you been blessed in the light of the Solum God?"

"I think so?" Tyel replied.

Omanon stopped his rummaging, and turned to Tyel with a furled brow. "That's no answer! Did ye father have yeh blessed or no?"

"I – don't know for sure. I never asked. We don't really worship any of the Gods."

"Never asked. Pshhh." He sighed and shook his head again, eyes widening for a moment, and started for another wall of arms. "Well, I'll trust y'r father did right by you and the Solum God, surely enough. Some of these weapons cannot be wielded – well, not fully, by the unblessed. We'll soon see."

And with that, he returned with a cloth-wrapped item. Would it be a bastard sword? Tyel wondered. It looked too short. A dagger of some kind? He had his iron dagger – but a second, perhaps of finer edge, might be a terrific aid. No. It was too broad…

Omanon laid the object down on the workbench, then, carefully as a father might handle a baby's swaddling, he unfolded the cloth.

Beneath it, laying before both of them, was a weapon the likes of which Tyel had never seen: a circular, golden-hued blade—the diameter of a large dinner plate, with small serrated teeth and a long handle wrapped in fine brown leather. A small stud of blood-red gemstone capped the pommel. The entire blade seemed to radiate warmth – a subtle inner-glow that went beyond simply the sheen of the fine metal – whatever it might be. It couldn't be gold, Tyel pondered. It would be far too soft. He wondered if it might not be orichalcum.

"An anointed weapon, this. A *circuitris*," Omanon said, as if picking up on Tyel's thoughts. He'd heard of these, but never seen one before. These were ancient weapons – practically religious relics now.

The Quartermaster lifted the blade, this circuitris, and slickly spun the neck of the blade in his hand, pointing the grip toward Tyel, who began to reach for it. Omanon hesitated and pulled it back. "If yer not blessed, this'll hurt some. It'll burn."

Tyel looked at Omanon; he searched his weathered face for trickery but found only solemnity. After a beat, Tyel reached back out for the handle of the circuitris; at first, he barely touched the leather wrap, stitched together and wound tightly around the grip. He certainly felt nothing in that moment – save for an overriding eagerness to hold this strange weapon and give it a swing.

Tyel held his breath – unsure what to expect. He allowed himself to wrap his fingers around it now and, as Omanon released the neck of the blade below the bladed ring, the full weight of the circuitris rested in Tyel's hand. He took the blade and carefully raised it in front of him, looking through the centre of the ring and back at Omanon, who was watching closely – unblinking, waiting.

And nothing. Just a beautiful ring of deadly radiance. The brushed golden hue reflected a dull distortion of Tyel face.

"Well 'n. Good; you've had your sacrament at least. That's somethin' anyway. Might be it keeps you a bit safer when you're facing who-knows-what ou' there."

Omanon held his hand out once again, motioning Tyel to return the circuitris. With a moment of hesitation, which did not go unnoticed by the Quartermaster, he placed it back down on the unfurled fabric.

"Oh – you thought this was *fer you*?" Oberon chuckled. "Lad, that cir-cuitris is worth more n' just about all the kit in here combined!" His chuckle built into a chortle. Tyel felt his cheeks redden. "And older than the capital, probably. Tyel! I think somethin' a bit more – straightforward – might be a starting point for ya'." And once more, he returned to the wall of arms.

Tyel watched, but his mind was on the circuitris. If an object could feel sacred, surely this one had that essence. It felt protective – *preventative*, even, in a way that was hard to pinpoint. But the Solum God had powers, or so he was told, and sometimes you could feel that touch. He'd never felt that kind of irresistible pull before; it was dominating his senses.

Omanon returned; this time, two pieces he held in his hands: a buckler as long as Tyel's forearm and perhaps three times as wide, and a short blade around the same length in a simple leather sheath. It could very well have come from his family's workshop at some stage. He deposited them in front of Tyel without a lick of ceremony.

"There yeh go my boy. These'll keep you alive—and maybe take a few lives too. Who knows."

Tyel picked up the buckler first; though small, it was heavy – hard wood, with an edge of banded iron. Small square rivets lined the outer edge. The centre curved gently and came to a point that would cover his elbow. Tyel looped his left arm through two bands of thick leather and gripped the metal handhold. It fit nicely and, once he was strapped in, the weight felt more distributed and natural.

"That buckler… it might serve to deflect alrigh' – but in truth, it's as much a weapon as this." He nodded toward the sheathed blade. "Give something a solid smack with your buckler and you'll do some damage, no question."

Tyel nodded wordlessly. With his other hand, he lifted the short sword and parted it from the sheath with a reassuringly smooth clack. His jaw fell open.

"Wiped the disappointment off your face, did it?" Omanon jibed.

He wasn't wrong, Tyel mused. This was fine gear indeed. Bluesteel, flawlessly forged and honed to an oily, dark blue finish. Two straight edges with a broad fuller. The taper to the point began quite far down the blade – about half way, which was unusual. It gave the impression of a long, narrow leaf, or the sleek body of a spindlefish.

"Listen to your master, Tyel. Learn to use this; it's a fine blade – prob'ly too fine for a squire, but your father is a good man, and a fair one. And I want him to know I did right by yeh. If you come back short an arm or – not at all, it won't be for my outfitting yeh poorly."

Tyel sheathed his shortsword. "Omanon! Thank you. They're both beautiful." And they were; the buckler was unique; his family produced round, simple bucklers–simple to construct, simple to stack and ship. This buckler's long, curved kite shape was elaborate and Omanon was probably right – almost too much for him.

"Alrigh' lad. Don't keep the Knight Commander waiting. And – His Grace, the precious Luminary. Ride well, Tyel. Do your family proud now."

Tyel gave the old man a deep nod of thanks. Omanon smiled warmly, then shooed him out with a laugh. He shook his head once and resumed his ledger work.

~ ~ ~

Tyel was flying. His leather jerkin fit like a charm; the thick cotton pants less so, but the leather belt was doing its best to keep them up. And now, he was fully armed. He felt a part of something larger than himself; a new world that came from nowhere, but here it was before him just the same.

Back into the outer yard he spilled; the company was filed in twos, astride. There alongside the Knight Commander at the head was his pack horse, saddled and kitted with side bags. Hardly a mighty steed, but he would serve well enough. Tyel was immediately filled with renewed excitement.

"Quickly, boy." Ser Filip beckoned and held out Tyel's horse's reins. "You're holding us up."

Next to the Knight Commander, atop his ivory warhorse, was the man he now knew was the High Inquisitor's son: Omanon had called him the Luminary. At once, the impractical pomposity of his shiny armour made sense. But something else caught Tyel's eye, and his reaction was immediately and inexplicably gutting.

There, in the Luminary's lap, was Alyse. He had his hands around her.

CHAPTER 6

VANGUARD

The sun was high and shadows fell short by the time the vanguard set out and away from the Solumbryan capital.

Luminary Gehard Fendrigar counted twenty-two mounts, not including his own, plus the ageing Knight Commander and this young man who seemed to have fallen out of the sky and into Ser Filip's grip. It mattered not at all; twenty-five or twelve or three–if the threat from the north was true, it would take more than this small troop of outriders to make a dent. Part of him hoped his father's downplaying had been more than just his usual incompetence and deflection.

He looked forward to the day when he sat at the head of a true formation – a galloping vee of thousands of soldiers and horses, cutting a swathe across the countryside to drive their foes back and crush them into the dirt. It would cement his name in history as a great leader. Perhaps the *best* leader. A leader of truest renown and sharpest steel – not like his soft, powdered father, who had never sat astride a horse (for fear the horse might collapse, he supposed), who never led a vanguard, who had fallen so far outside of the ring of political power as to be almost irrelevant. Almost.

He knew the truer purpose of this sojourn, even if Ser Filip did not. This was not a mission to gauge a veiled threat. Rather, something had pinched the delivery of resources into the capital, and now storehouses were beginning to squirm. His father was a fat fool, but it must be said that his immense appetite pointed toward the beginnings of a major issue for the region, let alone the capital.

"Ser Filip," Gehard spoke over the clomp and clang of their procession. "The High Inquisitor has given me fresh counsel this morning."

He turned to his right, swivelling as best he could while holding Alyse and wearing heavy plate. Ser Filip cantered alongside him; his new field boy trotting behind and to the left like an obedient whelp.

The Knight Commander eyed him warily. "Is that so?"

"It is," The Luminary replied. "There is to be a change of direction; we are heading north–but not directly so."

"Your Excellence, my understanding is that the nature of the threat needs to be determined – and swiftly." There was a tone of restrained frustration in Ser Filip's voice.

"Your understanding has just been further illuminated, Knight Commander." Gehard dismissed him; the old blowhard might be decent with a blade, but it was not his mission to command today.

"As is your prerogative, Luminary," the old man replied, warily.

"I am to lead this – *mission* – and secure for the capital additional resources from our northern settlements."

"Resources? Of what nature?"

"Foodstores and livestock," Gehard replied, flatly. "Cattle and hens. Dried meat, fish, sugarcane, milled grain, that sort of thing. We must all tighten our belts together. However, the Capital demands stability and stability it will have."

Tyel listened intently, not daring to speak. He watched the gentle motion of Alyse in the Luminary's saddle with distaste. *He did not like this man* – a most immediate dislike. Part of him knew from his childhood the divide between the opulent and wealthy families, and the ones who worked the fields and tended the cattle and forge. Coins always seemed to magically roll uphill towards the capital's elite families.

"Gehard—"

"Ser Filip, the High Inquisitor has spoken. I am merely acting upon his wishes. If we encounter resistance of any kind, I am sure we will dispatch it." Gehard narrowed his eyes slightly, before returning his focus forward. "In whatever form it takes. Now, please inform our men." Gehard's features hardened.

"At once, your Excellence." Ser Filip replied curtly, before withdrawing down the line. "Come, Branson."

The Knight Commander slowed the procession and delivered the Luminary's briefing. A voice Tyel knew from the night prior spoke out from behind a faceplate.

"If I can't blood my blade, I'll bury my staff instead. Plenty o' fat, young milkmaidens out there in need of liberation!" Royne snorted.

Another voice joined in. "We'll liberate 'em, and maybe gift 'em with a babe or two!" And a chorus of voices cheered in agreement.

"Enough of that," Ser Filip boomed. "Any man who pulls his member out for any reason other than to piss up a tree loses it."

"Oh, piss on that," Royne grunted.

"What did you say?" Ser Filip pushed his steed through to the bulking figure on the mud-brown mare. "I'll have your *balls* too. Believe it. Now shut your useless trap or you can walk home to your mother and tell her why she now has a eunuch for a son."

Royne huffed and kicked at his horse's side. He pulled away from the other riders who had begun to pick up the pace again.

"Same goes for all of you. Do as you're ordered and there'll be spoils plenty. And if we're favoured by the gods, we'll spill some black blood and you'll all earn your share of gold and glory. Then you can pay for your ladies or win their hearts for all I care. Until then, keep your eyes open and mouths shut."

The Knight Commander raised a fist into the air and motioned forward. "Onwards!"

Tyel spurred his horse. It occurred to him then that he really ought to name him. The colt was one of four horses his father owned – he'd learned early not to get too attached to the livestock, however. A horse was a tool – not so different to a cart, hammer or anvil – or, at least, that was how he'd been raised to think of them. You kept your tools in good order; scour and oil your iron; feed and brush your horses. Milk your cows and goats, slop the pigs, run the hens and sow the fields. Keep your life in rhythm and your house in order. *Good care now would save good coin later*, his father said.

Now, however, he felt a sudden jolt of care for the brown and white colt. He'd endured near as much as Tyel had – and he had all but neglected to think of him while he himself fed and washed and rested. Thankfully, the stablemasters had done right by his horse. He was fed, combed and saddled by the morning.

"*So – a name, then,*" Tyel pondered, his horse's rhythmic clop-clop carrying him along.

He let his mind ponder it for a while, watching the sun slowly making its grand arc across the early afternoon sky. He watched the silhouette of the towering central Citadel shrink and fade into a haze of lilac and blue as they left the capital territory behind them.

His mind went to great heroes of the wartimes; he knew their house names and their sigils. He knew the names of their blades and hammers. But not one stallion's name could he recall. It didn't seem right, somehow. A warhorse deserved a name, if not a line in an epic poem.

He considered a few noble names – famous houses of the Eld Age: Silverstride, Doverlund, Keening, Coryd. He recalled old friends from his village–perhaps he could honour them. But nothing seemed to fit just right. For now, it would just remain Horse. He gave the colt a little pat on the shoulder. When he looked on ahead, back to the head of the vanguard, he spotted Alyse looking back at him. Just for a moment. By the time he realised, she'd turned away again.

He wondered if she was reading the minds of the other soldiers; of the Knight Commander or the Luminary. He wondered if she was reading *his*.

~ ~ ~

Rolling farmland and uncleared scrub seemed to stretch on towards the horizon; the vanguard had begun north out of the capital, but soon had taken a road called the Westerling Trail; a looping pass that crossed over the long River Reedsrush via a wide stone bridgeway. There was an Easterling Trail, too – though he'd never taken that route before. That easternmost coastline was a mystery to him.

The hills of the capital lands flattened out as the Westerling tracked alongside the massive Marshtide River. On either side, sloping down into the valley carved by the river system, were muddy estuaries, marshes and floodplains. Inland, small hamlets had cropped up that traded their harvest up and down the river.

As they rode, Tyel could smell the rich, upturned earth, fresh with new-ly-seeded crops and young grains. The seedlings were still many moon-turns away from harvest, as it was early in the season.

However, there should have been at least a few farm hands in the fields, planting, clearing, protecting. They saw none. This struck him as odd.

Nor did they encounter caravans, traders, peacekeepers; the roads were entirely empty. Though the River Marshtide allowed for fast trade between ends of the land, these mainland trade routes were always dotted with enter-prise. Tyel knew this from his own dealings; food carts could be relied upon to station at major crossroads; families would pass in their wagons and farmers would sell directly to them between villages and outposts.

Ser Filip was not oblivious to the quiet. It worried him. He knew the settlements out here were more sparsely populated – but to see no one?

Unheard of. He furrowed his brow, which was beginning to turn a shade of pink in the afternoon sun. He turned to Tyel with an outstretched hand.

"A drink, Branson."

Tyel snapped back to the moment. "Ser." He twisted in the saddle and unclasped the flap of his side-bag. Within, he had stores of smoked fish and dried meats, fruits, seeds, nuts and rounds of tack. He also had bladders of wine and boiled water. He considered the wine, but selected the water, handing the bladder to Ser Filip.

He drank eagerly, capped the neck and thrust the water bladder back to his squire. Tyel stowed it. He was thirsty too—but his own ration was small and he could wait.

"Tyel – your family. Tell me more of them."

"Well, Ser – I have a father, Dain. Southron Solumbryan-born and native," he began.

"Aye. Siblings?" Ser Filip asked, eyes fixed down the road.

"Just a brother, younger by four years. Dilain," he replied. "I had a sister, Carille – but she died when she was very little. In the years of the Red Flux."

Ser Filip looked at Tyel now, reading his face. Tyel glanced at him, but returned his focus to the horizon. "The Flux hit many of us. I'm sorry to hear that, though."

"Kind of you, Ser." Tyel was surprised by the sudden interest in his roots. He had no problem sharing his tale, but he wondered what had prompted it. Maybe Ser Filip meant to just pass the time and break the monotony. "My mother near-died during her birth, and she was a sickly babe, Carille," he said, quietly.

"At first, she refused to nurse; she would be sick from milk. My mother was weak and still healing – but the worry of her daughter growing thin… it took a toll on her." His knuckles tightened on the reins. "I don't think she was the same after that."

"Go on… if you wish." Ser Filip's demeanour had changed; he seemed genuinely engaged with Tyel's story now.

"Yes, Ser. Eventually my mother did heal, but it was my father who would feed and care for Carille. He would suckle her on cow's milk and, when my mother was able, she would feed her too. But Carille struggled at the breast. Even so – it was all for naught and she…" He trailed off.

"But your mother still lives?"

"She does, Ser." Tyel rubbed his neck. "Not sure if she wishes differently – hard as it is to think."

Ser Filip was taken aback by that. His squire held some pain and he'd accidentally brushed against a tender spot.

"Loss and grief, boy. You cannot replace that loss, and you cannot hasten her grief."

"It consumes her, though," Tyel admitted. "I wish I could do more for her. I know she misses her daughter."

"Aye. She might always. A person must choose what they live for. Sometimes grief can keep a person alive."

Tyel sensed there was more beneath the surface of that statement.

"Anyway, Ser. That's my family. If our roaming brings us to County Keep…"

"It won't; not this ride. We'll follow the Westerling and come through the northern towns, then back south again, following the river."

"Aye Ser." Tyel missed his family – more from the atmosphere of uncertainty that was rising in the vacant roads and untilled fields that branched off the Westerling Trail.

The sun was low in the sky now, throwing long shadows of spindly horse legs across the hard-packed dirt. They'd been riding only five or so hours – which was plenty – but the nearest settlement was still a good hour away. They'd reach it by sundown. Still, he was starting to feel the effects of the saddle's constant impact.

"Halt, company!" The Luminary wheeled his horse around

and flagged down the troop, who slowed and fanned out across the road. "We break here." A small mercy, Tyel thought.

"Boy! I'm ready to dismount." Gehard raised his face and peered down his nose at Tyel.

"You will ask me before making requests of my squire," Ser Filip interrupted, pulling in between Gehard and Tyel. Tyel couldn't help but smile at the comment; it was sure to rankle.

"I am your *Luminary*! I command whom I please!" Gehard was indeed rankled. The sour response only served to amuse Tyel even more. Clearly, there was little love between Ser Filip and the Inquisitor's son.

"Of course," Ser Filip retracted. "Forgive me, Your Excellence. The road has tired this old man."

The Knight Commander dismounted, making a point of doing so himself – and with ease; old and salt-haired he might be, but Ser Filip was unquestionably in great shape. He nodded to Tyel. "Go and help His Excellency."

Gehard bit back; he knew when he was being slighted. "Perhaps old men are best left to duties more befitting their condition."

Ser Filip bowed at the waist. "As you say, Your Excellence."

Tyel threw his leg over the saddle and slid down the side. His legs and lower back were stiff from maintaining his riding posture – the sensation of motion still coursed through his muscles and standing on solid ground felt strange. It also came as a great relief.

"I don't know why I feel the need to explain my actions – but if you must know, the elf requires your assistance down before I can dismount. See to it. She's... unwell."

"Yes, your Excellence," Tyel replied, coldly. He did not make eye contact with Gehard. His attention was on Alyse, who appeared to be fading rapidly. Alyse looked parched; at some point, she'd raised her riding cloak over her head to keep the heat of the sun off her fair skin. Now, as the heat of the day began to fade, she lowered it. In the setting sun, her normally luminous eyes were pale and her cheeks were flushed.

"She needs water, your Excellence." Tyel ran back to his horse and found his ration; he hurried back over. She looked down at him. "Help me down, please." Her voice was thin as spider's silk. She reached out and, carefully as she could, turned herself around on the front of the saddle.

Gehard folded his arms and scowled. "Hmpf. Perhaps bringing you was a misstep, elf. You've been a burden to carry and poor company."

Tyel quickly wiped the grime of the day on his sleeves. He felt a sudden rush, making this fleeting contact with her as he took her weight, his hands holding her carefully around her waist. She let herself slip down.

"Yes, Luminary." She looked up at him, not bothering to search him, for there was only pride and ugliness to be found. She turned to Tyel. "Thank you."

Tyel handed his water bladder to Alyse. She held it for a moment, as if it were a sacred object, then carefully uncorked it and drank. She raised the neck to her pale lips as the contents emptied completely. There was something about even that simple action that Tyel found mesmerising. She lowered it, then whispered a few clipped words, so hushed, nearly inaudibly: *"Terr aquis inifi enil solum."*

She handed the vessel back to Tyel; it was full and sagging.

"How?" He whispered – a mix of confusion and wonder plain on his face. But he already knew. This girl was special in ways beyond his understanding; he desperately wanted to know all and more about her.

Alyse turned back to Gehard; he was struggling to lift his heavy legs over his saddle. "I'll ride with Tyel now," she spoke firmly. Gehard stopped his fitful dismount, mouth agape; the Luminary was most displeased.

He huffed like a petulant child denied a plaything. "A tender weakling, aren't you? Go; now you can dawdle as you please with the other help."

She brushed his comment aside; her attention now drawn to Tyel's horse. She rested a small hand gently on his muscular neck, moved her palm up along the arc and ran her fingers through the colt's brown mane.

"Tyel. Call him Mancer. That is his name."

Chapter 7

LEVERAGE

When Brea E'lario was released from the cell, she was by all outward appearances on her dying breath. The hold was cold and dank; no bed to speak of – not even an elevated seat to keep her off the floor, which was perpetually damp with saltwater. A thin slit of daylight cut into the barred cell each morning from high on the wall above her – peeking in from sea level, and she could track the hours as the beam slowly traced an undulating path as the ship rocked back and forth.

Until she took ill, the most she had to contend with was boredom. The scrap had left three men with broken limbs – one without an eye, or so she assumed when the town guards finally tore her off of him. The broken bottle was wedged into his socket fair-deep.

She'd set out on a shoreman's transport from the Elstemer Ports, far from her people in the Solsetter Isles, a small amount of coin concealed on her from her benefactor and a mission to complete. The longship had six levels and carried dock workers and supplies from the isles to the Solymbryan mainland. There were plenty of spaces to stow oneself, which was good because Brea didn't exactly buy a ticket.

Getting inside had been easy enough; she knew enough fade-magic to make herself unseen and unmemorable when she was. However, she still needed to eat – and needed to urinate. It was with her long, wrapped skirt down, squatting over a bucket that the three men jumped her. At that point, it was far too late to use her fade and simply blend away – they'd seen her in a moment of vulnerability; she'd let her guard down, along with her drawers.

"I ne'r been with a dark lass afore," said the first, before she dove on him. She crushed his windpipe. He didn't get up. She dispatched the second one before he knew what was going on. One second, he had a hand on his belt, trying to loosen it. The next, his nose was pressed against his cheek as a burst of red covered his flushed, sweating face.

The third, the largest man, was a little harder to take down. "You – you shade whore! You killed 'em!" He bellowed, spittle flicking down the front of his thick, grey-streaked beard.

"They're not dead," she replied, lifting her bloodied fist from the front of the second one's face, "Yet."

They collided like rams: his enormous belly rolling like the swell of the seas as the ship rolled with him, sending them both sideways. A bottle slipped from his hands – half-full. Brea swiped it mid-air, which caught the drunk by surprise. He was more surprised when half of it ended up jammed in his face.

His screaming only subsided when he lost consciousness, and by then, two guards had her pinned with short, curved scimitars pressed against her pumping jugular. She loosened her hands from around his thick neck. Her fingertips had drawn blood.

"Assassin," One of the guards barked.

"No," Brea corrected. "Spellsword."

"A filthy stowaway, more like," said the other. And she couldn't fault him there – she was both of those things at that moment.

"We should let them finish the job." The first guard pressed the point of the blade into her neck. She could feel the sting of the tip as it cut into her. Then he relaxed and withdrew. Brea scrambled backward. She made no effort to draw her own concealed blade; her green eyes wide and scanning for options out of this situation. None presented themselves immediately.

The men she'd beaten down were beginning to rouse now.

The second guard pulled her up. "Throw her in the hold. We'll work out what to do with her once we dock in Dawnport."

And that's exactly what they did. They took her four throwing daggers and her small pouch of thirteen gold coins – her partial compensation and retainer. She knew she'd not be getting any of this back; the gold was easy to come by, but nicely weighted throws were not.

She was fed, barely, and kept awake by the knock and roll of waves. After seven long nights, she awoke from a violent bout of vomit and knew she was in a bad way. She felt hot and dizzy – and the little water she had consumed had gone through her at both ends. She tried to stand and found it hard to keep upright.

She touched the small wound on her neck – barely a puncture, but the site was swollen, viciously sore and hot to the touch. Her throat was slowly closing up, as if choked by invisible hands. After strangling that thug before, this seemed an almost poetic end, if this was how she would meet it.

She could hear the buzz of activity above her on the deck. The voices seemed to ring unnaturally in her ears though. Brea felt another wave of nausea ripple through her as a rush of vomit came up again. She heard sea birds and a bell somewhere distant.

When the guard found her, she was fully unconscious.

~ ~ ~

A bright light and a soft bed. That was how Brea awoke. The room was small, yellowed walls that reflected a sheet of morning sunlight that broke through a glass-paned window looking out onto a busy street.

As she squinted, trying to focus, something else came into view: a short, aqua-skinned man, stout and bespectacled. His ruddy-brown hair was long, braided simply and shot through with strands of grey. He sat hunched over on a stool, like some sort of enormous mushroom, at the far end of the bed. Behind him, Brea could see an assortment of apothecary equipment: all manner of flasks and vials, small sealed jars of black substances, blue-green glass pots of thick viscous liquids and odd poultices.

"Ah! She wakes." Dust-in-His-Eyes made no move to get up.

Brea tried to sit up and found she was bound at the ankles and wrists to the wooden bed posts. She thrashed harder.

"Untie me and I'll end you quickly, dwarf," she seethed, wrenching against her bindings.

"A generous offer, but I'll pass for now. Good to see you have your senses back, however. You fought like a demon last night," he said, warmly. "You're somewhat better now though, it seems. Mostly."

She strained and thrashed, trying to wrench her head toward her wrist and chew the knot loose. "Free me, Dwarf, or so help me—"

"I *did* help you. That's why you're alive," he replied matter-of-factly. "Settle for a moment, would yeh?"

She said nothing to that, but she did stop her violent gyration. She still felt woozy; her head felt off-balance.

Those bindings are there to protect both of us. Hold still and I'll let yeh go. You're lucky they didn't toss you overboard into the brine, you know. Those Southron Seas transporters are notorious for live burials at sea for stowaways. They'd dump you and not blink twice. It's a wonder they didn't, honestly."

The dwarf pulled both ends of his bushy moustache to each side of his face and rubbed his eyes. Then, turning away from Brea, he retrieved a small roll of parchment from the table beneath his wares.

"This is you, is it not?" He unrolled the parchment.

Brea saw herself, a badly sketched version of her likeness at any rate. It had her high, full cheekbones and wide-set, angular eyes on dark skin. These days, she wore her thick black hair in two round buns toward the back of either side of her head, rather than bouffant as it appeared in the drawing. But it was her – her eyes, high cheeks that pointed towards her lips, her gently curved nose.

"Brea E'lario, the bandit sell-sword-turned-assassin," he proclaimed. "Quite an ill reputation. There's a fair bounty on your head to match, you know."

She did not, but that amused her some. Apparently, her exploits over the south seas had made the long journey ahead of her.

"I prefer 'freelance agent', if we're bandying terms," she replied sharply.

"And I prefer free pints, easy company and all my gold for nothing, but here we are," he laughed and stood up. He started to undo an ankle, but stopped.

"Perhaps that's why they didn't dump you over the side rail – someone caught a whiff of how much you might be worth. But then, your illness took hold. You've been in and out for three days. And in this port, a lot can happen in three days."

"You haven't yet turned me over for the bounty, but that's your intent," Brea barked sharply.

"It's a tidy sum, I'll admit. But alas, I've already collected it."

Brea puzzled at this.

"I retrieved you at the order of the captain of the ship. If he'd truly known the extent of your background, there's a good chance he might have taken you to the authorities instead. Alas, I agreed to hold your body in something of a quarantine." He resumed undoing her ankle binding. "I told him you did not survive treatment—and your body was cremated to prevent spreading the disease."

"Treatment? Disease? Who are you, exactly?"

"Ah! I haven't introduced myself. I'm Dust-in-His-Eyes – a modest medicinal practitioner and alchemist, among other things. You are most fortunate, you know. The world thinks you're dead, Brea E'lario. Therefore, you are now both alive *and* dead." He started towards one wrist. "And that is good for both of us, I think."

"What are you blathering about, dwarf?" Brea withdrew her legs, pulling her knees up to her chest.

"You can call me Dusty." He squinted at her through his round lenses.

"I'll call you whatever I damned well please," Brea spat back. "As soon as I'm free, I'm gone."

"Simmer down, coin-killer. Hear me out," Dusty sighed. "You are dead in the eyes of the authorities. I have your half of the bounty—" he hiked a thumb over his broad shoulder to a pouch on the table. "And you are free to take it." He freed her wrist and began toward the second. "But I have a *proposition* for you, Brea E'lario."

He undid the last knot. "A business proposition."

Brea rubbed her wrist. He had her attention, but she was waiting for the catch.

"And why should I not just cut your throat, take my bounty and run?"

"You could do that, but I wouldn't advise it."

Brea was all ears now. "Why not?" She sat back against the bed head and watched this Dust-in-His-Eyes like a raptor. "What leverage do you have on me, dwarf?"

Dusty laughed.

"You see, when the ship's guards brought you down, you were on the verge of death. They thought it was a contagion; I knew better. A blood-born miasma – most serious and very difficult to treat."

He sat down on the edge of the bed, which sagged slightly under his weight. "It's your good fortune that I too am something of a hired blade. Except, of course, my means are far more, ah, subtle… than stabbing and brawling."

Again, Dusty looked over his shoulder at his wall of ingredients.

"I happened upon your bounty poster and, after paying off an informant – two actually – I knew you'd be landing in my port. It's *my* good fortune that you were already incapacitated. Not dead, but well on the road down." He stood up again and walked to his table, retrieving the coin pouch.

"I treated you in two ways: once to induce death – or, at least, outwardly so. Then I called for the Justicar, who confirmed the bounty kill, paid the sum thusly, and left me to dispose of the infected corpse"

"And the second way?" Brea was horrified and fascinated. Who was this man? She knew many of the players in her field, yet this dwarf was not one of them.

"The second, the curative course of treatment, is why I suggest you stay put for the moment."

Brea did not like where this was going.

"You are alive because of my actions, but I must confess, you are also, *ah*, shall we say—"

"Say it clearly," Brea snapped.

"You are going to need treatment for some time to come. Your days will be numbered without it."

"What did you *do to me*, dwarf?"

Dusty scratched his head. "I saved you. The infection is gone. But in order to imitate death, just before the Justicar's evaluation…"

"You've doomed me."

"No, you were doomed *before* I intervened, Brea. Fate finally caught up with you. But, and here's the upside: I can treat you. Over a period of some months, we should be able to reverse your condition." Dusty glanced at her. Brea looked mad as a cut serpent, which was more than fair, he supposed. Her mouth hung open and her eyes burnt holes in him. "Each full cycle of the moon, I must administer the correct dosage of this medicinal concoction."

Dusty held up a phial of thick, white liquid.

"Or I'll *die*?" She was mortified.

"Or you'll die. Yes."

It took a moment for the words to sink in. She sat there, mouth agape, ready to talk, ready to bolt, but unable to do either.

"With that said, Brea, as I mentioned, I do have a business proposition for you." Dusty tossed the sack of coins toward Brea, who made no effort to catch it. It landed with a clink on the woven blanket top. "You can make this situation work to your advantage, and mine."

He turned from her. From above him, he retrieved two ceramic mugs. And below the table, he scooped two cups of wine from a stoneware pot.

"Here. Drink this." He tipped the contents of the medicinal phial into the wine, swirled it and thrust the mug into her hands. She sniffed it warily. "Why would I poison you? I just got done fixing you up. This is your first dose – the wine makes it a bit more palatable."

He took her mug back, took a sip from it, in overtly theatrical movements. "Mmm. Ah. Good. It's safe – see?" He handed it back. She sipped it, then, eyes widening, opened her throat and swallowed the cupful.

Dusty paused and let out a laugh. "Ha! Here. There's plenty more." He filled her mug again and returned to the bed.

"The authorities think you're dead. You're now free to live a new life. A new identity. And I *need* that new identity to help me with some very important… research."

"Why me?"

"You're convenient, for one. And, for now, you need me to live. I need you to protect me. I need *you* to live."

Brea pondered this for a moment. She hadn't forgotten her task; she'd been paid to perform that special service – but if word reached her client's ears that she'd died en route…

"I'm not changing my name. I won't run from myself – or anyone else.

Yourself included, dwarf. But I do see opportunity."

She had no obligations now, other than keeping her head down and remaining off the agenda of certain powerful figures. She looked down at the sack of coins. "This is my half, huh?" She said, quietly. She untied the drawstring and looked into the sack. She smiled. That was a foreign feeling.

"That's all of it. Take it. It did cost you your head, so it's yours. I have coin enough for now— and if we accomplish what I will shortly be setting out to do, we'll be sitting on a mountain of gold. You and me both."

Brea stretched and turned sideways off the bed, eyeing the door, the window, the exits. She could still run, she knew. Then she remembered the leverage. This death sentence that now ran in her veins. The smile slipped from her face. She would press him for more information -and perhaps she could procure and reproduce this medication of his. Then she would kill him.

"And what is it you mean to research? Dusty, right?" She softened her features. *'Fine, then. I'll dance this dance for now,'* she considered darkly.

"Word has come from sources I trust," he said, firmly. "From far in the north, over the mountains, in the cities of my kind – and below them. Something has returned that we have not seen for a long time. A threat to you, me – all of us. I mean to end that threat for good – and be rewarded handsomely for it."

The morning light had shifted across the floor and Brea knew exactly where the Dwarf had been and who he'd been consulting with. A ball of dread in the pit of her stomach was forming. She knew it was the dwarf's doing either way.

CHAPTER 8

THE TOLL

The eastern town of Dormanstar rested nestled between the gentle slopes of the curving foothills of the Atheron Ranges. The Atherons wrapped the north in a crescent of thick pines and crags; the largest towns in the north drew their resources from its ancient forests. Dormanstar's community were proud loggers and miners – but the village was still far enough south that it also grew fields of apples and hearty pumpkins, tubers and wandering vine-plants. On this evening, the final hour of sunlight settled between two ridges of the Atheron, spilling golden-orange and pink glow across the first long runs of apple orchards that guided travellers into Dormanstar.

Twenty-five horses travelled down this road now; the only signs of life in the region were two ebony crows perched along a stretch of rough-hewn fence palings doing their dogged best to discourage roaming fruit pickers. One winged scavenger cawed, flapped and departed; the other cocked its head and eyed the sudden stream of activity – then it too was gone.

The golden glow of the evening light seemed apt to Gehard. He knew something most Solumbryans beyond the Inquisitor's walls did not.

The mountain range was cavernous – and mining operations established by the church had begun to reveal rich veins of orichalcum and gold – both essential in forging sacred arms and for basic commerce. The extraction of these rare minerals had slowed of late – much the same as the transportation of produce. However, it might pay to line a wagon with ore. Perhaps he'd line his pockets too; this would become a fruitful errand if he could return with carts of orichalcum and not just bushels of apples and kegs of cider. He laughed to himself; it was so easy to be rich when you were under the protection of your father and the Solum God itself. Doors would open on command; none could be shut to you. And those who resisted?

The smile slipped from his face. Gehard shot a glance over his shoulder. Alyse; the elfkind girl. He would have her tonight; she would pay for embarrassing him in front of his men. How dare she reject him so? She should be grateful to be under his protection.

Tyel caught the glance; Alyse felt it. She held Tyel's waist with one arm; she found this much more comfortable than straddling the saddle horn. Mancer trotted smoothly, unlike the jarring clomp of Gehard's enormous beast. Each bump had sent the horn into her abdomen; she could feel the tender bruise the repeated impact had formed. She was sure she'd felt his fleshy lump pressing into her from behind as well.

The Luminary's wandering hands were repulsive. She'd dealt with worse, but was grateful to be away from him just the same.

Even now, Alyse could feel Gehard radiating a slowly-simmering resentment that bordered on petulance. *Fine. Let him come for me.* He would sooner lose control of his faculties – *at her command* – than lay another finger on her. Of all of her growing abilities, the one she needed earliest, a mind-sway, had saved her from lechers and killers alike.

"Once we reach Dormanstar, we should find the Templemaster," Ser Filip spoke over the cawing of distant crows and soft rush of wind through the apple trees. "We'll make The Inquisitor's requests known. The trees are bare; the harvest is done. So we should be able to load ourselves with apples on the morrow and continue on."

Gehard nodded nonchalantly. "See to it, Knight Commander, if you think your diplomacy skills might extend beyond exchanges of blades and fists."

Ser Filip bristled. "In my experience, Your Grace, words are often more precise than sword strikes. Diplomacy is always preferential to blunt force. There is power in diplomacy."

"In your experience." Gehard uttered. "In *my* experience, I ask, and it is given. If not, I take it. *That* is true power, Ser Filip. Divine authority."

These words, this sentiment, troubled Ser Filip. He said nothing as he breathed heavily and pressed forward. The Solum God was a very real, tangible being; this he believed firmly. And his appointees, it was known, were birthed into a sacred bloodline; accomplishments were irrelevant and fealty demanded by the position.

But the Solum God was a fickle one. This too was known. The will of the Solum God could not be known until it was made manifest. This was as much of a threat to the High Inquisitor's bloodline as it was to the realm, should the deity be unmerciful.

'Highborn or low; both burn the same,' Ser Filip mused. It did not bring him comfort.

Now the sun was setting on the day, the night bringing the sounds of locusts and the distant rush of the River Marshtide back to the west and south. As quickly as the steepled terracotta roofs of Dormanstar rose into view at the horizon, a sound rang out; a deep, long, tolling echo of a town bell.

The beating of metal against metal sent a wave of chime reverberating through the riders. It unsettled the horses; it unsettled the men. On and on it rang; *clang-clang-clang-clang.*

Tyel felt no good could come from a long-tolling bell at dusk. He read it as a warning.

"Ser," he called out. "I… don't think that bell means to welcome us."

Ser Filip turned to him. His face read of equal concern. "I agree, boy. Keep sharp. I don't like this."

"Will you two soft ninnies keep quiet? It's a tolling bell. We're in the north; it signals the end of the day—that's all. Nothing more." Gehard huffed and spurred his horse. "Come! I imagine my father has sent word by wing ahead of our arrival. They are probably signalling our approach." Gehard sped down the roadway; his men, encouraged at the thought of hot meals and cold drinks, began to quicken their pace.

Tyel whispered over his shoulder to Alyse. "What do you think?"

Alyse weighed her words carefully.

"If the bell rings out to welcome us, surely a rider on approach would serve the same?" She replied. "We've barely seen a soul on the road – at all, all day. I don't think it tolls to welcome us," she paused, as if resisting finishing her thought. "I think it might be the opposite."

Tyel nodded. "True enough. We'll find out soon either way."

The bell continued to ring out across the land as the late evening enveloped them.

"Torches!" The Knight Commander shouted. "Royne! Paldrick! To the front!"

'Royne.' The name sent a ripple of unpleasantness through Tyel. The largest man with the largest horse came galloping past on Tyel's right. "To th' side, runt." He snapped. He pulled in alongside the Luminary and drew out a tightly bound and oiled torch. Paldrick, a man whom Tyel hadn't seen before, drew a small self-igniting flint-lighter. They slowed the progression of the riders down now, slowly, slowly. Royne tilted the wrapped torch-end to Paldrick. The flint-lighter was loaded on a spring; he pulled the flint back in the chamber and it snapped and slid along the steel. As he did so, an arc of sparks shot out along the chamber and ignited Royne's torch. Paldrick pocketed the device again and unclasped his own unlit torch and lit it against Royne's. It was a marvellous little contraption, Branson thought.

The dark had settled in fast; the surrounding peaks of the Atherons grew around them as the town emerged from the din. Louder and louder the bell clanged as they approached.

Not a soul was out on the street to receive them as they passed between stone pylons that marked the town entry.

"No guards posted," Ser Filip noted to the Luminary. Royne and Paldrick, whose features Branson could now discern more clearly, scanned the landscape from side to side. Paldrick was thin to the point of being gaunt and pale as a sheet. A long, sharp nose stuck out on a bony, angular face. The bones beneath his cheek skin were like folds on paper; hard eyes were sunken deep in their sockets. In the light of the torch, he looked like a Deathreaper come to collect.

"I see no one, M'lord," Paldrick whispered, uneasily.

"We'll make for the town centre. Royne, tell the men to prepare to dismount and form up." Royne nodded sharply and turned his horse around. He trotted back around the other side, past the Knight Commander.

"Branson," Ser Filip pulled up next to his squire. "You and I will find the Templemaster. Girl, you will stay here."

Alyse shook her head. "No. I ride with Tyel."

"As you wish." He replied curtly. "Branson, she's your responsibility now, is that clear?"

Tyel nodded. "Yes, Knight Commander." He wasn't sure he wanted the extra responsibility – or even knew what this might entail. But he would of course protect her if it came to that. Gehard frowned but said nothing in response to this, which Tyel supposed meant the Luminary had perhaps moved on to more pressing matters.

"Good, fine." The Knight Commander turned his attention to Gehard now. "Your Excellence, might I recommend you wait with the men while I conduct these affairs?"

The Luminary sniffed. "I have no intention of waiting, Ser. You may do the talking, but I'll escort you. I wish to know what's said. And how."

Ser Filip puzzled at the comment. "As your Grace wishes." What was he implying? That he might somehow betray the commands of the Inquisitor? He knew not what he meant; he had to work with this man – setting him at odds was not an option.

Mancer whinnied; the young horse began to become unsettled. Alyse patted his hind and Tyel leaned forward to shush him. The clack of horse hooves on cobblestone reverberated between the plastered and bricked walls of the town's buildings. Shuttered windows showed lamplight and hearth-fire, but nothing stirred. It worried Tyel as much as it did his horse.

"Alyse, can you… sense anyone? With your… mind?" Tyel hesitantly asked – unsure of what to call her abilities.

In truth, Alyse had been trying to read anyone she could find as they approached; the nagging feeling of unease had been steadily building.

"I'm not adept. All I can do is sift for energy traces. It's… hard to explain. Even so, I can't read *anyone*, Tyel. And I can't understand why that would be, unless…"

Tyel didn't need to hear anything else. "Ser, we need to stop."

But by then, the path had opened out into the town centre; a large stone statue of a hand holding aloft a golden ring, tall as an old pine, sat on a wide-stepped plinth in the middle of the square. Around the plinth was a deeply recessed moat of dark water; it rippled with a current from some unseen channel that fed into the square.

The ring of the Solum God glinted slightly with the reflected shimmer of torches. The vanguard circled in front of the monument and began to dismount in a chorus of chatter and clatter. Several men led their horses to the moat around the plinth. Ser Filip did the same. This time, Gehard made no requests for assistance down from Tyel.

Alyse tugged at Tyel's sleeve; he turned his head as her voice invaded his mind. In that moment, her gaze was set far away.

When the time comes, you run.

Her eyes burned blue; her pupils seemed to disappear in ripples of flaming azure.

"… Alyse?" He looked at her, startled.

He did not get a chance to finish his thought.

"Branson! Dismount!" Ser Filip was already on his way over; he'd lit his own torch. Tyel immediately felt guilty about that. He should've had one ready for him. Quickly, Alyse slipped off Mancer, guiding herself over his hindquarters. Tyel pulled himself out of the stirrups and down, immediately feeling the stiffness in his legs as he landed on stone.

Ser Filip thrust the torch into his hands.

Gehard trundled over; he carried with him a drinking bladder, half-full. He wiped red wine from his mouth as he noticed Alyse standing just behind Tyel. He would perform his duty first; the fun would begin later. And if this boy should try anything foolish – something sad, sorry and storybook-noble, then he would teach him about his place, and firmly.

"I'm going to find the bellringer and ring them," Gehard laughed. "Royne! I appoint you as my personal bodyguard for now. There's a good man."

Royne was chewing on something; he took little notice of the Luminary; he finished his bite, took a long drink from his vessel, capped it, and with deliberately casual pace, stowed it away and belted his horse's side bag. Gehard was not amused.

Royne sauntered over to the Luminary and positioned himself in front of him, face-on. Royne had a solid two heads' height on Gehard. In that moment, the Luminary looked very small and meek, even beneath his ornate armour, as Royne looked down on him.

"Aye. I'll protect you," Royne muttered. "But I expect compensation."

Gehard was taken aback by this man's bravado. *The gall! The sheer bombast! This man knows how to wield power,* he thought. *I like him'* The Luminary laughed, shook his head and slapped Royne's chest with a broad hand. The soldier frowned as Gehard pushed past him. "Come. I'm sure the Templemaster and the bellringer are together."

"And what of the rest of the town, your Grace?" Ser Filip replied, fastening his longsword to his belt.

To this he had no answer. The Luminary didn't need the townsfolk, not exactly – just their stores. People could be moved from town to town, enlisted in servitude; forced if necessary. He didn't see it coming to that, but it was certainly possible.

The Luminary brushed Ser Filip aside and instead began to walk toward the Solum Temple, at the far end of the square. An ornate stone building, the Solum Temple had two spires that rose from behind an enormous grey stone facade. Behind round, stained glass windows, the faint glow of some inner light could be seen. High above, the circuitris of the Solum God capped the central spire, high above the square. Just beneath it, a bell, as large as a man, continued to clang away – pulled by some unknown arms.

The thought crossed Tyel's mind to take Alyse and run. Her words raised the hairs on his arms. What had she seen? What did she sense? There was no time to ask her now – for the small group had splintered from the rest of the soldiers. Royne and Gehard took the lead; Ser Filip followed closely, one hand resting warily on the pommel of his sword. Tyel and Alyse joined behind.

The square was lit only by the crescent moon, small and high above them, and the torches carried now by Branson and Royne. Their shadows danced in wide circles around them, leaping around like dark fingers grabbing at the cobblestones around them.

As they reached the steps of the Temple, looking up at three sets of doors clad in hammered copper, a dog barked from somewhere far off. That was the first distinct sound they heard, aside from the cawing of crows and endless chiming of the Solum Temple bell.

Then another dog. And a sour howling from a third.

The Knight Commander knew the howls of dogs could oft be for nothing—but equally something very grave. He knew his young squire was very much on edge; he couldn't fault him for that. The town appeared abandoned and with no good reason to be so. The happenings in Reedsrush and the return of great evils – had it spread to Dormanstar so soon? What had they walked into? Surely the Solum Temple, a holy space, would be safe from unclean interlopers.

The Luminary paused by the entry doors. As he raised his arms, Ser Filip interrupted him. "Your Grace, I don't like this situation. I strongly suggest we gather our men and set up a site south of the town."

"Retreat? From what? Nonsense. I say we find the Templemaster. Let us get a full account of the situation." Without waiting for a reply, Royne and Gehard pressed their palms against the filigreed doors.

They parted with a squeal as the heavy click of a latch mechanism reverberated through the towering chamber. He didn't realise it until he was already through the threshold, but Gehard had been holding his breath. *What a soft fool this old man was! His spine has all the strength of a handful of wet straw,* Gehard observed. He let his chest relax.

Tyel looked to Alyse; she seemed to be focused deeper into the heart of the temple's dimly lit interior. He wondered if those eyes could see things humans could not; perhaps through the darkness. Perhaps through people themselves.

Ser Filip shook his head and followed the Luminary, with Tyel and Alyse close behind. Tyel closed the doors behind him and, as his eyes adjusted, what he saw within took his breath away.

He'd never stepped foot inside such an ornate Temple before. Above him, the vaulted ceiling was supported by a dozen carefully carved, narrowing arches of wood that twisted and swirled like tufts of cloud as they swept toward the centre beam. Between these beams, the ceiling was a marvel, painted in shades of blue at the base, starting with aquamarine and transitioning darker and darker as it rose towards the apex. Golden stars, of different shapes and patterns, some with tails and some without, were dotted across the ceiling panels. These reflected the light of a thousand candles, a hundred or more at the base of enormous stone pillars that ran down the length of the space—twelve on each side. The impression was of an ornate night sky – one reaching infinity.

At ground level, rows of simple hardwood pews, in four long rows, ran from the back of the temple to a white marble altar, raised on steps, far at the back. Behind the altar, another carefully constructed, lead-lined window of stained glass in shades of yellow and orange. This was ringed by wrought golden metal; twists of copper sun beams radiated out from the Circuitris across the far wall, toward the edges of the room. These too caught the light of the glittering, glinting candles, slowly burning down.

Such a space was designed to overwhelm with grandeur and to inspire reverence for the Solum God; the god of all creatures born in the light. However, vacant as it was in the din of the night and lit only by candlelight, it felt discouragingly foreboding.

They continued into the chamber, along the centre aisle, down which ran a deep crimson carpet. High above, the bell continued to toll, now muffled slightly by the thick stone walls.

To Alyse's ears, it sounded as if the bell had begun to slow now.

"Let's find the bellringer, if not the Templemaster," Ser Filip suggested. His unease had not subsided upon entry – but perhaps some answers to his most immediate questions would quell it. "How does one operate the bell? Within the tower? Or beneath?"

Gehard did not answer – though this did not surprise Ser Filip. Tyel studied the room. There, at the back, a long, thick cord of rope ran through a pulley and down one of the columns. "Ser," he pointed toward the far-left corner column. "I see the rope. Looks as if it runs underground. See?"

"Just so," Ser Filip replied. "Then there must be an entry passage nearby. Let's go."

The five figures made their way towards the altar; the rope, it could be seen clearly now, continued to shift up and down; it ran into a metal ring in the floor; the edges where the rope met the metal was polished like a mirror from the repeated brushing of the fibres.

"Tyel," Alyse whispered. "The bell is slowing. I don't feel anything. This isn't right."

Tyel nodded. "Nothing's felt right since Reedsrush. This whole town, it's just as empty." He looked at her gravely.

"There," Gehard motioned. A square of double-hinged wood, divided in the middle, sat beside the hole in the far corner of the sanctum. "Royne. Go. Open it." And, after a beat, he added quietly, "Carefully." He glanced sideways at Ser Filip and peered at the hatch.

"Take it." Royne grunted in reply as he thrust his torch toward the Luminary.

"I don't *carry* torches," Gehard insisted.

"Of course not, Your Grace," Ser Filip replied, dryly. Why he would bother explaining this was beyond him.

Royne gritted his teeth in a frown. "Give it to the girl, then."

Alyse held out her hand and Gehard passed her the torch with a heaving breath of disdain.

Royne ignored Gehard's painful mummery. If anything should leap out of there, he would cut it clean in half. He partially unsheathed his bastard sword, his favourite implement for parting creatures from their souls. Then, without hesitation, he bent over the hatch, worked his fingers under two metal handles and yanked the doors open. A puff of pale dust plumed upward. He stood back, hand immediately on his blade, ready to pull.

Tyel's right hand reached for his short sword. All five stood braced.

Nothing.

"Listen." Alyse's voice made Gehard jump, and he turned to her. The bell stopped its toll completely.

Then the smell hit them. Unmistakable. Sweet, coppery, sickening – the fume of blood and decay.

Royne grabbed the torch back from Alyse. He took a knee and peered down into the dark chamber below, holding one hand over his nose. He withdrew just as quickly, dropping the torch to the stone floor with a clank. His wine came up to greet them as he scrambled on his hands and knees.

"What? What is it?" Gehard pressed, his voice now a mixture of excitement and fear.

Royne wiped his mouth with the back of his hand and got to his feet. "'Ave a look." He kicked the torch over the edge of the trapdoor and down into the dark.

Tyel and Ser Filip crept to the edge and peered over.

"Gods." Tyel could barely speak. Alyse pulled him away. She already knew; part of her had known since they entered this town – but how she desperately wished to be wrong now.

"Your… Grace." The Knight Commander gagged, but composed himself. "I believe we've found the villagers."

CHAPTER 9

NIGHT HORRORS

Captain Paldrick Vilimer had a terrifying face. It wasn't his fault of course, but for as long as he could remember, people would ask him who cursed his parents. His eyes were set deep in his skull; his hair fell out when he was barely in his twenties – and his mouth was permanently in a tight frown that pulled his sharp, high cheekbones into even sharper relief. Small children would cry; old ladies crossed to the other side of the road.

After a while, the frown became a fair reflection of his feelings.

Tonight, however, on the ride, he felt alive. Part of a band of other scary men, paid well enough, given due respect. He didn't care so much for the cracking of skulls and enforcement of the laws of his Inquisitor, but it kept a roof over his head, and food in his stomach. He'd lived better than his dear 'ma, to be sure. And though he'd never known his father, he was confident he'd surpassed him as well.

"They've been in there a while," a young soldier remarked to another. Paldrick listened half-heartedly. "Aye. Probably drinking and eating by now. Could be a time more. Could be all night, really."

"Best have some sup while ye can," Paldrick replied to neither of them in particular.

"Right you are," the younger of the two replied. He uncorked a flask, took a long swig and passed it to Paldrick.

He nodded and pulled a mouthful of the sour wine. "Better 'n nothing," he scoffed, but he had to admire the kid. He was barely older than the squire, but a man willing to share his ration was a man to keep around.

Paldrick sighed. While his Knight Commander broke bread with the head of the town, he would sit back and share a laugh with the men. They would talk of women, naturally – bedded and wedded and fled, and pit-fighting – human and non-human. This was his real passion: gambling. He had far more wins than losses betting on The Pits in Elstemer, across the seas. He could pick a winner on two things: their eyes, and how recently they took a shit or piss.

Near enough to the Pits is where he wanted to retire when his arms were too old to hold a sword. He'd spend his days drinking in the circle, maybe in the good seats by then. He would have enough coin to get fat and take a young wife or two. Ah, Elstemer. On the edge of the sprawling Southron deserts, warm and far from the roaming eyes of the Inquisitor. It was how his life began; he would make sure it would close out his chapter. Maybe by then, he'd learn to shift his downturned mouth upward without conscious effort.

The men stood around, some leaning or sitting on the steps of the statue in the centre of the square. The night was clear and the Lunum provided just enough light to wash the square in silver-blue. He felt tired from the ride, but the wine took some of the edge away. He settled back against a stone step. He'd close his eyes for a moment.

Dogs. Barking. There was a murmur from around the side of the plinth, across the moat.

"… the horses." He missed the rest. He opened his eyes again.

"Captain." Paldrick looked up; Cayleb, a foot soldier of little note, was standing over him, casting a shadow from the Lunum behind him.

"Cayleb."

"There's something wrong with the horses. You better come see," Cayleb's face looked grim. Now that he'd been roused, his senses sharpened quickly and at once he saw three horses bucking and neighing.

"What happened?" he pressed the foot soldier, as they strode over.

"I don't know, Captain. They were just drinking at the moat edge." Several soldiers were now trying to calm their steeds, pulling at the leather harnesses, attempting to bring them to ease.

The moat ran around the base of the plinth; it reflected the dark night sky as he saw himself reflected in it. The water was rippling. A current, from beneath the Solum Temple, and perhaps from the mountains behind the town, was carrying fresh water into the moat and through the underground channels below the town.

As he looked at the horses, then back down at the water, he noticed something that disturbed him.

The water had begun to cloud.

The cloud was a deep wash of crimson. It was feeding into the moat from the direction of the temple. He looked back at the horses; one, the enormous white stallion favoured by the Luminary, caught his eye. His snout was soaked wine-red from blood-tainted water.

The barking of village dogs came from all corners of the town. The horses screamed and stamped, bucked, protested. A soldier, desperate to control his horse, was knocked from his feet as the beast reared up and hooves came down on him.

"Men, at arms!" Paldrick shouted, and the sudden confusion rippled through the troop as the conversation died and the panic of the horses only increased in intensity, muting the sounds of steel being drawn from scabbards. The men scrambled to ready themselves. Water bladders and half-eaten sup fell to the ground.

Then there was a scream of a very different kind that split the air like a knife.

It pulsed in Paldrick's head, setting him off-balance. As he clutched at an ear, scrambling to draw his own sword, there came another shriek.

Black creatures poured and clawed themselves along the rooftops, down the laneways, from beneath the ground they stood on – somewhere in the black passages of the city, the shrieking cry of many inhuman creations in a dark chorus. He could see them; they looked right back at him. Glowing crimson eyes in pairs and fours – dozens of them, shades like gargoyles on the crenelations of a castle, dotting the terracotta rooftops. Down they came from the walls of buildings; up out of the sewers they crawled.

Shrieks pierced the night like the sounds of the underworld from both men and monsters. They engulfed the troop like waves rushing the shore.

Paldrick watched as the square exploded in violence. They were less than twenty; the monsters numbered in the dozens–and they just kept coming. Frantically, he swung at the closest of these—a glancing blow that struck bone. He could see his men falling, one by one; these strega could move on a nerve-twitch, shifting from spindly leg to leg, diving on his soldiers in twos and threes. He focused as he finished the job.

As he pulled the blade back out, slick with thick, black blood, he could see this creature's details come into the light. It was as the boy had said – a strega. An abortive creation from long ago. They took many forms, it was said – some on wing, some that were able climbers. Others were hulking brutes that towered over a man. But all needed the cover of night to emerge from wherever they spawned.

None had been seen in many ages; the last oppressive battles against such beasts were waged and won a century ago or more. When painted on plaster or written about in books, these horrors seemed disconnected from reality. They were very real now.

No sooner did he pull back from the first fallen strega than another was on top of him. He screamed as teeth bit down into the top of his skull, blinding him with a mix of pain, terror and blood. It ran into his eyes and down his face as he screamed. He dropped his sword and fell sideways, thrashing and pushing against the sudden burst of horrible rotting muscle that had clamped onto him.

He scrambled for his sword with one free hand. He could feel his end coming – but he would take this one with him into the next world.

The last thing Paldrick Vilimer thought as he blindly drove his sword through the chest of this blood-monster, this strega, was of how much gold he could've made betting on this creature in The Pits. Oh, the fight in them! The relentlessness! Another was already upon him now. And another. His fight was escaping him. He was alive long enough to scream as his arm detached, torn from its socket.

He was gone as his neck spilled open and his life drained away into the moat.

~ ~ ~

"I can't believe we're doing this," Gehard pouted as he lowered himself down, rung by rung, into the chamber below the Temple. He was the last to do so – and only after rejecting the prospects of being left alone above, without his escort. Below, the stench of decay mingled with faeces as insects in the hundreds swarmed around them. Royne retrieved his torch and relit it. Between his light and Tyel's, the flames revealed more than any of them wished to see.

The chamber was long and half as wide as the Temple boundary. Down the centre, a flowing channel of water, sunken three feet down and equally wide, cut the passageway in half. It flowed from one dark tunnel end to another, from north to south. However, the northern iron grate had been pried away from the stonework; its bars curled outwards, warped and bent like leaves hanging from a branch.

The strega Tyel dispatched had been strong – but relentless more than powerful. However, the raw power of whatever had done this to forged iron must've been enormous.

The floor was slick with blood, pooling in recesses, settling into cracks and splattered up the walls. A long, thick trail of blood ran down directly into the stream in a thick rivulet, to be carried out and away.

As Tyel turned his torch deeper into the chamber, they saw piles of dismembered bodies of men, women – even swaddling-wrapped infants, piled into a mound nearly as high as the stone ceiling. Branson had never seen anything so disturbing; their faces were ashen and distorted – when they had a face at all. Their clothes had been shredded.

He closed his eyes, trying not to notice the smell, which was impossible, of course, or the buzzing of bloatflies.

"I don't wish to be down here any longer," Gehard remarked. He took one last cursory look around and started for the ladder.

"Wait." Alyse interrupted. Gehard stopped mid-step. "Listen."

And they did. A few things made themselves apparent in that moment: for one, Alyse's hearing was exceptional, Tyel thought, as he couldn't hear anything. Two, she just told the Luminary to stop – and he did so. She held some influence over him – be it through her disposition or some other less tangible means.

Tyel turned to her. "What can you hear?"

She merely pointed to the bellringer's corner. The solitary arm that had once been pulling the enormous rope cord, sticking up as it was from the mound of bodies, had begun to move again. Slowly. The fingers were trying to close around the thick line. Gehard nearly fell over trying to move away from the arm.

"A survivor." Ser Filip moved to the corner at once. "Branson, Royne – help me shift the bodies." Alyse said nothing, but the expression on her face remained troubled.

"We're getting you out. You're safe now," Ser Filip consoled the buried figure. The arm looked thin, venous and covered in soot and blood. And yet it struggled against the rope, trying to pull it down once more.

Tyel exchanged looks with Royne. Neither looked pleased to be mingling with the half-desecrate dead – but they made their way to the corner and began to shift bodies. Limbs on limbs; the weight of the limp corpses made each removal a trial. After a few minutes, the three were covered up to their elbows in thick blood and unknown seepage.

Beneath it all, the figure of a small, balding man emerged, beaten and purple down the left side of his face. His left eye was completely swollen shut, and he made no attempts to open his right eye. But there he sat, propped against the wall; how he'd managed to survive, stuck and buried under this mound of death, only this man knew. He moaned quietly and let his arm drop back down. Even through the muck and blood, his skin was snow-pale and waxy in the torchlight.

Gehard too looked pale. However, rather than starting back up the ladder, he crouched between it and the figure on the ground. "I know this man."

"Templemaster?" He extended his hand, as if to take the shoulder of the old man in front of him, but stopped. The man's head lolled to the side; his one good eye opened as it searched for Gehard's face. Gehard extended and took his hand.

With a coughing wheeze, the old man started. "M-My Lord. The... *water.*"

Ser Filip looked shocked; he'd not known Gehard to be a sentimental fellow, but it appeared as if he held this Templemaster in some personal regard.

"Your Worship–just rest. You're safe now." Gehard turned to the party. "Bring him water. Now."

Tyel brushed past Royne and started up the ladder.

"What happened here? What can you tell us?" Gehard continued. He let the Templemaster's hands rest in his lap. Blood had pooled there

– but he knew not whether it was from the old man, or the bodies that had lain on top of him.

~ ~ ~

Tyel surfaced and immediately the sounds of combat met his ears. He sprinted toward the heavy doors of the Solum Temple. As he approached, the indistinct sounds grew louder and more disturbing. Screams – more like shrieks – and a sound that immediately brought him back to Reeds-rush village just days ago.

He parted the door slightly as a reverberating screech seemed to cloud his head – his eyes blurred as if trying to focus on something very close to his face, yet not there. He peeked out. It appalled him. He closed the door. His heart was beating furiously now.

~ ~ ~

The Templemaster lifted a hand, with great effort, and pointed down the underground passageway. "You must – leave. There. Warn the south. I rang the bell – to bring attention." He was struggling to stay focussed. "I'm so sorry." His eye was beginning to tear up. "The... village... was overrun."

Gehard said nothing. Ser Filip now knelt down next to the Luminary. He could see genuine upset in Gehard's eyes.

"Don't apologise," Gehard replied. "What did this?"

The Templemaster's eye rolled toward Gehard, then to Ser Filip. He was weeping now.

"I... watched them die." He turned his head and spluttered a bloody cough. "I watched... I couldn't... prot... ec..."

His ragged breath slowed; his heaving chest issued forth one more expulsion of foul air and then he lay still. The Templemaster's one open eye was left to gaze off into the infinite.

Gehard's mouth hung open, crouched and motionless, unable to find the words.

Just then, the hatch above creaked open. Tyel's head peered in.

"I really hope there's another way out of this Temple," the squire shouted down.

"Why?" Ser Filip replied, but he suspected he already knew the answer. Tyel was on his way back down, not bothering to reply.

Instead, it was Alyse who spoke. "Tyel is correct – we cannot return to the square." She stepped toward him. Gehard's face soured.

"What are you talking about, elf? I'm not leaving my stallion."

"Or your men, your Grace?" Ser Filip rose to his feet. Gehard disregarded him.

"We're overrun, Ser. The guards are lost." Tyel called out as he reached the floor. "And if we linger here any longer, we will be too."

At this, Gehard worked himself to his feet, straining under the weight of his armour. "Did I not make myself clear? I'm not leaving my horse and walking back to the capital."

Royne sniffed heavily, spat, and took to the ladder. "The pissant is just a coward. And who believes the word of 'n elf? A liar by birth. I'll get the true sense of it."

Tyel looked over at Alyse. Her eyes flared blue. "And you are a fool. Makes no matter," she seethed. "Go then. Meet your bright god all the sooner." The way she said *'bright god'* made Tyel's skin crawl. The three men stood stunned; none had seen Alyse flare like this before. *She seems so… meek,* Ser Filip thought. *A handservant. Halfbreed at that. But she has bite. Then, there was more to Gehard – mayhaps more to his maid as well.* Gehard looked amused.

Royne bared his teeth and pointed a gloved finger at Alyse. "Open your mouth like that again and I'll close it fer good, elf."

He stomped up each step and threw open the hatch so hard, the left door came off the hinge, crashing onto the stone floor. The soldier's heavy footfalls faded into nothing as he crossed the Temple.

For a moment, no one spoke. All eyes were on the elfkin. She only looked at the floor in front of her.

"He won't be returning," she said quietly. "And now we must away.

RITE

Royne could hear the sounds of a losing battle as he spilled out into the square, bracing for a fight. As the scene before him revealed itself, he skidded to a halt. All around him, chaos. He drew his low-slung bastard sword, mouth agape. It was dark in the square – only moonlight betrayed the scores of creatures crawling, leaping and thrashing. He'd never seen beasts such as these before. *'Gods, that Branson kid had the right of it,'* he had to admit. That just made him angrier. He was hungry for a fight before; now he felt a little ill.

He saw Paldrick laying on his back, unmoving. Three more bodies lay at the bottom of the stone plinth. Arms. A leg. One black creature was straddled and hunched over another fallen soldier, its back to Royne. He couldn't see what it was doing, but he could guess. Things had fallen apart while he was away, playing fool-games in dank basements with half-pint heroes.

One thing was clear: this was not a winnable encounter. What he needed now was a fair retreat strategy, and one that preferably led to a warm tavern somewhere far from this mess.

He considered returning to the safety of the Temple's blessed grounds; surely these bloodspawn, if that was what he was witnessing, couldn't pass the threshold. But then, how did they enter the basement? He didn't know –

and it didn't much matter now. There was no escape from that underground waterway, and the streets were overrun with these things. The Luminary, the Knight Commander and their green cohorts, were as good as fly-bait now.

He needed a horse; any would do. One lay dead – a large brown mare, torn into pieces. The rest were gone – fled or freed. So that was not an option. He would have to fight his way out and leg it back south. It was not a pleasant prospect; it might take him two full days at a decent clip, and that was without supplies – and all assuming he made it through the town unscathed.

He had already lingered too long on the Temple foresteps. The time for decision was on him. He felt the cold rush of anticipation surging through his veins. His legs carried him forward without conscious thought and, before he even knew what he was doing, he was swinging hard into a walking corpse, as best as he could tell, planting his steel into its back with a heaving swing. It buried itself halfway into the beast. It shrieked as it collapsed sideways, black blood pumping out onto the stone.

'*On to the next,*' Royne thought – and rushed forward past the fallen foe. He felt his vision narrowing as adrenaline carried him on. From his left, a human cry. He turned to the sound; Haylor Gefrey – a seasoned fighter. He was propped up against the far wall of a grey stone building, below the shuttered windows. A single bloody handprint marked the wooden window frame. A long trail of blood ran toward Royne. Gefrey's pale face was drawn tight as he raised an arm to Royne and let it fall again.

He started toward him, but another creature darted into his path, crouched and ready to spring at him. Its eyes glowed faintly red as it opened its jaws, which unhinged like a serpent ready to feed. It screeched – a sound like the dragging of old wooden chairs across the mess hall floor. There was something else in that sound too – something deeper, that seemed to affect his muscles, making them clench; his eyes blurred and he had to fight to stay upright.

'What in the gods' names—' he thought, and then it was on him. He was knocked backwards, hard onto the ground. The screeching stopped as Royne raised a mailed fist and planted it into the side of this strega's head. The stench! He felt its wet breath in his face, across his cheek and away, as it rolled to his left and off with a yowl. He rolled toward it and got on top; it thrashed at him with fingers like tree branches, claws like a jungle-cat's razor talons. He pushed the arm back down against the stone pavement with his left hand.

In that moment, he could see this thing clearly. A strega, no doubt. If it had been human once, as it was understood to be, it had since transformed into something animalistic and single-minded; its eyes were black almonds, glowing red from some unknown means, on a long, almost snout-like face. It was a face he would enjoy crushing, Royne thought. He did so. His right hook was a punishment and he left it twitching on the ground as it bled out.

He would head south, the way they came in, but off the main road. However, to exit the town, he would need to beat a path out. He was angry before; the night was supposed to be a lark – a fetch mission for the Inquisitor and a simple escort duty. There would be wine and food. Now his friends were dead and dying and his anger felt left to dangle limply against too many enemies. He could keep this up for a little while, but sooner or later he would tire. And when he did, that would be his end.

He pushed back to his feet, glancing toward Haylor Gefrey. He was still now; his eyes sagged and visionless. Another gone. *'Okay, time to go.'*

There was a side-alley that ran between the block next to Haylor Gefrey's last stand; he would make for that, round the corner and head south on a backroad. Perhaps he could avoid confrontation.

He scrambled for his wayward blade and dragged it back up. Pooled blood had begun to dry in the fuller; he dragged the blade across the cuff of his doublet and darted toward the alleyway.

~ ~ ~

Gehard looked appalled. He twisted and adjusted his waist belt, shifting the sheath slightly. "Of course he's returning, girl! He's–he is my appointed protection!" The Luminary's concern betrayed him as he stammered. "He's under oath to serve."

Alyse ignored this. "I feel something happening above us. Something is pulling the – strega – away from the square."

"They're being drawn away?" Ser Filip pressed. "I don't know how you know these things, but I'll take you at your word. I'd rather not head to the surface and find out the hard way that you're correct once again."

The elfkin nodded. "But more will come."

"They came in through the underground channel – that's the northern end." Ser Filip motioned to the badly warped water grate. "Can we pry open that other grating?"

Branson jogged toward the rusty, slotted grate, embedded in the channel at the far end of the chamber. The bars were finger-thick iron; they could perhaps bend them wide enough apart to squeeze through, he figured, but it would take time they did not have, and there was no way the Luminary would fit through so fully plated.

"Ser, it would take more strength than all of us have to warp the bars," Tyel replied.

Ser Filip scratched his chin, looking up at the hatch to the surface; reconsidering, continued, "Then we head north, underground."

"In – the *waterway*? You must be joking," the Luminary spat. I'm not getting in there like this."

Ser Filip walked over to Gehard and leaned into his face. "You're right. Remove your plate. I hope you had the sense to wear more than spun wool 'neath. Branson, assist the Luminary."

"Branson, hold. Absolutely not. I will not leave house-blessed sacred plate armour here, to be befouled by only the gods know what – in this,

this *sewer.*"

"Then you'll rot in here with the rest," and he turned away. "To stay is your choice to make, your Grace. Whatever you command."

Gehard's eyes darted to the waterway. Things had spiralled rapidly away from the mark now. *His* command? Not exactly. He rode at the head of this folly; he would be completely accountable. He simply could not return to the capital without supplies. It would almost be better if he cooked in a funerary pyre on the road south than fail the High Inquisitor. To fail his father's command was to slight the Solum God – and he'd seen the bodies strapped high up on the golden rings of the Solum Temples to roast in the cleansing fires of the Solum God's touch. A horrible end – and not one he relished experiencing.

The Luminary turned to Tyel. "Boy. Be careful with the straps. And set each piece against the wall. When I return – or, perhaps a courier, should I send one, I want these pieces back in perfect condition."

'Perfect condition,' Branson thought darkly. *'It's armour.'* Clean armour was either worn by a coward or a poor fighter. Gehard was more concerned with his appearance than a powdered mummer on a Caravanerie stage. The Luminary lashed his tongue more than he'd ever cleaved a sword, he felt.

"Alyse, Branson—we'll have to fight our way out if we should happen to encounter more. Are you both up to this?"

Gehard was nearly out of his breastplate. Beneath, he wore a thick, white cotton tunic with a high neckline of thick leather. His armpits left stains of pale brown that ran down his sides. Next, Tyel helped him remove section after section of leg plate, undoing black strapped leather from their notched fastenings.

Tyel was grateful the Luminary opted to wear britches.

"This will not be pleasant," Gehard hesitated. "But the Knight Com-mander is right. We must salvage this mission. We head north, then, once out of the town limits, we will head above ground and make our way back south. We must warn the High Inquisitor."

Ser Filip took a lingering look over the edge of the waterway and, pinching air in his chest, jumped in. The cold mountain water, now tainted a dull red, immediately tensed his muscles; he felt his skin turn to gooseflesh. The water came up to just below his waist; the flow was gentle, but a slight current pulled at him, teasing him southward.

"Your Grace?" The Knight Commander sloshed across to the edge of the waterway and offered a hand to the Luminary. He ignored it and with one last look over his shoulder at the Templemaster – or perhaps his armour, Tyel noted, he was in the water.

Tyel took Alyse by the hand. "Ready?" He wasn't sure if he was, himself.

He started forward, one hand on his sword. She stopped him. "Tyel." In a whisper, she spoke. "Remember. When the time comes, you run. No matter what."

As she dropped into the waterway, it parted around her. She landed feather-gently on a perfect circle of dry ground beneath her, and only her.

~ ~ ~

There was a sudden and definite lull in action as Royne sprinted across the square; he could feel dozens of red eyes instantly upon him. With his back arched, he sped past his fallen brother-at-arms, nearly throwing himself around the corner – and he let the momentum carry him forward. The wind seemed to pick up now – a scattering of leaves and branches blew and shook. The alleyway was narrow – barely wide enough to extend his arms to either side, crooked like a creek-bed and undulating the same.

His footfalls slapped against the cobbles and echoed against whitewashed walls. They seemed to bend inward in the dark like a terrible bower. Behind him, above – in all directions, the sound of claws scraping against stone, the flapping of heavy, leathery wings – and insect-like chirping and tittering. It almost sounded like laughter to Royne's ears. *Some of these bastards can fly,* he realised. It did nothing to improve his mood.

Harder and harder he sprinted. The alley continued around one blind crook and into another. It was nearly high-nightfall now and the slit of a Lunum shone down, giving just enough silver light to keep Royne from breaking his own neck on a jag in the road – and denying these foul beasts the chance themselves.

The alley spilled into a crossroad – a small intersection of thin town-houses, two and three floors high. A few pale lights snatched for his atten-tion. Royne was more preoccupied with a new sound – heavy, determinedly pounding foot-stamps from somewhere across the street. The next alleyway was pitch; he was about to leap without looking. The sounds of strega filled the air.

He skidded to a stop in the middle of the street as something enormous, broad as a bullock, filled the mouth of the alley in front of him, emerging from the shadows like a grotesque tongue hanging from the maw of a skull.

Royne had never felt fear like this. Not once; not to the point where rational thought slips away and the hollow space that's left behind is at once filled with the need to run away. This thing was nearly twice his height; bound in rags and chains. It squeezed out of the alleyway, one arm against the wall of a slanting terrace, and the other dragging something behind and to its side.

Six eyes, two sets of three, ran down its huge elongated skull. The eyes were small and black, rimmed with the same red glow as the other strega. This one, however, was as different in build as could be. It revealed itself fully, issuing a wet, rounded roaring from deep within a broad, hyper-mus-cular chest. Its arms were as thick and rounded as stacked boulders, split-ting at their ends into two sets of wrists. Two hands on each arm, clasped together like a clamp. To Royne, it looked like three strega had been stitched together, seamlessly; a blend of the power of three blood-monsters.

From overhead, the behemoth swung something downwards into the road between it and Royne. It splattered on impact. It bellowed again. All that remained in the monster's gigantic dual-hands was a severed leg. The rest of the person was smashed completely and drawn broadly across the cobblestones. Whichever poor peon this thing had grasped would've died of fear, Royne thought, darkly.

The splash of cold blood against his face brought Royne back to the moment; his already-tense muscles awakened in a jolt. The cold fear gripped him, so he grasped for his sword and rounded to the right of this giant.

There were horrors in this world that even horrors would fear to cross.

Royne was breathing like a furnace; in his peripheral vision, he saw the streets fill with dark movement. He knew this was it.

"I killed y'r brothers and sisters," Royne screamed at the abomination. It raised thick lips in a twisted smile of too many teeth. It was laughing at him; an undulating, hollow laugh like an echo in a long chamber. It laughed slowly and loudly. An ugly sound.

He raised his filthy bastard sword – he hoped someone would find it when he was gone and bury it in his place.

"Aye, so y' *understand* me, you dirty pigscrewer?" He yelled back. He laughed as well, which surprised him in the moment.

"Good! Let's see if ya bleed like the rest!" He charged forward.

Three things happened at that moment, though Royne would only live to know two of them.

First, the rotting tower-behemoth stepped forward on its tree-trunk legs and grabbed Royne with all four hands, like a child might with a stitch-doll. It raised him off the ground, holding him at length as it compressed his chest. He could feel his ribs snapping and he dropped his blade feebly. He couldn't breathe, let alone scream.

Second, as it did so, the beast spoke. "I will *raise you*. You will head north." Guttural and dark as sin, it uttered these words. "Now you will die." It squeezed and the life slipped from Royne as his bald head rolled back on his thick neck, limp as wet cloth.

Third, beyond the gaze of a hundred unblinking strega eyes in the street, lining the walls, crawling along the rooftops and screeching in the laneways around this doomed confrontation—two more sets of eyes watched.

Two were human and green. Slightly below and to the left of them, two were dwarven and grey. They spied from an unlit upstairs bedroom vantage down the street with great fascination and equal horror. Brea E'Lario peered through the window. She spoke. Dust-in-His-Eyes fixed his spectacles.

"It's happening," she said curtly. "We're about to witness the rite."

~ ACT II ~

CHAPTER 11

REFLECTION

The morning seemed to arrive too soon for Melodis Fendrigar's liking. She rose and habitually pulled the satin drawstring of her servant bell. She threw the thick downy quilt, intricately stitched with pink roses and golden butterflies, forward over her legs and rolled over and out of her four-post bed. The sun was peeking through the middle of the heavy curtains, giving the room a warm and comfortable glow that bounced off the pale pink walls.

A few moments later, a young woman rapped on the door and entered carrying a gleaming copper basin of warm water mixed with dried flower petals and scented oils. Melodis always took her morning refreshment this way; the perfumed oils cleared her head and set her straight for the day.

She was dressed quickly and carefully by two handmaidens who knew better than to dawdle in the chambers of the daughter of the Inquisitor. Today, she had the inner chamber to herself; her father was already breaking fast and her brother was off playing the gallant knight somewhere north. She could only guess her mother was out of the city, as far from her father as possible. It was clear their marriage was barely more than a formality these days.

Melodis scrunched her brow at the thought as she watched a handful of servants sweep the marbled halls and change out the evening's candles for fresh ones.

Peering down into the sheltered garden courtyard, she took in the cool morning air. The sun was still low in the sky and not yet hitting the small square of carefully clipped grass and tile, lined with boxed hedges. A simple pool of prayer and reflection lay in the very centre, filled by the constant flow of river-water from the north. The gently rippling waters splashed against the centre-stone monument, a hand-wrought golden Circuitris.

"Oh servant! Servant!" Melodis chimed. A young man, barely old enough to drink with adults, looked up from a cart of stacked tallow candles. "Please tell the kitchen I wish to sup in the gardens today."

"Very good, m'lady," the young man replied, bowing as he did so. He skittered off to deliver the message. *'Handsome young thing. Mayhap I'll send for him tonight,'* she thought, with a smile, *'To pray with me.'*

Her duties were few: be a model of chastity and modesty, keep the Solum God's laws at heart and serve the realm. She knew she failed most completely at the first two, and the third was loose enough to be interpreted as she pleased–and mostly she opted to serve the realm by keeping the scullery maids in work to do.

She bobbed down the spiral stone stairs, from bedchamber hall to ground-floor foyer, passing the watchful eyes of posted guards and handmaids. The high-ceilinged grand foyer allowed access to the gardens on one side, and all other doorways led to various halls, amenities, staff quarters and spaces she'd never bothered to peek into. Rarely did she see faces not paid to be there.

The garden was divided into quarters; each corner hemmed with carefully-clipped hedgerows. At the far end of the courtyard, a tall weeping willow arched three long limbs gracefully over the middle of the space, its long dangling leaves rippling with the slightest breeze.

This morning, the courtyard was still in pale blue shadow, but by high-sun, she'd lounge beneath that tree and sip something cool and refreshing.

She positioned herself by the pool of reflection and sat heavily on the broad, curving stone lip. Gingerly, she leaned over and peered into the water. The fractious drift of white wisps of cloud rippled behind her own distorted reflection. She didn't like how she looked in polished metal; she felt her face was too round, her chin ran down her neck in steps that reminded her unpleasantly of her father. She had her mother's blue eyes, from what she could recall – but it had been so long since she'd seen her mother's face that she appeared like a far-off dream when she tried to recall it.

She was no vision of beauty, she knew it, but she was never short of company. Blessed gold could afford the finest companions: company that did only as she wished, who laughed with her and poured honeyed affection on her.

She dipped a hand in the chilly water and let the current tickle her fingers. Then, looking up and around and seeing no one, she turned that hand into a bowl and scooped a mouthful. She'd done it since she was little; a kind of strange and forbidden treat, to drink from the flowing waters of the pool. Gehard would scold her when she was younger, teasing her for tainting the sacred waters. But she did it anyway.

Her thought was interrupted by a gentle, elderly woman's voice. "Your… Gracefulness! River water is for the likes of peasants and livestock! Please, if you thirst, summon one of the servants!"

Blushing immediately, she quickly wiped her stocky hand against the lap of her day-dress, a butter-yellow long gown with a meticulously embroidered pattern of suns around the hem and sleeves. Melodis shrivelled her features.

"I was just—" she blurted, but stopped short. Why should she answer to a kitchen worker?

"Your Grace, presenting your morning sup; I wanted to apologise personally for the… simplicity of it," the woman said, meekly. "We have supply shortages." She approached Melodis and slipped a wooden tray to rest beside her. On it sat a meal that by reasonable standards appeared to be rich and diverse: pan-cooked eggs on thick-cut slices of buttered oatbread, a bowl of cream and stonefruit slices, three cuts of cured pork glazed in a fragrant sauce of lemon and butter beside a large glass of pressed solfruit juice.

"No sweet course! Again?"

The kitchen matron bowed low, pressing her hands together against her soiled white apron. "I'm sorry, Your Grace. Sweetcane is becoming hard to source, and—"

Melodis cut her off. "And solfruit causes me vapours most repugnant – the kitchen knows this. You do this to *tease* me, do you?" Melodis lifted the pressed juice and poured it into the pool of reflection. "I'd rather drink river water," she moaned, scooping a glassful back up. Spitefully, she drank a long, glugging gulp.

"My— my lady! No!" The kitchen matron slapped the glass from her hand. It clinked once against the stone lip of the pool and shattered on the pavers.

Melodis gagged. At once, she knew something was amiss. She looked down at the pale square of stone pavement. Among the shards of glass, the water spread in a puddle tinged with brown. She could taste something sickening at the back of her throat.

"Qu-quickly–fetch me clean—" and then she vomited; a fountain of thin, white liquid came pouring down her front.

Repulsed, the kitchen matron turned heels and darted away as quickly as she could. She needed clean water. Through the foyer, she hooked a right turn and sped past a guard, who flinched and pulled her up.

"What?" He pressed.

"The Inquisitor's Daughter is – *unwell*," she huffed, catching her breath. "Quickly. Attend to her. I'll fetch help."

The guard blinked at her for a moment and adjusted his helmet slightly.

Then, with a puff of indignant breath, he looked at the matron with scepticism. She returned the look with panic that prompted him to take this situation more seriously.

Descending the steps into the courtyard two at a time, he saw Melodis doubled over, on her knees, one hand clutching at her distended stomach, moaning in pain like a tortured piglet. Into her other hand she coughed. She raised her head to him pitifully. Around her mouth, he saw blood. It trickled down her neck like a run of wax.

~ ~ ~

The High Inquisitor hobbled down the stone steps into the cool of the subterranean pools. His sandaled feet struggled to keep a grip on the moisture-slicked floor. As he approached the edge, he carefully lowered himself down on one popping, straining knee. He nearly fell backwards, but steadied himself against the lip of the pool. His weight shifted and he slipped into the cool waters.

The effort of descending the stairs left him sweating. He felt his skin prickle against the sharp contrast in temperature.

Two towel-bearing maids stood wordlessly on both sides of the arched entryway, observing. They exchanged glances as Boff waded out into the water. He turned to them with a face of disinterest. "Leave me to my prayers," he commanded. Bowing wordlessly, the two women set their towels aside, gathered themselves together and departed beneath the archway that led back up toward the ground level.

As their footfalls faded into nothing, the Inquisitor sat back down. '*Good.*' In these healing waters, flowing through his lands from high in the Atherons, he could feel himself cleansed of his misthinkings and sinfulness.

The ceiling glittered with the undulations of the blue-tinged water of the sacred pool. Boff watched the play of light and let his mind wander for a moment.

Water and life. Water and death. Water to cleanse. Water to extinguish.

He would bless the waters, anoint it with smoky duskwood oil and crushed leaves of the kaffir. He would burn a candle down to the base and make an offering to the Solum God of his prayers. Sometimes he would bathe daily. Other times, he could only stand it weekly. It really came down to how pious and charitable he had been in the days before. He had not been particularly pious this week. The news from the north had been dwelled upon too long before action. And once confronted with cold fact, he knew he should act with swiftness and decisiveness, but his sinful appetites had tugged at his attention instead.

His stomach's hunger was an unscratchable, intractable itch, so he had sent his only son north under the pretence of surveillance – but in his heart, he knew the people would soon grow hungry. And hunger bred reactionary, desperate and violent circumstances. Gehard would bring resupply; this would quell the uprising before it began, and then – yes, then he would bring the full strength of his forces north to stamp out the godless blood-monsters. *'Yes,'* he consoled himself, *'A generous and loving ruler, am I. I have the grace of the Solum God upon my shoulders.'*

His thoughts turned to his son and the vanguard that he helmed. He'd been gone two days now; no word had yet come from north, which was not unusual, but he would expect a pigeon soon. And on those wings, good tidings would bring him some mental relief, shortly followed by fresh edible delights. The kitchen had been struggling for some time, he had noticed, but until just recently had always managed his full accompaniment of courses.

He smiled to himself, feeling the sting of cold water against him as he pictured the trays of brightly coloured confection and racks of baked pies, carefully layered cakes and sugared fruit. His favourite were summer-cherub rounds; sweet and sour berries in a thin crust of sweet pastry.

Footsteps rushing downstairs interrupted his gastronomic fantasia.

"Your Grace! Please!" A voice he recognised to be that of the kitchen matron, a grey woman he knew as Dorothea, called from behind him. He spun around in the water, furious at the interruption. He opened his mouth to thunder at her, but as soon as she rounded the stairs beneath the archway, he stopped. Her front was covered in crimson.

"What happened?" He blurted out, struggling to find his feet and leaning heavily against the lip of the pool to balance himself

"Please, Your Grace! You must come quick! It's your daughter."

"Melodis?" A hundred thoughts went through his head at once; none were positive.

"A towel! Now!" he barked, and the matron complied, rushing to retrieve a large folded length of thick cloth.

He snatched it from her thin hands, noticing the crimson palm prints she left behind. His stomach lurched. *'My sweet Melodis…'*

The matron averted her eyes as the High Inquisitor stepped out of the pools and wrapped himself from generous bosom to knee. He began to reach for his underclothes, unaccustomed to moving about his grounds disrobed as he was, but was cut short.

"Quickly. There's no time." The matron stood aside and directed him upward. He hesitated, but then, something was wrong with Melodis. He nodded uncomfortably and waddled toward the stairs, grasping for the iron railing to pull himself along with more haste.

By the time he made it to the courtyard, his knees ached. However, they stopped supporting his weight completely when, as he pushed through the circle of helpers, healers and onlookers, he spied his only daughter. He fell down on his knees next to her.

She had barely the life left in her to turn her head.

"F…ather." Her baby-like features were smeared with dried blood. Her eyes, usually a dazzling blue, were shot through with blood and looked hazy.

"How did this happen – Melodis! Oh Melodis. My child!"

A healer, an old woman in a tall white headwrap, addressed him gently, if stiffly.

"When we found her, she was quaking and vomiting. This turned to blood; something inside her has given out, your Grace."

The Inquisitor turned to her now. "Do something! You're a healer, are you not? Heal!"

"But for the Solum God's grace, we cannot do anything. I am truly sorry, Your Gr—"

The Inquisitor slapped her, full-handed, across her face. The Healer recoiled, pain and terror on her face. "*Worthless! All of you!*" He screamed. "Find me another healer. Now!"

Melodis was having trouble breathing. She groaned pitifully as she looked up at her father. Her eyes rolled here and there, trying so hard to keep focus.

There was a flurry of movement around them; able bodies scattered to find help. Boff Fendrigar looked down at Melodis Fendrigar and for a moment, he felt powerless, stripped of his title and clothes, unable to help her.

"Th… Wah-ha… she tried to speak, her eyes rolling upward. "Wah-haa…" But her tongue was swollen now; a trickle of blood spilled over from the side of her lips and down her round cheek. Her pretty day dress was a battlefield of spilled blood, as she lay there barely moving, her hands spasming, trying desperately to reach up towards his face.

The Inquisitor was shaking now as well; a quiver that started in his chest and seemed to run outwards down his arms, then his legs, and finally up his thick neck, to his broad face, which had turned wine-red. He shook uncontrollably, the breath in his lungs unable to escape. His eyes began to quaver. Tears. At first a wiggling, glassy line on his lids, then, like a saucer of spilled cream, they flowed down. He let out a low, lingering groan that grew and grew as he sobbed. Staccato spasms of upset punctuated his anguish.

And she was gone.

He howled.

"*...H... H— How...*" was all the mighty man could muster, broken through sobs. And no one remained who could answer – save for a single soft hand now gently resting against his shoulder. The kitchen matron knew how.

He flinched at the touch, but did not turn – could not turn – from Melodis. Through his weeping eyes, he saw his sweet, harmless daughter depart this wicked world. A loving and good girl, she was. Any father would be proud. *How could this happen?* Her time was snuffed out, blotted away into nothingness. The sun shone down on them from above, warm and indifferent, glistening in the Pool of Reflection.

"It's in the water, Your Grace."

CHAPTER 12

ESCAPE

In the water was exactly where Tyel wished he wasn't. Everything he wore, everything he carried, was now waterlogged to the point of hopelessness. His newly acquired leather was oiled, sure, but now saturated and heavy, soaking up the dirty brine of the waterway. Every step felt as if weights were tied to his legs, with both arms above him trying to keep his blade and buckler dry. Alyse had no such trouble. As she walked, water seemed to wick away from her at arm's length, in a perfect circle around her. Not a droplet of liquid touched her fair skin.

True magic, he thought. *Such an incredible thing to see.*

The Elfkin spoke little as it was, but her face read of deep concentration. Tyel thought it best not to interrupt her.

He thought of his horse now. He hoped Mancer had the good sense to run; Alyse had told him to do the same when the time came.

In front, Ser Filip progressed slowly. He ran one hand along the curved wall of the underground waterway: a long, straight tunnel running north to south, intersected here and there with smaller pipes and flow-throughs. At first, Ser Filip had tried to maintain a lit torch, but dripping water eventually extinguished the light. He let it float away in futility. Gehard frowned as it bobbed past him.

Now they travelled in near-darkness; only dim beams of moonlight spilled down into the channel from intermittent drainage above.

"Did anyone see that flash?" It was possible his eyes were tired, but for a moment, there appeared to be a brilliant spark of purple and green. There and gone before it registered.

The Knight Commander nodded uneasily. If the Luminary saw it, he didn't acknowledge it.

"Aye," Alyse replied. He glanced at her, but she showed nothing but continued focus, her eyes pale now. Branson knew it meant something, that flash – but what exactly was beyond him now. It was unnatural to be sure. He put it from his mind as he weaved to avoid the down-facing body of an old man floating downstream.

"How much farther?" whined Gehard, quietly. "We need to get back above ground and make for the south again. Each step we take is farther from that."

Water gently sloshing against his waist, Ser Filip paused to consider. "We must be nearing the northern skirts of the town by now. The flow of water is faster. Certainly louder."

And he was right about that, Tyel thought. Progress was slow in the dark, and even then, this was a large town that worked its way upward into the foothills. At first, the bodies that floated past were disturbing; now that they were farther north, they thinned considerably. By count, Tyel tracked more than forty before he stopped counting. It was just too morbid.

"Listen."

When Alyse chose to speak, now they knew to heed. At once, they knew why. There, above the reverberating, soft rush of water around them, there was something else. They turned to Alyse. Her eyes burned blue.

She looked at Tyel alone.

"Now we run."

~ ~ ~

Dusty's eyes were poor in daylight, but at night, things came into sharper focus – to the point where he could remove the thick lenses he wore strapped to his large head. Born under a dark moon, so his parents said, with Lunum dust in his eyes, so Dust-in-His-Eyes they named him: afflicted he'd been with poor vision, even for a mountain-dweller.

He never knew otherwise, so it didn't bother him. The dark suited him just fine; working by candlelight, mostly travelling by night – in Dusty's experience, the most interesting things happened after sunset. The fondest encounters with women, the best time to drink or smoke or think. The easiest time to get away cleanly.

The road north had taken them nine nights, mostly by road, and generally in darkness and silence. For the most part, Brea felt entirely fine – which annoyed her, since it was so tempting to slit this dwarf's throat and be done with the whole affair. But as the Lunum had not waned, she waited to see how her condition might change. Dusty seemed all too comfortable having a ruthless killer for a road companion as well – though, she supposed, he too had dirty hands. If they fought, she knew she could take him. But without his remedy, whatever it was, the risk of ending up cold and stiff was too great to chance.

And so, she found herself playing the part of hired muscle. Dusty was informed, specifically by whom she had her notion, but informed nonetheless—that a clan of blood fiends and abominations had taken root in the caves within the Atheron Ranges. Worse, it was said they'd been raised by an elf of some social standing. A traitor of the lowest kind, and a dealer in magics of the darkest nature.

It was Dusty's contention that, like most spreading infections, the affliction could be slowed, then stemmed or stopped completely. An exacting and clinical view, befitting a dwarf of medicinal background.

For her part, Brea believed she knew of the target of whom he spoke. Be it coincidence or the guiding hand of fate, she felt certain threads of her existence being tugged when Dusty spoke of the details. He did not know how intertwined they might be. Brea too had been paid by the Oracular Magisterium of Nine to infiltrate, then eliminate this betrayer – this Necromant.

The Magisterium was the highest office of power, whose reach extended beyond even the High Inquisitor's in each region. The Oracles were said to be inhuman, which allowed them to be conduits of higher powers. Three of the Nine praised the Solum God; three, the Moon. Three others, The Void. In Brea's mind, they were all opportunistic hacks at best, and at worst, a dangerous syndicate of criminals, exploiting religious fervour for protection and gain. But they paid well, partially in advance, and this was how she preferred it.

Now she realised, even if Dusty hadn't worked it out yet, she was likely one of multiple hired swords working this assignment, all hired by the Magisterium. That was fine; she was prepared to beat a path north fast and claim the rewards herself. It also meant the Oracles thought the task extraordinarily difficult with low likelihood of success.

Even though Dusty thought *he* was leading the way, holding all the keys and answers, Brea knew better than that. Really, it was *she* who held the knowledge of the target they sought; *she* had the skills *he* needed. And in the end, that meant she had her own leverage; perhaps more than him – save for the means to keep herself alive after an unwitting dose of this dwarf's own black medicine.

If that meant taking the dwarf along with her for now, resisting the urge to end him, then that was how it would be.

And here they were. Tonight, in the town of Dormanstar, for a brief moment, night would vanish in a blinding flash of amethyst purple and jade green.

"There," Brea whispered. "The Necromant." In some sense, she knew they were lucky to find him here; in a truer sense, they were also deeply unlucky to be in the middle of what was unfolding.

Down at street level, a hooded figure with a long, twisted staff glided slowly into the middle of the lane, past a hulking behemoth of muscle, tendon, bone and blood. They'd just watched this beast, replete with two forearms, lift and crush a footsoldier as wide as a door frame as if he were no more than a down-stuffed pillow.

The flash of green and purple light cast outward from the Necromant's staff – a curl of black, warped wood crowned with a gem of blood red. The blooming sphere of light rippled in a wave from the gem; it lit the entire street from one end to the other like a flash of lightning – and kept going. Beneath the hooded figure, the ground ignited in a ring of indigo-black flame. The tongues of fire licked at his draped cloak but did not ignite.

Crouching behind a smokestack, Dusty leaned on the upturned handle of his axe as his eyesight was overwhelmed by the brilliance. He winced and turned away, feeling the sudden shock of heat as the light ran through him.

A choir of shrieks and clicks and shrill screams began to echo and, as the pulse of magical light vanished, a warm breeze blew against Dusty's plaited beard, as if an invisible horse and carriage had wheeled past them at speed. His eyes adjusted to the night again but what he saw made him wish they hadn't.

At first, the Necromant made no other movement. The ring of black-fire around his feet dissolved, flickering up and away. The screaming died down and it seemed nothing dared break that moment of stillness – perhaps from the shock of the light, or reverent awe at this black magician.

Then, slowly, something stirred. Then some *things*. Then a great many things. Brea could hear them before she could see them.

"Dusty," she hissed. "The dead of this town. He's raising them."

"Aye, tends to be what a Necromant does."

The Necromant outstretched one hand above the fallen soldier; the corpse was spasming, trying to right itself. It moved one broken arm around to its side, then another. Crumpled legs began to snap back into form.

"Sure. But he's not just raising them." And Dusty could see the truth of that.

The body pushed itself upward–or was raised by the Necromant; it was hard to tell. Suddenly, the body was suspended upright; this time, no spectacular show of light, but there he was, pinned and hanging mid-air, just a step above the cobblestone.

As Brea watched in fascination, she began to piece together the bigger situation transpiring. Fascination quickly became dread.

The soldier's body began to warp and crack; blood poured out of burst seams that split the skin as the Necromant waved a hand and tilted his staff. He mouthed low, dark words that were lost in the air.

Again, the gemstone glowed a sickly red. The blood that poured out did not run down the corpse's body – but hung in thick spherical globules, like gnats around a lamplight. The body continued to distort and contort; the soldier's spine emerged from a seam which was rapidly tearing away from the back of the body. The arms swelled; the legs, too, ripping the fabric. Flesh stretched and tore and more and more blood seeped out and hung in the air, swirling around him.

Behind the Necromant, the huge, muscular horror began to laugh. Even from their vantage point, it was low and loud, carried to Dusty and Brea on the breeze. Brea nudged Dusty and the pair scurried along the rooftop, from chimney to chimney, getting as close as they dared.

Then, much to their surprise, the Necromant spoke aloud.

"Oh, but you *are* a large one, aren't you?" He laughed. It was a loud and bleak voice; a raspy sound, but not without an animated, almost melodic quality. "You are *raised*, my loyal servant."

With beckoning of his thin hand, the blood that had been held suspended in mid-air pulled inward toward the staff.

"I thank you for your contribution."

The gemstone seemed to draw the blood into itself, illuminating brighter and brighter as it did so. The glow licked at the Necromant's features. From Brea's view, she could finally begin to make out the face of her target. Large eyes; small nose. High cheekbones, flooded in red light; a small, thin mouth high above a long chin and even longer neck.

"An elf," She noted in a hush. Dusty said nothing; his large eyes stared unblinking. It made sense, she figured. Handily magical by birth, with a distaste for humans. Of course, Necromancy was by its nature condemned and outlawed across the lands and seas. Such a practice went against the basic laws of nature – and it was not the place of mortal beings to meddle with the process of life and death.

It took a dark and daring soul not just to learn about it – but to master it so utterly, as this Necromant had. Brea almost admired that bold contempt for the law – and people in general.

He set the soldier back down; no longer was it human, exactly – only vaguely did it resemble the bald-headed warrior it once was. The head remained bald, but below the thick neck, the torso became something bloated and tumour-like. A mass of muscle, extra appendages and jutting, angular bone. The man-beast's spine poked outward like the tops of fence posts; the arms split into two forearms, much the same as the behemoth already behind the Necromant.

"Now," he continued, "You shall call me *Master*. For that is what I am. Let me hear you say it." For a moment, the newly-formed beast said nothing; its bald head hung low. Then, it raised its head. "Speak!"

"Ye-sh… *massher.*"

"Good. Close enough." He waved his hand once more and the beast looked back down. "Now you will be silent and remain so. Here; a taste of life – you will crave more and I shall deliver it to you."

He tapped his staff once, firmly. At that, a thin stream of blood arced like a tendril toward the man-beast. It raised its head and opened its deformed mouth, which split wider into the cheeks of its pale face. It fed on the stream. The Necromant tapped the staff again and the funnel of fluid ceased.

"And to *all of you*!" He bellowed, like a rake against a bell. "When the waters of this land run red, you will feed. Now come! There is much to do."

The Necromant raised his arms high above him; the staff lit up like a star. At once, there was movement below and all around them. The simple bedstead they occupied had been empty; the alleyway beneath them, however, had not been. Brea flattened herself down on the tiles and peered over the edge of the roof. She motioned for Dusty to join her.

The town was littered with fallen and dismembered corpses. They were moving again – and most had taken new, distorted, almost animalistic forms. Some appeared as the thin, wiry strega that crawled along other rooftops and scurried like scouts into the streets and lanes. Others remained corpselike, but upon their bloodied foreheads, new eyes burst open. Second mouths split open like gaping wounds on the sides of their faces.

"Look!" Dusty nodded back toward the Necromant now. He'd turned his back, his staff still raised high. "A portal!" Dusty squinted as an oval of blue-white light opened from the surface of the road up past the head-height of the Necromant.

"North!" he shouted! And, with a swirl of his staff above him, he stepped through the portal. The oval collapsed inward and disappeared in a small burst of static sparkle. He was gone.

Out of laneways the dead spilled; some took flight on leathery wings; Brea held her breath. All it would take was one pair of eyes on their position and things would fall rapidly to pieces.

The streets teemed with un-life. With the Necromant's final command, every creature – dead, two-headed dogs, mutated, long-limbed cats, ratty bone-pigeons and even one large, white horse – torn at the mid, intestines dragging – a caravan of the most horrific kind, ambled toward the north end of town. Toward the mountains of Atheron.

CHAPTER 13

UNION

Below the streets of Dormanstar, Alyse knew they were no longer alone. In the water around them, behind and in front, bodies of the fallen had begun to rise to the surface. Alyse screamed as a grey, swollen horror rose up behind her, reaching with dead fingers.

The grey, decomposing hand came off cleanly as Tyel brought his blade down on the wrist, flopping onto the ground inside Alyse's protective bubble. The bleeding stump withdrew. Recoiling now, the unfortunate being in front of them resembled a bloated, grey sausage, rather than the person it once was. It went again at Alyse, who this time was better prepared. She moved to the side and past it, leaving it shambling and disoriented in the darkness.

"How is this possible?" Ser Filip balked, but there was little time to dwell. With a grunt of effort, Tyel thrust his sword deep into the gut of the corpse and withdrew. It retracted with a scream that was somehow more terrifying than the monster itself. A black fan of blood poured from the wound.

Gehard turned to see, far behind them, the shifting, undulating heads of more of these beings, wading through the passage. "Let's go – now, please." They wasted no time – but moving through nearly waist-high water was slow – and these horrors were gaining.

"It's no use! They'll be on us before we can get out of here." Tyel trudged forward. Alyse led the way, unimpeded as she was in her dry void. "Alyse!"

She turned as they moved forward.

"Can you…" Tyel struggled to articulate the thought. "Use magic to make your, um, dry, ah…"

She read him instead. It was faster.

"I don't know—I can try, but I need to stop."

"We can't stop! Are you *warped*, elf?" Gehard gasped, splashing water with every lunging, lurching step forward. "Move!" He pressed past her, feeling the odd sensation of his bare legs momentarily moving into her dry circle and then back out.

She stopped. Tyel followed suit behind her, water gently splashing against his waist. Ser Filip came up beside them both. He raised his sword – motioning Tyel to do the same, and turned to face a throng of arms, heads and torsos fighting up the underground stream, thirty paces away. Even against the current, they were moving rapidly.

"Do what you need to, girl," The Knight Commander uttered. He locked eyes with Tyel. "Ready to scrap, boy?"

He wasn't sure, but what did it matter? Either they tried and lived, or they all died together. He shook his head. "No, but that isn't really a question."

Ser Filip laughed darkly. "Aye."

Twenty paces.

He glanced back at Alyse long enough to take in her face once more – maybe one last time. She raised both her arms, palms out, tilting her head back slightly. Her blue eyes burned – they glowed with a rising corona of heat and plasmic energy, drifting upward like pipe smoke. The curve of the stone waterway reflected that eerie blue.

Ten paces.

"Whatever you're doing, elf, do it fast." Gehard reluctantly drew his steel. He stayed facing Alyse, at the front of the line.

All at once, the manic crush of the dead was upon them: a thrashing, chaotic mass of reaching hands, bloated flesh and dead eyes, numbering dozens. Seemingly all of the unfortunate bodies floating downstream, ravaged by strega and dumped below, had risen by some means.

Terror rose in Tyel's throat.

"Branson! Steady!" Ser Filip shouted. "Target the neck!"

They tried to hold their ground as the tide of corpses pressed in on them; the flowing water slapped against their distended, rotten legs. At this close range, the putrid smell of decay and blood punished their nostrils. Ser Filip took one more step forward, bracing himself. He raised his sword in front of him, then twisted his torso, giving him just enough room to swing sideways.

Tyel saw this, took a step sideways and back, nearly against the wall, and tried to emulate the stance. However, he was a head shorter than the Knight Commander, and his blade was shorter than that of Ser Filip's. His swing wouldn't have the same reach nor impact. He would have to move up and do his damnedest to press as many back as he could.

He threw himself forward as bare arms reached out for him. He could see glassy eyes, some black as night – others milky white. Mouths open, teeth exposed – some with teeth like nails. Hands tipped with bone jags – claws or talons like a beast, clutched at his face, scrambling for contact. Branson brought his sword sideways, as hard as he could; the blade planted deep in neck tissue. He could feel bone reverberate through the grip as he pulled back and swung again. His foe's clawed hands went limp as it collapsed into the water, causing the corpses behind it to stumble. Behind it, more came to take its place, clambering over the body.

There was no way they could keep them pressed back for long.

"Ah, hell." Gehard trudged forward, alongside Tyel. "Look out." He thrust his blade between the ribs of a deformed, tumour-laden woman, gnarling and pressing through the water. It was beginning to take on the sharpened, exaggerated features of a strega now. Tyel stumbled backward as he tried to swing again. Something was beneath his feet – something soft, wriggling and yielding. At that moment, he was pulled under. His mouth, half-way into a shock-induced shout, clamped shut, forcing water away. He could feel hands around his ankles, pulling him off his feet. His eyes drowned in an instant as he was dragged under.

I mustn't swallow the water. Branson scrambled to think straight, but he knew that much. He pinched his eyes shut, feeling himself sliding down onto the bottom, pulled by clawed hands. He still had his sword – a small miracle.

Eyes shut, he stabbed in the direction of the arms holding him down – with as much force as he could manage. He struggled to find the hands holding him down; he could feel the air in his lungs starting to escape as panic set in. Water in his ears, he could hear muffled shouts and the violent thrashing of creatures on all sides. The more he kicked, the tighter the grip on his legs became.

Alyse gasped. *'Tyel!'* She could feel his panic. She had no time. She had to do this now.

"*Branson! Grab him, Gehard!*" Ser Filip pulled backward, his face streaked in blood. He hacked away any appendage within the reach of his edge: stiff fingers, dead hands, misshapen ears, broken noses, decomposing faces.

Gehard ignored him; what did he care if this boy fell? He glanced down. The boy was thrashing violently in the choppy soup of muck and entrails. Besides, he was a little bit preoccupied with his own situation, which was rapidly deteriorating.

"Stand *back*!" An uncommonly forceful voice issued from her thin lips. Her eyes blazed with potent magic – and so too did the palms of her hands. A glow of aquamarine formed a ring of sparking energy that emanated outward in a pulse. With it, the circle of protection around Alyse expanded outward, wicking water away from her. She clenched her teeth, feeling the icy burn on the palms of her hands, trying to ignore the pain and focus only on the outcome she desired. She did not know the words for the magic she needed to use – she knew only the desire to stop the water. Sometimes that was enough. She hoped this was one of those times.

Beyond the dead fingers around his ankles, Tyel could feel the dark and dreamy sludginess of unconsciousness begin to take hold. But now, he could feel something else–something frigid, like a burst of winter air. It brought him back to conscious awareness.

At that moment, the air around Ser Filip bit with icy chill; the water around him became a slowing slush of ice as it rushed away from him. He could feel a burst of freezing air as a bloom of aquamarine light enveloped Gehard and himself both. It pulsed around, pressing the rapidly-freezing water backward, sweeping it up in a curl, like a wave against a cliff-face. The water held there, locked in a frozen wave of dark, thick ice that curved up to the ceiling of the tunnel. The glassy surface caught the last of the spell's glow as it faded.

Arms and legs writhed in this wall of ice; dead eyes, partially submerged, wriggled and rolled in their sockets. Even in the low light, they could see the ice extending away, thicker and thicker and finally freezing the bodies of their attackers mid-movement.

Tyel kicked hard, working to free himself – suddenly aware he was no longer submerged. His muscles felt unencumbered – free of the weight of the water. He opened his blurry eyes, ignoring the sting of foul water. He now found himself in a circle of dry ground, one end held in place by a thick frozen barrier – the other held off by Alyse. Tyel lay gasping, sucking air in a fit of coughs, scrambling back, kicking away from a pair of arms reaching out for him haplessly from the ice. They became still.

Gehard offered him a limp, dripping hand. "There. See? He's okay." Tyel took his hand and pulled himself upward. Gehard gave him a firm pat on the back, sending the squire lurching forward. The sound in the tunnel, of coursing water and moaning, screaming death, was muffled now by the wall of ice. Instead, he could hear blood pounding in his temples and his lungs heaving.

He turned to Ser Filip, who was panting like a beaten dog, hunched over, and who had turned his attention toward Alyse.

"Girl, when this is done, I will see you rewarded. Remarkable," he puffed.

Except it wasn't, not to her anyway. She felt soul-sick – like something had torn inside her that would take some time to mend. She stretched herself, pulled tight the parts of herself that she drew on to conjure. She'd never performed like this before, but there must have been a cost to this. This she felt in her mind. Alyse didn't want them to know how close they came to drowning, or how much it had hurt her to cast this spell. She looked at her frost-burnt palms, then quickly hid them behind her back.

"I don't know how long this will hold," she cautioned. We must hurry."

Tyel turned unsteadily on his feet; his ankles scraped and wrenched from thrashing against the grip that held him underwater. Alyse looked tired; her eyes had ceased their glow now, as if the fire was extinguished as the water froze. He came over to her side and gently tried to take her hand. She flinched and withdrew.

Tyel felt an immediate pang of guilt.

Her reaction was cut short by the sharp crack of ice splitting.

"Go!" Tyel yelled – and, with the bubble of water protection now in front of them, Alyse laboured a jog. As she moved down the way, water seeped in behind them once again, splashing against the ice wall. 'This will speed the thaw,' Ser Filip realised. He heard the popping, splitting ice, threatening to burst, as they moved as quickly as Alyse's pace could afford them.

"Faster!" Gehard wailed. "Go!"

Tyel put an arm around Alyse; she was limping noticeably now. Something was wrong with her – he could tell, even if the others were otherwise occupied. The floor was slick, the way ahead dark, only faintly visible in the light from the drainage grates. Tyel could feel his feet slipping in age-old slime-moss.

They needed to surface – there had to be another ladder coming – a pipe upward, something. Anything. They were fifty paces or so away from the ice barrier. Alyse was weakening. The more she slowed, the more Tyel held her up.

"Ser! Help me here." The Knight Commander at once saw the young pair struggling. If the elf should fall, and the water barrier fail, this would surely slow them again. They might not survive another confrontation down here.

Tyel put his arm around the girl; she was so slight. He could see she was faltering; the water was beginning to close in around their legs once more.

"Hold on Alyse," Tyel pleaded. "We're getting out of here." She said nothing. He afforded a glance at her; barely visible. The only water droplets that touched her were two thin strokes of tears, pulling away from the far corners of her eyes. Tyel could feel his heart wrench. She was trying to keep it together – the pressure she was under he couldn't imagine. He didn't know how magic worked – he'd love to know. If they lived, he would ask all he could, if she would share. But it clearly put her under terrible strain.

They were well away from the ice barrier now; if it held up at all, it must be close to dissolved.

With Ser Filip taking Alyse' side, Tyel could lift her up beneath her arm. They carried her along like a totem, as fast as they could. The water was beginning to trickle in around their feet. He noticed something else too – the tunnel had begun to incline. With the steep angle, every step forward became twice as hard. They must be surfacing now.

At that moment, Gehard heard something else – something that slowed his footfalls.

"Waterfall," he shouted. "Hear it?"

At first, Tyel could hear only his breathing. But there, hushed like a soft breeze in the ears, came the sound; the consistent and rising white noise like wind tunnelling through an alleyway.

Then another sound – far behind them. A piercing shriek. This he *had* heard before. Strega – in the tunnels. The ice wall had failed – at least in part.

At long last, barely perceptible in the dark – a speck of white light. Each step upward brought it closer and closer; so too it brought the water barrier closer around them. The barrier was barely in front of their waists, creating a meniscus of water sliding along the invisible force that kept them separated.

A waterfall.

If there's a waterfall, it must lead back upward to the surface – to the base of the mountain range, Tyel figured. They just needed to reach it.

More sounds behind them – closer now. The incline steepened. Three sets of feet pounded against wet stone, sending water splashing; Alyse was suspended, doing her best to stay focussed, but weakening by the moment.

Light faded in, brighter and brighter. Silver moonlight, reflecting off a tumbling sheet of whitewater, cascading from above and out of view.

Water lapped their knees. Still Alyse barely held the water in front of them at bay; a small indentation compressed the flow, keeping it from splashing against their waists.

Tyel felt his throat tighten. In the pale light, he could see Alyse's almond eyes were shot through with blood. Her tears had become streaks of deep red.

The tunnel stopped abruptly, as the roar of water filled their ears. The underground tunnel's opening fed into a cylindrical stone chamber, filling a pool that ran into two other channels seemingly identical – one on each side of the tunnel they emerged from. *These must send water through different areas of the town,* Tyel thought. Perhaps they fed back into the River Marshtide–through Reedsrush, maybe down to the Capital itself.

With one more step, Alyse was done. Whatever strength she had left was gone. The water crashed into their midsections like a wave slapping a child at the seashore. Ice cold – but mercifully clean, compared with the sickening, rotten stew they'd endured.

They were immediately uplifted by the strength of the surge now; the floor had fallen away beneath them as the four drifted out of the tunnel and into the pool. Alyse was barely keeping her face above the water's surface, even supported as she was by Ser Filip and Tyel.

Can elves swim? Tyel considered. He had no clue. They were desert-faring people, after all. So many things he wanted to know about her and her people.

There, on the left of the curved wall, were rungs of iron, rotted through with rust, dropping down into the water. Each rung was driven into the grey, slick stone, creating a path up. A way out. Tyel wiped water from his eyes as he stared up. The surface was only perhaps thirty rungs up, behind a mesh of iron bars. A small space above each ladder allowed for passage in and out.

It was impossible to hear anything but the steady roar of tumbling water now. If the rush of dead and risen were approaching, their cries were as drowned now as they themselves were.

Gehard reached the iron rungs first. He made no effort to help Tyel and Ser Filip with Alyse. Instead, he threw himself up the ladder with a newfound energy. The heels of his waterlogged boots clanked dully against each bar.

Ser Filip reached the ladder, his arm slung under Alyse's torso. Her eyes were closed; her pale face was dotted with blood, thinned from a mist of falling water.

"Branson. We'll need to carry her. She's in no state to climb."

Tyel nodded as Ser Filip moved to the side of the rungs. The squire took the other side. They would share her weight and climb up together. Tyel could feel rungs below the water, so he propped himself up on one and, with a groan, began to climb his side. Ser Filip mirrored his movements on the other, glancing upwards and grateful to see hazy sky far above, beyond the bars.

As The Luminary reached the middlemost-rung, he stopped.

He looked down at Ser Filip.

"Wait."

"What now?" The Knight Commander's exhaustion was growing proportionally to his shortening temper.

"I thought I saw movement. *Shadows.* Above. What if there are more of those things up there?"

Ser Filip sighed. "Then we… *fight* them. What else can be done? We cannot stay here, Gehard. They will be on us again from within."

Tyel spoke up at this. "If we have to fight, Alyse won't make it. We cannot defend her and ourselves, same. We barely made it out without her."

"Then the girl is lost," Gehard snapped coldly. "She proved useful, but mayhap she's beyond that now."

Tyel threw a dagger with his eyes. This Luminary, Gehard, was graceless for a highborn, and as far as he could see, less useful than even Tyel's own lowborn self. Graceless and cowardly.

"There's none here less essential than you," he snapped. "Climb and run away, then."

"Enough! Tyel, you forget your place. Don't make me take your tongue." Ser Filip shot him a look. "Your Grace, we take a chance either way. But we cannot delay longer – and fighting in water will be far worse than on dry land."

Gehard looked back up, tightening his grip on the rusty rung. The Knight Commander had a point. "Fine. My blade is still hungry."

With that, he began to climb again. "Squire. Listen to your betters. It would be a shame to bleed you slowly and leave you to die after you've come so far."

Tyel scowled bitterly – he hated that Ser Filip was right. He had nothing to show for himself yet, really. And he *was* a lowborn. If he died in a dark waterway, the world would move on without remark. He would be forgotten to the ages, not even a name remembered on lips beyond his own family. The rich and powerful were lamented for their loss of status in death as much as their accomplishments in life. To be wealthy was to be remembered. To be poor? Condemned to be so for all-time, even in passing. Poor and forgotten.

Alyse's head lolled backward. *Please be alive,* Tyel urged her. *If you can read me, hear me, then please hold on.*

Gehard eased himself up to the last rung, breathing heavily.

He looked up through parted strands of matted blonde hair – hair he feared might never be free from the stench of decay. A figure loomed over him, barely discernible in the dark.

The shock sent Gehard reeling backward with a yelp. He slipped a rung, then another, trying to hook his hand, his foot, anything–to keep from falling. He did not.

He narrowly avoided clipping Ser Filip, who shifted his position, and Alyse with him, as the Luminary plunged back-first into the water.

For a brief moment, no one said a thing. The shock of the fall stunned Tyel and Ser Filip as much as Gehard. The Luminary wiped his face in a flail, paddling toward the ladder like a child in a pond. His face ran pink with embarrassment. Branson grinned at him – but his attention was pulled upward again.

"No further," the gravelly voice from above shouted down at them. From their viewpoint, all that could be seen was an indistinct black silhouette of a round head and shoulders.

Then a second shape appeared, alongside: taller, thinner.

"If you're a foe, know this: you will die here," came the second voice; a woman, higher pitched, but accented from the far south to Ser Filip's ears.

"Not foes," he replied.

"But we are pursued by them," Tyel added. "We're no threat to you."

"I have a blade to bury in you, boy, if you should cross me," the woman said. *Seems fair enough, on balance—since I have one too,* he thought.

"That's fair. Lay down your arms and we will come up." Ser Filip made no movement up the ladder. Alyse murmured quietly in their arms.

"We stay armed, or you stay down there," came the man.

"We have no time to stand-off," Gehard retorted, panic rising in his voice. And he was right. There, from the depths of the tunnel they'd escaped from, came a screech.

"You have my word as Knight Commander of the High Inquisitor of the Capitol. We will stay our blades if you stay yours."

Two more shrieking screeches, now clear above the foaming turbulence. They waited for a response. It came flatly. The two heads receded from the edge of the waterway.

"Come, then," said the woman.

Tyel took a deep breath, adjusting his hold beneath Alyse's arm and around her back. He looked over at Ser FIlip. He looked impatient more than concerned. He could understand that – the threat was very much at their very waterlogged heels; they could chance a fight with two humans more than another encounter with a tunnel full of blood-monsters.

They began their climb; this time, Gehard remained close at their feet.

Ser Filip crested the lip first; he saw before him a stocky dwarf of reasonable stature for a mountain-man. Next to him, a tall woman, well-toned and dark-skinned, holding a curved dagger. Their posture was wound tight as a tripwire.

Are they highway thieves? he pondered. It felt amiss to turn his back on them, but Tyel needed help with Alyse. She was drifting back to consciousness, but weak and disoriented now.

Tyel lifted her up, feeling himself blush as her backside brushed against him. He'd never so much as held a girl's hand before; now he felt a rack of shame in having been so close to Alyse. There was nothing untoward about this – he was trying to help, trying to keep her safe – but the confusing feeling of arousal rushed into him. It came as a relief to feel something beyond acute fear.

At last, Gehard surfaced, frowning, brushing his hands against his soiled linen. He slicked his hair back, and reached for his blade.

At once, the dwarf leapt at him. The woman readied to throw the knife.

"Hey!" Gehard tumbled backward, onto the ground. "Stop!"

The dwarf pressed a foot onto his chest. "Try that again," he said, "and I'll only break your arm. She'll take it clean off."

"Get off him, dwarf," barked Ser Filip. "This is the Capitol Luminary, Gehard Fendrigar. Son of High Inquisitor, His Grace, Boff Fendrigar. He could have you disembowelled for this."

The dwarf sniffed and peered down at this half-drowned figure. His small eyes squinted in the dark. "Doesn't look like him. Isn't the High Inquisitor a rather rotund fellow? I've heard he's round as a melon. This man looks… rather *underfed* by regal standards."

Gehard shoved the dwarf's foot off his chest. "My *father* is cursed with a large appetite. My curse is a short temper and quick swing – which you'll soon witness if you speak ill of your High Inquisitor, dwarf."

"That lordly butter-dish is not *my* Inquisitor, sewer rat," the woman interrupted. "Now stay put, like a good pup, while I determine whether you should all live to see the sun rise."

Tyel crouched by Alyse. She sat, shivering, by the stone-walled edge of the waterway. Branson removed his leathers, then his shirt, despite the chill in the air. He wrung the cotton out, before draping it around Alyse's shoulders.

He shot a glance at the woman with an equal chill. "If we don't all leave now, none of us will."

ATHERONS

The waterfall spilled from a rocky valley in the undulating hillsides of the Atherons. At the base, a large lake had formed, surrounded by tall needle-pines and cone-firs, crops of reeds and marsh grasses. They had taken shelter north-west of the town, where the thickening treeline gave them some means to camouflage themselves. From their viewpoint, the lake's black surface reflected the moonlight in shimmering crescents.

Dusty knew somewhere deep in that mountainside ran a warren of tunnels and caves, originally carved by his people in times before counting. The first dwarven settlements had taken root there, safely nestled between dense peaks, hewn into the grey granite over countless generations. In the many years that had since come to pass, his people had worked their way north, out of the mountains and into the foothills, then into the tundra itself. The North Sea was their dominion now – and a naval fleet of some reckoning had begun to form – mostly out of necessity. Their trade favoured mining, construction, raw materials that the far reaches of the land demanded. Food was plentiful, water was pure – and isolation served to keep their kind safe.

Now, staring at the peaks of the Atheron Ranges, the dwarf was not so sure of their safety.

He'd heard with his own large ears the Necromant draw up his forces; he'd seen the stream of claimed souls rise and follow his command to head north. North meant through the mountains, almost certainly – for a long detour around the base of the mountain ranges seemed impractical to say the least – and perhaps impossible for night creatures such as strega. They'd be too exposed – and great evil needed sheltered darkness to thrive.

So fresh questions now emerged: what had become of his northern kin? The mountainous, stone city of Yrkanh remained the seat of power; most of the population had long since moved north, but the magically-reinforced walls and runed barriers still held their council chambers, libraries of sacred texts, ore banks, large forges and ancient tombs. Surely a fortification that had stood unperturbed for aeons would remain so; the last strega threat had never come close to breaching it.

The situation was growing in complexity, Dusty felt – and he was certain Brea would agree. Did they follow the serpent into its den? And what then? Could they do the job without bringing down a mountain of monsters upon them in the process?

Dusty stroked his beard as he lifted the flap of his leather apothecary satchel. He ran his thick fingers across the stoppered vials as they clinked together.

The elf girl was in bad shape, to be sure. Sick and exhausted, barely conscious. He had treated enough elves to know that, while hearty and resistant to most sickness, when they did take ill, it sometimes took a great deal of time to heal. It was far harder to treat a magical race – or magical ailments – with non-magical means, after all.

Wortcrafting was a fairly common practice, but it did not mean that it was particularly effective most of the time. Only skilled chemists could harness the recombinant healing properties of the natural world. He could, though. He knew what he lacked in sight, he made up for in wit.

"So. An old knight, a greenling squire, a… Luminary… and a very sick elf." Brea crouched in the fallen needles, swirling at them absently with a twig. "Sounds like the beginning of a poor joke."

She looked at the three men before her. Not much to behold, she thought. "What happened down there?"

Ser Filip sat shivering, but said nothing. Gehard shot her a miserable glance.

"Well, I left behind a set of plate steel worth more than – look, we barely escaped a stampede of reanimated dead. I can't say the same for my men."

"Our men," Ser Filip interjected. He sighed heavily. "We were tasked to confirm sightings of strega in the area, foremost."

"I'd say that's well and fully confirmed, old man," Brea laughed and tossed the stick aside. He nodded.

The Knight Commander could feel exhaustion creeping in. In truth, tonight he did feel his years clipping at his heels. He wanted now to be warm and dry by a hearth; to take in a bath in the copper soaking tubs and sleep the deep, still sleep that comes from the stress of a battle concluded. Except it wasn't. It wasn't even really begun, as he saw it.

"Confirmed, sure. But that does nothing if we cannot warn the south. Twenty strong soldiers were near-as-nothing to these things. A siege of two thousand may put an end to it, however."

Brea raised her eyebrows and rolled her eyes.

"Or one well-placed blade," she replied. "You think too big, Ser. Too bold. Too loud. Armies work against armies. This – these – are something else. They may require different solutions."

That gave him pause. "And that's why you're here?"

She ignored this, instead turning to Dusty. He was crouched next to Alyse as she curled in on herself, her head resting on Tyel's thigh.

He had mixed two small portions of a clear fluid together in a third empty vessel, no larger than a sewing thimble. The concoction turned a shade darker and fizzed. He turned her head upward slightly, her damp hair falling back across her forehead. Then, careful not to spill a drop, brought the tiny vessel to her lips. She swallowed it without complaint – or much recognition at all. Her eyes remained closed. Tyel put a hand against her forehead. She felt too warm for the chill in the air tonight.

"The girl. Will she live?" Brea asked. This surprised Dusty; she had shown no interest in the girl back at the well – pointedly so. It seemed as if she was ignoring her failing condition back there.

"Why the sudden interest?" Dusty fixed his glasses on his nose and peered at her. "She'll live." he said softly. "I'll see to that." Tyel felt himself relax slightly at that.

"Like you saw to me, dwarf?" Brea snapped.

"No. Not like that. Not at all. Though yeh may well be sick for some time to come."

Brea narrowed her eyes. "Perhaps you enjoy the power you have over women. Over their lives."

The off-exchange was not lost on Tyel or Ser Filip. They looked at each other. There was something sour between these two. Perhaps they were not necessarily in league with each other – not exactly.

The dwarf was unmoved. "I take no pleasure in hurting others. And healing them is my gift of balance."

"Gift of balance?" Tyel interrupted.

"Yes lad. I take lives and I grant them. A balance."

Tyel's eyes widened at this.

"You can relax, lad. You've nothing to fear from me. Can't speak for her though." He hiked a thick stub of thumb at Brea.

A gust of rising wind blew through the thicket. Pine needles rustled in a wide ripple as clouds, illuminated by the moon, slipped across the dark sky. High above, like the eyes of a million night creatures, stars of white and yellow, pink and blue, twinkled softly. In any other context, it would seem a moment of serenity. But the chill was biting and there was a feeling of being watched by more than just stars.

Tyel looked at the crouching woman; her lanky physique reminded him of Alyse – but her skin was much darker – as was her demeanour.

The elfkin stirred as the potion began to take effect. Alyse's eyes opened for the first time in the hour or so that had passed since their narrow escape. She looked up at Tyel – both reading confusion in each other's faces.

"Tyel," she spoke softly.

"That young man hasn't left your side, girl. I'm Dusty. That's Brea. And you're lucky to be here."

"What happened?" Alyse sat up slowly, feeling stiffness in her neck and a distant ache from somewhere deep inside her skull. "The last thing I recall was being down in the waterway."

"That's it?" Tyel replied.

"That's it."

Brea stood back up from her crouched position and walked to her now.

Alyse studied this woman in front of her. She began to prod gently at her mind; as if peeking through heavy curtains.

"Stop. What are you doing?" Brea burst out. "Are you… reading me? How dare you!" Brea leaned over her. Alyse withdrew and recoiled; Brea softened, feeling a tiny bit of remorse at frightening her. Perhaps she hadn't meant to intrude. Or perhaps she very-much meant to. Both were intriguing possibilities. "So you know some spellcraft, girl? A sensitive, we call your kind. And a *marktongue*."

"A… marktongue?" Alyse had never heard of this. "I don't know—"

"Marktongues are spellsayers, girl. Sometimes Elfkind are known to possess the gift – but it's rare – and rarer still to find a sensitive one. Who was your Elder?"

Alyse had never heard any of these terms before. "Elder? You mean, a teacher?"

Brea sighed and rolled her eyes. "Elder, teacher – some wizened old crone or sleepy magemind. Who taught you to read minds?"

"No one. I've never had an… Elder. Or a teacher – or anything like that."

Dusty raised his eyebrows. "Quite incredible. Truly. What was your name again, girl?"

"Alyse."

"*Alyse*. Indeed. Southron Elf, but so fair-hued. Quite rare." He adjusted his spectacles slightly. "And how do you feel, Alyse?"

In truth, she felt awful. Exhausted, sore and certainly confused. There was a gap in her memory now that felt like a page torn from a book.

"Tired."

"Tired is fair. From what Tyel here tells us, you performed quite a remarkable conjuration. Elemental, in fact. Let me see your hands, Alyse." Dusty held a hand of his own out to her. She complied, raising her palms towards him, and he leaned in, examining the reddened, irritated skin.

"I see. You've sustained an ice burn."

Tyel knew she'd hurt herself to save them. "An ice burn? Can ice burn?" he asked the dwarf, genuinely mystified.

"Certainly so. Practiced conjurers – spellswords among them – tend to wear conjurer's gloves for that reason. Often magically sealed to prevent such injuries. Ice burn is more common in the far north. Here. I have a salve for this."

Once again, the dwarf shuffled clinking vials in his bag and returned with a thin blue-grey paste in a clear jar.

"Is there anything you don't have in that bag, dwarf?" Brea ribbed.

"I'm running a little low on patience for you." he laughed. "Now then. Allow me to apply this." Tenderly he ran a thick dab of the ointment across both palms. "Good. Now rub that in gently and allow it to absorb."

A wave of cool swept across Alyse's palms. Immediately she felt some relief from the lingering sharp ache of the burn.

"Thank you, Dusty. Brea?" Alyse turned to the woman still standing in front of her. "How did you… know I was reading you?" Her words came out meekly, feeling almost shameful to ask.

"You're not the only sensitive here. Nor the only marktongue." She replied flatly. "I wasn't born with it, however. I had to work for it. And, there's this." Brea stuck out her tongue. An ornate black spiral, almost floral in design, graced the pink flesh. She withdrew. "See the symbol? Getting it inscribed hurt like you wouldn't believe. And it cost me…well, let's just say it cost a lot. But that's the price if you're not a natural spellsayer. Hence – *marktongue*."

Alyse's mind raced with potential. She'd never met another marktongue before. Could this Brea teach her to use these gifts? Improve them?

Ser Filip stood up, dusting off his backside. "So, what now?"

Gehard scoffed. "What now? *Now* I try to find my colt and ride south." He stood up next to the Knight Commander, pulling pine needles from his legs with animated frustration. "South to a warm bath and a hot meal. I shall inform my father that we require the full force of the Blessed Legionary Guard." Gehard trumpeted.

"As for the rest of you, well – you saw as I did – the threat is very real. And I'm not inclined to encounter them tonight."

"A horse might be harder to come by than you might think," Dusty countered.

"And how so, dwarf?"

"Dusty, if you please, your Luminary."

"Dusty, then. Say what you know."

"We're dealing with a Necromant. A dark sorcerer of the highest order – or lowest, depending on your view of things. And what we saw – well, they slaughtered a score of horses – just to raise them again as their own. So too, dogs and birds and just about all else in the town."

Tyel thought of his own steed. *'Mancer.'* The dark irony of its name hit him squarely. *Did Alyse know about the Necromant? Is that where she drew his name?* He didn't know, but it wouldn't surprise him if she had. Now he supposed his poor horse was gone. He felt a pang in his chest for his young mount. Whatever his fate, he hoped it was quick.

"A Necromant – *here?* In Dormanstar? This backwater town?" Gehard scoffed. "Why would they bother?"

"You said it yourself. The threat is very real, Luminary. We watched the Necromant raise his defeated dead. He's raising an army utilising blood magic – drawing blood from their bodies and harnessing it."

Dusty stood back up, leaving Alyse. Brea joined him.

"He's correct in this." she said. "It is the Necromant we sought to find – and find him we did. We watched him transfigure some poor soldier – a huge man, into – *something else.* Something monstrous."

Royne. Tyel thought. *If there's any justice, they took his bald head off at the shoulders.*

"We have a decision to make," she said. "If the Necromant now resides in the Atheron Ranges, then the dwarf and I have business in the north."

Dusty nodded.

"So what do you propose, then?" Ser Filip pressed.

Brea looked at Dusty. They both spoke at the same time: "We travel south," said he – and "We split up," said she.

"I mean—"

"I *said*—"

They looked at each other.

"South? Why?" Brea balked. "We can still do this."

"We take a chance either way. Time is a precious thing – but so are information and strategy. To my particularly *keen* mind, it is clear that venturing into the Atherons tonight would be unwise," Dusty replied. "We're unprepared for this new development."

"*You* might be. I'm more than armed."

"Ah, but you need me if you want to keep using those arms." Dusty smiled wryly.

Gehard huffed. "Will you two get it together? What either of you want to do is of no consequence or worth. You're merely sellswords who I could rightly dispatch now and be done with it. It would be a service to the realm."

"We're *in service* to the realm, Luminary." Dusty was beginning to share Brea's irritation with this puffed-up blowhard.

Gehard began to protest, but instead shook his head and straightened his crumpled shirt and started for his sword.

Fast as slick ice, Brea drew her throwing knife. "Don't make me hurt you, your *Excellence*."

The Luminary looked at her, frowning.

"Oh ease up, would you? I'm not going to lop off your heads. I was just saying."

"South?" She looked at Dusty.

"South. Yes," he replied.

She turned back to Gehard, slipping her blade back into its leather sheath high on her thigh. "Stow your fat tongue, then. If we're going to travel south with you," she shot a sour look at Dusty, "I don't want to be second-guessing your every posturing."

She turned and began to walk toward the tree-line, downhill. "Come then, if you're coming."

Geherd reddened. He glanced at Ser Filip. "Posturing? What'd she mean by that, Ser Filip? I don't know what she meant by *that*."

"Come, Branson. I think you've earned a commendation, squire."

Tyel smiled. He looked at Alyse, his head filled with a strange mix of impending dread and flushed relief.

"Are you okay to walk?"

Alyse smiled. "I'll be okay," she started. "Thank you, Tyel. For a lot of things."

He could feel himself blushing. *Oh how pathetic. I'm sure she can tell.*

She barely made a sound in the fallen brush. "But most of all," she said, "thank you for listening to me."

"Thank you for saving us," he replied. "Because you did, you know. Save us, I mean." His words felt clumsy. Why did she have this effect on him? "I'm glad you're safe too."

They caught up to Dusty and Brea who paid them little mind. Ser Filip trotted behind them. Gehard sulked quietly as he fell in line.

"Oh Tyel – we're not safe." Alyse looked at him with her blue irises of disarming sincerity. "We're far from it."

CHAPTER 15

NORTH & SOUTH

The ancient keep was hewn from the grey stone by sure-handed dwarves long since turned to bone dust. It was richly appointed, which suited his tastes, but the scale of the tables, chairs and surfaces were a little small for his long limbs and uncomfortable beneath his slender frame. Still, it cost him nothing to acquire it; nothing beyond the spilling of blood and the time it took to do so. It was this blood that afforded him the means to take the first of the villages.

Vimnir Delcryth drummed his bony fingers on the curved stone arm of his high-backed throne, the surface worn smooth by aeons of pudgy backsides and tightly-gripped dwarven fingers, clinging to this seat of power and casting their rule from the cowardly safety of the mountain's dark womb. No longer; he had driven the dwarves out and crushed those who were arrogant – foolish – enough to stand against him. Rockbreakers; it was a pleasure to grind them into the earth they greedily plundered. Now they were at one with their ancient relatives in this dark, cavernous complex. Piles of dust and decay and nothing more.

And now he would rule the north. However, unlike the dwarves, he was no coward. He had no fear, no hesitation in raising hell here. He had taken the keep by force and would keep it through the same, if necessary. This was his stronghold now; an essential point of operations, away from the eyes of the Oracular Magisterium of Nine and their agents. Oh yes, he knew they would come for him.

They could try.

He tossed his hood back, shaking free his long black hair, shot through with grey, and letting it settle again around his shoulders.

He sensed them as he portalled into the foothill town. He could taste the mixed-blood woman's trace, and that of the man – a dwarf, pure. A strange pairing. How compelling.

And there were others, still. Harder to read – but he could sense them too. Another elf, somewhere in Dormanstar, just beyond his reach, sticking up defiantly like a bright dandelion in a dry, dead field – such a strong essence. He drummed his fingers again.

Perhaps he should reach out – try to read the elf women, both – even that half-class one. He might get a better sense of, if not their *plans* – then at least their capacity to act on them.

It was late in the day – or now quite early in the next. In his past life, he might have craved sup and sleep; the cold might have bothered him, this far from the deserts of his people.

The best part of being dead, he considered, was the freedom from inconsequential matters such as rest, hunger, sickness. It did nothing to alleviate certain other hungers, however. Those of the soul; the appetite for power and pleasure, the craving for order in the chaos. A hunger for control and a return to old ways of things. Death brought such clarity to simple matters. After all, everything was life or death in the end. Anything else was simply a means towards one or the other. He made his choice. His master saw to the rest of the ritual.

His master.

If only he could inform him of his successes and revel in his Master's delight. His master had already rewarded him richly, of course; an indefinitely long existence, free from pain or fear, free to harness power and, in return, use that power to bring order and change. Yes, his master had been most generous – bestowing a final gift beyond his master's own knowing, after the end had finally come for him.

Vimnir waved his hand, and with an index finger, traced the divine shape. He spoke his words. Before him, a small wooden cask and a shallow baked clay cup.

There was great pleasure in knowing that he need not drink or eat, but for the pleasure of it. The simple earthenware cup filled slowly from the bottom up, a rich wine-red, but the warm, thick liquid did not come from juice-of-the-vine. He drank.

There was much to do, he thought – and he laughed. If all that stood between them now were a handful of small souls, he would lay them flat and through his righteous momentum. Through sheer force of his will, like a firm hand that knocks the pieces clean off the board.

He looked out from his claimed throne at the comings and goings of his blood-risen children.

The chamber pulsed with such beauteous death-energy! These feeble humans and beasts, freed of their unproductive and meaningless lives. Now they were granted purpose! Once peons, now warriors; able bodies of the freshly restored. All shapes and all sizes, he would take them in and change them out. In return for his gifts, they would provide him an army to retake his lands. An army that would mark the end of the ages of men and dwarves and all others who had turned from the old ways. An army to end the world.

"A feast! A feast for my friends! Bring them in!"

At once, six soldiers, stripped bare and bound at wrist and ankle, were dragged on short ropes across the floor by two behemoths. Their jutting bonespines pointed toward the high ceilings as their skulls tilted down at the writhing, wailing human figures before them.

"Help yourselves, now!" Vimnir chuckled. "Feast!"

Within moments, the sea of deathforms descended upon them until nothing remained.

His cup refilled, he drank again and smiled.

~ ~ ~

His Grace wept.

The night had been a long one and the morning brought no relief from The High Inquisitor's terrible woes. The agony in his heart! The bleed at the centre of him! Last night, he cried himself dry, so he drank wine and supped on suckling pig, but even the sight of the round creature, the luxurious, sweet and buttery fat, nothing could stem his tears. For the life of him, the poor creature reminded him of his daughter. Sweet and innocent, round and soft.

His Melodis was done. She lay in state, wrapped in cloth, cold on a stone slab within the crypts. Today he must oversee her consecration and immolation that the Solum God might take his humble servant into the beyond.

So unexpected. So confusing and cruel.

'It's in the water,' The kitchen crone told him. He could still hear Melodis struggling to breathe, desperately trying to speak. *'Wah-haa'*, she gurgled, limply. Then she left him.

Water. And it may have been true; there were words on winds that told of a spreading illness in the lands around them. Strega in the north, now a waterborne pestilence in the south. Famine and death kept close friendship.

His thought drifted back to the dark omens so forcefully fed to him by the Oracular Magisterium as another round of tears welled.

As he lay in his spacious bed chamber, he fought the overwhelming urge to slit his wrists and be done with this. They could cremate him in the ring alongside Melodis and perhaps he would find peace.

He lay there, tantalising and torturing himself with this morbid imagining; his form naked for all to see as the rays were focused in and his flesh blackened and he was reduced to cinders in the sun. A breeze might carry him away, spreading his remains across the fields that grew sweet fruit and sugarcane.

There came a gentle rap against his chamber doors, followed by a small voice.

"High Inquisitor?"

He ran the back of his hand across his eyes, to and fro.

"What is it?" He uttered quickly, feebly trying to compose himself.

"Your Worship is requested in the Temple square. We have prepared your Legionary escort. They await you by the outer gates."

He rose from the bed. "Send two handmaidens so I may dress quickly."

"At once, Your Grace," the voice replied. And it was so; almost immediately, two women knocked and entered. Although he had washed only yesterday, when he raised his arms, the ripe, pungent smell teased him. Perhaps a soak in the pools… Then he remembered the water. Would his pools be contaminated? Surely not. It was understood that fresh water was cycled out regularly – but under these circumstances, he hoped they had not changed the water yet.

Water. How could his lands survive without water? He would need to strike up relations with the Elven Council and shore supplies. Those pointy, lofty bastards; their uneasy relationship would shift in their favour when news of a water crisis crossed the south sea.

His black robes donned, he found his armpits already damp. Sweat had formed on his brow and upper lip and his heart pounded.

"Your… Grace?" One of the women offered him a small fold of cloth. He snatched it and dabbed at his brow.

"It's nothing."

"Of course, Your Grace," she replied. They helped him to the door; a train of black silken finery, hung from his shoulders, trailed him.

Pestilence, famine, drought and plague. On four sides he found himself pressed. And a fifth, death, danced in front of him now. As he moved through the adjoining sitting room, he looked out the window into the capital streets beyond the curved walls. Blue sky, scattered with tufts of cloud. Birds in pairs and threes, darting from one place to another. A day like any other, but only in the most superficial ways. In his heart, he knew things were very much in flux now.

Downstairs, the atmosphere was notably sombre. Servants who usually lined the halls, cooking, cleaning and attending to the needs of the house, were nowhere to be seen. Only a handful of guards, posted at the entryways to the central courtyard and the long hall out to the Capital grounds, remained. They averted their eyes respectfully as The High Inquisitor passed.

On the other side of those doors, sitting in an ornate wooden chair, waited Central Templemaster Kyrus Eogan.

Upon seeing the doors open, Templemaster Eogan rose with some effort and bowed at his waist, as low as his ageing bones would afford. He looked as old as the outer battlements of the Capital, and just as lined and worn.

"Your Grace. Please allow me to express my profound sympathies."

The old man took The High Inquisitor's arms to steady his unstable legs and together they walked down the long hall, toward the double-wide doors.

Fendrigar resisted the urge to roll his eyes. The doddering, skeletal man was practically ingrained in the woodwork of the building now, but served about as much function as the chairs in the halls or the tapestries hung above them. A perfunctory, decorative human – there for ceremony and tradition; present at sacred births, marked occasions – and anointed deaths.

"Your sympathies are noted."

"Yes. I— *ah*, if your Grace would accompany me to the forecourt, we will begin the ceremony at High Solum."

The ceremony, the Inquisitor mused darkly. He'd been to enough of these to know he did not relish the thought of watching another. But to let poor Melodis' passing drift by without appropriately marking the occasion would be a slight to her memory and an affront to their god – and the people who worshiped him. A sacred death required such a ceremony. It had always been this way. He never imagined he'd outlive his own progeny, however. He felt another swell of heartache lump in his throat and he turned his attention to the guards in front of him, who parted the doors.

Sunlight greeted him as the courtyard spilled away and down the steps toward the outward protective walls. Green grass, running long down either side of the pathway, dotted with white and yellow flowers, shone in the brightness of daytime. Fendrigar found it overwhelming; the intensity of green, the dots of hot-white and yellow – it all seemed to clash; it made him dizzy. He was not made for outdoors.

A procession of finely cloaked and heavily-mailed guards, his Holy Protectorate, lined the long laneway beyond his keep, leading to the city beyond. Rarely did he make such ventures – and even less commonly on foot. But such was the tradition; a minor discomfort of walking in quiet reflection to focus the mind on loss and sacrifice.

His joints protested each difficult step, but the heat of the sun made it worse still. He could feel his ungainly heaviness, the sag and bob of his over-hanging stomach, the perverse wobble of his neck as beads of perspiration formed and ran in rivulets down his face and onto his black-cloth garb. The temperature! It felt as if he was standing in front of an open furnace! He could feel his heart pounding, blood pumping in his temples. At least the old man he escorted was a slow-walker. He could manage this, just.

"High Inquisitor," Eogan spoke quietly, from beneath his ceremonial hood. "I must tell you. Prepare yourself."

"For… what," The Inquisitor puffed.

"Your daughter, your Grace. She… is not as she once was." The High Inquisitor certainly heard the words – but their meaning was lost on him.

"Templemaster. I do wish you would say what you mean." It was clear the old man was choosing his words carefully.

"Melodis, Your Grace."

"Is," he caught himself, "*Was* my daughter, yes."

"She… appears to have… changed." Fendrigar stopped. He pulled away from the Templemaster to look at him, as much as he could beneath the layers of robes.

"Changed how, exactly? Speak."

Evidently it would be easier to extract words from a woodmole than this man. "Fine, fine. Where is she? Where is my Melodis?"

"She's… contained. Prepared upon the Circuitris. We will raise her when the moment comes." They began to move again. "It came at some cost."

'*Contained? Cost?*' More flowery riddles. The Inquisitor furrowed his brow. 'Who has the patience for this on a day such as this?'

Sensing the High Inquisitor's unease, the Templemaster elaborated. "She… lashed out at two of my oil-bearers." The High Inquisitor said nothing to this, but the concept twisted a knife in his gut. Was she somehow *alive*?

"So you mean to tell me that my daughter lives?"

"Not exactly, your Grace. Perhaps it would be best to show you."

The line of escorting guards repositioned themselves either side of the High Inquisitor, allowing the Templemaster to lead him up the wide-set steps. Behind their high shields, wide eyes watched the pair closely. A large crowd of gawking, murmuring onlookers had begun to gather now, as word spread throughout the capital streets of Melodis' passing. Such a thing was a dark occasion, but it seemed this particular ritual burning was not to be missed. Perhaps it was the spectacle of great wealth being met with even greater suffering that drew them today.

Temples were ornate buildings by their nature, but the Capital Solum Temple was the most elaborate structure in the city, nearly as tall as the spire of the High Inquisitor's own tower. Each of the five spires was crowned with a slightly different form of the Circuitris; some were ringed with flames, others a simple golden band. At the centre of the building sat the central spire. This incredible structure of engineering prowess allowed the raising and lowering of a sacrificial ring – a Circuitris upon which the energy of the Solum God could be focussed.

The High Inquisitor made the arduous path up the central steps, sweat pouring from him. Guards swung the doors open into the antechamber. Beyond, he could hear screaming, screeching, wailing. From the tone of her voice, he recognised Melodis – except, there was something else in that sound that was distinctly different. Animalistic; like the sharp yowl of a wounded cat, or the squealing bray of alleyway dogs in heat.

There, beyond the high arches that led to the Temple sanctum, lay his daughter – or what had once been her. Her nakedness showed the extent of the changes her body had undergone. Her cheek bones protruded and stretched the pale, blueish skin on her face; her hair, a point of pride for her, had all but fallen out. Below, her arms and legs were bound by leather in a large cross to the golden ring – but all over her body, her skin had begun to necrose. Juts of rib bone, hip bone and thigh were warped as if something had pushed them violently outward. They no longer fit the generous confines of her round body.

There, on her contorted face, he saw her eyes were now different too; black, glossy and soulless, but wide like chasms. Too large for her face now. Some horrible metamorphosis had begun to take place – and she was somehow conscious once more.

"M-Melodis," he whispered, disbelieving.

At once he understood the Templemaster's words. The High Inquisitor was immediately struck dizzy and nauseous. He reached out for something to stable himself; he found the curve of the stone arch.

The Templemaster took his other side, the little he could do to support the large man's frame.

"I'm sorry, your Grace, but we must raise her. It's time."

High Inquisitor Fendrigar walked toward the ring, not consciously doing so, but drawn forward. His steps were small and quivering.

"This – horror. This cannot be her." Melodis thrashed against her restraints, screaming sickeningly, twisting her head from side to side. Her twisted mouth opened as she did so, revealing small, sharp juts of teeth, where once were small, elegant pearls.

He raised a hand, not sure whether he wanted to reach out and touch her, to comfort her as a father would, or cover his own eyes, his ears, and block out the disturbing sights and sounds before him.

The Templemaster stopped him. "Please. Your Grace. You mustn't approach. This is no longer your daughter."

Fendrigar looked at the small man to his side. He fought an urge to slap him, bring him down to the ground.

Instead, he found himself weeping once more. He lowered his hand, turned and walked back toward the archway and the foyer beyond. Then, he stopped short and with a wet sniff, issued his command to the Templemaster.

"Raise it."

He would not stay to watch this; curse the Solum God, curse the Temple. It might bring the ire of the Magisterium down on him but they could be cursed too. He would not watch this – this *thing* – that had once been his own blood be raised and burned and forgotten as the foul peasants of his city cheered her unmaking. The lice-bitten, workshy gutterfolk! He felt his sadness shift toward broad, unfocused rage. Someone must surely be to blame for this. If he couldn't find that person, then the city would wear the burden of responsibility.

Behind him, the sound of chains being fed into a winding gear system. He knew from here the Circuitris would be raised up and up as the curved ceiling opened. The clanking gears and chains rattled and reverberated through the Temple, turned by hand. The metallic sound of each link was a sickening countdown.

Once the beams of High Solum struck the ring, it would be aflame, and so would Melodis.

A sudden thought overtook him. He did not want Melodis to be seen like this.

He exited the Temple as the sound of the crowds around him intensified his loathing. He turned to one of the many guards either side of him.

"Find your commander. Tell him to disperse this crowd at once."

"Your— Your Grace?"

The High Inquisitor clenched his jaw. "Now, or I'll have your head. All of you!" He shouted. "Clear the streets!"

The Protectorate guards looked at each other in confusion. Never before had they been asked to shift a crowd away from a burning ceremony.

"Now, curse you, *now*!" He screamed, tears streaming down his red face. "Get rid of them!"

The guards complied, at first uneasily – then with violent vigour.

Back inside the temple, the Circuitris ring reached the ceiling. The split in the roof began to open; a tiny slit of white-hot sun drew a line down Melodis' body. The line of sunlight grew as the panels parted.

On the streets, tower shields and drawn swords pressed the throng of onlookers backward, away from the square, toward the adjoining streets and alleyways. There were small pockets of resistance, but in futility. Mostly, confusion.

Fully extended above the forecourt, raised in between the five steeples, the Circuitris was now glowing like the sun itself. The light of High Solum had already begun to focus, drawn into the metallic ring of polished gold and orichalcum. Melodis' skin had already begun to blacken.

Against his own will, or despite it, the High Inquisitor turned and raised his eyes to the sky. He heard her screaming; the appalling blend of her high-pitched voice and the nightmarish creature she was becoming.

All at once, it peaked – and went silent. He watched as the ring was engulfed in white-hot flame, from the inside-out, a ripple of fire like a stone thrown into a still lake. The focused energy was so pure, the heat so intense, that only ash would remain; carried away on the winds to be spread across the land.

The ring of flames guttered and dissipated. She was gone.

The High Inquisitor found himself staring at that ring, watching a small mote of smoke spin upward and into nothingness from the top edge of the symbol of his rule and his own subservience to a greater power. So much fire and fury now dissolved into nothing.

A scream of a very different nature, in the sept beyond the arches, jolted him back into the moment.

CHAPTER 16

MAGISTERIUM

Though they were exhausted, Brea insisted they reach the southern border of the northern town before sunrise – and do so without passing through the city. That meant a loping, wide arc of traversal around and across the rocky foothills, among thick pines and ferns that sprang up between the outcrops. In the low light of stars and Lunum alone, it was perilous – but an encounter with strega would be more dangerous.

Dawn would not be far off, and with it, a burst of thawing sunlight. Morning also brought the reassurance of fewer horrors hidden in shadow, waiting to strike out at them.

No one much talked; in these dark, small hours, it felt somehow wrong to interrupt the quiet chirp of insects and the rushing of soft wind. It didn't stop Tyel's incessant inner-voice from filling him with questions. Who were these two new wanderers in their midst? Was Alyse going to heal? Was his family safe? Mind-noise fed a deep well of anxiety – but one question sat at his heart: *what was coming?*

The only prophetic beings, he thought, were oracles. But Alyse seemed to have shades of that magical aspect herself.

The question raised another idea. It was worth a try.

Alyse? He reached out to her with his mind as they walked together, their feet crunching on gravel and fallen leaves.

Tyel.

Despite suspecting it might work, her voice in his head startled him. The sensation of another's voice tunnelling to the surface in his mind, somewhere deep between his ears, felt extremely odd.

Could she hear his every thought? How did this work? How could he control it? If there was one thing he knew to be impossible, it was holding back a thought; once it emerged, it was too late. And he knew that some of his thoughts about Alyse ought not be shared. And there, in that image his mind had conjured, he knew he'd overshared some raw and suppressed feelings.

She said nothing in return. If she was blushing, it was too dark to tell.

He tried to move his mind along. *How are you feeling?*

Her words drifted in. *Tired and… in need of healing.*

Healing?

I think something is… wrong with me. With my mind.

How can we heal you?

His question seemed to hang in empty space for a time. Either Alyse was pondering privately, or she simply didn't know the answer.

Tyel looked at her, searching for words. *If I can help you, I will help.*

I know. She looked up at him now. *But I don't know how to fix what's wrong with me.*

The intimacy of sharing a person's thoughts and feelings, directly like this, brought with it a flood of emotions. Tyel could feel her pain in those words; a blue desperation. He could feel her searching herself for something, like grasping for an unlit candle in the pitch.

The sun was beginning to crest the rise of the hills to the east; a small slit of golden light, just below a band of thin grey cloud. The sky looked ashen in these early hours.

"We're beyond the city now." The first words in some time came from Ser Filip. Though quiet, they came as a relief to Tyel.

"D' you have any food?" Dusty enquired.

"Seems an odd time to be thinking about that, dwarf," Gehard scoffed.

"I don't suppose you know how to conjure a roast lamb and a few rootspuds, girl?" Dusty laughed. Alyse only shook her head gently.

"Well perhaps we can come up with something else, then."

Tyel hadn't noticed how famished he was until Dusty had brought it up. But now, it was all he could think about.

"I suggest we make for the river, beyond the hills and along the marshway," Brea nodded toward the west. The lands south of Dormanstar were largely agricultural, but toward the east, where the lands sloped gently toward the River Marshtide, the banks became marshy in areas.

"I used to pick saltberries and cressgrass from the waterside when I was younger," Tyel said. "And go hunting for mudcrabs."

"And much more besides. There's plenty to forage if you know what to look for," Dusty nodded.

"We will cut through the farmland and break-fast along the way," Brea continued. And once we reach the banks, we'll find ourselves a vessel or two."

"Find, or take?" Ser Filip raised an eyebrow.

"I don't see a distinction," she replied. "Especially right now." She picked up her pace slightly. "But if you prefer to walk…"

Tyel laughed at this. It felt good to be away from the gloom that had settled over Dormanstar. Though exhausted, the thought of a rapid return to the Capital buoyed his spirits.

"Can we… rest for a time?" Alyse asked softly.

A look of concern ran across Brea's face. Whether that was concern for Alyse, or her own timeline, Tyel didn't know. Brea exchanged glances with him.

"If you insist," she said, but the request was clearly an imposition.

They settled down in a grassy field, beneath an old, knurled oak tree. The sun was just beginning to throw long shadows behind them as a cool breeze rustled the broad leaves above. The dotted stars had begun to fade now.

Alyse lay on her side, curled in the grass. Within moments, she was asleep.

"Bran, why don't you get some rest as well?" Ser Filip suggested. "Perhaps we all ought to."

"Suit yourselves. The dwarf and I are moving on."

"Are we just?" Dusty dropped his rucksack. "I don't think we are. I think I'll sit for a spell."

Brea shrugged. "Fine. I'm not tired. Head southeast; meet me at the trading post by the riverside. There are always full moorings."

"Have it your way, Solsetter," Dusty nodded and yawned, taking a knee and opening his rucksack.

In actuality, Brea E'Lario was also exhausted; she'd barely had a moment to herself in weeks, and now that they'd found themselves conjoined yet again by another group of wanderers, it made for a great opportunity to foist Dust-in-His-Eyes on them instead. Time to herself meant time to think.

As she left, Dusty settled himself into a small grassy groove in the earth. Gehard, ever painfully vociferous, declared he needed to relieve himself – and chose to do so behind the great tree they circled under, raising the ire of Ser Filip. And the swooning fawn, Alyse, was being doted over by the boy. *What a doomstruck, forlorn pair they make,* she thought. She could sense the tragedy already; he would die for her, or her for him, or they would both fall victim to some terrible happenstance each at the expense of the other. It was too obvious; too dully poetic. Too pathetically storybook.

~ ~ ~

Ser Filip was snoring away gently, his arms folded and legs crossed in front of him. Gehard, now relieved, had settled into the same position, but wriggled uncomfortably on the hard ground.

Tyel, content with sitting for a time and not feeling under the immediate threat of death, watched Brea depart. She was so strange; he couldn't make heads or tails of her.

Once the strange Solsetter was out of earshot, Tyel turned to Dusty.

"What makes you think she's going to wait for us?"

"She will."

"But why would she?" Dusty's flat answers left him more and more intrigued. The Dwarf once again had rummaged and retrieved some equipment from his leather satchel; a wooden bowl slightly larger than an outstretched hand, three phials of various sizes, and a small, drawstring pouch. "What's going on between you two?"

"Who?" Dusty didn't look up as he unstoppered a phial of white-brown powder and tipped half the contents into the bowl.

"You and the Southern woman, of course."

Dusty laughed and shook his head. "The less you know, the better for all of us, sonny."

"That's not an answer."

"Well, that's not a question I *want* to answer," he replied, cocking his head. He uncorked a second phial – this one containing something dried and dark green – and sprinkled a dash into the bowl. "But I have a question of my own. Are you hungry, lad?"

The final phial contained a light green liquid. Dusty held it up to his eye, squinted, nodded. He tipped it in.

At once, there was a white-hot flash.

From the bowl erupted an expanding plume of off-white dough. It burst upwards on a thick stem before spilling outward like the cap of a cream-coloured mushroom. Branson's eyes lit up. The enormous loaf began to turn a lovely shade of golden-brown before his eyes.

"Bread?"

"Quite incredible, isn't it?" Dusty whispered. "I learned this little concoction from a half-dwarven minstrel of all people, from the frozen north where grains cannot grow – or, at least, that's where he said he was from. Said it kept him alive through the years of the Dark Wintertide, but who really knows, eh? That's bards for you."

And it was incredible, Tyel thought. He could smell the sweet, toasty aroma of freshly baked stonebread, as rich and pleasant as the loaves his mother would make in their stone oven.

The dwarf tipped the bowl over and gave it a gentle jiggle, catching the underside of the mushroomed load in his other hand. He bounced it slightly in his palm. "Still warm," he said.

He tore a large hunk from it and handed it to Tyel, a puff of steam rising pleasingly from it.

The warmth was equally pleasing to the touch – and as Tyel hungrily took a bite, the flavour surprised him. The flecks of green were some kind of dried herb, onjion or garlicairn. The consistency was fluffy; just firm enough to provide some chew as he bit into the top crust.

"We'll save some for the others when they awaken," Dusty noted, and pulled a hunk for himself. "It'll do until we can properly forage later, anyway. Do you fish?"

Tyel almost missed the question, so enamoured was he with this marvellous foodstuff. There was something else in the bread, some aspect of it, that seemed to scrape away the cold and the exhaustion he had felt. He could feel warmth spreading throughout him; his sore feet and nagging pain around his scraped, bruised, battered body, which had been plaguing him for hours, were beginning to dull.

"Fish?" Tyel replied, through a mouthful of bread. "Sure."

"Aye. Live by the riverside, do you?"

"Closer to the sea, actually. A small town – well, not much of a town – more a village. West of the Citadel." He took another bite.

"And what was the name of your village?"

"County Keep – just inland from Feldstone Inlet, where the ports receive post."

"But now you're squired to this man?" He nodded toward Ser Filip.

"Apparently so," Tyel replied quietly. "It's not exactly something I aspired to be, but – here I am."

"Quite so. Here you are." Dusty gave him a puzzled look, as if he didn't quite know what to make of his story. "And the girl? How did you meet here? An elfkin, but she's not of a pure line – and powerfully… capable. Quite interesting."

Dusty could try to pry, but so could he. "About as interesting as your relationship with Brea," Tyel smiled. "Wouldn't you agree?"

Dusty laughed.

"This is what I think," Tyel leaned in. "You're assassins."

"Me? I'm just a humble apothecary!" Dusty chuckled. "And as for Brea, she's my assistant. That's all."

Branson shot him a look. "Assistant? I doubt this, somehow."

"About as much of an assistant as you are a squire, no doubt."

"I'm more of an indentured servant than a squire. I'm in service to the realm for – well, I'm not exactly sure. Befouling the High Inquisitor's chambers, officially. Unofficially, I think Ser Filip just did us a mercy." He nodded toward Alyse.

"Sounds like there's a story in this," Dusty replied.

"The short of it is, I killed a strega and brought its remains – a hand, anyway, and some fangs – back with me as proof. I wanted to raise a warning."

Dusty hung on a word. "Fangs! Did you now? Tell me you still have them!" Branson nodded that he did. From his leather waist belt, provided to him by Ser Filip, he unbuttoned one of the small folded compartments. From within, he plucked two long, thin, needle-like fangs. The broad end was forked and faintly brown from dried blood and tissue.

"Tyel, these teeth – they're quite potent – quite valuable to an alchemist, such as myself."

"I thought you said you were an apothecary?"

"I'm many things, depending on need."

The dwarf held out his hand. "May I examine them?"

Tyel tipped the two teeth into the heavily lined palm of the alchemist-apothecary-assassin. Dusty squinted through his thick lenses at them. "Fine specimens. Note the inner core, running through to the tip; a fine channel that wicks blood upward – or injects it." He turned the teeth over in his hand.

"Tyel, these teeth can be turned into several extremely powerful medicines. In the right hands, of course."

"Your hands, I assume," Tyel smiled.

"You assume correctly. I would be indebted to you – though, seeing as I am keeping you fed today, and your friend here is alive, I'd say the scales are more-or-less in balance. So. What do you say? May I work with these?"

"Dusty, if what we saw back in Dormanstar is any indication, we're not going to be running low on strega teeth, or eyes or bones or entrails or anything else. But yes, you can have them."

"Great!" He closed his hand around them and quickly tucked the fangs into his satchel.

"But tell me something in return," Tyel continued. "If you're an assassin, who hired you?"

Dusty stopped his filing. "Tyel, if – and I say *if* – I was an assassin, I would never reveal my charge – nor my commissioner."

Tyel expected as much. However, to his surprise, Dusty continued.

"But you seem a smart lad. And you've a good nature about you. Perhaps not world-wise, and not smart enough to leave certain things well alone, but smart enough."

Dusty's expression was deadly serious now.

"Have you heard of The Magisterium?" he asked, quietly.

Tyel looked at him flatly.

"Don't tell me you've never heard of them."

"I – *haven't* heard of them."

"The Oracular Magisterium of Nine. What can I tell you? Wherever do I begin, even?" Clearly Dusty was astounded by Tyel's lack of knowledge.

"For a start, they're not human. They merely possess – take host – within their corporeal bodies. And they are very rich indeed. They pay well – and in advance. But to cross them, or not perform the task, whatever that might be, would be a suicidally poor decision."

"Are you a Solum worshiper, Tyel?" Dusty pressed. "The blessed Circuitris and all that?"

"I'm not anointed, if that's what you mean."

"Aye. Well, there's the Solum God, of course. And most north of The Elstemer Sea favour the Solum God. But, Tyel, this is just one of the Aspects of Trine. My boy, I surely hope you've heard of the Trine before."

Tyel nodded. Of course he had heard of the Trine. Sun, Moon, Void. Dawn, Dusk, Night. The aspects of the world distillate, it was said.

"Good, thanks be for that," Dusty jibed. "The three Aspects of Trine are represented by the Oracular Magisterium of Nine."

Dusty grabbed a stick from beside him. To his front, in a small, oblong clearing of dirt, he drew a triangle. At each point, the lines intersected then overlapped slightly.

"Outwardly, they seemed opposed, do they not? A trine of elements forever in opposition. But a trine also intersects, too – you see?" He pointed in toward the middle of the triangle. "All faces pointed inward to a centre, and outward toward the infinite." He drew a line outward from the centre of the triangle through each side.

"This is the nature of our world – and beyond."

Dusty blinked at Tyel through his lenses, studying the face of the young man. Tyel sat absorbed in the story, crouched in slightly, trying his best to understand.

Dusty lowered his voice. "To grasp infinity is beyond the minds of us simple beings. We're blacksmiths and barbers and cheesemakers and poets and lovers. Creators and killers. We're creatures of flesh and blood and bone."

Tyel nodded. "So are strega, for that matter," he added.

"That's true enough, to a point. But the Oracles – they're not like this; not like us. They are not bound to this physical realm."

"What does that mean?"

"Many things. They possess abilities beyond reckoning. It means they're extremely powerful, Tyel. And extremely powerful beings are also inherently extremely *dangerous*." The words hung heavily in the cool morning air.

"So I'll tell you this. Whatever you should do in this life, the Magisterium likely knows about it. They move pieces on a board before you've taken your turn. They cast their counters before the rules are even known."

They looked at each other, unblinking for a moment, before they realised three more sets of tired eyes were also watching them now.

"Do you understand the implications, boy? The horrible futility of pre-destiny?" Tyel did not – not fully. But there was an unsettling look in Dusty's eyes now. "And their agents are everywhere." Dusty turned to Gehard, who sat dumbfounded.

"*You're…* working for The Magisterium?" he swallowed hard, rubbing his eyes.

"Yes. I am." He picked up the half-torn loaf of bread and tossed it to The Luminary as Alyse and Ser Filip pondered Dusty's final words. "Hungry?"

CHAPTER 17

BREA'S FOLLY

Under the lavender and fuchsia dawn, Brea unfurled a small, ink-embellished paper map, turned it about, squinting at the horizon and comparing the tree line. The sun was now clear of the curve of the far-off hills and treetops. She eagerly awaited the radiance, warming her half-frozen skin.

Satisfied with her orientation, she folded along the heavy creasing, stowed it once more and continued across the field, over an old and crooked fence, down a hillside and up another.

She noticed the brushing of long grass on her bare legs above her boots as the soft ground gradually sloped away in declining undulations towards another thicket of oak and needle-pine trees. Far off, she could see, just beyond the ridge lay the smokestacks of a small trading village, barely a strip of homesteads and fishing shacks – common enough along the riverside.

Critically, however, they were a water-faring fishing village by reputation. Fisherfolk meant watercraft, which meant a means to head south to the capital with ease.

She plucked a long, thick reed of green dewgrass and popped the base in her mouth. As she chewed it, the sweet juices did little to revive her, but it helped give her mind something else to focus on, beside her aching arches and burning resentment towards Dusty.

How could she have allowed that diminutive, bespectacled bastard to undermine her? Moreover, how could she get out of this situation now? For two weeks, they'd been travelling together – and for two weeks, she'd been carrying some secret blight in her veins that, according to the dwarf, would be her undoing.

The thought made her livid; she felt more violated by this intrusion than the sloppy attempts the thugs on the cargo ship had made to over-power her. The Dwarf went further; the dwarf *had* her. He had saved her life, but inverted it in the process, placing himself on top of her like an immovable weight.

Could she kill the dwarf without dooming herself in the process? That was the question she now wrestled with. If she could master the formula she needed in order to hold this malignancy at bay, perhaps. By her reckoning, she had at least seven more nights before she would need another dose; if she was careful, she could work out the ingredients, proportions and preparation.

If she couldn't discern the ingredients, she would kill the dwarf anyway, take the phials to another apothecary and see if they could determine what they were and their method of action.

They were both tasked with the same target, too. While the dwarf might think it easier to surmount and fell a Necromant with a partner, Brea absolutely preferred to work alone. A person cannot completely depend on another person; it left no room for mistakes, unpredictability and the indomitable will of a person to keep on living in the face of threat of death. Even more so when dealing with a being who can harness life and death as Necromants do.

Either way, the dwarf's days are few. There was a brighter thought. She would kill him, cure herself – or treat herself, somehow – and deliver the head of the Necromant herself to the Oracular Magisterium. A wealth of coin beyond imagining – this was promised. She had no reason to doubt they had it, too.

She was far from camp now; even though the air was cool, she felt clammy, worked up into a state. Brea wiped her brow, spat out the last of the sweetgrass and looked behind her. Nothing but still, open fields of green and yellow. Ahead, a tree line. Once she was obscured by the thicket, she would try to reach out to the Oracles and provide them with an update of their situation.

It wasn't a requirement – when they contacted her, it was clear that they wanted a satisfactory outcome at any cost. But as she reached Dormanstar and witnessed the extent of the Necromant's power, that outcome was far from assured. Brea felt a certain professional responsibility to provide the Magisterium with a fresh insight.

She considered that for a moment. *Oracles are supposed to be all-knowing.* Something didn't sit right with her about this. Brea had heard the same tales as all others had – of the Magisterium's omnipotence, their near-godliness separating them from all others. A chosen council of nine. But now she wondered exactly how far they could see; how widely and how deeply too.

Why then did they not know the Necromant was building an army? Why did they not warn her?

She would ask them – though, she did not expect transparency.

She was nearing the edge of the thicket now. The needle-pines of the northern lands were interspersed with birch and cedar. Small brown sparrows tittered in the tree branches. The grass was thinner here, beneath the canopy, and dotted with rocks, fallen branches and an assortment of orange and brown dried leaves.

Brea found a knee-height stone, weathered and pitted, and sat down on it. She took a moment to remove her boots and gave them a solid upturned shake. A tiny grey pebble tumbled out of the left. It felt good to let her small feet decompress for the moment, and she squeezed and flexed her toes.

Taking a deep breath, she quieted her mind, stilled her body and closed her eyes.

While she was an adept spellsword, her powers were still fledgling in some respects. She could play with elemental powers, such as fire and water – conjurations that invoked and transformed the energy around her. She could ignite edged weapons, pull fire from dead wood without effort. Like many Solsetters, manipulating water was easy enough too; it was no different from any other tool to be manipulated – but it took a combination of mind-mastery and inherent magical ability.

Somewhere, generations earlier, Brea's line had bred with Elfkin. However, unlike elves, who were inherently gifted psychically, her traits were passive and she worked hard to grasp even the fundamentals.

This extended to transcommunication; one of the easiest – or so she was told – concepts for a sensitive to grasp. For her, to reach out and connect with another person's mind, felt intensely foreign and uncomfortable.

Now, sitting in the stillness of the thicket, she knew that connecting with the Magisterium would be a challenge. They had approached her, after all, and she had no idea if the reverse would even work.

Brea treated her mind as both an extension of her own voice and a muscle to be flexed. With her eyes still closed, she flexed her mind and asked the Nulum to connect her with the Oracular Magisterium. Over and over. A chanting kind of mantra; a focussed and forceful request.

In the moments that followed, two odd things happened.

One, her mind felt penetrated by something not her own. Something with prying fingers, like dark roots foraging in the soil of her being.

Two, she heard the elf girl in her head. *'You need to stop.'*

'Alyse?' But the words came too late.

The dark thing–with its reaching, creeping fingers, also spoke.

And who… are you? A raspy tone, far off and echoing in the infinite void, funnelled into her mind.

Brea yelped and fell backwards off her stone seat. Her eyelids felt heavy, as if the tiny muscles had atrophied, but she forced herself to part them. What she saw now froze her.

"Brea." It said – this time, aloud.

A black, swirling, tendrilous mass of vapour; undefined but identifiably proportional as a man.

"E'Lario."

And just like that, it was gone in a twisted swirl of black, cloudy nothingness, as if it had never been there at all.

"Wha- what in high hell was that?" she said aloud, if only to reassure herself that she could still speak. *That voice…* She put a hand over her mouth, eyes wide as window panes.

Brea knew then where she'd heard it. A voice as dark as the figure itself, he had spoken as he drew blood from the reanimated soldier in the streets of Dormanstar.

She fought a sudden urge to vomit – which was not uncommon after a transcommunication session. Her head hurt, spun inside itself to the point of dizziness.

He saw her. He knew who she was. Where she was.

Her mind turned to Alyse now; the elfkin had somehow found her way into her mind – just before the Necromant had. She had tried to warn her; how did she know?

Questions upon questions, Brea tensed. She felt drained – no, worse. She felt scared.

Fear was not a feeling she was accustomed to.

Fear and dread.

~ ~ ~

Alyse had woken with a start, sitting straight up, mouth open, eyes burning brightly. It was jarring enough to cause Dusty to flinch – and he did not startle easily. She blinked twice and looked around, trying to pull herself back into the moment.

"What? What happened?" Tyel, who had just started to nod off, was violently awake now.

"I don't know, exactly." Her heart was racing. "I think I reached out to Brea."

Dusty looked at her flatly. "You what?"

"It was an accident! But…" Her face carried a disturbing upset now. "Someone else was already in there as well."

"What does that mean?" Dusty stood up and walked to her side. "Tell me everything, girl. Tell me what you saw."

In truth, Alyse wasn't sure what she'd seen – it was more what she'd felt. Sound asleep, Alyse found her mind freed from her body for a time. This happened occasionally – particularly when deeply exhausted, that bone-tired feeling of being overexhausted – which she certainly was now.

"I… accidentally read her. I was asleep and I felt myself reaching out to her – or she was reaching out to someone else and I was swept inside."

Ser Filip was awake now. "What did I miss?" No one rushed to answer him.

"She— she was what? Reaching out?" Dusty puzzled over this. "To whom, Alyse? Did you see?"

"I'm— not sure. But I could feel something else watching from within her." She lowered her eyes. "It felt evil. Just, darkness in presence."

Dusty chewed on those words for a moment. A darkness in presence. His mind immediately went to that of the Necromant. An agent of life and death, with an elfkind lineage – such powers to intrude psychically made a great deal of sense. It also made him wildly threatening – particularly if they had just lost the element of stealth and surprise. *Did Brea just reveal herself to him?*

Another darker thought occurred. *Did she do so on purpose?* He had little trust for the Solsetter – only an obligation to keep her alive and well, and see their shared mission through to the end. But was she somehow playing both sides?

Dusty scrunched his brow, which forced his lenses down his large nose, and turned to Tyel, Ser Filip and Gehard.

"And did all of you know Alyse is a sensitive?"

"Of course!" Gehard replied. "Why do you think the High Inquisitor kept her for his own? Certainly not for her looks."

If Alyse cared about trivialities of superficiality, or such comments aimed to cut at her, she didn't show it outwardly.

"Why would you say that?" Tyel interjected. Ser Filip shot him a look that clammed him up tight.

"It's okay, Tyel. I don't need defending." Tyel felt a pang of embarrassment.

"No offense intended, young lady. It's just – the High Inquisitor prefers humans as bedhands."

The image turned Ser Filip's stomach. He knew the High Inquisitor's tastes were hardly exotic, but he also knew that rarely did he have bedhands. He took his pleasure in the privacy of the underground pools. Often, stories would circulate of the High Inquisitor's penchant for receiving – and sometimes doling out – pain.

"Besides, Alyse is far more valuable to him than a simple servant," Gehard continued. "She's an extraordinarily useful set of eyes and ears that none see watching or listening."

"I can imagine a sensitive person is highly prized in seats of power, aye," Dusty scratched his chin. "How came you to the Capital, Alyse?"

Tyel didn't need any special abilities to sense that Alyse was uncomfortable with the question. "Why don't we get moving," he suggested.

"In a minute, in a minute. I want to hear more about our special friend here."

Branson opened his mouth again – but in fact, he too wanted to know more about Alyse. And as she said, she didn't need defending. That was more than true. It was evident she was tremendously powerful in a number of ways. He did want to know how she came to be under the thumb of the High Inquisitor.

"It's – *complicated*." Alyse shifted uneasily.

Gehard cut her off. "She's a vassal of the state of Elstemer."

"So – wait," Branson interrupted, "who *are* you?"

Alyse tensed slightly, as if cornered.

"I'm the eldest daughter of Elfking Thirandyse of House Elsteme," she replied. There was sudden burst of pride in her voice as she uttered those words.

"My dear!" Dusty exclaimed, awed. "You're High Elfkind royalty? Remarkable. Truly most remarkable!"

Tyel was stunned; even Ser Filip had clearly not known. In fact, only Gehard looked unmoved by the revelation.

"That would make you – a princess?" Tyel grinned. "I knew there was something about you."

"Except, she's not – not exactly," Gehard remarked. "Are you, girl?"

Alyse watched as Gehard folded his arms, satisfied that the point he was trying to make was somehow putting the elfkin in her place.

"My— mother. She wasn't a pure-blooded elfkind."

"Meaning what, exactly?" Dusty was less than familiar with the intricacies of elven bloodlines and their social implications.

"It means I'm not— *titled*," she said.

Gehard let slip a slippery smile. "The King took a human lover, once. She was a halfbreed. Halfbreeds cannot take the throne. Therefore, her father was most willing to send her across the seas as a vassal. Now she forms part of the transnational treaty between Elstemer and Solumbrya. We keep her in good health and reasonable comfort, and she aids us in negotiations by simply existing under our dominion."

"You hold her there as captive?" Tyel frowned. "That's appalling."

"That's political manoeuvring, boy." Gehard's smile slipped away. "It's the way of the world. Besides, she's proven herself much more useful than even my father expected."

Alyse resumed her solemn mood, but her eyes remained bright, unblinking. It was true that she was taken care of. She had her own quarters, assured to her father as part of their dealmaking, and was only rarely mishandled. But she was not *cared for*. She remained separated from all others, through their mistrust of her or simply her other-ness. There was an invisible wall that existed between her and the other servants, never articulated to her by anyone, and seemingly impenetrable. Tyel had been the first person to take any interest in her at all, she realised – to take interest and give her care. All others wanted or expected something in return.

She looked at Tyel. His quiet wonder was tinged with sadness that emanated from him in delicate waves.

"You all speak as if I'm not here. Well, I am." Alyse shot a look at Gehard. "Mostly."

"Mostly?" he replied.

"I can read minds. Often without trying," she stated, as if it were simply a casual fact.

"Can you read *my* thoughts, then?" Gehard smirked.

She could. Alyse's eyes blinked as she frowned and turned from him. "That's disgusting."

Dusty, clicked his tongue and shook his head. "Alyse, if what you say is true, and I haven't seen enough to know one way or another, but if so – then Brea has revealed her hand to the one person we do not want to know about it."

"I believe she needs to go now. And so do we." she replied, standing. Dusty joined her, and the others followed. "What I saw, what I felt – had nothing but ill intent for her."

~ ~ ~

At first, a rustling. Brea's chest was pounding so hard, she barely noticed it. The ground around her writhed beneath the fallen leaves. She heard disembodied laughter in her ears – that of the Necromant's mockery. Beneath her feet, something stirred.

A hoof. The top of a skull. A fallen sheep carcass began to pull itself together out of the ground, bones sliding into place, black and rotten tissue slipping along the smooth rib cage.

Just a few feet away, another creature was rising – a crow. Tiny vertebrae slid into place in a short chain, as it hopped along the ground.

Then a hare.

Another bird, smaller – a finch or jay.

Behind her, something much larger stirred. Brea turned, a gasp caught in her throat.

A... a... bear! Unmistakable. The enormous shape of a forest bear, long skull downturned, two massive shoulder blades capping a rib cage large enough to house a person.

At its feet, dozens of rat carcasses, now scurrying. Reborn.

Terror rose in Brea's throat. All around her, deceased animals were crawling up through the earth silently, save for the rattle of dry bones and crisp crush of leaves and grass as they parted the earth and worked their way up to the soil. The writhing body of a snake coiled around her foot, causing her to flinch.

Horrid, dry laughter came at her from everywhere and nowhere.

It was time to go.

She ran.

Chapter 18

HARROWED

It had been a most pleasant evening.

Sated, the Necromant's resurrected blood-children had been sent away and now the chamber was still at last. The night's blood-letting had energised him, but as the day had now worn on, Vimnir began to pay more consideration to the woman in the forest, the dwarf and their companions.

He now knew they pursued him with murderous, final intent – that rang clear as a bell. He read it the first time he spied them watching him in return, back in Dormanstar. Now it was underlined when he read the woman again this early morning.

This time, however, he viewed them through his seer-lens. The sacred device was an involuntary parting gift of the previous dwarven tenants of the mountain fortress. The seer-lens was a hand-polished anointed lens of wrought gold, decorated with precious gemstones of red and blue, sitting pinned by five golden hands. Who crafted it originally, he could only guess – but neither dwarven or human hands. Vimnir felt a certain entitlement to it, then.

Without the proper incantation, the lens was little more than a deco-rative curio. Of course, he knew the words to allow him to view whatever he desired, when he desired. This morning, he'd turned his seer-lens to his would-be assassins. He'd spoken the words aloud, and the lens had become a remote eye into the world.

Toying with the woman in the forest had been amusing. She'd been reaching out to someone when he first found her trace. He enjoyed watching her confusion bubble to the surface – it was just a shame the bear was slow to recorporeate; it would have fought her mercilessly, and perhaps finished her off for him. The thicket was alive with the dead now; a wonderful dark miracle.

Now, he watched with some amusement as two parties struggled to unite; the woman in the forest had run away, which he had expected. However, instead of heading deeper into the forest, she'd turned her own tail in retreat.

From a high disembodied vantage, he watched the woman pound her feet against the grassy fields, beating a fresh path. A few of his resurrected animals followed her trail, ambling.

Then there was the elf. The dandelion-bright girl. He drifted his eye across to her – a beacon of energetic light, like a bonfire on the horizon at dusk. She had so rudely intruded on his prying eyes. The elf girl was powerful, but unsure of herself.

Now the elf led her small contingent across a field toward the forest edge. Before long, they would intersect. She would tell them of what she saw, what she heard – both within and without. And then they would take arms against his animal playthings, press them back into the thicket, break through and make for the village beyond.

No matter, he thought. He knew what he was up against now: very little.

He laughed and stood up, walking over to the centre of the grand room. Crusts of dried blood, haphazardly splashed here and there like spilled wine, painted the floor like a mosaic.

Vimnir stood there for a time, looking down at the patterns it made. He stood, and stood some more, head down, two hands at his side, just thinking. There was much to consider. In some ways, to clip the rot now might be the simplest and best action. If the interference of swarming gnats cannot be endured, then they must be swatted down. Yes. But then, somewhere deep inside himself, killing other elves was antithetical to his core, to his cause.

Perhaps minds could be turned, the coil twisted the opposite way. And, of course, if those minds resisted – well, death was always a solution, and one he could control whether they willed against it or not.

He rubbed his narrow chin and took in a ragged breath.

An idea came to him at last. He would keep them guessing. Sow the seeds of doubt: the tangled wandering ivy that can never be stripped away completely.

They would play their games. Fine, then. He could play his.

From the waist belt of his long robe, he unsheathed a small copper dagger. He extended his arm, rolled his sleeve back, revealing a thin and heavily scarred forearm. Years of carving rune-rituals, and retracing those runes over and over, had left his pale skin a patchwork of thick scar tissue. Each rune held powers; each drop of blood was a cost incurred to use it.

Carefully, he planted the tip of the blade in a raised circle of skin. He traced the outline of the ring, crossing back and forth, following the lined pattern within it. He closed the circle's ring with the blade tip as warm blood ran smoothly down his wrist, toward his palm, pooling there. With the knife still in-hand, he conducted the blood outward from the small pool, into the air, in a perfect crimson sphere. It hovered there, in front of his blade tip, bobbing obediently.

The sphere of blood began to split into seven smaller spheres, each no larger than a thumbnail.

The spheres flew from Vimnir now; they slapped heavily and burst against the stone floor, then swirled smoothly into a perfect circle of red. The blood ran, at Vimnir's command, from the outer ring of the circle in zig-zags, mirroring the route the blade tip had taken on his flesh.

The trace of the rune was complete. He spoke the secret word, a hidden teaching, and the blood rune burst into indigo-black flame.

He would return his blood-creatures to the earth. Make them disappear.

From the black fire, small globules of potent, energetically-charged blood seeped upward, like drops of inverted rain, pooling in the air.

Vimnir held his palm aloft and grinned.

~ ~ ~

Brea sprinted so hard, she worried she might break her ankles, sending herself spiralling on a slip of dew-damp grass. She needed to warn them – about everything. Across the familiar field, between a scattering of oak trees, over the hill and down the other side.

She spotted Alyse first, who halted immediately, followed closely behind by Branson the boy, creaky Ser Filip and the blowhard. The dwarf trailed.

They were within shouting distance, but she was breathing like a blast furnace, so she kept moving instead.

Alyse picked up pace again, and the group broke into a jog to meet her.

"What happened?" Gehard shouted.

Brea skidded to a stop, fumbling forward from inertia, doubled over, gasping for air.

"He— knows—" she started, gulping breaths. "The— Necromant."

Brea rose up, sweat running down her temples. She pointed at Alyse. "You!"

Alyse took a step backward.

"You were in my head! How dare you!"

"I didn't mean to!" She raised her hands defensively. "It happens some-times – it's not easy for me to control!" The elfkin appeared ready to scrap, which took Tyel by surprise.

Dusty stepped in between them. "Enough of that. What of the Necro-mant? What did you see?"

Brea's mind raced back to the treeline, to the thicket. Much happened in a short span of time – and she was still processing it.

"I sat to rest for a moment – and the girl was suddenly in my head. She was telling me to run." She recounted the dark presence's laughter; the oppressive heaviness in her mind – and then the rising horrors. "So I ran," she said. "And here I am."

"And here you are, indeed." Dusty's eyes narrowed. "Do you know what you've done?"

"Of course I know, Dwarf. We're not safe now. And… we've lost the element of surprise."

"*And*," he interjected, "Sounds like there's a trail of risen creatures coming our way now."

Ser Filip drew his blade. "Branson, arm yourself."

Tyel did as instructed; Gehard likewise. Their faces were tired and grim. In Tyel's mind, he conjured images of the skeletal bear; facing down against animalistic strega and other horrors after a day and night of fighting, escape and exhausting travel. The notion of another conflict, or a desperate sprint through the forest did not appeal.

"Should we not turn around and make for the Westerling Trail?" Tyel suggested. He knew it was wishful thinking.

Ser Filip shook his head. "Without horses, the trip would take days. We don't have time enough to waste. We need to make for the capital directly – the river will carry us to the heart."

"And besides," he considered, "If what Brea says is true, then the village may be in danger. We have a responsibility to the realm – we cannot cast our eyes to the side."

"Fisherfolk." Gehard frowned, displeased. "They better have an inn and good food. Come on, then."

Brea took a deep breath. When this was over, she was going to need a long soak in some very salted waters. "We'll crest the hill and get down low.

The vantage should allow us to see how many creatures pursue us. I left them in the dust, but we've tarried now." She removed two short blades from her thigh-strapped hilts.

With speed, they made their way across the field, retracing the path of crushed grass left by Brea's sudden return. They were sensitive to every rustle of branches and the rush of breeze through the long grass. Thin white clouds, high above, streaked the pale blue morning sky, drifting slowly and indifferently to the increasingly chaotic world below.

Soon they came upon the largest of a series of the broad, domed hilltops, some eight hundred paces from the edge of the thicket. From here, the rooftops of the far village just beyond could be seen. Beyond, lay the wide and shimmering run of the River Marshtide, which ran south from the Atherons, in a loping, undulating cut across the lowland. It branched here and there, feeding rivulets and farmland, but the main artery pumped directly into the capital, nourishing it.

"I see smoke in the chimney stacks, just about," Tyel noted quietly, as the six lay on their stomachs in the grass. "That's a good sign, right?"

No one answered him.

They lay there, parting the green-yellow stalks of grass, watching the treeline for movement. A breeze blew softly; the grass swayed as the morning sun warmed their backs. In any other context, it would make for a blissful moment of respite, Dusty thought. His eyes were hopelessly outmatched when it came to distance viewing. He turned to Brea.

"What do you see?"

She frowned. "I don't understand this." She cupped her hands, focussing the light into her eyes, sharpening her already exceptional vision.

Dusty studied her face. Doubts about the Solsetter had already begun to form earlier – the way she departed struck him as most peculiar. Now, with the revelation that she'd been in some form of communication with the Necromant, and that Necromant had certainly been aware of her location, worried him greatly. More still, and worse, she'd drawn this Necromant's vision back south, to them. There was no telling what their target knew about their plans – but if he could read minds, then their loosely-formed plan was already worthless.

Was she playing one side against the other? He bit his lip beneath his large moustache pensively, then stopped himself. If she was, what was the benefit to her? He wanted to confront her about this, but now was not the moment.

"I just don't see anything now." Brea lowered her hands, but did not break her long stare at the tree line.

"It's possible that, like strega, they simply cannot enter direct sunlight for long," Dusty suggested. In his heart, Dusty wondered if these resurrected animals even existed in the first place. Perhaps she'd simply created a cover story – one that would drag them along, put them even more on edge – make her appear nothing more than a victim of circumstance and psychic intrusion. Was it possible that even perpetually shrewd individuals could stoop so low as to side with a deathpriest?

Alyse's elf eyes scanned the tree line. "There's nothing to see. It's still dead."

"A poor choice of words, but the girl is right," Brea agreed. "I— don't know what to tell you. I know what I saw."

"Aye." Dusty considered a few wise retorts but continued to button his own mouth to that end. Instead, he opted for a more neutral view. "Could it be a trap of some sort?" And if it was, she would know it. He watched her eyes. They were unwavering, unblinking, still fixed on the horizon.

If she flinched at all, it was imperceptible. Dusty wondered if Alyse might have more insights. Perhaps he would take her aside quietly and ask her.

The six lay still for a moment, like toppled statues, none quite ready to declare the situation with any certainty.

"We cannot stay like this all day," Gehard raised himself up on one knee. "If I lay any longer, I'm likely to fall asleep again."

Tyel had to agree. His side was aching again, where his dislocated rib was still gradually healing. He was slow to lift himself up, and as he did so, he thought of Omanon the Quartermaster – his round face and long beard, a gruff man – but one who had cared enough about Tyel, even for a few minutes, to set his injury to heal properly. He thought about the mess hall fare, the copper baths of steaming water, even the thin bunks and linen coveralls. It all seemed very removed, very remote.

He thought of his mother, and his father – and his brother, Dilain. He ached to know if they were safe in County Keep. The Westerling river branched south, but also to the west in a broad fork that ran into the sea, bypassing the port town of Feldstone Inlet.

A thought occurred; he wondered if he might be able to travel to see his family – depart from the company for a time, on promise that he would return swiftly – and with arms. He knew his family's storehouse was provisioned with all manner of arms and armour. If the realm was truly under threat, surely every able-bodied man and woman would be tasked with its defence. And those hands needed good iron; those heads needed helms.

He would ask. But not now – maybe once they'd reached the waterside.

Tyel joined Gehard and stood up. Ser Filip joined him. "I see nothing – but best to be prepared for anything."

At last, Brea broke eyes away from the distant trees. "Fine. Agreed." She sighed, pensively.

Dusty worked himself up to standing, a little stiff in the knees. He offered Alyse a hand, which she took out of courtesy, but his squat stature offered little additional support. It was a kind gesture though, she thought.

They started down the western slope of the hill, a knoll of white and yellow flowers reaching upward between the grass. Here and there, the hillside was dotted with large grey boulders. It provided them just enough ground cover to make their way, crouched and controlled, toward the tree line.

An undulating vee of kressenbirds passed overhead, almost directly pointing the way toward the riverside village. Branson took that as a positive omen, but he did not loosen his grip on the hilt of his drawn sword.

Aside from the kressenbirds, however, the land was still; the wind had died down, blocked in part by the thicket of trees. The treeline ran for at least a farthing to the north and south, thinning towards each end.

Suddenly, Alyse stopped short.

"Wait," she pressed, and got down low. "Someone is in there." She needn't say more; though none could see who or what she was referring to, they knew enough of Alyse's powers to heed. "They're searching for…" and she trailed off. Her eyes were closed now, reading.

They dropped to a crouch, though they were exposed now. The air hung heavy with unease.

"What can you see?" Tyel whispered.

"Something is blocking me out," she replied. "I can't read them. I can't sense their intent."

"That's not a good sign," Dusty spoke softly. "If they have some sort of psychic shielding, something that protects them from intrusion, then they're either well-trained in magic, or know we're coming – or both."

"It's a man; that's all I know for certain," Alyse concluded. She opened her eyes again, revealing their aquamarine glow.

"So what, then – we go around the forest?" Gehard sniffed. "I don't think so. Whoever is waiting will taste my blade should they face-up against me. My mood is foul from all the stop-start-stop we've endured." He stood up again. "I will cut through them and anything else that gets between me and my path home. Now stop tiptoeing – get up and let's go."

And so they did. There was no sense in spending another long day taking a wide berth around the forest – costing more precious time and energy. Tyel's nerves were on edge, and he could see the focus on Ser Filip's face. Gehard just looked tired and miserable, his sword drawn and held low.

The canopy let dappled morning light scatter here and there, but beneath the trees, nothing stirred. The fallen leaves carpeted the mossy earth in shades of brown and yellow and green; the density of tree trunks, mottled with white and orange lichen, made it nearly impossible to see deeply into the forest.

"I see no skeleton bears or strega-moles, Brea," Dusty noted, dryly. The Solsetter only shook her head, frowning.

Tyel led the small group around a grey fist of moss-covered granite, over a fallen tree trunk and through a winding natural cleft in the earth, where ancient roots broke through the rich, dark soil, threatening to snag loose fabric, or graze careless elbows and knees and shins. The air was damp and loamy with the rich smell of ancient decomposition. Unlike the befoulment of the Dormanstar streets, or the putrid waterway itself, this earthy smell felt oddly comforting to him. It reminded him of wandering with Dilain and exploring the forests south, near County Keep–though, those regions were less densely overgrown. After a heavy, soaking rain, you could almost smell the land reacting to the water; the sprouting of small delicate undergrowth and the blooming of mushmarrow fungus on old logs. The scent of pure, indifferent nature in balance.

Alyse had never set foot in such dense woodland before. Her people were desert-dwelling, and her time before her indenture had been spent largely within the walls of her own capital, Mar Elstemeri. The Elfkind cultivated trees, of course, and her castle had a private orchard and pleasure gardens. The conjuration of pure water was their race's greatest ability, and it allowed their empire to thrive and remain independent to some extent, even in so harsh a clime.

Now, even with the ache of a possible threat in their midst, she couldn't help but marvel at the scale and variety of the trees – the sheer beauty of unconstrained growth. She ran her hand along the trunks of broad-limbed oaks, touched the fractious ruddy-brown bark of towering pines; she studied the papery shed of shale-bark elms. She had no names for these, of course, but the wonder was all the greater for not knowing.

How nice it must feel to be free to grow and climb and wander like these, she mused. *To chatter as trees do amongst themselves, feeding and sharing life and water among them. Spreading life instead of pulling selfishly at the edges of anything within reach; endlessly accumulating like we do.*

She looked at Tyel and sent him a thought.

It's lovely in here, isn't it? Peace and life.

Branson was startled by the voice, and turned to her. *It is, my lady. Your... Grace.* He wasn't sure what the proper formality was when addressing her now.

She sensed a touch of embarrassment at that and betrayed a giggle.

"What?" Ser Filip stopped.

Alyse smiled and shook her head. "Oh. It was nothing. Just a thought."

The Knight Commander raised an eyebrow, sighed and continued on, with a shake of his head.

Brea interrupted the quiet chirping of insects and distant rush of wind in the treetops.

"There. This is the spot. Look." She pointed towards a small clearing, not ten yards onward, where the canopy parted; a diffuse beam of sunlight filtered through in a conical shaft to the ground beneath. The trees themselves were different here; they were lean and withered and grey, and the lichen that ran up their trunks was dry and brown. No carpet-moss covered the soil, which was badly upturned in places. Even the air took on a sour quality. All six could see, feel, smell the corruption.

"I *told* you," Brea spoke softly, almost in resentment. "I spoke true. This was where I saw the vision of the Necromant; where he spoke to me and where he raised the animals."

A black, glossy substance lay at the centre of the small clearing – though, what it was, Brea couldn't say. Perhaps dried blood, perhaps something otherworldly. She saw the Dwarf eyeing it greedily and she rolled her eyes. "You mean to collect that?"

Within moments, Dusty had his side bag open and a small phial in-hand. He made his way gingerly into the clearing, rounding a grey stone, stepping over the disturbed earth.

"Of course," he replied, and he bent over the strange circular substance, adjusting his lenses.

On closer inspection, he understood what he saw. The substance was glassy as chipped ebony, but smooth like melted wax. The ground itself was burnt with such intense and focussed heat that it had indeed crystalised.

"Fascinating," Dusty uttered to himself. "A crystalline manifestation borne of the actions of the Necromant himself." He felt around in his bag for a pair of tweezers, found them, and pulled them out. He began to reach out toward a small slip of the black, glass-like material when a shadow fell over him.

"Dusty!"

Alyse let out a cry of surprise; her Elfen synapses seemed long moments faster than the others'.

He fell backwards and looked up into the cone of honey-hued daylight. The silhouette of a looming, squarish figure materialised into his field of vision as if a sheet had been dropped to the floor.

"*Don't.*"

A loud, rounded voice; a voice of authority.

"Do not touch anything. This is harrowed ground."

CHAMPIONATE

Up here, the air was gaspingly thin. Ice storms left gashes on even the smallest patches of exposed skin that froze before they had a chance to bleed.

Away and across the white-water of thrashing seas and high upon the snow-crusted alpine peaks of the Northern Sprawl, in a land so remote that no trace remained of the obscure, bygone path that led there, resided the chambers of the Oracular Magisterium of Nine. Permanently obscured in thick grey cumuli, even keenest eyes could not see the circular stone tower, a third artificial peak between two ice-hardened mountaintops.

In this way, long after the lands to the north shifted to the frozen wastes, the only possible access into the Magisterium's solitudinous abode was remotely – or by express invitation via teleportation chamber.

The Sacred Championate opted for the latter, for as nauseously disorienting as the portal gate could be, it was far preferable to bleeding from the eyes, nose, ears.

The azure-lit portal disintegrated behind him with an electrical snap.

Before him, as with all other times, sat a semicircle of tall, dome-topped thrones of fine green malachite, shot through with pale white impurities – nine in total. These matched the nine towering twists of green marble pillars that supported a domed ceiling far above. At the base of each, a burning blue-orange hearth-fire, endlessly aflame, slowly consuming a vapour of magical energy drawn by some means from the ether.

Each of the nine Oracles assumed a similar posture; arms either in their laps or upon burgundy armrests, veiled faces further obscuring heads beneath cowls; backs pressed against the deep red leather of the throne-back that finished in an arc to match the top of the throne. Three marked by the golden ring of Sol, three silver crescents of the moon, three of the swirled black void.

How a grandiose space such as this could feel so deathly, the Sacred Championate could only attribute to its seemingly permanent inhabitants. Behind him, if he had dared to look, he would have seen an arched door. Aside from the portal, it was the only other means into or out of this space.

"Our Championate approaches."

Solum Three spoke; the low, hushed voice of an elderly woman – but there was no way of knowing for sure if what sat concealed beneath the robes was even human. It was said they could inhabit human forms – or needed to – but what resided within, only they themselves knew.

"As always, I am at your service." He knelt, the plate steel shifting and clattering as his knee impacted the thick, woven carpet runner.

Another voice: male, younger. He tensed at the unpleasant tone. He could feel their eyes watching his subservience and relishing it.

"Restate your commitment," came another voice. "We wish to hear it."

"As your designated Sacred Championate, I swear my sword and shield to the divine Oracular Magisterium of Nine. Through your counsel, I serve the needs of the realm. I uphold and defend the aspects of the Trine and in doing so, I protect the balance of the land. I am the blade that acts for justice, and justice is impartial."

"Rise." Lunum Two leaned forward. He did so.

"Our Sacred Championate. You are most blessed this day, under the protection of the Trine. Today, you act for the Solum God. Will you heed our request?"

"I will hear it."

Solum One leaned forward; a young woman's voice, clean like a bellbird chime.

"There is a new, dark reckoning of our age. A coming storm. One that will wash away the leagues of man and woman and child. A dawn and a dusk and a nightfall forever."

The Sacred Championate did not respond. He did not so much as blink. But deep inside, he felt the words propel the cogs of his beliefs, the roots of his holy training. It angered him, sickened him and prompted him to action.

"Tell me what I must do."

"A Necromant – most powerful. A being of great and terrible reckoning. He must be intercepted and stopped. There is no cost greater than failure."

"It will be done."

"Begin at once in the harrowed land beyond the portal we set. You will find aid and resistance both. We cannot intervene, but know this: agents of our own tasking are operating in both the light and the dark. And we cannot influence the outcome; merely advance our physical expressions upon the great plane."

Much of this was rhetoric, but it disturbed him that there were other agents already in deployment. He could cleanse harrowed land easily; untangling the poor work of others was more difficult.

"Thus your task is before you. Do you understand?"

"I do."

"Then may the Trine point the path for you and all." Solum One relaxed her posture. There would be no further instruction, this he knew. This was the Magisterium's way: vague, veiled and threatening, but he would be paid for his time and his ability – and imbued with power to accomplish his task.

"Then remove your helm and approach." A low voice from a Nulum oracle, dark and thick and slow like syrup.

The trio of Nulum Oracles, pointedly silent, stood now on their raised marble dias. The six of Solum and Lunum remained seated.

He removed his ornate gilt helm crown by the crest of Solum and Lunum and Nulum in Trine; he pinned it in the crux of his arm. His long, brown hair spilled over his plate neck guard.

"Kneel and receive."

Once more, The Sacred Championate took a knee.

From the three outstretched arms, a ball of golden, plasmic light emanated towards his head; small and delicate, like a perfectly formed soap bubble, caught in a breeze. It drifted towards his downturned forehead. He closed his eyes. The heat of impact caused an immediate sting that dissipated into a soothing warmth that penetrated deep into his flesh, before running down, like tendrils of warm water, through his torso and limbs. Sacred energy, like a sensory meal. But this gift came with payment to be collected later, he knew.

"Go now and uphold the balance, Championate."

Behind him, he heard the static crackle of a portal being raised. He rose once again, and in customary fashion, bowed to each of the three groups of Oracles in turn. Nothing was said or elicited in return, but that too was expected.

Placing his helmet back upon his head, he turned and looked through the shifting portal plane, like an ovular window ringed in sparking energy. Beyond, he saw a blurry and wavering vista of dappled sunlight falling in a forest meadow.

With a deep breath held in his broad chest, stomach muscles clenched, he stepped through.

~ ~ ~

At the sensation of cold steel pressed to the side of his jugular vein, Dusty dropped his satchel. The figure in front of him was coming into focus now.

"Declare yourself."

Dusty was prepared to do no such thing. He raised his hand and, with the confidence of age, swatted the blade edge to the side. "You have five blades levelled at you, soldier. Cut me and you bleed too." He glared at the figure.

The Sacred Championate was taken aback. Who was this half-man to undermine his authority?

"I am no *soldier*," he said, with certain disgust. "You address the ordained Sacred Championate."

"You say this like it's s'posed to mean something to me," the dwarf laughed. "All I see is a bell-end in plate steel, thrusting carelessly into our private business."

The Sacred Championate levelled his blade against the dwarf's neck once more, and held it firmly – unwaveringly.

"Choose your next words wisely, halfman, or I'll lance that hairy boil you call a head. You. In the shadows. Come forth, or the dwarf dies."

"Let him," came Brea's voice, with a laugh. She made no advances from her vantage.

"Such loyal associates you're joined by, dwarf."

"It's Dust-in-His-Eyes. *Dusty*. And the Solsetter is not representative of the whole, to be sure. It's no accident that you've found this grove, however, is it?" Dusty pressed.

The Championate nodded.

"Sacred Championate, you call yourself."

"It is the title granted to me."

"An agent of the Magisterium, you would be, if I had to guess." Dusty winced at the growing sting on his neck.

"Hmm. You say true – though this is none of your concern."

"Oh, but there you're incorrect. We are most *certainly* aligned by cause. Mayhaps a mutual concern."

The Sacred Championate reflected on those words for a moment – grateful now for the steel that covered the majority of his puzzled expression. He had not expected to encounter anyone so immediately upon arrival, let alone a band of strange and vaguely threatening vagabonds, seemingly intent on playing a game of three truths and a lie.

"Go on." The Championate pressed his blade's edge in slightly, that the pressure might issue more sensible answers. "I have not yet decided whether to spare you."

Dusty could feel the sharp edge digging into his neck. The slightest increase in pressure would part his skin like sun-softened cheese, clip his artery and that would be the end of him.

"Lower the blade," Dusty winced. "Dead men do not make for great storytellers."

"I want no tales from you; only truth." He withdrew the edge, but only slightly. Dusty felt the quick sting of drawn blood on his skin. He hoped the blade was not edged in some foul element. He sensed not. He raised a hand slowly to his neck and pressed it against the cut.

"What brings you here, then?" The Championate levelled the question toward the edge of the clearing, over Dusty's head. "Speak."

To his surprise, from the din emerged a slender, pale elf. A woman of indeterminate age, as all elves rarely show their age outwardly. He could see she was beautiful, however. Striking in a way that exceeded her physicality. It was something about her eyes; piercing and disarming, but vulnerable too.

He could also sense she was powerful; magic seemed to radiate from her like heat from a bonfire. She lit up like a candle to his senses.

At once he realised what he may actually be sensing.

"No further." He held his sword aloft, pointing the tip toward Alyse.

She felt dangerously capable. That was it.

"I am no threat to you, Ser."

"I think, there, you may be wrong. I think you're very much a threat."

Alyse stopped, her feet crunching on grey, ashen leaves.

"You may be right," she replied softly. "But not to you."

He cocked his head sideways, watching her closely from the thin eye slit of his bluesteel helm. "You're an odd one. I can sense much tension in you. More than that."

"Why have *you* come here?" Alyse made no movement towards him; she worried less for the blade than the powers of the man wielding it. She likewise could sense radiant magical energy emanating from him. He was awash in it; more than she had ever felt before, in fact. It was potent to the point of intoxicating, like skin rubbed deep in rich perfume. Her mind cast back to the High Inquisitor's chambers for a moment. His quarters smelled of sacred oils, pressed flowers, wood shavings. He wore a lather of patchouli and smokeweed blossom, anointed upon his bulbous, pink flesh, daily.

She shook the thought away.

In the here-and-now, the man before her was the physical opposite, in steel plate that was, at least in part, reminiscent of the sleek and finely shaped prow of a tall-ship, or the killing-end of a lance – both things she'd long ago encountered on her voyage across the seas. The surface of each pauldron, the chest plate and each flat surface were intricately inlaid with sacred geometry – the powers and symbolism of which Alyse could only guess. It was, without doubt, extraordinary and magical garb to match an equally potent person within.

Hearing her words, reading her demeanour, or simply out of patience with the protracted conversation, at last, the towering man began to soften his stance. He slowly lowered his sword until it rested, tip-down, by his side. He did not yet sheathe it.

"As the Sacred Championate of the Realm, I have been appointed by the Oracular Magisterium of Nine to investigate the infiltration and possible proliferation of corrupting evil. This site has been harrowed. As such, it is my sworn duty to cleanse this land and restore the balance – both beneath our feet and wherever great and unholy evil lurks."

He seemed to inflate with those fanciful words, as if his sense of duty could propel him through solid stone walls. Though to Alyse, those words sounded rehearsed, his voice was undeniably beautiful and melodic – almost theatrical. It reminded her of one of the choral performers who entertained with song in the Inquisitor's dining hall in the Capital.

Alyse nodded. "You seek the Necromant. So do we."

The Sacred Championate did not reply. Instead, he at last sheathed his broad blade in his waist-mount. With his hand now free, he reached up and behind his right shoulder. With a twisting motion, he uncoupled something else.

To his front, he smoothly drew down a golden blade wrought into a broad, circular shape.

Tyel's eyes widened at the sight and he took an involuntary step forward, eager to better view it. He immediately recognized the weapon as a variant of the unusual circular blade on a short, leather-wrapped handle that Omanon had produced in the armoury. A *circuitris*, he called it – a name it shared with the religious symbol of the land, not to mention the sacrificial rings its believers gathered around. A blessed weapon, the Quartermaster said. This one, however, had a cross-guard just below the ring, and the ring itself was perfectly without serration or embellishment. The blade's edge was bevelled slightly, however, and a dazzling shade of fine gold.

The Championate raised this sacred blade high above his head, like a shining beacon along the shoreline, catching the diffuse, white morning shafts of sun in the shallow fuller that ran the circumference of the ring.

Suddenly, the blade's golden-hued metal took on a sudden unnatural iridescence as the open centre of the ring ignited from the middle outward. It rippled with vibrant indigo and orange flame. The light it cast seemed to grow and grow until it became difficult to look at directly.

It takes into itself the light of the Solum, Tyel thought, and at once, he knew he wanted one of these for his own one day. He felt as if the radiance it produced was in some way cleansing; there was a purity to it as measurable as the quenching of clean, still water or a candle's protective, illuminating flame in the dark.

"Stand back. All of you. Witness the power of the Solum God's wrath."

Dusty's mouth hung open; he caught himself in a gasp, grabbed his leather satchel in haste and, as he scurried past Alyse, also deeply entranced, the dwarf dragged her by the hand. The force of his pull nearly sent her reeling backward.

From just a foot beyond the treeline, Tyel watched with fascination – a feeling palpable among them, for none had seen such a rite performed.

Not an eye among them dared to blink.

Slowly, methodically, meticulously, the Championate lowered and rotated the blade until the ring of the circuitris was held out at his arm's length, level with the ground. Under his breath, he uttered the blessing.

Like a puff of breath might instantly smother a candle flame, the circuitris' ring immediately extinguished.

Then, just as instantaneously, with the almighty fury of a summer thunderstorm, the ring burst into brilliant white flame. The space was lit to blinding, like a monumental and heart-rending strike of lightning. There came no heat – just a flash of impossible luminance the likes of which none of them had ever experienced before. The sound that followed was deafening, and as he reflexively grabbed his ears, a thumping, round wave of pressure knocked Tyel backward, off his feet and into the trees.

The trees swayed; leaves blew backward. Far away, the rolling, thunderous echo of the blast reverberated into infinity. Somewhere, birds took flight, cawing in shock.

Tyel came to, wincing, several feet farther back than where he began. He registered hazily that he was not alone on the ground. Gehard too was pressed against a tree, a look of appalled horror on his round face. Ser Filip was sprawled on his back, struggling to right himself. Brea was breathing heavily, clinging to a tree trunk, her teeth clenched and eyes like a screaming wildcat. Only Alyse remained standing, joined by Dusty. Around the pair, a familiar protective sphere shimmered slightly, almost pearlescent, before fading away to nothingness.

"I told you to stand back."

The Sacred Championate spun the circuitris around on its handle like a door-knob, then flipped it end-to-end, before raising it back up and stowing it behind his shoulder. Beneath his angular helm, he smiled.

"What – in the three *hells* – was *that*?" Brea screamed. "You nearly killed us, you— you—" She struggled to find a curse foul enough to encompass her boiling rage. Instead, she let out a frustrated, huffing groan and reached for her blades.

"Let's scrap, goatlicker!" she roared.

The Championate laughed. "Cool your fire, Solsetter. Not today. I have saved you. Look around."

Brea slowed, then stopped. Tyel joined her side. They shared a sideways glance as they absorbed what lay before them.

What was once a dry and deadened hearth was gone. No trace of the blackened residue; no brown and failing undergrowth, or disintegrating grass and moss. All that remained now was exposed earth: a broad, brown circle, like a raw and exposed wound on the land, radiating away from this odd Champion of the Magisterium.

The Championate removed his helmet, allowing clean air to refresh him.

"You – destroyed everything in here!" Tyel protested. "There's nothing left!"

"No," he replied. "Wrong. Everything in here was marked by death. The Necromant, of whom your elf speaks, harrowed this land through his dark rites. There was a blight upon it – to even touch this ground with bare flesh would be deadly to you."

He shot a look at the dwarf.

"Now I have cleansed this land; redeemed it. I have allowed it to flourish once again, stronger. Hallowed.

"As Sacred Championate, I am an instrument of higher powers – ones you cannot hope to comprehend. And today, I am tasked to channel the Solum God and deliver his righteous blessing. This is what he offers: life anew and a scourging of all those who oppose."

He placed his helmet upon the freshly upturned soil and, with one hand resting upon the pommel of his sword, he finished his florid prose.

"Now," he slid the blade slowly out of its hilt. "Do you oppose?"

CHAPTER 20

BLOODLINES

I t had been a most unpleasant day.

High Inquisitor Fendrigar regurgitated his long, late lunch into a heavily stained wooden chamber bucket.

This was, of course, partially intentional, as he often tickled his throat with a feather to clear the way for another platter of edible finery. On this day, though, his mind was elsewhere and his stomach seemed unable to overcome a crippling nausea. The feather merely aided the inevitable.

"Your Grace – another course?" A young tablehand approached his side. He swiped him away. "Go. Leave me. All of you." The High Inquisitor's dining hall, lined with guards and housekeep, evacuated rapidly.

He was alone to reflect on the morning; the choices that led him here.

The aftermath of the impromptu riot left the streets splashed in lashes of blood. Growing discontent in the capital was beginning to express itself in odd and unnerving ways. Antisocial and aggressive ways. Trends that must be clipped before spreading, he felt. The Solum God had seen fit to bludgeon him with a famine, and in denying the simple peons of the streets and alleys and cellars the chance to watch the burning of his tender Melodis, some final filament, a fine and invisible tether, had snapped. Like a single pebble that starts a landslide, he watched as pushing and shoving gave way to thrown fists, then to thrown clay-bricks. This led to drawn steel and drawn blood.

At first, he meant to retreat to the safety of the Solum Temple, but by that point, even inside the sacred confines of the sacred structure, something had overcome the young priests. As he agonised up the stone steps, he watched two pale figures, in a state of frenzy, descend upon the ancient Templemaster, Kyrus Eogan, like hungry hounds on a bow-legged, bearded goat.

The dusty, crook-backed man bleated like a goat too – not one soul attempted to wrench the young priests, lost in a mindless frenzy, off of him.

The High Inquisitor averted his eyes to that horror, choosing not to let the image settle on him. It was too much to comprehend. Too strange.

He started back down and away, feeling hot and heavy and unsteady as he descended the steps. Before him, his city guard, some of them anointed, and others simply paid security, were roughly forcing a throng of villagers back, swords drawn. He watched through eyelids running with salty sweat and tears as bursts of violence had begun to flicker here and there, and then continuously, like sparks from a smith's wheel.

Something – a strange and indefinite *something* – was happening around him now. He could feel his day upending as he retreated from the Temple. Faintly, in the back of his mind, he knew something had broken back there that could not be mended. Down in the street, he could faintly smell the rich, fatty bubble of burning flesh that wafted in from far above, on the golden ring. The scent hungered him, which he knew was appalling, of course, but perversely alluring all the same. Two pairs of guards, covering his front, back and sides, escorted him back toward the keep, as hurriedly as Boff could muster the energy to do so.

The streets thinned and the sounds of discord faded into grey indistinction as they reached the gates.

Crossing the threshold, he felt a soothing wash of relief. Whatever was building out there, threatening to bubble over, he wanted no part of it and as much separation from the wider world as possible today. Within these walls, he could not be touched.

Once inside, hand servants brought him cool tea to sip and a fold of damp cloth to soak his reddened brow. Both helped distract him some, but the sting of unsated hunger gnawed at him. He took in a luncheon meal – another welcome distraction, but there was unease in the air even within his tower. The servants hurried here and there with long, worried expressions, as he settled into the cool of the dining hall. It was far too early for dinner, but the kitchen prepared a series of platters of cold-cut meats, pressed white and green-veined cheeses, dried and fresh fruit, sugarloaf and sourloaf breads and a large freshly-caught pink Salamana, stuffed with citrus and fragrant herbs, cooked tableside on a bed of red-hot coals. He did occasionally enjoy watching his meals gutted and prepared over flames. It took on a sacramental quality.

And so he dined, vomited, gorged again and thought heavily on the day. He missed his children; no more would he dine with his son and daughter together; no longer would she laugh and jape and recite her songs and poems (he never cared for her singing voice, but did as all fathers should do and humoured her passion for it).

Where was Gehard right now? His vanguard was, he knew, purposefully removed from the capital – a choice made for him, and enacted *through* him, by the Magisterium. Now Gehard was his only living heir. How would he tell him that his sister had gone? What if Gehard was gone now, too?

He could feel his eyes welling. He bit down hard on the inside of his cheek to pull himself back together.

He thought about Melodis and Gehard's mother, Lyssy – his estranged wife. Of course, Lyssy Fendrigar was not a *Fendrigar* at all, though he could just as easily have wed a blessed niece or aunt. His own mother was wedded to a distant relation – his father was High Inquisitor and also his mother's cousin, three times removed.

All of this was in service of keeping their family in power, and in the good favour of the Solum God. His own mother had wanted to find a suitable woman within the limbs of their tree, but he had insisted he choose based on his particular tastes. He wanted a hard woman. A woman who could wield authority of the most brutal kind in private, and be softer than dew drops in the watch of the public. A wife who would punish and please him.

He found who he sought – in the same long trip to Elstemer that netted him his vassal, Alyse. The servant girl. Oh gods, why had he agreed to let her go with Gehard? She was precious as leverage – and a powerful psychic; her insights during negotiations were invaluable.

He felt his mind drifting back and forth between Lyssy and the elfkin of House Elsteme; of the blood feud and the fragile treaty that now existed.

Lyssy was of the family Delcryth. Her Southern bloodkin were ancient and distantly elfish; an older-than-old House, though heavily interwed and crossbred with humans now. Not all of them, however, had taken human partners, or birthed human offspring. The High Inquisitor's own kin had very few traits, save for the blonde hair. Their body shapes couldn't be farther removed from those lanky sand-dwellers and water diviners. Those that adhered to the strictest dogma of their race stayed pure-blooded.

The family Delcryth were the ruling house for many turns of the age; a name synonymous with supreme magical ability and unfathomable wealth. A house that could punish and please.

Mar Elstemeri, the Elstemer Capital, endured a ghastly civil war – and it was Delcryth blood that soaked deeply into the fabric of the throne, undoing the King's hold on the South. It was said the entire immediate royal Delcryth family had been murdered by agents of the usurper Thirandyse of House Elsteme. They claimed the throne by birthright – and, Boff supposed, history was on their side. The city was founded in their name, after all.

It was during this uprising that House Delcryth had been violently unseated by House Elsteme. Dethroned, the House now had no seat through which to wield their power, making House Delcryth, in some respects, ideal for a blood-union with House Fendrigar. It would serve to strengthen both houses and quell tension.

After the fall of House Delcryth, the surviving Delcryth family went into exile. Most travelled farther south – but not all. His wife had remained in Mar Elstemeri as an ambassador of sorts, while Boff Fendrigar brought his holy might and the Solum God's influence to the capital. By the time a peace treaty had been agreed upon, he left with his young and beautiful wife, a woman with a stonelike resolve, and a young vassal of House Elsteme as surety that the uneasy peace would hold.

Boff's wedding of Lyssy Delcryth was widely regarded as a stabilising factor for the blessed line of Fendrigar. Worshipful Fendrigars, imbued with holy righteousness, were a beautifully corresponding match to the merciless and magical Delcryth.

Then there was the matter of his missing wife. He knew rumours were circulating in the halls of the Capital citadel that Lyssy had been missing for many weeks. She supposedly had fled in the night, though it had taken some time to be notified of her leaving. Before then, she kept to her own quarters; rarely did she sup with her family, and it was rarer still to encounter each other outside of meals. She escaped by carriage, he was told, in a cloistered carriage, via the Easterling Way. From there, she might have headed north, south or farther east.

He had the entire regimen of night guards stripped, beaten and left to burn on rings as punishment for their incredible, galling ineptitudes. Nine betrayers. Not only did they undermine him most directly, but they undercut the order of the House; they allowed a seat of power to become vacant – and politically vulnerable – on the flippant whims of his ill-tempered wife. The notion made him feel queasy all over again and he eyed his bucket.

He considered allowing the roast fish to surface once more, but kept himself together and placed the bucket of vomitus down on the floor with a grunt of exertion.

Where are you, Lyssy? he asked himself. But part of him knew. She'd gone south; back to her people. Perhaps, back to her uncle – though he knew not where he resided now.

Lyssy's Uncle, she claimed, held many keys – some metaphorical, many literal – to opportunities of great wealth, that the old man had promised would be redistributed his way – and even greater power. That her uncle was a potent wizard merely gave the High Inquisitor more reason to support him at the time. Lyssy claimed his abilities were unique in all the land; a man of connection and fearsome influence across the races.

He just needed a seat through which to act.

In return, Boff would allow – in fact, fully *support*, the Family Delcryth, in taking certain liberties in the North and beyond.

Turned out, another's seat of power can be just as potent as your own, if you can control the one who sits upon it, the High Inquisitor pondered bitterly. He took another gulp of wine. And in the end, it would be he who would be held to account; no others were party to the strings that pulled his machinations remotely.

At first, he thought he held control; now, it was becoming clear he was merely a supplicant to the Solum God on behalf of foreign interests.

Oh, Lyssy – what horrible, shadowed gateway did you open? What broken bridge had she built between her blood and his? And what now crossed it to the other side? *But that isn't the truth of it, is it?*

Boff's head spun with the pleasant disconnection that came with a bellyful of wine. *This is my making; I undid the knot that held together the Seat of High Inquisition.*

He had chosen fleeting pleasure and sacrificed his power to the manipulations of another.

Tonight, he needed a firm beating. And to repent. Again and

again. Oh yes.

Vimnir had promised him so much. So far, death and disorder were his only recompense.

He grabbed for the bucket and, in horror, swore he saw Vimnir's thin face smiling back at him in the reflection.

~ ~ ~

It was deep into the daytime – approaching evening, now – though it could hardly be known from closed shutters deep within the mountain fortress. The Necromant rose from his reclaimed, dwarfly-proportioned bedtress in his resting chamber, a room of plush magnificence. The high ceiling was draped with fine burgundy sateen, an extravagance that softened the hewn stone of the walls and beam-lined wooden arches. He kept those large shutters firmly latched. Unlike his strega progeny, he could tolerate sunlight – but he despised it all the same. It proved a distraction to the senses.

Vimnir found the reduced scale of his surroundings all rather poetically amusing; a great man among the small of the world; a proud figure out of time and place, forced to adjust to the relative discomfort of the age.

Though he rarely slept, the day's energetic expenditure drained his vitality greatly. Now, upon waking, Virmir could feel his dark work unmade. It infuriated him. His carefully laid deathspring, designed to spread his influence, had been cleansed away. It was as if it had never been – and removed by whom he did not know – but he would have his insight soon enough. Seeds had been planted that would bear fruit in due course.

He wrapped himself in a thin, ash-grey cloak and made his way down a curving staircase to the chambers below. Doors parted at his approach, and the conference room opened out before him.

A long table of twenty-four high-backed chairs ran neatly down the middle of the space. Vimnir jabbed a bony finger towards a wide-set blackened hearth and it ignited, flooding the room with amber and permeating warmth.

Sliding away a chair and working his way into the plush cushioning, he took a seat at the head of the table. In front of him rested his seer-lens, in opulent gold, catching the fire light. He closed his eyes and focused on the target of his contact.

"Present to me the Grand High Inquisitor, Boff Fendrigar."

The seer-lens bloomed to life.

~ ~ ~

The day had been utterly abysmal so far; the appearance of this glowing portal merely added another bleak colour to a dull palate of unpleasantness.

The High Inquisitor noticed his hands were shaking. Perhaps from the vomiting, he thought. Surely not his nerves. He wrapped his hands around a pitcher of wine and tipped it down his throat. The sharp kick made him gag slightly, but it would serve to steady him.

He did not take this unannounced visitation as a positive portent.

Now, dabbing his mouth with the table cloth, he found himself staring at the shifting, phantom-haze form of the last person he desired to see.

"Vimnir."

"High Inquisitor. I interrupt you at meal time. Though, when are you not leading into, or out of, a meal of some kind?"

"Oh, leave off, Vimnir. I am in mourning."

The visage of the Necromant hung framed within the small ovular portal. Through the energetic distortion, Boff could make out an odd sort of frown, head tilted, but eyes raised, as if searching for an appropriate emotional response.

"Is that so?"

"I… lost Melodis. My sweet one. My innocent child!"

If Vimnir was moved by the revelation, it wasn't betrayed by his expression.

"Then you have my condolences, your Grace. How?"

The flatness of the reply; the callousness of it. The High Inquisitor crumpled the table cloth, stretching the skin across his knuckles taut. He wanted to reach through the small portal and wring Vimnir's thin neck, if only it might bring some small satisfaction and relief to the blackness in his heart.

"I held her as she died." His eyes filled once more, but rage simmered more than sadness now.

He searched for the words. "Something in the water… overtook my fair daughter. An affliction." A sudden burst of adrenaline coursed through his veins; he felt his muscles, buried deep within, clench.

""There's something in our waterways, sorcerer, and I think you are aware. In fact, I think you are very much responsible."

"Whatever are you talking about, your Excellence? That's a profoundly dangerous accusation."

"What have you done to the water supply?"

The Necromant cast his mind back to the streets of Dormanstar – and more specifically, the supreme annihilation that filled the alleys and drains and sewers with corruption and decay. In his nostrils, such thoughts conjured coppery odour; the red pools of blood that ran downstream, out of the town, aortic, throughout the body of the land.

"Oh, I see," he gestured the idea away with a thin hand. "Melodis. Sweet and porcine, wasn't she? A weak constitution. It was only a matter of time before her heart gave out. A tragedy, but also, an inevitability."

"How dare you! What have you done, Vimnir? You— you know you have damned us all!"

At this, the Necromant uttered a single, pointed and rusty laugh.

"Damned you? Oh, for the melodrama of it. Please, your Grace, you should exercise some decorum. You betray your fragile feelings. Your hate is showing and it is most unflattering for a man of sacred birth. It makes you appear… petty."

The High Inquisitor sputtered at the insolence.

"You *dare* to call me petty, blacktongue? I'll have it removed from your head! I'll take the head with it – why not?"

The Necromant tutted. "Now, now. Let's not say things we might regret later. Your Grace, the mood of this conversation has soured. However, I have come with good tidings! Perhaps your mood shall be lifted as you receive this word."

The High Inquisitor's blood pounded in his temples; he felt faint, distant. Such ugly confrontation – and none to bear witness to the verbal spar.

Vimnir smiled thinly through the portal.

"Let us not dwell on unpleasant words. I can forgive a man in mourning, besides." He ran a hand through his thin hair. "Great progress is being made. It is most unfortunate that such change often comes at great cost. Your Melodis was a victim of change, High Inquisitor. You do remember our discussions, do you not?"

Sudden shame rushed to Boff's cheeks. He knew very well that he had agreed to support Vimnir's taking of the northern towns and mountain dwellings. He knew not the manner in which his claiming might occur – only that the sorcerer's methods were likely to be dark and swift and violent.

"Of course I remember," he replied, stiffly.

"Good. And you recall, of course, that when I come into my seat once again, your compensation would be as richly golden and eternal as the Sun itself?"

"I… do." The High Inquisitor clenched his jaw like a vise.

In his heart, he knew he was lost to this man's whims. More than angry, Boff was frightened of him; a fear that penetrated his core. He barely let himself accept this. It disturbed his sense of power – undercut his sense of worth.

"Then allow me to show you your great reward. Follow me, if you will."

The glowing ring of the portal's view expanded. Vimnir was on his feet now and walking away from his long table, out and down a winding stone staircase. The view showed only what passed behind the Necromant, tracking him as he navigated the stone archways and passages, down and down. The glow of the portal lit the dark wizard's features, highlighting the recessed eye sockets, thin and high-set cheek bones – a long, narrow nose like a razorbird's beak. As he smiled, rows of small teeth appeared washed in an oil of blood.

Through one dimly lit hall, down another staircase.

There came a sound, soft at first, like the indistinct sound of wind in boughs, but building with each step the Necromant took.

At last, Vimnir stopped; behind him, all the High inquisitor could see was a dark hallway, stretching far away, untouched by sunlight.

"Look upon what our fine union has afforded us, High Inquisitor."

With a small puff of exertion, Vimnir pushed against something heavy – large doors, Boff assumed. They shifted slowly, achingly, with a dry dragging scrape along ancient stone.

The sound, that was once indistinguishable, burst into a roaring cacophony of screaming, moaning, rejoicing, lamenting. A horrific chorus of agony and rage and misdirected misery.

Vimnir turned, spinning the view of the portal with him.

The High Inquisitor's jaw flopped open, like a soft-minded fool. He could not help it. Cold terror crept up his spine like corpse-fingers.

Behind his cloaked shoulders, beyond the back of his laughing skull, Vimnir presented his gift. A thousand-thousand bodies – some barely human, others barely contained within a distinguishable form – writhed and shifted and scrambled in a monstrously deep tomb. Blood-horrors beyond reckoning, and more numerous than the blackest nightmare.

"Your Grace, meet *my* children. They departed this mortal realm just recently, much like your daughter. Though, no need to mourn them, dear Fendrigar."

He turned his head and waved his arm broadly, triumphantly. "This is a time for rejoicing! Look at them! Countless, ageless, fresh-reborn and *so very hungry.* With my children, I will free this land of the blight of old, tired thinking. The fall of House Elsteme and humankind." He turned to face

Boff Fendrigar once more.

"And to you? Your reward. I bring you this freedom." He smiled. There was no goodness in it.

"I will liberate you of the burdens of constant human fallacy: the gluttony, the greed — the endless lust for power and pleasure — though, I hear you prefer pain. This is good. I, too, admit a preference for pain."

His cackle was an ugly blight.

"High Inquisitor, I bring you death. This is my gift to you."

~ ACT III ~

CHAPTER 21

COLLAPSE

The ageing innkeeper worked and scrubbed the dark wood of the wet-bar countertop, her furrowed brow as red and heavily-lined as her knuckles.

She worried.

She worried so much, and so intensely, that a small circle of wax-varnish had begun to strip away. She paid it no mind; her eyes were fixed on the top of the staircase: on the thin, closed pine door, separating the dining room from the simple bed-rests upstairs.

At last, as her fingertips began to ache and numb, she caught herself in the repetitive motion.

The odd caravan had reached the small village of The Westwater Run the previous day, as the sun was setting, raising ire as they did so, for the strangeness of them.

The proud, tall knight had insisted he bless the town before stepping foot beyond the threshold, causing a stir amongst the odd assortment of fisher-folk, their children and grandchildren playing in the streets with foxglove reeds brandished like rapiers.

From her hazy window, she watched as the odd knight – or so she assumed him to be–anointed the ground with flame from a blade shaped like the sacred Circuitris. The children squealed with delight at the show of magical bravado.

Trailing him came a stocky and half-dressed blonde man, a dark-skinned woman, a squat and bespectacled dwarf, an old and battered-looking soldier of some sort and a late teenager, red-faced and frayed as the old man. And then there was the elf-girl – she irked her the most. She never much liked elves – and there was something deeply, intensely off-putting about this one in particular. It was in her eyes – unblinking, darting and scanning… as if absorbing everything she saw.

The sudden appearance of the strange wanderfolk was not the cause for concern so much as the fact that they came traipsing into The Westwater Run on the tail of another odd happening: a dreadful pox seemed to be taking root.

She wandered, half-absently, to the bucket of grey water in the corner of the under-bar and dropped the rag in with a plop. She watched it distantly for a moment as it disappeared below the surface of pearly suds and was gone. She sighed heavily and looked back up at the door, as if expecting it to burst open at any second.

Now, upstairs, filling every one of her vacant rooms, the odd travellers had not emerged since paying for their keep, the evening before. The dwarf had handed her ten heads of gold – far more than she'd taken in all season. She nodded her thanks warily and produced pints of sweet ale and three loaves of yesterday's seed-bread, with clotted butter and honey. Aside from the knight, or whatever he was, the group looked famished and filthy. The loaves were gone within moments, so she produced two more rounds.

While they tore hunks from the bread, she studied them cautiously. The young man was sporting a number of bruises and cuts; the old man looked ready to collapse. The elfkin ate only little, and her mind seemed elsewhere, far from the candle-lit interior. The blonde man gorged himself as the dark-skinned woman frowned and drank her share. All had been through some kind of brutality.

Part of her wondered if she might not find their corpses upstairs if she dared check on them this morning. The compulsion to take a peek was irresistible. She started for the staircase, feeling a twinge of prying guilt and doubt. Surely she was overreacting; reading too much into these visitors. She hoped so.

As she closed in on the top step, short of the recessed doorway, she heard the front door squeal on its hinges, followed by heavy footsteps. The sudden noise made her heart leap into her throat.

"You'd better lock the doors, Sylvie."

Her husband, Raynald, ran a simple sundries store, barely more than a shack lean-to, out on the shore, next to the docks. Ray's usually jovial, ruddy face looked pale and peaky. He was breathing hard.

"Ray? What's happened?" She lowered her hand from the doorknob and made her way down to him. He pulled up a stool and helped himself to a bottle of white spirit.

"It's a little early for that, isn't it, my love?" He ignored her and unstoppered the corked neck with his teeth. He lifted the bottle to his lips; she noticed the blood on the back of his hairy, calloused hands.

"Ray! Your knuckles're exposed! Tell me – what's going on? What happened?"

He set the bottle down on the bar top and turned to her. The look in his eyes could've knocked her backwards. "Latch the door and get my leathers. I'll deal w' my hands."

She didn't take her eyes off him, but rounded the bar to the solid door, taking a moment to look out at the morning light and the road beyond. She couldn't see much of anything through the grime, but she could hear some kind of disturbance down toward the dockside. Raised voices. The rising feeling of unease was back in her chest. She swung down the wide wooden barricade into the hammered iron rungs, securing the doors with a satisfying clang.

"Bo Briar – that crooked tax collector up from the South – he was *wild* this morning, damn near tried to kill me."

Sylvie came over to her partner. He had fished out a long run of old linen rag from the stores beneath the bar and had begun wrapping the knuckles of his right hand. "I had to lay 'im out. It was either 'im or me – and it warn't gonna be *me*."

"Why would he—" Sylvie put a hand to his cheek and turned his face to meet hers. "He tried to strangle you! Your neck's raw!"

"That hoary bastard's blood was up. No idea why. His eyes were shot through with blood and he looked like the very grave. He jumped me as I was opening up for the morn. Sent the bread rolls for the day rolling."

Sylvie sighed. "Those were fresh this morning, Ray! Tell me you picked them up."

He tucked the loose end-flap of the wrap under itself and flexed his hand with a wince. "I was a little busy being assaulted. I beg you pardon me, Syl."

He picked up the bottle once more.

"But that's not all," he continued. "Something was wrong with the catch overnight as well – I o'erheard the netterfolk talking." He frowned. "A catch of dead fish, nearly all of 'em.

"It's all very wrong-faced this morning, I'll tell yeh. So keep the doors locked." He took a swig. "And sorry 'bout the penny-rolls. But y'can blame that louse Bo Briar. He's gonna have one hellbound headache when he wakes up."

He smiled darkly and picked at the bandages, which were beginning to dot with red. Sylvie found the whole situation as grim as the sudden arrival of her current patronage upstairs.

"Ray, do you think it has something to do with…" She trailed off, but nudged her head up towards the stairs.

"Aye. As soon as they stepped foot into town, things went well queer-sided. I trust no dwarf who wears lenses, for one. And the old man looked like he'd been pounded into leather."

He laughed at his witticism, feeling the numbing effects of the highly potent spirit on an empty stomach. "Those outlanders – they brought something down on us, woman. I tell yeh true."

Sylvie kissed his forehead tenderly. It was good to know the old salt still had some of that youthful fight in him. "You're getting on in years. Y'too old to be scrapping, Ray. Now, leave your leathers where they are and help me bake some fresh seed-buns." She smiled. She couldn't remember the last time they'd baked together.

The thought was cut short by a scream from somewhere beyond the main street. It was impossible to know for sure. Ray jumped off the stool and took Sylvie's side, unsure quite what to do now. They looked at each other with shared grim eyes.

There were sudden footsteps on the floors above, like falling pine cones on a slat-shingle roof.

"I want them out."

As if in perfect response, the door at the top of the stairs creaked open.

The odd knight, Sylvie noted. *Shirtless. He cuts a fine figure.* She felt her cheeks turn rose as he leaned around the door frame, allowing her a first proper look at the man, now no longer in his fine armour – or much else.

"Why is the door barred?" the man asked, an edge to his question.

"We're closed for the day." Ray grumbled. "If you and yours are up and awake, I suggest you leave soon. And keep away from the docks."

"We're leaving, as soon as we're dressed." He looked down.

"Well, no need to hurry on that count," Sylvie smiled and gathered herself together with a small shake of her head. Ray shot her a look. She took a small breath.

"I heard a scream," the knight studied the pair. She could feel his eyes reading her somehow. More deeply than she cared for, in fact.

"No idea." Which was true enough, she figured.

"And what happened to your hand, fellow?"

"Hurt it," was all he was willing to share. Anyway, what business was it of the knights?

"Thank you for your patronage," Sylvie finished and turned from him. There was more than a hint of bite in her words. If the knight noticed, he did not react.

"People scream for good reason. So too do they bleed," he replied, quietly.

With that, the odd knight turned and was gone. More footsteps in the eaves, muffled voices and the sounds of rummaging and dragging and thumping. Six pairs of feet all gathering themselves together.

Ray finished the remains of the spirits and joined Sylvia behind the bar. His hand ached, but he was more concerned now about the spoiled catch he overheard. It was a poor sign; the river's health was the lively-blood of their town – and the rest of the lands beyond.

Before long, the dark-skinned young woman emerged from the door at the top of the stairs. She regarded the innkeeps cursorily and made her way to the bar.

"Any more seeded buns?"

"Fresh out," was Sylvie's curt reply. In actuality, she had a half dozen beneath the bar, but the sooner she could get these folk out of her premises, the better for it.

Brea knew she was lying, but let it go.

"Come from far, have ye?" Ray asked, half out of expected courtesy to break the awkward silence, and half because he worried what this heavily-armed young woman might do if she were slighted, or found herself provoked. "Over the seas, I expect?"

"Far. Far and long." She adjusted her thigh hilt, tightening the strap. "You sure you don't have any more rolls?"

Sylvie gulped audibly. "Aye, well – how about that. I forgot about…

ah, these." She fished around beneath the bar, not taking her eyes off the woman, and drew up a pan of six conjoined rolls.

A voice from the top of the stairs caused them both to turn.

"Perfect! A bite to break my fast. Let's eat and run." The dwarf smiled warmly and winked at Sylvie. "Oh now, what happened to your arm? Want me to take a look at it?" He tapped his leather satchel, reassuringly. "I'm quite a seasoned practitioner of the medicinal arts."

Ray lowered his hand below the bar and out of sight. "No, no thank yeh. Just an accident's all," he replied.

The dwarf continued down the stairs and pulled alongside the young woman. "Accident. Aye. And what about the other guy?" Dusty laughed. "No matter. Suit yourself, then."

Brea turned from Dusty with a huff and helped herself to a roll from the shallow pan. It was sticky with baked sugar glaze over crushed solflower seeds. She was not above licking her fingers as she finished it off in a few eager bites. "Thesh're *goob*," she chewed out a few thick, stodgy words as she swallowed.

Dusty reached for the pan and grabbed a hunk.

Sylvie smiled meekly, trying to hide the building anxiety and minor frustration at their own meal now being committed to the guts of these strangers.

Another scream.

Suddenly, a procession of four more figures appeared in the doorway.

"It's here too," the elf-girl spoke softly. Sylvia did not like those words; their knowingness, their loaded inference, and the weirdling waif delivering them.

"More screaming. I think it's time we left." Tyel started for the door and lifted the wooden latch plank. Alyse followed closely behind.

"I don't like what I feel out there, Tyel. I think the town is being overrun."

The words sent a chill through the room, like a gust of icewind. Ser Filip approached now.

"Our path is South, Alyse. We cannot delay longer, even if the threat has spread."

"Excuse me, but what threat?" Six heads turned to Ray. His face read of bristled bemusement and a little bit of confusion. To their surprise, he turned his nose upward, sniffing the air like a pack dog. "What is that?"

"Is that… smoke?" he asked, not really wanting to know if his senses were on target.

Gehard smacked his palm against the bar. "What now? Can we not just enter a village without things immediately turning sour?"

Tyel had to agree. "Ser, I think I see flames across the way." In fact, he could see more than flames: he saw – then heard – the frantic commotion of dozens of bodies to-ing and fro-ing, blurry and indistinct through the weathered, filthy glass pane.

"Careful, Tyel. Once you open that door, I think we'll be entering a fast-flowing current." Alyse's eyes glowed intensely – a telling giveaway that Tyel knew meant she was connecting deeply with some kind of invisible magical ether. *She must be reading – or sensing – the situation,* he considered. And he knew to heed her words carefully.

Ser Filip motioned him away from the door. He let his hands drop as he gauged the blanket-seriousness of his Knight Commander's expression. The innkeepers looked on dimly, unsure of exactly what they had suddenly found themselves caught up in. Ray glanced down at his hand, connecting points in his mind. Nothing good, he was sure of that much.

"What did you bring down upon our town?" He looked at them grimly. "Things were fine until you showed up. I want you out of here. Out of our stead and out of our town."

"You don't need to tell us twice," Gehard sneered. "Come, let's make for the docks and commandeer ourselves a vessel away from this… this…" He waved his hands around the room. "Hovel."

"Out! Out, damn yeh. God curse yeh!" Ray grabbed for the empty baking tray and hurled it at Gehard. Alyse's eyes flashed. The pan clinked against an invisible barrier in front of them.

"Thank you, my dear," The Luminary flashed a smile at the elf and bowed at Ray. "We've overstayed our welcome. Don't let your fine abode burn to smouldering cinders, now." Sylvie's face looked like a crumpled rag as the front door opened and the party ventured forth into unfurling chaos.

~ ~ ~

The Westwater Run was little more than a trading port and a one-street row of stores and distractions for the netters, their fishwives and urchin-babes living in small hillside cottages to spend their coin in after long days trawling the wide river up and down and out to the Dividing Sea. Loggers floated strapped parcels of boughs and timber past ships of all manner and purposes. Masts draped in every colour of sail and spinnaker dotted the wide-set river that flowed steadily and gently down from the Atherons and out to sea.

A patchwork of wooden docks and bridges extended at various points along the riverside; these were occupied by many small ships and the occasional large longship, docked in their own berth. These long, zig-zagging jetties ordinarily buzzed with trade activity – but now, they teemed with another kind of energy.

The small row of thatched tenements that lined the main street burned in the hazy daylight, throwing unimpeded black smoke into the sky like a hellborne fissure. Small children wailed at their parents' ankles and nobody quite knew what to do.

Buckets were being carted by hand from the river, tossed haplessly into burning windows. The buildings were so basic in their wooden frame and thatching that the flames were spreading rapidly.

"This isn't working! The whole town is going to go up!" Branson looked around. Only one solution came to mind.

"Alyse…"

Alyse closed her eyes and extended her hand outward, palm forward.

There, in the space in front of her, just beyond her open palm, miniscule droplets began to form. Alyse was drawing moisture from the air around them, pinpoints of water coagulating together into perfect translucent spheres. With her other hand, she raised her index finger and, with a deep breath of concentration amidst the chaos, drew a perfect circle.

The droplets began to pull together, more and more and greater and greater in volume and speed.

Ser Filip watched in amazement. Within moments, dozens of eyes were transfixed on this strange girl.

Then, with a sudden flourishing swish, she tilted her hand forward and to the side, fanning her fingers apart. The spheres of water that she drew together became a spray of projectiles. They flew like a swarm of insects towards the flames.

Alyse slowly opened her eyes now, allowing herself to see her spellcraft in action. She took a small step forward as moisture continuously gathered in front of her and was launched outwards in a smooth arc of spheres.

At once, by her side, she found another spellcaster.

The Sacred Championate raised a mailed, gloved arm.

Alyse glanced to her right in surprise, only momentarily allowing her focus to waver. The droplets slowed, wavered, then continued to pummel the thatch. Suddenly, the sheer volume of water dramatically increased. The Championate focussed intently on the stream of water, manifesting a solid pressurised spout of pure crystalline liquid.

Together, they pressed forward, directing the flow in tandem, smothering the flames, which had begun to spread to adjacent rooftops. A few villagers had dropped their buckets of water in shock; it was exceedingly rare to see acts of conjuration such as this.

Then, like a rampaging bull, something large and livid emerged through a crumbling wall, where a simple wooden door once sat, from within the burning building. The side of the building gaped open like a cannonball impact.

Brea and Dusty recognised it immediately, but it was Tyel who acted first. The bald, deformed behemoth surged forward, straight at Alyse and the Sacred Championate.

Brea and Dusty watched all of this from some ways back; while Brea was certainly a capable fighter, she had no desire to stick her neck out only to have it snapped by large, dead hands.

"Look out!" The squire hooked an arm around Alyse's waist, dragging her sideways. The Championate lunged the other way. The force disrupted their magical influence, and the stream of water faltered and began to fall in a drenching sheet straight across the stone street. Horrific shrieks went up from all around them. This enormous creature was burning in the sunlight as it heaved dead lungs and swung its deformed forearms at Tyel. He raised his buckler and deflected the first blow, Alyse just behind him. The force threw him backward; his arm slammed back in on his own chest.

In that moment, the beast recoiled and Tyel saw a face he recognised; a face of malice on a hulking disfigurement of a body.

"It… can't be," he said, gasping through the sudden jolt of pain surging through his forearm. He drew his short sword as the back of this monstrous creature surged with unnatural flame. The smell of roasting flesh filled the air. "Royne?"

The familiar bald pate, with its broad, broken nose and fence-post teeth of the anointed Soldier stared him down. The whites of his eyes were blood-red and wide as the sun that burnt his exposed skin. The not-Royne behemoth bellowed in pain and confusion as it raised both arms, readying to bring them down like warhammers upon him. Its fists were candles.

Royne had become something else now, and that something was under-standably angry at being on fire in the hard daylight.

It brought its fists, two sledges on each forearm, down like a hammer pounding steel against anvil. Branson tucked his legs and rolled sideways, barely avoiding the blow. The impact reverberated, sending grey flecks of hard stone shattering outward.

He drew his sword in a twisting motion and scrambled backward, working himself into a sprung crouch.

Royne's dead eyes rolled to him as it drew back up, readying to scrap. The over-stretched skin on his head was blackening now.

"Stand aside, boy."

Royne groaned and swung toward the voice as the Championate thrust cold steel, in a downward motion, deep into the twisted, blackened knots of its exposed backside. Bones like spines jutted around its shoulder blades, as if it had merged with something else wildly inhuman, absorbing its skeletal features into its frame.

The behemoth screamed as the sword stayed planted, but immediately twisted its torso away from the Championate, wrenching the hilt from his grip.

For the briefest moment, Tyel could see the faint spark of humanity still buried deep within him, and he felt a sudden sting of betrayal. In life, he hated Royne for his needless cruelty and single-minded machismo. In death, he was pitiful and mindless, like a prisoner locked in a cage, carted onto the battlefield. And yet, he was an anointed soldier, serving his rulers. He did not ask for this end.

The Championate scrambled to retrieve his sword, but, thrashing, not-Royne evaded his grasp. It twisted and jerked back and forth, trying to grasp at the blade embedded in its backside, but unable to retrieve it. Not-Royne rushed back inside the broken building, through the side from which it had emerged, beneath the steaming shade of the now-extinguished thatched building.

Appalled, the Championate stole after him. "That bastard has my blade!"

Ser Filip, sword out, helped Alyse to her feet. She brushed herself off; her clothes drenched in splashback. *I just bathed, too.* she thought. But she had more pressing concerns.

She turned to Tyel. He looked at her standing there, radiating strength and, in her large and luminous eyes, clear doubt.

"You saved those buildings," he reassured her.

"And you saved *me*."

She embraced him, both arms wrapped around his own. He tilted his short blade away from her, nearly dropping it, almost unwilling to enjoy the feeling of her touch and the warmth of her acknowledgement. He could feel the soft vibration of the energetic field around her still; some fragmentary magic lingering from her incredible conjuration. At least, that's what Tyel assumed – though, part of him wondered if he was feeling an expression of something else: a deep and growing emotion – empathy or, dare he say it to himself – affection.

He pulled away from her.

"No, not really. Just returning the favour, I guess." Part of him wanted desperately to hold her again. The stronger feeling, now, was to leave her, lose her now so he would not feel the pain of rejection or loss later on, around unseen bends and rises.

She puzzled at his reaction.

"Tyel," she began. The thought was interrupted by the sound of a splintering crash; a sickening creak of warping wood and heaving weight bearing down to the ground most suddenly.

The smouldering, steaming building the behemoth had retreated into had begun to collapse on itself. The Sacred Championate was somewhere within its charred interior.

"Brea, Dusty – look alive. Help us," Ser Filip implored.

"Nuh uh. No way, old man," Brea balked. "I'm not stupid. I don't relish getting crushed by a ceiling beam this morning."

Dusty nodded, but it was clear he had no intention of rushing into the collapsing building. "I fear there are others besides that hulk. I think we're best placed to act as lookouts right now."

"Gehard! Are you a coward, or a man of holy strength?"

The Luminary smiled. "Coward, is it?" He drew his sword. "Come then. If our almighty and fanciful champion is still wearing his helm, perhaps he lives. But then, so might the behemoth."

He and Ser Filip started toward the collapse.

Tyel began to move, but stopped short. He looked at Alyse. "Are you okay?"

"Are you?" she replied.

"I will be once we're on a boat and headed south, away from all of this."

She nodded, but there was something off about her. Then, of course, she rarely seemed to be fully in the moment. Her consciousness danced between places simultaneously. Perhaps she was reaching out to find the Championate.

Or perhaps something else was reaching out to her. He cocked his head and looked at her intently.

Tyel swallowed hard at the dark thought.

"Are you… alone in there?" He found himself asking. "I mean…"

Alyse's eyes widened; she looked struck by a blow that Branson did not mean to issue.

"Tyel – I… we should talk. Not now. There will be time. But not now. Not today." A cold, strained response, Branson felt. He had touched upon something buried and secret, almost intuitively. He did not know why exactly he asked this question, or why he phrased it so. But it struck the core like an arrow.

She turned and left him hanging on that response; a puncture deflating his careless words into limp nothingness. The thought trailed away as he followed her to the sagging entrance of the collapsing house.

CHAPTER 22

BOLERO

The Sacred Championate was furious. The rotten meat-bag had absconded with his blade, retreating out of the sun and into the rapidly more ruinous, fiery innards of the building. Strategically, he knew he had just broken two rules: one, never lose grip of your sword. Two, never follow your enemy into a building of which you do not know the layout. Worst of all, never rush into a building on fire without clear cause to do so. The blade was blessed, and the finest weapon he'd ever held, but it was, after all things, just an object. Now, as the roof threatened to come down, and he was choking on black sooty ash, his anger was beginning to give way to regret. That, and the immediate urgency of trying not to trip, break a leg and be cooked alive inside his suit.

"I want… my *sword* back, pit-fiend," he growled, eyes stinging from the thick, black smoke that billowed from the open wound in the building's side. While their magic had stemmed the spread of the flames to other structures, this simple abode had been gutted and was still alight. A thatched roof and wood-lined walls became tinderboxes when flames gnawed at them.

Inside, he could see the remnants of shelves of tools: mallets, shears, augers, planes, draw-knives and flat-tipped shovels. Beneath lay neatly stacked piles of cut timber in different thicknesses and dimensions. All of this was rapidly becoming fresh feasting for a gout of fire.

There, laying in the middle of the room, face-down, was Royne. A thick beam of wood lay across his waist, just below the protruding sword. He writhed like a beached and bloated toad, once pale skin burnt to char.

The heat was intense and worsening as the Championate approached. He coughed and put a hand to the slit-grill on the front of his helm, futilely attempting to obstruct the burning air flushing inward.

From distantly behind him, he could hear shouting; the voices of his recent company. It occurred to him then that they did not know his name, for he never provided it. The idea of them calling "Sacred Championate!" over and over amused him slightly, for the ridiculous, unwieldy nature of it. But the thought passed in a sudden creak, then snap, the fracturing of a giant's bones, from above. *That's not good,* he noted to himself, rightly.

The Championate darted toward his sword, feeling reassuringly for the wrapped hilt. As he wrapped both hands around it, Royne gave one final screaming, deathly outpour of anger and sadness, shifting his body onto its bulking side. The fiery ceiling strut rolled down his back and off to the side, next to his gigantic body. Royne was dead already, to be sure, but clearly he was journeying down that black and final path one more time. Black sludge poured from the wound as the Championate pulled his blade back out. Unfortunately, in one horrible final lurch, Royne returned the favour. The Championate felt his legs swept out from beneath him by the kick of an enormous, deformed foot. He went straight down, legs suddenly in the air and head thumping painfully into the ground.

His head spun. He took a deep breath, trying to find his wits, lost in the smoke haze and the shock of impact. He found his blade and, gripping it tightly, it returned him to the moment.

He got to his feet once more; Royne's eyes, all three pairs of them, had rolled up into their sockets; his enormous, split-wound of a mouth hung open. The Championate, not one to leave a job unfinished, stiffly ambled to

Royne's front. The monstrosity's eyes pulled down again, all six taking one final look before the sword plunged into its tree-trunk throat. The Championate pressed his weight against the blade until he felt the hard impact of bone and thick tissue, then pressed harder.

Through blurry, burning eyes, he could see Royne was no more, again. That brought him the most fleeting satisfaction, before an almighty crash, like a great clap of thunder; the triumphant moment was cut short by a downpour of cinders.

All at once, the air was pure fire. Another ceiling beam came down, followed by the floorboards of the second floor, and all of the contents they held up. He felt the crushing weight of something large and wooden, a hutch or a wardrobe perhaps, bearing down on him, and he was buried in burning oblivion. He could not see, he could not hear, save for the grey roar of flame and the crackle of disintegration around him. He could not feel, he realised. Nothing below his waist. He knew what that surely meant.

Tears streamed down his red cheeks and turned to steam. The world beyond called to him by name. Voices in harmony, old and young and beyond creed or gender.

The voices of the infinite Trine.

May this be it, he thought. The flames felt warm, then cool, then he felt nothing at all.

And that was it.

~ ~ ~

Outside, calmer eyes watched closely.

"What kind of fool rushes into a burning building – for a *sword?*" Brea watched, bemused, arms folded. "Must be some sword."

Dusty only nodded; he felt altogether useless in the face of acts of bold valour – the kind that either get you killed or make you a hero of song – or both. He wondered which hand the Sacred Championate would be dealt.

"Why would he do that?" Dusty agreed. "No fool was he. A strange compulsion for a trained warrior."

He turned his eyes to Alyse.

"Look! She's faltering. Come, let's take her side."

Alyse continued to pull water from the air and direct it into the collapsing building. This drawing down of life-liquid was the first magical technique she'd ever learned – the only piece of true energy-magic that she felt immediately comfortable with. Her family were water-sowers; her people needed such techniques to flourish in the middle of a sprawling desert. The filling of water glasses was easy enough, if slow when the air was dry and warm. Thankfully, this far north, and this close to a waterway, it was much easier to draw water from around her. The hardest part, as always, was feeling the connective line between her own energy – what she felt was her own vital life force – and the cost of metering it away on complex magical tasks.

She could feel herself wavering; it had been remarkably easy to amplify her powers when the Championate had joined with her. It had felt like a magnification of sorts, like reading through a looking lens. But when he left her, the weight pulled at her essence more greatly again.

Alyse's eyes glanced to the side as Dusty sauntered to her left. Brea joined her on the right.

"It's okay, Alyse. You've done what you can – but the building is lost."

She knew he was right about this. "But the Championate—"

Ser Filip and Gehard had only barely made it beyond the threshold as a blast of flaming debris forced them backward.

"It's no good," Gehard shouted, recoiling from the shock of impacting wood and stone in front of them. Tyel darted to their side, as a growing crowd of townspeople gathered around.

"We need to drag him out," Tyel shouted, and he knew he was right, but not in a position to follow through. He was wearing thin, tattered fabric – and even from outside, the heat was intense. Alyse's magic had saved the other buildings from significant damage, but the flames were just too overwhelming here.

"It's too late, boy," Gehard snapped. "Save your breath. It's hard enough to breathe out here as it is." He looked at Tyel with hard eyes. "Look. The man made his choice, and it was a poor one. He's gone."

Alyse's eyes were faint as she was pale. What energy she had expended was now used up. She came up to Tyel. "I can do no more."

"Can you sense the Championate in there?"

She closed her eyes.

"No. Nothing lives within now."

Ser Filip hung his head. "So that's it, then."

Brea observed the Knight Commander's slouched posture and knew at once the reason for it. In the street, a heavy pall fell over the community that spread like a contagion. Many watched the tall, heavily-armed man race into the building. All saw it collapse. None saw him emerge.

One final burst of embers brought down the second floor entirely. A sparking gust of red-hot flume sent those gathered reeling backwards.

The walls were a blackened stone husk; the thick grey stone held the fire within, like an enormous hearth, churning on the last remains of wood fuel and fallen heroes. The ashen plume had begun to thin and spread into the sky, diffusing the light, transforming the burning glow of Solum into an angry, crimson eye. It loved what it saw; it danced against the shadows, a manic bolero of fury and obliteration.

Far away, all-seeing eyes raised their stolen hands to that same sky, saying their secret words and working their magic, manipulating the slow turn of time and reality steadily, gently – as if pulling loose a thread, one stitch at a time, in an endless strand. Three aspects in opposition, yet forever connected in the push and pull of the way of the universe. A Trine of all things good and bad and old and new and now and then and of those still to come.

As the smoke smouldered away into steam, the sun crawled in its long arc across the sky. Ashes replaced piles of timber; hammered iron tools returned to the lumps from which they had been drawn. It would be some days before even the white-hot ash had cooled enough to be scooped away and the ruins of the building gutted and slowly rebuilt.

Timidly, the Innkeeper and her husband emerged from their abode. They crossed the street, dotted with onlookers, and came upon Alyse first.

"Girl. We saw what you did back there," Raynald spoke quietly. He exchanged looks with Sylvie. "Appears I misjudged yeh. Y' and yer kin are owed some debt of thanks."

"It's nothing. I wish we could have done more," Alyse replied.

"Aye, well – you stopped the spread and fought that bald bastard off. More than the rest of this lot did. And I'm… sorry about your friend. We watched him go into the blaze."

Alyse said nothing to that, but she didn't need to.

"Your lot mentioned you were heading toward the dockyards," Ray continued. "I don't know if it's connected – I would guess so, but I was attacked by a man down there. If I was you, I'd watch yourselves."

Tyel found himself eager to be away from here. The sun was bearing down on his shoulders, adding to the feeling of mounting pressure. He pictured for a moment the charred remains of the Sacred Championate, his defined features burnt away to blackened bone, mouth open in a silent scream as his lips peeled back and way. It turned his stomach.

"Let's go, then. I'm ready to be away from here," he said. None argued with him. Alyse looked almost relieved by his burst of decisiveness.

They began to walk down the sloping, gently curving street. Around them, a sick kind of energy flowed; there were unnerving sounds of weeping women, shouting men. Somewhere nearby, a stack of ceramic fell and shattered. The village was alive, but the tension had replaced what would ordinarily be a buzz of trade and conversation.

Around the bend, the road forked; one path led gradually down toward the docks, and another ran up along and behind a long row of shacks and shanties, set against each other like crooked teeth in a rocky, sloping gash of land. It was here that the Innkeep had his run-in, Tyel thought.

The waterway sparkled with the sparse motion of deep flow and steady current. The docks themselves ran as far as the most distant of the shanties. The meandering path was made of hearty but weatherworn planks and pylons. Between stretches of a hundred strides, large ships were moored; the water here was calm, but clearly deep enough to allow the tall-masted shipping vessels to safely anchor.

On any other day, at most other times, this would be the centre of activity for the trade outpost. Now, however, the smell of rotting fish filled the air, and the docks appeared devoid of life. The ships bobbed gently in silent protest to the chaos in the streets.

"Gods, the smell," Ser Filip winced. "Reminds me of—"

"The sewers," Alyse finished.

"Indeed. The sewers."

"Do you see the wake?" Gehard pointed as they approached the steps down onto the docks. "It's brown. That's not normal."

"Neither are those." Tyel nodded toward a discarded pile of silverfish, rotting in the sun. The mountain of putrefying fish, eyes clouded and covered in flies, looked as if they'd burst open. Some had two heads; others had too many eyes, too many mouths. Others simply ceased to resemble fish at all. "That's a sight."

A voice from behind made them jump.

"Stay out of the water."

Behind them stood a pudgy, rodent-like man with a receding hairline and a weathered face. Through a salt-crusted beard, he spoke with a high-pitched, almost squeaky voice. He looked like the sea had swallowed him up and spat him back onto the shore. "They come from the water. Stay away from it."

"And which crypt did you emerge from, old man?" Gehard laughed. "We dispatched the threat in town."

"Pah!" The old man waved a calloused and gnarled palm at him. "More the fool than you look. See for yourselves and be damned if it pleases."

And with that, he turned and made for a simply hewn set of wooden steps leading up the hillside toward the trade shacks.

"Gehard," Dusty shook his head.

"Don't tut at me, dwarf. There's nothing to see in there—" he turned and his mouth hung open.

The wake splashed against the side of a longship, its cargo ramp down, deck deserted. Something else was in the water. *Many* somethings – drawn, it seemed, by the noise of conversation. The surface of the water undulated, but just beneath the murk, curved backsides and white limbs wriggled toward the shore, beneath the raised boardwalk.

"Don't say it, dwarf." Gehard scrunched his face and groaned. "Haven't we been through enough?" He began to unsheathe his blade.

"Luminary, I don't think we've even seen the worst of it," Dusty replied. "Dormanstar was just the beginning of something most heinous."

"How can there be so many?" The Knight Commander asked. "Did they all come downriver from Dormanstar?"

"There will be time for questions, but this is not it," Dusty snapped.

"Do we make for one of the vessels?" Tyel asked.

"That's the plan, boy," Brea replied. "The *only* plan right now."

As she said that, the sounds of screaming issued from behind them, from within the weathered lean-tos. It could've been the old sea-farer; it could've been anyone. It didn't matter. It wasn't a welcome sound.

All at once, the water seemed to erupt into whitewash as a surge of bodies broke the surface and scrambled onto the shore, toward the boardwalk.

Alyse tensed. Tyel drew his steel once more, feeling a sickening surge of fear and energy intertwined. *This won't be pleasant,* he thought to himself.

It won't be, Alyse replied, in his mind. He laughed aloud. Ser Filip shot him a queer glance, then drew his own blade. "Don't lose your mind now, Branson. You're not allowed to die here – or allow Alyse to come to harm. That's a command. Make for the far end of the boardwalk."

Within moments, they would be surrounded.

He could see a smaller vessel, a skiff of sorts with a long prow and a single mast, barely peeking around the bend in the boardwalk. It would be small and agile, and manageable with only one or two able bodies. It would do. They just needed to get to it, kick off and follow the wide, undulous river south.

"Go!" The Knight Commander shouted.

They were travelling in the waterways, he realised. From the mountain ranges, down the rivers, into towns, through sewer systems, down south. The dead had no need to breathe and the water protected them from the sun's burning, destructive qualities. In a certain way, it was brilliant. In all others, it was horrific and damning. If these things could travel day and night, sweeping through hamlets and towns like the winds of death, the land would be overrun.

In the old man's heart, he wondered if he had the muscle-tensing, blood-pumping fight in him to survive this. He couldn't see the end of the throng of corpse-like bodies shambling out of the rotten, briny water. But he could certainly see a dozen ways that this might be his own undo-ing. He could feel every one of his years in his angry joints and torn and never-fully-healed muscles.

He thought of his wife. Her young face framed in lovely mountains of copper hair, barely a sketch in his imagination now. He might see her soon enough, on the other side of the grave. He hoped the Solum God would cast a ray of light in the dark and lead him to her once more.

No, he thought. *Not now.* He shook away the distracting morbidity. *One day, but not now.*

"Lend me a blade, Brea!" Dusty held out his hand.

"When you lift my curse, dwarf!" She drew her curved blades, flipping them upside down in her palms so each edge faced outward and away from her. She laughed and moved away from him, leading the six down the wooden path.

The first of many bodies scrambled up onto the docks. Out of the water and in the purifying heat of full sunlight, its skin began to sizzle and brown.

Another, and another, and yet another scrambled onto the boardwalk. The first strega was aflame – an orange ember with legs and a pitiful scream of pain and misplaced rage.

It charged at Gehard, clawed fingers outstretched and wanting. Like the resurrected Royne, the longer it remained in daylight, the more intensely it burned – but it did not seem slowed by what must have been utterly mind-dissolving levels of pain. Gehard kicked it backwards and followed through with a solid swing that cleanly removed the left arm and embedded cold steel in its side. It went down, but scrambled, shrieking, back to its feet.

The severed arm continued to burn like a log in a campfire.

"Gods. They burn in the sun!" Tyel shouted.

The squire dodged the second strega as it dove past him, like a hound after a hare. It scrambled on long limbs, charring the surface of the wood beneath it.

"They're going to burn the bloody docks down," Gehard grunted. "Alyse!" He turned to the elfkin. "Do your magical waters-pinning tricks, would you be so kind?"

Alyse raised her hands, biting her lower lip as her arms shook. Something was wrong.

"Girl! What are you waiting for?" He struck a final blow into the neck of the strega. Its head came clean off and rolled into the water.

Ser Filip booted the body, long and lanky, but surprisingly light, into the water alongside it. The waters embraced it, dragging it down and extinguishing the flames.

"I— *can't!* I—" her eyes, usually saucers of blue energy, were dull and, increasingly, welling with tears. "He's here! He's in my *head*!" She screamed. "He won't— let me!" This brought the combat to a skittering halt for a fraction of a second.

"What do you mean?" Gehard turned to Tyel. "What does she mean?"

A fresh plume of grey-black smoke was blowing across the sweep of the town. Tyel could see tongues of fresh flames that had since sprung up, presumably from strega pouring from the waterway and spreading through the town. He glanced at the hazy sky and, with a sick realisation, understood immediately that the farther the fires spread, the more that resulting smoke would block the sun – and the easier it would be for the strega to traverse in daylight. It would be a self-perpetuating and constantly renewing plague.

He came crashing back to reality as he was knocked sideways in a burst of blinding pain. He could smell the fetid stench of decay as his peripheral vision filled with the bodies of the dead. He scrambled for his blade, which had fallen from his grasp as a deformed man with five eyes and too many mouths rolled on top of him, searing fingers digging into the exposed flesh of his back. He screamed as he felt the fiery, pressing weight of the man-demon scratching and gouging at him.

At once, the weight disappeared as Branson turned to see Gehard plant a solid kick into the side of the man, launching the strega, burning and flailing, onto the boardwalk.

He pushed himself forward on his stomach to grab his blade, feeling the thin cotton shirt smoldering against his back. He did not feel fear – just anger now; every bit of him wanted to return the pain and frustration tenfold. He saw a mess of legs around him, dozens by quick count, licked by orange flames, and more still reaching out from the water in an attempt to breach land.

"This is hopeless – we must retreat," Dusty shouted. Tyel struggled to his feet and, two hands around the hilt of his sword, began to swing. The dwarf met his back, following behind him. "Don't stop now, lad. Press on!"

Horrified human shrieks issued from twisted mouths as sharp metal parted flesh and bone. Tyel could see the masts at the far end of the dock above the chaos, but there had to be a hundred bodies between here and there. Alyse was screaming. He could hear Ser Filip grunting and cawing with exertion. Somewhere behind him, Brea was shouting and twisting like a wildcat, working her curved daggers into exposed necks and doing her damnedest to keep from being overrun.

Yet more and more foes entered the fray; the boardwalk, though wide enough to accommodate twenty large men side-by-side, was filled with movement. With these bodies came more fire and smoke. However, as the air filled with ashen plume, it cut the rays of the sun so greatly that the unnatural flames had begun to diminish. The violent chaos did not taper with them.

Gehard held back a laugh as he recalled his entirely wonderful and extraordinarily expensive plate steel laying useless beneath the streets of Dormanstar. He watched this young squire, such as he was, fighting with all his might, his skin split and bleeding, burnt in places, but his resolve undiminished. The boy had shown mettle, even if he was greener than fresh goat shit.

He took a lunging thrust, driving his sword forward with both hands. It connected and pierced cleanly through the midsection of a fat woman with three chins and six lunatic eyes. The squelching gave way to a chunky, slaughterhouse chock-chock sound of meat being sliced as he withdrew and took aim for her bulbous neck.

The blackened blood sizzled on the flat face of his blade, welling and bubbling in the broad fuller like a witch's brew.

It went on like this, much as it had in the sewers – though, as tomb-like and claustrophobic as the Dormanstar waterway had been, at least the throng had rushed at them from one direction, and the elf-girl had been able to construct a barrier. Gehard felt beads of hot panic beginning to build on his forehead. What was she saying about her head? The moment was lost in the ensuing blood-frenzy.

Dead heads rolled and warped limbs fell limply, for every vicious aggressor that faced them down was met with unrelenting resistance. *But we could not possibly last long, could we?* Brea's hands were coated in black blood; her fingers were gummed together in the rotten substance as she took to the left of the group, trying to afford herself enough space to fight effectively.

Even with just two small blades, she knew her agility would keep her alive – for now. Only if she faltered would she come undone. Her years of training – building her tolerance for exertion and pain – were her other vital weapons now. If she could out-manoeuvre them and outlast them, she would beat them back, one at a time. She ducked beneath the outstretched arms of a thin, bony strega, a spine of nubbed bones jutting from broken skin. As she weaved around it, she extended her left leg and swept her calf under the strega's legs, causing it to tumble forward. In one smooth motion, she arched around and came down upon its backside, crossing her arms and bringing the curves of her blades beneath its throat. With a wrenching pull, she scissored the skull back and off its body. A jet of black blood shot forward in a pulsing spray. She clenched her teeth and rolled to the right as another beast leapt at her. She let it pass over the top of her.

With a kick of her knee against the corpse below her, she launched forward and planted both blades deep in the shoulders of another blood-horror. It raised both arms above its head in shock as the Solsetter cut away at its spine.

Smoke filled the still air, making breathing a chore. Brea choked down a gulp of soot and gagged. It would do, but if the very air betrayed her, even her skills would fall away to nothing before long. At least the beasts were barely aflame now, she noted.

On the far right of the group, Alyse was crouched and weeping. *The pain,* she thought. *I cannot take this.* She could sense him in there, just beyond her grasp, beyond her reasoning, out of reach – an itch she could not scratch. A waking nightmare that she could not shake for all her trying. *How? How did this happen?* Over and over, she asked herself this, small and balled up, head down, hearing the sounds of fighting around her, but unable to rouse herself. She felt very far away from her own body in that moment, lost in the shadowed backchannels of her mind.

She searched for him. He evaded her.

He toyed with her, laughing. She could retch at the nauseating pleasure he took in his games.

Then, his voice filled her, like dry leaves, moss on granite, old wood splintered apart: *Your blood opened the door, my little one. So thoughtful a gift*

He laughed.

Alyse screamed deep within and so very loudly without, and the world twisted into enveloping blackness around her.

The embers of burning lean-tos danced in the grey haze. The town of Westwater Run was failing before them; a force of six could never hope to hold back the tide of countless monsters such as these, Tyel thought. Could they really hope to navigate a vessel down the riverway if the waters teemed with death? He could feel his arms growing tired; he had fought off more than his share of these creatures so far – but, bleeding and exhausted, he could feel his concentration slipping.

If not for the piercing wail of Alyse's voice, Tyel might not have noticed the beginnings of a portal forming. At first, a small ringed void, purple-aquamarine and swirling, had opened in front of her. It grew in size, forming a perfect oval, about his own height. It crackled with energy, swirling like a whirlpool of emanating plasma that lit the ashen, heavy atmosphere around them.

The threshold begged to be crossed. To where it led, he could not know.

"A— *portal*—" he barked at nobody specifically. His sentence was caught in a wheezing cough that nearly caused him to fall. This was hopeless.

Somewhere far away, Tyel knew that the Necromant watched them and, with detached passivity, allowed them to depart. Why? Had he been the one to conjure the portal? Was his hand guiding their journey into his palm?

Ser Filip caught his eye; the old man looked thread-worn, but still he fought on.

Dusty was the first to make his move. "Get the girl! Get her up, boy! Move!"

Brea was on the wrong side of a large strega; this one appeared connected to another by some strange umbilicus at the side, and both shared a third leg. What had caused this warped mashing of limbs and torso, Brea could only guess. Her more pressing concern was how to take down a foe with two heads and four thick, tuberous arms. It grappled for her, two heads wrenching on their fat necks as she skittered backwards, evading it. The twin-torso beast twisted sideways, muscular and fast for its size. Two long legs propelled it forward as the third ambled forward and backward.

This is the ugliest thing I think I've ever— but the thought was lost as quickly as it formed. The thing had picked her up, collecting her before she could pivot and attack. Brea groaned as she felt the air being compressed in her chest as two arms swept her up, as a child might with a straw dolly.

She tried to lever her arms to the side, working her way from its hug, but her limbs were pressed against herself.

"Brea!" Ser Filip exclaimed. From ten strides, the old man paced, hunched over, barely dragging his longsword.

A large hand gripped Brea's skull from above. With slow, deliberate pressure, it began to pull.

Ser Filip's eyes were blurry with blood and grit. Trails of sweat guided black blood down his face and into his nose and mouth. He had long since accepted that the blood was most likely in his body now, coursing through him, infecting him, claiming him. He felt immediately sick, but let his legs guide him toward the Solsetter.

"No— you *don't*," the Knight Commander grunted, and, shifting to the left, then right, avoiding reaching limbs and salivating, black-eyed faces, he fronted the conjoined behemoth. "You can't have her."

He raised his sword, as high as his stiff shoulder joints would allow. In his mind's eyes, he was twenty-one again, with fire in the belly. He could feel the last burst of adrenaline, that battle elation, that dizzy-sick excitement of all great encounters.

The twin faces turned to him, and for the briefest moment, the right arm that held Brea close to its midsection relaxed. The left hand, which held her skull like an apple plucked from a branch, released her head.

Fighting through the crushing, wrenching pain, Brea thrashed at the air beneath her, trying to connect. She still couldn't move her arms away from her side, as the vice-like hug had her pinned to one of the behemoth's two broad chests. However, she could, in that moment, take a ragged breath.

The Knight Commander brought the sword down, slightly off-centre, in an arc that sheared the air, cleaving heavily just past the arm that held the Solsetter in place.

His objective was not to remove limbs; rather, he wanted to separate the two halves of this monstrosity, like an axe might split a log. The blade connected. It drove down diagonally into pale, venous skin until it hit resistance. There was a harmonized roar of displeasure and surprise from both heads. The behemoth didn't so much release Brea as use her to fend off this sudden attacker. Unlike the Sacred Championate, the Knight Commander held firm on his hilt and wrenched it back. The wound gushed blood from deep within. The behemoth staggered backwards and, in that moment, seemed to lose interest in crushing the life from Brea. It tossed her aside as its two heads turned inward toward its waist, arms raised, inspecting the damage.

Brea landed on her side, sliding along the wooden pathway. The surface was slick with the dark product of the encounter, coating her in black blood and entrails. She looked up, head still pounding and neck badly tweaked. What she saw filled her eyes with salty tears.

"No!" She cried. "Don't!" She raised a blood-slicked arm in futile protest.

The two halves of the behemoth had grabbed Ser Filip by the waist. His sword had clattered to the planks at his feet as he was lifted upward.

Brea dug at her thigh-hilt and retrieved a long, weighted throwing dagger, but her fingers, slick with filth, struggled to cooperate.

In that moment, the Knight Commander knew life was forfeit. He closed his eyes and clenched his teeth, tensing his muscles. He tried to press through the pain, the hellish sounds and graven smells. He thought of his wife and her face. How she looked at him and only him. Her loving eyes.

It would be his final thought as the end of Brea's dagger found its mark. It struck cleanly in the back of his neck, just below the base of his skull.

He didn't even have time to register surprise. Ser Bolfred Filip's grey-haired head tilted forward as he left his body. He was long gone as the behemoth tore him in half at the waist.

A clean strike and a swift release were all she could offer him. It was little compensation at all for his risking – sacrificing – his life for hers. She blinked back tears, but they came. Brea's eyes streamed, disarming her with the sudden and violent wellspring of emotion. She lowered her arm.

There was no time, she thought. *No time.*

No time to think – only to react. He had reacted to her dire predicament with the bravery of his title and responsibility. She had reacted with an act befitting her own path: a clean death; a mercy kill for a hero. Her gut twisted at the thought. That was a first – killing an innocent. He deserved better, but this was all she could do to prevent a far worse fate.

Get up, Brea, she told herself. *There will be time to over-analyse your actions later – but only if you survive.*

Blearily, through the haze, she saw the horde scampering around her, picking away at the Luminary, the boy, the elf. The dwarf – where was the dwarf? She scrambled to her feet – her curved blades long gone now, and she was down to just one throwing dagger. It was then that she saw the portal. *Dusty,* she mused. *Did you conjure a portal, dwarf?*

She darted toward it.

"It's time to leave, girl," she scooped a battered and filthy arm beneath Alyse. The elf was unconscious, slumped over in her own lap. "If we survive, I'll show you a thing or two."

Tyel stopped her cold. "Ser Filip – what did you—" He looked at her with miserable disbelief. "How could you do that?"

"Scold me later, kid. If you want your friend here to live, take an arm. We're going."

"Get away from her," he snapped.

"No. I won't. Now grab an arm."

Tyel looked aghast. He'd watched her murder Ser Filip. Even if the Knight Commander was fighting for his life, he deserved to have that chance. She had no right to take that from him.

He pointed his sword at her.

"Don't make me disarm you, Tyel. If I do, you'll lose a hand."

"You can try," he replied. In the impasse, the fray around him seemed, just for the moment, to fade away.

Brea looked at him, at first coldly. Then, another unexpected emotion overtook her: pity. He looked afraid, but so loyal. Needlessly loyal to a dead man.

She softened her features. The tip of his blade wavered. Branson blinked twice, feeling every pain that had been inflicted upon him all flooding at once. He was tired of fighting. Tired of struggling in a conflict that he had no business in – not really, anyhow – but had been dragged into, like the silent surging undercurrents of the sea shore.

"It's… okay," she said. "I'm sorry." And she was.

Tyel sheathed his blade; his arm muscles twitched with strain. He felt sick; his broken leg from many years past ached in protest.

Brea turned and shouted over her shoulder. "Gehard! We're leaving. Come on," she shouted. The Luminary had pushed the seething, hissing line of strega back as far as the edge of the boardwalk would allow, but it was hopeless. He nodded. It was then that he realised the Knight Commander was not among them.

The town of Westwater Run that rose above the hillside, beyond the edge of now smouldering lean-tos and trading posts was no longer the same village they'd entered. If the inhabitants survived, they'd surely fled – or were in the process of doing so. The strega would eventually swarm the streets and rooftops and byways as they had in Dormanstar. They would draw out those foolish or unfortunate enough to remain behind, and add yet more legions to their growing cavalcade.

Brea lifted Alyse below her arm as Tyel joined her. "Where's the dwarf?"

"No idea. I thought he was with you?" Branson replied.

Brea felt a certain unease at the idea of misplacing the only person who could prevent her untimely demise. Where had the little blighter run to? What if he'd been dragged down and into the water?

"Gehard! Where's Dusty?" She shouted.

The Luminary was chopping wildly, a brutal hacking downward slash, into a wiry, hideously malnourished-looking strega. As soon as it fell, it was on to the next.

"No idea," he panted. Maybe it didn't matter. She had to hope there were other ways to cure her of the dwarf's well-meaning malpractice.

The portal beckoned. Gehard turned and ran toward them, unsure of what lay in store next. He hoped for nothing more than a breath of clean air. All else was secondary.

Together, they stepped through the portal, carrying Alyse, deep in unconsciousness, with them.

CHAPTER 23

REDUX

One moment, he'd come face-to-face with three strega, snapping and screeching, ready to remove his arms from their sockets, and the next, he felt himself falling – or rather, being pulled.

Dusty was swept inward, dragged at his midsection by some invisible, powerful force as the world seemed to invert and shrink before him. Hazy light smeared in streaks across his eyes. The air in his lungs was compressed. All at once, cold stone floors met the dwarf's face as he opened his eyes to an unfamiliar space. He sat himself upwards, squinting.

He fought nausea. Above him, stooped in the shadows, loomed a large figure. Dusty gathered himself, squinting, grateful his thick lenses made the sudden journey with him. He immediately felt for his satchel and, with a short exhale of relief, he twisted it around from his backside.

The figure spoke. "If you're going to upchuck, aim for the portal."

"No." He whispered. "Impossible! We saw you burn!"

"And yet here I stand, redeemed," A demure and familiar voice replied. "Many and more things are possible than most would believe."

The Sacred Championate crouched down and offered a hand upward. Dusty took it hesitantly, as if offered by a spectral being. He half believed it to be the case.

"How?" Dusty took to his feet. "And where am I now? What happened?"

"I summoned a portal. It would appear you fell through it as it materialised. You're in the Northern Sprawl," The Championate said. "Chambers of the Oracular Magisterium, so watch what you say."

As his eyes adjusted to the soft light within the space, Dusty could see, fuzzily, beyond the Championate's frame, nine tall-backed thrones. All were vacant.

"And what of the others?" the Championate pressed. Dusty shook his head. The last thing he had seen was his impending demise. He hoped the others were safe, even the Solsetter, but the odds were rapidly diminishing. "I know as much as you. Thanks for the portal. And, ah, nice to see you alive and well, I suppose!"

He looked back at the swirling ovoid of purple energy. A soft breeze, smelling faintly of smoke and burning meat, emanated from it. The bitter aromatics of a losing battle. The flow of soot-saturated air intensified as the glowing portal spun faster and faster.

Suddenly, a figure burst through the void, tumbling forward. Dusty reeled backward. Then, another. Brea and Tyel spilled over each other as Alyse slid outward like a tongue from a mouth. At last, Gehard joined them. He, however, kept his footing.

"My lad! You made it."

Tyel was breathing heavily; the transition from the suffocating heat to cool stone jolted his skin. He felt the disorientation of portal travel twisting his insides, making him want to vomit. He pinched his eyes shut, allowing himself a moment to breathe the cool, sweet air. He could feel Brea leaning on him with one side, doing the same.

"Where…" he began, but, feeling ashen grit in his eyelids, he dug at the corners of his eyes with his thumb and forefinger. He blinked in the din and what he saw stole the words from him.

"*Gods,*" Brea whispered.

The Sacred Championate, for a start, was there, arms folded and entirely *alive.* His armour looked unmarked which, of course, was impossible – as impossible as his standing there.

"Where's the old man?" Dusty enquired.

"I must close the bridge," the Sacred Championate took a step forward. "Where's Ser Filip?"

Tyel drew a small breath and cast his eyes downward. "He… didn't make it."

"No! How?" Dusty looked devastated.

"Depends on how you look at it," Tyel shot a look at Brea.

Dusty cocked his head. "And what does that mean, exactly?"

"The old man was as good as gone. I finished the job quickly. *Kindly,*" Brea replied.

Tyel frowned. "If I had seen it, we could have saved him. He was my…" He searched for the words. "Leader. My Knight Commander. You took that responsibility from me." His throat felt tight, like a small hand squeezing at his words. He didn't get to say goodbye, didn't get to thank him for taking him under his guidance. Ser Filip made the most of bad situation after bad situation. And he did it fairly and patiently. He was a man of honour in a dishonourable land, and that made him rare and fine.

Brea began to speak, but stopped short as all eyes fell to her, waiting for a typically curt response. Her eyes darted around for a moment, then walked toward the curve of high-backed chairs. She turned and looked back at the group.

"Close the portal."

With a nod, the Championate raised a hand and drew a symbol in the air. At once, the portal dissolved in a flurry of plasmic sparks that fell to the stone floor and disappeared. The indigo glow now gone, the atmosphere in the chamber shifted once more to something more sombre. Brea approached the line of thrones.

"So here we are. The other side of the wall, as it were." She ran a hand across the arm of one of the Solum thrones, admiring the finely polished darkwood, carefully and intricately carved by ancient Solumbryan hands and long-forgotten Solumbryan faces. "I don't know if we're safer in here, or back there."

The Championate nodded. "Watch what you touch. And watch what you say. They are surely watching us, and they will not reach out gently in return."

Brea withdrew her fingers and clasped them together by her waist.

"Alyse," Tyel whispered. The elfkin lay pale and still. She was breathing softly.

"How is she?" To Gehard's eyes, she appeared to be sleeping, were it not for the ominous outburst just prior to her collapse.

"I don't know." Tyel placed the back of his hand against her forehead. "What did she mean back there? *He won't let me? He's in my head?*"

Gehard crouched beside him. "She means the Necromant, surely. Dusty, can you rouse her?"

"Aye," the dwarf responded. "But if what she says is the truth of it, perhaps she's safer far off in rest right now. Perhaps we are, as well."

Gehard exchanged an uneasy glance with him. "Have you heard of anything like this before?"

Dusty shook his head. "Not quite like this. Transcommunication is not a lingering presence. A person's voice does not occupy space, as I understand it. No. What Alyse indicated sounds more nefarious. More... infective. Something I'm quite familiar with in other circumstances."

At this, Brea joined them. "Infective. That's apt, Dusty," she turned to the dwarf.

"You and me, we have dealings to discuss."

"What's she talking about? What dealings?" Gehard's eyes narrowed.

"I don't know if I can trust you, to speak precisely. But if you're playing at something…"

"Look, if we were double-dealing, or working together against you, you'd already be dead. Know that," Brea snapped. "But, fine. I'll tell you this. Our diminutive friend here has some leverage over my health and well-being, as it were."

"What leverage?" Tyel looked up from Alyse's porcelain face to meet the sour, exasperated expression on Brea's.

"I cannot go on wondering if I'm set to die if you happen to shrug off your mortal chain. Under the current circumstances, that seems likely," Brea scowled. "I haven't come this far just to keel over from slow-rot in my veins."

Dusty sighed heavily and adjusted himself, shifting uncomfortably on the spot. "It's a matter of perspective, lad. Brea was sick-to-dying when she was dragged from the dockyards as a stowaway. I was asked to treat her. As a person of medical tutelage, that is my ethical responsibility. It just so happens, I also knew she was a person of particular skills. And, what's more, her presence was conveniently timed with some rather abrupt contact from the beings who inhabit this very chamber."

Dusty looked squarely at Tyel. "We're assassins, Tyel. Beings of blood-work by trade – though I am sure you know this by now. What you might not realise is that there are a great many of us. As I have gathered, the Oracular Magisterium likes to play the game of odds. They want our Necromant eliminated, and they clearly do not favour the task being completed by one or two of our Guild."

He then nodded toward the Sacred Championate. "I'd say the reason our friend here is alive and well is due to our shared objective. Am I wrong, Ser?"

"Not wrong, but not wholly correct, either," he replied. "I am no assassin. I am a being of balance in an unbalanced plane. I'll explain eventually, but once again, this is not the space for this."

Brea laughed. "Your droll semantics aside, we seem to be ignoring my problem." She crossed her arms. "Cure me, dwarf."

"I cannot do that, Solsetter. But I can administer your treatment for now. Then, I suggest we move on."

Dusty opened his leather satchel and frowned. "Oh." He looked up, blinking above his rims.

"What now?" Brea groaned.

He looked back down and began to rummage, though more carefully. "Several of my phials have, ah, shattered."

"Dusty," Brea balked. "Don't joke. And do not tell me you can't give me what I need."

"Well, I won't tell you that, then." He began to carefully remove the intact ones and lay them out, stoppered as they were, on the floor. "But that's the situation, lass."

He tipped out his satchel with a clinking, clattering, shattering chime. The floor was scattered with herbs, white liquids, murky black ooze – and countless twinkling shards of glass.

"How… long do I have?" Brea's usually controlled manner threatened to give way.

"I will need to restock before I can treat you. Days at very most. We're in the last phase of the moon. You will begin to feel the effects of going untreated."

He tipped the last of the glass jags onto the floor. Then, gingerly, he plucked up half a dozen phials, two small glass jars, and the wooden and iron apothecary's tongs and spoons. Two strega teeth clinked inside a small, squared off jar that might once have held ink.

"I'm truly sorry, Brea. I will fix this."

"You better, or I'm taking you with me, dwarf." Brea shot arrows with her eyes. In truth, she felt fine – but if Dusty was right, and she would begin to deteriorate, they would need to move quickly.

Tyel bent over the assortment of odd ingredients. The smell was foul, like unwashed feet, fetid and cheese-like. A thin, white vapour rose from a gurgling black puddle. Branson half-expected the puddle to wriggle off, like a soot-sliglet, into a crevasse and out of sight.

"And please, nobody touch any of this now." Dusty raised his hand, motioning them back. "There's no telling what mixing some of these things together might do."

Alyse came to slowly at first, hearing the familiar voices rolling around inside her head before conjuring their faces and connecting the sounds to their owners. She felt cool stone beneath her fingers, grounding her in the moment and helping her fight off the dizziness in her head and the throbbing ache in her muscles.

"She's awake!" Gehard nodded to Alyse. She rubbed her eyes with the back of her thin hand and sat up more fully now. "You missed the fun, elf."

"Gods, girl. You're lucky to be alive," Brea knelt next to her. The Elfkin said nothing. She studied the group. They were one short.

"Sir Filip—" she started. Her eyes found Tyel. He returned her look for a moment, before his head dropped.

"He's… gone," Tyel replied softly.

She felt a pulse of guilt and sadness emanating from the young man.

"I'm sorry." She meant it – though the words crept out felt hollow and thin.

Dusty approached her, finding a space next to Brea. "It wasn't your doing, girl. He knew the price of his position. He's a hero of the purest kind, lass." He held out his hand for her to take. "Come on now. Are you in one piece?"

As she reached for him, the moment was broken by a blinding flash of pure white issued from the direction of the Magisterium's thrones. A booming voice issued, *"Who breaches this sacred chamber uninvited? Speak."*

"I think he's talking to you," Brea shoved Dusty's shoulder sharply. "Go on."

The dwarf shot her a sideways glance. He cleared his throat and, looking now at a tall, thin figure in a long, tan-hued robe, puffed up his chest. "To whom do I have the pleasure of speaking?"

"You are in the presence of Oracle Solum the Third," the figure replied.

The figure raised his arm, and from beneath the drooping sleeves a hand emerged. Within a fraction of a second, a pillar of scourging flame erupted in front of them. The twisted column of orange fire consumed the shattered remains of Dusty's satchel. As quickly as it had spun into flame, the dervish subsided. Only a pitiful pile of char remained.

"Sacred Championate, why have you brought these interlopers into our chamber?"

"No disrespect intended, Oracle. It is my understanding that the Magisterium has already been in contact with two of my party – directly or indirectly: Brea E'Lario and Dust-in-His-Eyes."

"And the others?"

"Address the Oracle," the Championate turned to them.

Gehard grunted. "You have the pleasure of being in the presence of His Excellence, Luminary Gehard Fendrigar, son of High Inquisitor Boff Fendrigar of The Capital. I expect you've heard of me."

The Oracle looked at him blankly. "You are quite unlike your father."

"What?" The Luminary looked gut-punched for a moment. "What do you mean?" Was this an insult? Compliment? He scrambled to decipher this.

The Oracle disregarded him. "Who else? Speak."

"Tyel Branson, squire for…" he stopped. "For the Anointed Knight Protectorate." It wasn't quite right, he supposed, as he no longer knew if he was a squire at all, since Ser Filip had passed. But it would do for now.

"Branson," The Oracle pondered. "Eld Age kin. And who is your companion?"

"Southron Elf, Alyse – of House Elsteme," Alyse bowed, with as much grace as she could muster.

"Alyse… Elsteme?" The Oracle took pause at that. "It has been a long time since we've had a delegate of House Elsteme this far north. The Magisterium's protection is at your command, your Grace."

Alyse went rose-flush. "I— You have my thanks, my Oracle."

The Oracle nodded. With a thin hand, it folded back the heavy hood obscuring surprising features. Tyel gasped at the sight. He'd never seen such a thing before; it seemed unreal – but then, many things he'd seen recently were beyond his sheltered understanding.

Beneath, a face of shifting features: at one moment, an old and age-spotted woman; the next, a young and olive-skinned man. Within an eye's blink, the nose lengthened and broadened. The mouth shifted up and down, warped and twisted. Each eye shifted from blue to brown and to hazel. The Oracle's face was a kaleidoscopic distortion of beings – genderless, indefinite, perhaps entirely inhuman.

"Sacred Championate, you have assembled a most unusual party. It is, however, not unforeseen, as all things are. Chance plays no part in this odd assemblage."

The Oracle walked toward Alyse, regarding her carefully. "I sense great energy within you, Alyse Elsteme. And great conflict. Is this true?"

Alyse cast her eyes down. "Yes. I suppose, yes."

"I think, Alyse, some intervention is required. I believe you carry a subtle infectant of a kind. A parasite of the mind. It seeps from you like a wound. It taints your very essence."

Alyse's eyes welled. "Yes."

"You know of whom I speak."

"Y-yes…"

"Then you know that while this parasite exists within you, none of you are safe. And no actions are private."

Branson took Alyse's hand. She pulled away from his touch. "Don't.

Don't Tyel."

"Father always said House Elsteme were duplicitous and weak – I knew you were no good," Gehard spat.

Brea cut him off with a raised palm. "Stow it, Gehard. Alyse, you've been compromised by the Necromant. How long have you been hiding this?"

"I— I'm sorry…" she began. Then, as a flood of bitter tears began to flow, she looked up at the Oracle – the indifferent eyes and inscrutable, shifting features.

"We can treat this, but I must caution that the outcome is binary. If the hold is too strong – and we cannot draw out the essence, the subject may not live."

"Do what you must," she said softly.

"Don't hurt her," Tyel growled. "Don't touch her."

The Oracle uttered a clipped laugh. "Your noble heart bleeds need-lessly, Tyel Branson. While destroying the host is one outcome, it is not the only one. We will take care. Alyse, lay upon the ground within the Mark of the Trine."

She looked at Tyel; his dirty face did nothing to diminish large and loving eyes. In her heart, she knew she would hurt something so tender. It would be impossible to handle with care something so delicate.

Alyse set herself down in the centre of the markings, then lay back-ward. She closed her eyes, feeling her heart pounding and the last loose tears tumbling backward toward her large ears.

"I must assemble the Oracular Magisterium. The rest of you will stand back and refrain from interference – no matter what. Is that clear?"

All but Gehard nodded. "I don't see why we can't just end her and be done with the whole affair. She's just a vassal."

"Luminary, your worth is great," The Oracle replied. "Hers is greater. Now you will be silent, or I will portal you to the Snowbarrens until we are through."

Gehard huffed, turned and walked to the curved rear wall, near the broad chamber doors. There he leaned, head low, arms folded. The others joined him, sitting with backs against the stone.

Tyel's guts churned. He mulled over the Oracle's words. A binary outcome. Life or death. Success or failure. Yet, Alyse willingly offered herself to the Magisterium, knowing full-well this may be her end. His heart ached for her – a life of servitude and ridicule, underestimation and isolation. All leading to this. It just didn't seem fair. It didn't seem right.

And yet, he thought, the Oracle claimed all things were known – foreseen. How could they not know whether she might live or die? How could they not already predict the success or failure of this undertaking? The rise and fall of nations; the births, lives and deaths of all beings – the Necromant included. His mind was an unspooling line of sacred questions and supernatural suppositions. He wanted to ask them all. Above all else, he wanted her to live.

The room glowed the same familiar blinding flash of white brilliance from the line of thrones. At once, eight more figures appeared – all hooded in pale garb, all veiled in shadow that Branson assumed hid their shifting faces from each other. The air in the room grew markedly colder, he noticed, as if a winter wind blew cleanly into the space from a large open window, sight unseen.

The third Solum Oracle turned to the eight seated before them.

"Why have you called the Magisterium to Order, Oracle?" came a voice.

"There are interlopers in our midst," came another.

"Before you is Alyse Elsteme. It has come time for intervention, to preserve order," The third Solum Oracle replied.

At once, a Nulum Oracle, seated at the farthest end of the run of thrones pressed themselves upward. "The sacred order cannot be threatened. You know this."

There was a murmur among them now; the Solum Oracle turned to the Nulum Oracle.

"The Necromant's injunction is insidious. I vote strongly for removal. Psychic corruption is a black casting."

"And a Necromant is a black caster. Your point is moot," The Nulum Oracle replied, snidely. "It is within the nature and calling of the Necromant. We cannot draw him out. It is against the Balance."

From the Nulum side, an echo of agreement. To their left, the Lunum Oracles nodded solemnly.

"Solum Oracles, what say you?"

"The Nulum Oracle is predisposed to chaos and shadow. We strive for order and light. We concur with you, Solum Oracle; psychic corruption removes freedom of choice. This removes balance. Thusly, the Necromant must be purged."

The sixth chair, a Lunum Oracle, now stood up to address. "The girl has keen abilities. She is capable of implanting emotions – is this not akin to psychic interference?"

"Her abilities are far from advanced," The third Solum Oracle replied. "Nor is she predisposed toward dark dealings. This is not a fair comparison. They are not on equal footing."

More murmurings and a flurry of nodding and agreement.

"Magisterium, removal of choice is what we are debating," The first Lunum Oracle spoke, leaning forward on their elbows, hands steepled. "It is in the Necromant's nature to exploit the black craft. Is it not also in the girl's nature to use her gifts to fight back against such craft?"

Brea and Tyel exchanged looks. Dusty squinted fixedly on the panel of Oracles.

"I concede this point, Lunum Oracle," the Third Solum Oracle raised a hand. "To the Magisterium, I declare an outcome has been presented and the balanced decision is clear. Do we all agree?"

The eight seated Oracles nodded, speaking practically in unison, with a perfunctory. "We do."

He turned to Alyse.

"The girl must fight to free herself."

CHAPTER 24

LYSSY'S LAMENT

"Dear Niece."

Vimnir Delcryth stood at the top of a long road that opened into a carriage circle of weathered granite beneath the early evening sky. Upon the stepped landing, the Necromant took in the commanding view of Atheron's valleys that were dimly lit in the final moments of the sun's afterglow. "A pleasure to see you again, and looking so vital. How was your journey?"

The canvas curtain window drawn back, Lyssy looked drawn and tired; her delicate features betrayed her Elfen heritage, but her heavily tanned skin spoke to the more dominant traits of her Solsetter blood.

Lyssy Delcryth opened the side door of a simple wooden carriage and stepped out. "Long," she replied. "I don't know why you wouldn't simply portal me here. Travel overland is just so *tiresome*. Worse than by ship."

"Tiresome, but assuredly necessary, Lyssy. We do not know who is monitoring the summoning of Portal Gates, do we? Many prying eyes." He extended his arms and embraced her, pulling her slight figure toward him violently. "You are far too valuable to me – too important – to have your whereabouts known widely. Even your fool husband doesn't know you're here – though, after our last encounter, he might guess as much."

She nodded, withdrawing from him, and pulling up the hem of her long, grey dress. She took the flight of steps carefully, looking up at the towering, cathedral-like arches of what was once the dwarven city of Yrkanh.

"I'll summon a porter to bring your things inside."

"How did you do this, Vim? How did you take Yrkanh? And what of Havrohd and

Minovarh? Surely the dwarves are mounting a resistance."

"Please, come in – there will be time for answers. For now, enjoy the hospitality of your new home. This castle is my gift to you – and my gift to House Delcryth. It is the start of a new legacy for our kind."

He took her by the hand and together they passed over the threshold and into the castle's entry hall. His fingers were unpleasantly cold, she noted.

Lyssy walked stiffly and wordlessly down the grand entry hall of the great castle Yrkanh. The cool, still air was a refreshing change to the stuffy carriage. Looking up at the arched roof, she pictured the countless generations of dwarves who had meticulously crafted raw stone into intricately carved pillars. Each pillar told a tale around its circumference. Some showed great legions of dwarves and men in battle; others showed elves beneath a burning Sol, working their magic to produce water for their crops. Others showed busts of great dwarven leaders and fabulous wealth. All felt lifeless now; relics left behind after a losing battle.

Vimnir's porters were odd creations, she thought – once dwarves, surely. Now, with their bloated limbs and distended bellies and bulging eyes, they looked hideous. She averted her eyes as they scurried past her down the hall toward the entryway.

"Oh, don't let them disturb you, Lyssy," Vimnir giggled. "They're nothing! Nothing at all. There are countless other creatures here – all of my own creation. Or resurrection, as it were. Now those – those would take your breath from you."

She wasn't sure if he was being literal. She feared he was.

"Is that what became of the Yrkanhan dwarves, then?" She asked casually, trying to downplay her growing discontent.

"Oh yes. The sub-chambers here teem with them. All of those tubby little aristocrats, bankers, diplomats. Dwarves of the worst sort; once feeding off the fat of the realm – now ready to serve it in a more… productive capacity."

"You have been busy then, Uncle."

He laughed at this. "My dear, you have no idea. The northern villages are now mine. And my reach extends south as we speak. Why, I do believe we have a foothold in the Capital by now. What fun!"

He reached the end of the long, wide hallway. To the left and right, two more halls ran.

"Your keep is down there, far end – through the double doors. There's a rather fetching view over the Ranges, and the scale of the space is a little more in line with our needs."

"Thank you, Vim. And where are your quarters?"

"Wherever I choose. I sleep little. Often not at all for many turns of the Lunum. I have no need now."

She knew it was true, then – he had taken the final step.

Vimnir read the concern on her face. "Oh Lyssy. Come now. I have merely embraced that which called to me, darkly. But in that darkness lies a pool of infinite knowledge. And power."

"You're… *dead*, aren't you?" She struggled to speak. She'd known he seemed off, from the very moment she slid back the drapes of her carriage window. During her private conversations many months ago in the communication chamber in the Capital tower, she'd only seen him faintly. Then, he still had his dark complexion. Now, he looked corpse-like.

"My love, everything in here is dead. This is my trade. But am I dead? Not exactly, no. Not far from it, I suppose."

She raised a hand to her mouth. "Vimnir, what have you done?"

"I relinquished my life energy. My essence – my sense of being – is unchanged, but that energy has been… *replaced*. It really is quite liberating. I have no further need for the contrivances of men. Sleep, food, lust, sadness – even the bite of cold weather – they're nothing to me."

Lyssy took a deep breath through parted fingers, then lowered her hand. Why was she so perturbed by him? It was still Vimnir, after all.

"You're right. I'm still me," he laughed.

"You're reading my— how dare you," she snapped, and raised a hand.

He swatted it down. "Don't." His eyes were cold now. Some flicker of life wavered far off in him, but a new and deathly spectre seemed to dominate him. She grabbed her hand. It stung now. She rubbed the pain out.

"Don't provoke me, dear Lyssy. I have a great many new powers. That is the least of them." He ran a hand through his long hair. "We are loved ones, are we not?"

"We… are," She stammered. "Of course. Of course we are, Vim."

"Good. And loved ones mustn't bicker. Be happy for your dear uncle. These are fine times! The start of something most wonderful, Lyssy. A new cycle for Solumbrya and a rebirth for our kind."

"I *am* happy for you. It's just all… very new to me. It's a lot to take in, that's all. Yes."

Vimnir softened. Something approaching a smile crept across his thin, pale face.

"It is. And you are tired, I'm sure."

"I am weary. I'm sure a good bath and bed will clear my mind."

"Indeed. I'll have the porters attend to your needs." Lyssy's skin prickled at the thought.

Suddenly, Vimnir winced, his face contorted as if struck by some invisible force.

"Are you—" Lyssy began. He cut her off.

"You must excuse me now. Something has come up – just now – that needs my attention." With that, he turned from her and headed towards the opposite end of the hall. She watched him hurry away, turning a corner back into the main hall and, with an odd sense of relief, she was alone again. She finished her walk toward her quarters and opened the door.

Within, she found a fire of blue-orange flame in the hearth, casting a blend of honey and azure light across the tapestries. At the far end of the room, wide-set doors leading to a balcony were set into the wall. Beyond, she could see the final moments of dusklight across mountain peaks. Vimnir was right – the view was fetching.

She wept.

~ ~ ~

It began as a headache, then it exploded. Vimnir collapsed into his preferred high-backed chair in the dining hall. He barely made it.

The girl.

This was most unexpected. He grimaced and closed his eyes. He would have to stamp this out immediately. With a focused thought, he reached out to her.

Like parting thick storm clouds, he filled her mind with his own. Before, there was little resistance, but now, something was different. He opened her eyes with his own.

From her viewpoint, he saw the high ceiling. He felt her skin against the stone, and the radiant heat of hearth fires. Then, reaching further in, moving her eyes to a better vantage, he saw The Nine. She had made it to the Magisterium.

Oh no.

"Vimnir Delcryth," a voice called to him – an Oracle, but he was unsure which. "You are hereby summoned. Your host will be given the opportunity to remove your essence, in accordance with fair balance."

"No!" His voice issued through her body as he sat her up.

"You will be given the opportunity to retain your connection. You will fight. Fair balance will be determined by the outcome," the voice commanded.

He could already feel the girl pushing back against him now.

"You may begin."

Vimnir had never felt push-back like this before.

It was not difficult to take a person's mind and feed them suggestions. That certainly had its uses when dealing with that oaf Boff Fendrigar. He was practically a plaything; a puppet on a string to be tinkered with at Vimnir's behest.

With Alyse, he'd taken things a step further. Perhaps too far to be subtle. He had interrupted her conjurations, pulled knowledge from her like the index of a reference tome, seeking people and places and things. He'd made her weary, pulling at her senses. To her credit, she'd held herself together and kept her condition quiet; she had tried to shut him out once or twice.

Now, he would have to dig his heels in. Something had changed within her; he could feel it.

I know your secrets, girl. I know your longings.

Deep within Alyse, she saw the form of him. He cut a black and insectoid figure, draped in a shifting cloak of smoke and void. Beyond him in all directions, the plane of her consciousness stretched to infinity. There was no sound but their thinkings. No feelings could penetrate this space. No light, no smells, no distractions. In here, it was an endless dreamscape.

I know you long for family. And yet, you resist affection. Why is this?

Get out of my head!

His form swirled around in the blackness *I know why, but do you? And you yearn to master spellcraft, yet are fearful of your power. You are full of odd contradictions, Alyse.*

She pulled away from him. *You don't know anything about me.*

There was no running from him here. The further she pulled back, the faster he was upon her. *You are most incorrect! I know much and more. Yet, you are as wild and untrained as a whelp.* His black mass swirled in front of her inner vision. *You could be so much more than you are now. Why fight against one who would teach you so much? Why fight against the blood of your own?*

I want nothing you have to offer, she spat back. *You're a murderer. A monster.*

No, Alyse Elsteme. His black form was dominating. *I have so much to offer you. Much to offer all of Solumbrya. Much and more. Elfkin of House Elsteme would be wise to listen.*

Do I have a choice? You're in my mind.

It's your mind, Alyse. It's your choice. It always has been. Part of you is curious about me. Part of you, I know, wants to listen.

This point dug its claws into her and it lingered there. Had she really been able to rid herself of him this whole time?

I can feel your confusion. I find it all quite amusing.

She looked down. He could sense everything she was feeling as she felt it. She felt a burst of shame and betrayal at her privacy stripped to nothing.

Then, she felt something else: surprise. Looking down, from her point of view and, to her amazement, she found she had a form. She could see her own body; a lithe glowing figure – shimmering with the same energetic blue that shone in her eyes. Now, her whole body was afire. She'd never seen herself like this before.

I am the future. I am the future that is coming for all of us.

Cold words, dark with malice.

I know more than you think I do, Alyse pushed back. *And there is no future for you.*

Alyse focused on her arms and pushed.

At once, a glowing surge of energetic force, like the rolling crash of a wave against headland, slammed into the shadow form of Vinmir Delcryth. The impact sent his form reeling backwards. His shade-figure, once defined and whole, spun backwards, disintegrating into tendrilous wisps of dark cumulus.

We're done, she murmured. And they were, she knew.

She looked down at herself, visualising a protective sphere of energy around her thought-form – much as she had when she was in the sewers of Dormanstar. Around her etheric body, she established a barrier – and she knew the door was closed now.

~ ~ ~

He didn't even have time to react.

In his high-backed chair, Vimnir thrashed and spasmed. His eyelids flickered like window shutters in the wind. His pale body contorted and he slid from the chair and onto cold stone.

An explosion of pain laced his mind as he opened his dry eyes. He lay on the floor. If he could still sweat, his skin would be clammy. Now, it stung. He sat up stiffly.

"H— how—"

She had ejected him! And with such force! Such beautiful control! His pain was matched by tantalising thoughts of her potential. The power she held was undeniable. He knew even she was unaware of the extent of her gifts.

He would reach out to her again.

He found his focus once more and closed his eyes. His body was still – no pounding of blood in his chest or temples to distract him anymore. He felt the familiar disconnected sensation of his consciousness stretching – or being pulled away, like an infinitely fine and filamentous arm, feeling in the dark for a hand-hold.

He felt others, yet – the boy, the dwarf, the strange Solsetter woman and the Fendrigar buffoon. None held the power he sought; none were worth his time. Now, however, he could not find her. It was as if her light, which shone so brightly, had been extinguished completely.

He pulled back, opened his eyes, stood and grabbed the thick edge of the table. He saw his dull reflection on the polished surface and frowned.

The connection was severed, he knew it. He roared.

With a broad wave of his arm and a bellowing yell of disgust, dusty cutlery, silvered dining plates and a five-armed candelabra scattered across the room.

With red, puffy eyes and tear-streaked cheeks, Lyssy watched her uncle from the crack in the door and knew the man he once had been was now very far away and gone.

Her voice was barely a whisper.

"Dear Uncle."

~ ~ ~

When she awoke, Alyse was on her feet. She had no memory of standing. She had only a vague recollection of what had led her to the chambers of the Oracular Magisterium. What she did know for certain is that she had faced off against a figure of extreme power and evil. His darkness pervaded through her essence like radiant heat.

Her heart was pulsing and her head swam as she stumbled backward. Spots of lingering blackness danced at the corners of her vision.

"Catch her."

"Alyse!" Tyel was already on his own feet and over to her side, sure-footed in her lack. He caught her with an arm around her lower back and held her upright. Her eyes were unfocussed and brilliant with magical bloom. "Alyse. Are you okay? What happened?"

Her eyes shot him a look of fear as she stiffened and recoiled.

"He— he's— "

"What did you *tell* him, girl?" Gehard was on his feet once more. "You've betrayed us, I know it."

"No! I— He's gone. Please. Let me catch my breath and I'll tell you what happened."

Dusty approached her. "Gehard, the girl has done nothing but face up against horrific evils with stoic bravery. And she's done it while protecting you and I – and the rest of us, I might add."

He turned and raised a finger at the Luminary. "And yet you repeatedly cast her down. Why? Are you so small a man?"

The Luminary scoffed. "You would know all about that."

"Oh, enough. Enough! Let it go," Brea interjected. She waved them both down. "She has more steel in her backbone than you, Gehard."

"Silence! The Chamber will have order." The first Nulum Oracle stood up. The third Solum Oracle did likewise.

A hush fell over the space as the Magisterium commanded. Tyel returned to Alyse's side; her furtive glance at him read of deep unease. Solum Three returned to the floor, approaching them.

"Alyse Elsteme, what of your encounter? Speak if you would, your Grace."

Alyse took a deep breath and began her recount, as best as she could recall it. Imagery came slowly at first. The Oracles watched wordlessly from a semicircle of anonymous eyes beneath heavy hoods, motionless in their thrones, as the elfkin described the smoke figure with his veiled threats and empty promises. Then, with a flick of her thin forearms, she told of repelling him, despite his protective sphere.

Tyel listened with fascination. Her abilities were beyond his understanding – he wondered if even the Magisterium genuinely knew the extent of her gifts. They certainly indicated they knew of outcomes before they occurred. Part of him doubted this too – but he couldn't pinpoint exactly why.

"And it was done. He's gone. I don't know more beyond this, I'm sorry. I do not know if my protection spell will last – but I am doing what… feels right."

At last, the Solum Oracle nodded. "So be it. The connection has been severed by fair confrontation. Balance has been decided. This can be agreed upon." He turned to the panel and was greeted with a muted chorus of agreement and nodding.

"Your Grace, I do not speak for the Magisterium when I say this, but I am most impressed with your aptitude for mental arts. I feel you have much and more to learn – and will. May you stand in the light of Sol." He bowed to her, low and long, with an arm bent below his waist in courtesy.

Alyse allowed herself the faintest smile, but the disorientation in her head – the cloudiness – persisted. She was ready to be far from here.

The Oracle flicked his wrist and, with a sucking whoosh of air pressure, a portal crackled into the space behind them. Nothing was yet visible on the other side, Tyel noticed.

"To Brea E'Lario–know this." Brea's attention whipped around, startled. "Your past deeds cannot be undone. But for now, few who seek to under-mine you believe you live. Use your gift of un-making wisely."

Brea nodded. 'Unmaking.' The dwarf was right. The world thought she was dead. Perhaps there would be great advantage to this after all. It was somehow reassuring to hear it from another, though.

"Dust-in-His-Eyes. Do not mislead your partner. Tell her the truth of things. This is the will of the Magisterium and you should heed this. Only together can you succeed."

Dusty swallowed hard and looked down.

"Dusty." Brea turned to the dwarf. "What are they talking about?"

"Luminary Gehard—" The Oracle continued unabated.

"No! Wait – we're not done here. Dwarf, what's going on? What are you not telling me?"

Dusty frowned. "Ah, Brea. Let's discuss privately—"

"No. Let's discuss *now*, shall we." She loomed over him. "Spill it."

Dusty looked around the room, as if measuring the space, or looking for a quick exit. The portal led nowhere – a connection point had not yet been established. The distance to the exit doors was too far. *And, really, what am I running for?* he scrunched his brow and scratched at his cheek. *The woman is a violent ally, but reliant on me – perhaps the best combination. I must handle this carefully,* he mused.

He didn't finish the thought. She kicked him. He crumpled inward and fell back to the floor, grasping at his nether regions.

"You've been lying to me, haven't you? I knew it. I knew it the whole time, you rotten—"

"No! It's not like that!" He wailed, rolling onto his side, reeling in agony from the impact of her pointed toe.

"Oh no? Then tell me how it is! I know I'm not dying, dwarf. I feel fine."

"I— I'm not lying to you!" He winced and rocked onto his back, clutching himself. Tyel stifled a laugh. "It's just—"

"What?" She shouted, leaning over him, readying another kick. "Talk! Or say goodbye to the family heirlooms."

"I didn't want to tell you like this! You— you *are* dying!" He staggered onto his knees. His face was a bulbous canvas of beard, sweat and pinched tears. "Gods, woman. That kick…" He wiped his face with thick fingers and adjusted his glasses. "It's just that, when I said I could keep it at bay and cure you over time – that may have been an… exaggeration. Of sorts."

"*Exaggeration.*" Brea's stomach lurched. "Explain."

"Your body is *dying*, Brea. It is. I have slowed it down through wortcraft and no small skill on my part. But you are dying and I don't know that I can stop that. I did what I could to save you. I still am. But you will die, Brea. I fear that death is unavoidable."

Brea's right leg returned beneath her as her face lost its intensity. Her eyes became unfocussed. She could've been looking at the horizon, ten thousand days travel beyond. She raised a hand to her mouth. The air in the room felt heavy.

"And that's the truth?" Her focus returned to him.

"That's the truth of it, I swear to you." He could no longer hold back the threatening tears of pain and shame. "I'm… sorry. I'm so sorry, Brea. Truly I am," Dusty's eyes met hers and she at last found focus on his face. "I take no pleasure in telling you this."

Nobody spoke for a long moment. Brea sat down on the floor next to Dusty. His face was long and full of shame. She tipped her head forward, arms resting on her grazed kneecaps.

"Your bollocks okay?" she muttered softly.

"No," he laughed weakly, and that was true. He would be purple down there.

He turned to the Solsetter. "I tell you true, Brea. You are a mean fighter and fierce ally. I don't mean to lose you – nor will I let death sweep you up without a fight from me."

At that moment, she believed him – perhaps for the first time. She nodded, stood and offered an outstretched hand which the dwarf gladly took.

"You better. If I die, you're coming with me."

"Aye."

The Luminary tutted. "Oracle. Please. What were you saying before this ill exchange interrupted you?"

The Oracle continued as if nothing had happened.

"Luminary Gehard. You will return to the Capital. Your father needs you now."

Gehard's face fell. He thought of his father and sister. Something must have happened. Worry filled him. He refused to show it. *Perhaps it is plain to see anyway,* he thought, and turned from the group. *Curse and damn it all.*

At last, the Solum Oracle turned to Tyel Branson.

"The boy Branson. Now a man. Your path is south to your family who need you, most surely. But not before your time in the capital is through. Trust your mind, but listen to the wisdom of your other senses."

Tyel looked at Alyse, back to Gehard and down at his feet. Questions swirled. He knew no answers would come. There was no comfort in that realisation.

Now," the Oracle continued. "Sacred Championate."

The Championate knelt, bowed his head and rose. "Your task remains unfinished. However, the fates have deigned to align you with these other agents of The Trine. In this, we see great opportunity – and great risk."

"You will serve the Magisterium by committing to protect our agents to the best of your ability. Your time in this plane grows long. Each revival strains the natural order that binds all beings to this plane. We cannot promise your next revival will come without cost."

Brea glanced at the Sacred Championate; his unblemished face was unreadable. If this was new information to him, he buried his reaction down deeply. *His days are numbered too,* she realised. *But all must die. Even handsome mystical warriors and sun-kissed assassins.*

"Henceforth you will serve Alyse Elsteme. Your blade is her blade. Your shield, her shield. Her life, yours. All will serve the balance. Is that understood?"

The Championate mulled this over. For a moment, a flicker of confusion glanced across his face, not unnoticed by Brea.

He nodded. "Understood." The Championate turned to Alyse. "I am at your command henceforth."

"I thank the Magisterium, but I have no need for protection," she replied flatly.

"It is the will of the Magisterium and it will be so."

She said nothing, but nodded. He raised his gloved hand. With grace and confusion, she took the tips of his uplifted fingers with her own and bent her knee slightly in acknowledgment. She knew there was no use in debating. There would be time to work things out later, she supposed.

"Now," the Oracle raised a hand once more. "Together you will rise or fall. The balance will preserve itself and we wish you well. Your time in the North is now concluded."

The portal crackled electric white. Warm light shot into the room. In a blink, the Oracles vanished.

It was time to leave.

CHAPTER 25

RETURN

Omanon's one good eye had seen much over the years, but until this day, he'd never seen an elderly scullery cook, pendulous breasts soaked in crimson, shrieking with three jagged mouths, attack an Anointed Soldier in full plate—and then *overpower him.*

But then, it had been a morning of odd and horrible things. He woke in his small but tidy bed-flat (gifted to him in perpetuity by High Inquisitor Fendrigar's late father), to the sounds of desperate wailing in the square. It was still dark, which was when he preferred to rise – but generally not to the sounds of butchering and wailing.

He readied himself quickly in his leathers, looping his scabbard through the thick leather belt he had worn for more than a dozen turns of the seasons (he was onto his final, farthest notch now, which was a worrying reminder of the slow creep of his waistline ever outwards).

With a calloused forefinger, he parted the roughspun curtains of his sole window and looked out. He did not like what he saw: a mess of men and monsters and terrified townspeople peeking from behind curtains and through shutters, much as he was.

Strega, he thought. And he knew at once that Tyel Branson had been right – he'd encountered just one, but one meant a nest of many. The vanguard, whom the High Inquisitor had sent far afield, had been surely walking into a storm front of resistance.

He dropped his hands, approached his front door, readied his sword, firmly unclasping the hilt – then stopped.

Think, fool. He knew better than to spill out onto the streets and get swept up in the rabble. He needed a strategy. He needed to get back to the keep. If the strega had invaded the capital in great numbers, and it certainly appeared that way, then he would need to ready as many soldiers as he could – and, perhaps others of a different sort.

He rounded the small alcove to the rear of his abode, past his many shelves of possessions, personal weapons, curios collected during his long years as a travelling soldier. He quietly exited the rear of the building, which backed out into a sloping alleyway of smooth cobblestone. From here he knew he could keep away from the majority of the fighting for now. He would round the square from a distance and work his way through the upper village and to the gates.

Omanon kept low, moving between waste barrels and stacks of shipping crates left haphazardly along the crooked stretches of alleyway. As he broke past the end of the corridor and through the intersection, his jaw dropped.

Screeching, crawling things, clawing away at the pave and leaping from rooftops to window ledges and on. There seemed to be no clear direction to their movement; why had they come here specifically? And how? Were they led in? How had they gotten past the guard towers and fortifications? There would be time for investigations later, he figured – if there was anyone left to question.

His eye darted up toward the skyline beyond the smokestacks. The cloudy early morning sky was taking on the first faint streaks of pinky-orange solrise.

Good, he realised. *These rotten things can't live in the daylight for long.* It was known, even if only loosely, that strega burned in direct daylight.

But then, this raised more questions. If they'd come from the northern village, which was where the boy Branson encountered one, had they only travelled by night? Where had they hidden themselves from the heat of the day's light?

He felt the pinching stiffness of his lower back as he jogged uncomfortably across the street. The path he chose meandered upward in a zigzag, working a route toward the gated citadel. Shouts of fear and pain and disbelief bounced off the walls of the lanes and streets as the citizens of the capital joined him in his rapidly rising dread.

At last, in a heaving, panting, barmy series of footfalls, he approached the guard tower gate. Four men in red and white leathers were positioned either side of the portcullis, which was closed.

"Ho! You men," Omanon puffed. "Open up and let me pass. It's murder ou' there."

"It's murder in 'ere too, old man. We ain' opening for you or none other," came the tallest, fattest of the four.

"Yes y' will," Omanon replied coolly.

"Are y' thick, old man? Head off or I'll remove yours."

The three other soldiers glanced at their designated representative, suddenly unsure. A smaller, bonier guard nudged his bulging side. "Why's an old man like him carryin' steel?"

"Oi, ain' that…" Another whispered to the fat guard.

"I'm the Quar'rmaster. Now open 'er up, you whore-bastards!'

"Oh blazes. It's One Eye," came another.

The rotund guard swallowed hard and stumbled backward.

"A-at once! Raise the gate!" the fat soldier shouted over his shoulder. There was a faint acknowledgement from somewhere inside the gatehouse and the portcullis began its slow ascent, one thick chain link at a time.

Omanon passed by the guards, then paused and turned to them. With a clamp-grip, he grabbed the collar of the fat guard and wrenched him forward and down toward him.

"You. Wipe the shit from between your ears and hear me good. You'd all be stripped and burned on th' ring if it were my call today. Seein' as we're under some kind o' godless threat, you pit-wipes better be ready t' fight for your worthless lives when I come lookin' for ye. Clear?"

"A-Aye, Quartermaster," the fat guard stammered. Omanon ignored him and pushed through toward the inner courtyard.

He was keenly aware that finding, let alone training, decent soldiers was hard during peacetime. Training routines were often just middlingly effective for preparing soldiers for combat. But one would make do with what one had — even these piss-weak dolts. All would soon know what it was like to fight and die for what little they had.

The inner courtyard was unsettlingly still, despite the early hours. Omanon spied torchlight in the halls through the shuttered eaves, but no movement besides.

Far above him, a sleepless High Inquisitor paced his quarters, slowly wearing a groove into the carpet.

~ ~ ~

Vimnir. The name had become a dark mantra. *Vimnir. Vimnir. Vimnir.* Over and over, the name gnawed at his mind as he shuffled. He had placed his trust in this man, his wife's own family. And that trust had run away from him, slipped away downstream like the infection that was spreading across his city.

What have you done, Vimnir? My — my streets are overrun! The waterways are teeming with the dead. We have nothing to eat, nothing to drink — what have you inflicted upon us?

He asked the question to himself, of course, but part of him almost expected an answer. Vimnir had a nasty habit of popping up in his thoughts, voice and form — almost as if Vimnir held a finger in the doorway of the High Inquisitor's mind, ready to return at any moment. He was grateful no word came this time.

First light was breaking. He knew his soldiers were already taking it upon themselves to form ranks in an attempt to take control of the streets – even without the oversight of the Knight Commander or his son at the front of the rank and file.

He doubted it would be enough.

Vimnir…

What he needed now, what the capital needed, were magical soldiers; a small circle of specialists. He needed to call upon the Battleblessed.

With that, a new name came to mind: *Omanon.*

Where was that one-eyed block of gristle and iron? Had he even survived the night? He put the idea out of his mind. There were few in the lands as weathered and hardened as Omanon; he was a stalwart barnacle who had evaded death and led many smaller battles – mostly territorial issues – in his early years.

Since then, Omanon had been granted a mostly ceremonial position as Quartermaster, supported by green-eared recruits not fit to carry a blade – with barely brains-enough to issue weapons to other soldiers, let alone accurately track these actions in the master ledger.

However, his most significant contribution, he knew, was in his mastery of magical arms and tactics. As such, one of Boff's father's final decrees had been the formation of the Battleblessed. The Battleblessed were few in number but potent in the extreme. If Omanon agreed, they would be summoned and the streets reclaimed.

A clear, singular scream stabbed the silence in the halls. The cup from which the High Inquisitor had been sipping tea clattered onto the floor and shattered.

"Guards! Guards!" The room was empty, but he knew help was not far removed. Or, at least, he hoped.

Within moments, two heavily-armed men threw open the doors to the sitting room. Each had a hand on the pommel of their swords hanging from their belts.

"Your Excellence?" spoke the first guard.

"What was that scream?" he pressed. "Am I safe?"

The guards exchanged glances.

"Your Grace," the second guard began. "It's nothing to trouble yourself with. We have the situation contained."

Fendrigar sincerely doubted that. "I see. Fine. What's your name?"

The guard blinked. "Korin, your Grace."

"Korin. Find Quartermaster Omanon and bring him here at once."

The guard bowed and turned to leave. The other guard turned to join him, but the High Inquisitor cut him off.

"Not you. You stay. If anyone other than Omanon enters, you are to cut them down."

The guard nodded, his eyes narrowing slightly. "Of course, your Grace." The guard-turned-messenger left quickly. Fendrigar regarded the remaining protection with a suspicious eye.

"And what's your name?"

"Me?" the guard replied, meekly.

"Yes, you fool. You're the only one in here."

"Aye, your Excellence. Tildor. Tildor Gefrey." The guard reddened. He was young, this man, Fendrigar observed. Soft features, but broad-set. His blonde hair reminded him of his own son.

"Gefrey. I know that name. Yes. Your father served this house once. I remember him. He was a fine fighter."

"Aye, your Grace. My kin, Haylor, also serves. He was part of the vanguard sent north with his Excellence, the Luminary."

"Fine, fine. A family of soldiers, I see."

"Aye, your Grace. It is an honour to serve the Solum God."

The High Inquisitor huffed once and turned away, returning his attention to the window overlooking the town. The courtyard below was begin-ning to fill as morning's first light allowed formations; ranks of soldiers, organised into small squads, began to ready themselves for what lay beyond. The sight of them made him most anxious. He was entirely reliant on his captains to oversee their men, and work independently of Ser Filip while he was away. He hoped their numbers would see them through the day.

His heart raced at the distant notion of what might happen if they failed. His hands clenched, released, clenched again. He needed distraction. He needed soothing. No. More than that.

"Tildor. What is your duty?"

"I beg your pardon, you Grace?" The young man stumbled over the question.

"Your duty. What is it?" The High Inquisitor inquired, almost sweetly.

"I—" Fendrigar turned to the man, his pale skin flushed. Clearly the soldier had never spoken with anyone of his virtuous standing before. "I am at the service of the realm and to your Grace, your…Grace."

"Yes. Yes you are."

The guard took the slightest step back as Fendrigar walked toward him.

"I wish you to serve me now," he murmured. Tildor's eyes moved down the High Inquisitor's front.

Fendrigar felt his impulse, his blood, rising.

"Y— your Grace!"

"Kneel. Kneel and pray to the Solum God that you might receive his blessings through me."

"P— please, your Excellence! I— perhaps a handmaiden might better suit—"

"Now." The High Inquisitor began to rummage at the waist of his off-white nightclothes. A small but pronounced lump had appeared at his groin.

The soldier backed away, not realising his hand had found the grip of his sword once more. The High Inquisitor closed in against him, close enough that Tildor could smell the salty pinch of sweat on his Excellence's skin. An abrasive, infective stench to match an abrasive man.

The room's atmosphere became frigid; the air filled with static, raising the hair on Fendrigar's arms. Parchment scattered; the curtains flung themselves from side to side and the candles guttered.

The High Inquisitor, at once distracted, stopped his pudgy fingers from fiddling with himself and turned towards a blinding flash of white that enveloped the space. He moaned and clutched at his eyes, which felt scalded by the intensity.

He stumbled backwards a moment, joining the guard with his back to the wall.

Tildor drew his blade, shaking off the disorientation.

There, in the centre of the room, upon thick carpet and between long lounges, a portal had appeared. Icy air ushered forth. The High Inquisitor rubbed at his eyes; black dots sat at the middle of his sight, as if he had been staring into a candle's flame.

A form shifted within the portal; he could just make out the figures beyond, in a space he vaguely recognised. *The Magisterium,* he muttered to himself. *Isn't that great?*

A large form emerged though the crackling blue-white ovular portal. Then another, and another, and others still.

The High Inquisitor's eyes focussed and, rather than the bemused and detached voices of the Oracles, another more familiar one greeted him.

"Father. I've returned."

~ ~ ~

Kneeling on tired joints, Omanon lit his storehouse's simple iron stove. Each evening, his assistants would shutter the store's front window and secure the most valuable items in their possession. Each morning, before he would arrive, they would prepare a fire, boil water for tea or cleaning– which was sometimes the same brown liquid – and unlock the chests for easy access.

This morning, however, his storehands had not turned up, so the task of setting up fell to him. Of course, he had no intention of sitting idle here when the enemy was already within their city. However, with the ranks of men filing into the square, he figured his services might be needed.

He latched the iron grate on the stove's front and, with a little too much strain, returned to his feet. He sniffed the leftover tea from the day prior with a modicum of disdain.

From outside, the sound of heavy slapping footfalls pulled him away as a voice called for him.

"Quartermaster! Quartermaster Omanon!"

Omanon dusted his palms against his leathers as a young guard entered the room. The Quartermaster approached his countertop, as the man bowed slightly in respect.

"Aye there. What d'ye need, lad?"

The young man took a deep breath.

"Quartermaster, your presence is requested by High Inquisitor Fendrigar most immediately."

There was no sense in asking why – the Inquisitor surely wouldn't share a reason with the lowly soldier. Then, it didn't take a wizened sage to reach a prediction. Fendrigar needed counsel. His control of the capital had begun to slip – what little he had of it in the first instance. Now, with strega running freely, and only the diligence of their small enclave of soldiers keeping them away, Omanon knew something would eventually give under the strain.

"That so? Then better not keep th' man waiting. Just give me a moment t' gather m'self."

He turned toward the back of the room and opened a creaking wooden trunk before returning with something wedged under his arm. The guard gave him a quizzical look but left it at that.

They crossed the yard quickly, though Omanon's thoughts were occupied with his old ways of thinking: strategy and timelines, capabilities and cost. He scanned the young, tired, confused faces and knew what the true cost would be of a protracted struggle.

~ ~ ~

Within the entry halls of The Tower of the High Inquisitor, there was notable disquiet. To Omanon's eye, the House hands were unusually few in number, replaced by a dozen Anointed Knights. Two were crouched over an emaciated body lying in a pool of red. He could see the same blood wash running down an exposed blade. They turned and nodded to him as Omanon walked past. The old man returned the gesture but did not slow.

He followed the young soldier through the door leading to the upper chambers, peeking into the kitchen block at women with red eyes and sagging shoulders.

At the top of the spiralling stairs, the familiar long hall terminated in closed doors leading to the High Inquisitor's private reception. As he walked the length and drew close, he could hear muffled voices. Omanon moved the young soldier aside and reached out to give the door a firm rap – but stopped short. He glanced down. The rounded toes of his boots reflected an unnatural glow from the gap below the door.

Portal, he realised, at once. Someone had tunnelled into the High Inquisitor's chambers.

Omanon unwrapped the parcel he held firmly under his arm. The soldier gasped and recoiled slightly as the circuitris burst into radial flame. He planted a solid kick against the handle of the door.

~ ~ ~

"My boy! Oh, my beautiful boy!" Boff Fendrigar threw his arms around his son in a bearish embrace. The largeness of his midsection prevented him from clutching him fully, which was just as well; his swelling was still present, though he felt his urge subsiding.

"Hello father." Gehard recoiled from the hug, immediately sickened by his father's pungent odour. The old man had not been caring for himself. Something was indeed wrong; even though the High Inquisitor was not known for impeccable standards of cleanliness, his face looked haggard and his eyes were sunken.

"Are… you well, father?" Gehard's focus was drawn to the soldier, a Gefrey kin if he recalled, pressed against the back wall. He looked pale and deathly afraid of something.

"I apologise for our sudden intrusion; it appears we interrupted you."

"No, no interruption. Come! You are in the company of strangers – though, I recognise the boy – and you brought back my vassal, I see. Good. Good."

"Father, we have much to discuss. Perhaps it would be best if you sit."

The High Inquisitor's arms dropped to their side. "I would invite *you* to sit, boy. Not the other way around. Some time away has stolen your manners."

The Luminary frowned. "Father, forgive my impropriety. I am weary from protecting the realm's interests."

The High Inquisitor's mouth hung open. "The girl I know, and the boy – but a dwarf – and, judging by the dark cast, a Solsetter? And who is this large fellow? You tread with odd persons, Gehard. Explain yourself. Where is Ser Filip? And the rest of your vanguard?

At that moment, the door to the chamber burst open, and a radiant glow of fiery golden flame filled the room. All eyes turned toward the sudden interruption as the silhouette of a stout man filled the door frame, leg lowered from a kicking stance.

Fendrigar spun with a wobble. "Omanon! What—"

The Quartermaster pushed past the High Inquisitor, circuitris elevated like a hand mirror.

The Sacred Championate was the first to act; he drew his own circuitris; the golden ring hummed to life. "No further," he barked. The old man saw the face of the Championate – and the blessed weapon – and knew at once he had the wrong of it.

There *was* a potent threat here – certainly – but not one aimed at the High Inquisitor.

Omanon passed a hand behind his circuitris and immediately the magical flames rippled away into nothingness. He inverted the blade and took a knee, bowing his head. "Forgive an old man. It's been a long time, Isidyr."

Tyel pointed his thoughts toward Alyse in something he felt approximated a mental whisper. *They know each other?*

"Rise, Omanon."

The Quartermaster staggered back upward on stiff joints, propping himself slightly on the upturned handle of his sacred blade. "The years have been good t' ye, I see."

"The Sol God has kept you alive, One Eye," The Championate replied.

"The Trine's not done w' either of us, seems." The old man laughed and extended a hand. The Championate clasped it warmly and released it.

"Where is Ser Filip?" Omanon pressed.

"Hold up," Tyel interrupted. "You have a name?"

"Of course I have a name, boy," the Championate replied. "Nobody asked – though it matters none. Only the oldest Solumbryan tongues might know it. *Isidyr*, they graced me. Though I do not know my family name – and there are none who live who would."

Isidyr, Alyse whispered back to Tyel's mind. *Eld Age name. Like yours. And like mine.*

Tyel knew immediately that this Sacred Championate must be at least as old as Omanon himself – perhaps far older. Yet, he did not age – through some magical means, he assumed.

The High Inquisitor slumped into a seat. He suddenly felt very faint. To Omanon, he looked deathly pale and far older than his years.

"Father?" Gehard took to his side.

"I'm fine. Just – you took me by surprise. I must eat. Yes. Regain my strength."

Gehard turned to the young guard against the wall. "Gefrey, right? Go. Fetch cold wine and sup for his Grace." Tildor Gefrey nodded awkwardly, looking almost relieved to be leaving. Another guard peered in from the hallway, but made no attempt to enter the room. The two soldiers scurried away.

"Someone – anyone – explain to me what's going on. Slowly." The High Inquisitor pulled a square of folded fabric from a pocket and dabbed at his forehead. "You ruined my door, Omanon."

"Apologies, your Grace. The circuitris reacted to magical presence. I also saw the portal light and thought you may be under threat."

At that, the Sacred Championate raised his hand, made a series of motions and the portal crackled out of existence in a dance of magical energy.

"Father, if we might discuss the threat? There's much to go over, and not much time."

"Fine, yes. So you say."

"Father, I regret to inform you that Ser Filip is… no longer with us. Which is to say, ah —"

"He's dead," Tyel finished his thought. His Knight Commander would have chided him for speaking out of turn, but he no longer answered to him. "We were surrounded by an army of strega. They were coming up out of the Marshtide – they swarmed us. Ser Filip— he—" Tyel found his voice wavering; he felt a sudden flush of heat in his face.

Omanon looked as if someone had planted a fist in his gut. "Ser Bolfred Filip was a good man. An' a fine friend. I'm cut deeply by this news, t' be sure."

Brea felt for the old man, but shook it off.

"Your Grace, my name is Brea. Brea E'Lario. This is Dust-in-His-Eyes. The boy Branson speaks true. We joined them far in the north; their vanguard was already in shambles. The threat is greater than you know—"

"You don't know *what* I know, Solsetter." The High Inquisitor slammed a balled fist against the arm of his chair. "I sent my son – the Luminary – north to assess the threat, among other services to his House and the realm. And now you mean to tell me that some of the finest soldiers we have – those of the Anointed Protectorate – have failed? And Knight Commander Filip is dead? Preposterous. I refuse to believe it."

"Your Grace," Brea clenched her fists. She already despised this ball of bloat. "You best believe it. Your Ser Filip lost his life saving mine – the size of some of these horrors – now *that* you might not believe."

"There's more, your Grace," Dusty began. "We, Brea and I, as well as– Isidyr, is it? We were hired by the Magisterium to eliminate the source of the threat. A Necromant – a very powerful one – perhaps the most powerful in this Age."

Boff knew of whom they spoke, of course. He tried to feign surprise.

"A… Necromant, you say?" He dabbed a fresh bead of sweat from his temple. This conversation was rapidly elevating his heartbeat. He shot a look at his vassal. The girl. He felt a sudden intrusion.

"Her. I want her gone." He motioned toward Alyse with a sweaty hand. "Go!"

She did not. Rather, Alyse stepped forward. "You are a liar. I *know* you are."

The High Inquisitor recoiled as if slapped by unseen forces. "How dare you! Guards! Guards! Seize this traitor! Guards!" He practically leapt from his chair, face blooming in swatches of red.

No guards were forthcoming.

"Alyse, is this the truth of it?" The Sacred Championate took to Alyse's side. "This is a very serious accusation."

"I swear it. I— I think I can show you. If you'll allow my… intrusion."

"Shut your mouth, blood traitor. Your kind is the reason—" Boff Fendrigar grabbed a handful of her long hair and wrenched her head backward.

In a flash of burnished bluesteel, the Sacred Championate levelled his blade at The High Inquisitor's neck. "Release. Or lose the hand."

At this, Gehard drew his blade. "You dare point your sword at my father, bastard?" His nostrils flared. "Whatever the truth, he is your High Inquisitor."

Isidyr cocked his head, his eyes still fixed on the High Inquisitor. "I do not recognise his authority over my actions. I answer only to the Magisterium and Alyse of House Elsteme." He breathed hard, eyes focused as if to poke holes though Gehard. Boff released her hair, but not before giving her a yank forceful enough for her to shift backwards. She caught her balance, reeling from the pain.

She turned to him.

"No more of that. Never again."

She raised her hand towards him, palm up. A glow, first at her fingertips, spread to her palm and along her thin wrist.

Omanon knew at once, if she followed through, it would be the High Inquisitor's undoing – and hers. He moved in between them.

"Don't. I know you want to, and you have every reason to, but don't." Gently, he took her hand, feeling the icy electrical shock against his thinning skin, and lowered it. Alyse's eyes burned; at their base, tears of blue flame wreathed them. "Show Isidyr what you've seen – what you've heard."

The glow subsided. With her free hand, Alyse wiped her eyes.

"Tyel," she said softly. "When this is over, we are leaving this place. I will meet your family."

Her face hardened. She turned once more to the High Inquisitor. "And as for you, your Grace, soon you will meet mine."

The menace, the coldness and directness of it, hit Fendrigar as firmly as her spell would've. Certainly, he didn't know exactly what she meant, but she clearly understood. He found that deeply unsettling.

"Now, Isidyr, if you'll close your eyes…" She took his large hand and clutched it between her slender fingers. Dutifully, he closed his eyes. The Championate's mouth, perfect pearls of teeth in impossibly perfect formation, hung open like a whitewashed fence. His eyes rolled back in their sockets.

Immediately, his mind flooded with an assault of overlapping images and sounds. Alyse drew upon her memories and unspooled them like twine.

The High Inquisitor, in conversation with a voice Alyse now knows well and one the Sacred Championate can guess. The girl is somehow within the High Inquisitor. She can feel his enormous body as she might sense her own, and the Championate is a proxy to this. She is reaching within his mind and drawing this memory up to the surface as a plant draws water.

Alyse glances though the High Inquisitor's eyes. His view moves to his left and down the long dining room table. Lyssy Fendrigar is there; equidistant between the two ends. She looks pale.

The Necromant speaks with his gravel-coarse voice. "You're barely a stone in the path that lay ahead for me. Would you care for me to step on you, or over you?"

Alyse feels the unease – and also deep contempt. Fendrigar feels played – outmanoeuvred in his own House, by his own family.

Family. Alyse stumbles over this as her consciousness stutters for a moment.

Back in the moment, the High Inquisitor started for the door. He could feel her inside him; she was probing his mind. He knew what she was delving for. He had felt the same sensation before – fingers flicking pages in his head, delving deeply into his thoughts, pulling out shameful memories.

"This is ridiculous. I'm leaving. Out of my way, dwarf." The High Inquisitor pushed past Dusty. Brea felt for a blade – one she kept in the small of her back for moments like this, and drew it, quick as slick ice.

"Stay." She pushed herself into his face, so close she could feel his heart pounding against the blade she held against his large chest.

Alyse focuses again.

"My children must be able to travel freely. The waterways will provide something of a refuge, but it's hardly practical, is it?"

Alyse doesn't understand — not fully. But she knows the strega have been rising from the Marshtide in great numbers. From the sewers and the understreets in the north, and down the great river system that is the lifeblood of the land.

"Why, my niece certainly agrees! Why don't you ask her yourself? Speak, Lyssy."

The High inquisitor swallows hard. His wife says nothing. Her face is downturned, hands in her lap.

"Niece. The High Inquisitor's wife is the Necromant's blood relation. His niece." Alyse speaks; the Sacred Championate utters the words from his mouth.

When the moment is right, and that moment is coming, dear Boff, you will look to the Sol in the sky, your precious and fickle god, and you will see the fullness of my vision. The extent of my power. The finality of it.

What of my family? You assured us safe passage north!

The Necromant rattles a laugh.

No. When the time comes, I assured my family *safe passage north. You promised me riches! Wealth beyond measure—you said this!*

Wealth? I have more wealth than you can imagine. A mountainside of gold and gems and precious niceties. All of that is yours. Come and claim it. Send a party north. I care not. Those are trivialities in the face of what I stand to gain.

And what of my family's safety? Boff reaches for sour wine and swallows too much in a choking spasm. The cup falls to the table and rolls to the ground, leaving a streak of burgundy down the cloth.

Alas, you must take your comfort in wealth, for you are not my family, Boff. I cannot assure your safety. But if you do not obstruct me, I will not be forced to step on you. That is my promise.

Fendrigar is coughing wine. Something deep inside him is deeply unwell. A voice in his head is screaming.

Your black-tongue issues only lies. Do what you will, gods damn you." He *stands, slamming his puffy fists on the table.*

And you, woman—you brought this deathspeaker into our House. Be you damned too. Leave, then. Be gone and be damned, both of you.

Lyssy erupts in wailing tears. The Necromant is smiling his wicked smile.

Guards! See that the Lady Lyssy is packed and gone before morning. To where, I do not care. But you will not see the south again, whore of Delcryth. You will not see your children again, betrayer.

The Necromant stands. He draws a sign and a portal opens. The stone he keeps on a chain around his neck emanates indigo light. He steps through and is gone. Lyssy wails, but the sound is growing distant.

The images departed like smoke haze into the atmosphere and were gone, replaced by fresh images. These were buried deeper still.

It's dark in the bedroom. Alyse is exhausted, but his fluffed mattress is so plush. It's the first comfort she has felt in some time. That feeling disappears under the pressure of his weight on her thin body, smothering her. The stench of stale breath huffing rhythmically. He promised to treat her better. To give her her own quarters, to allow her more freedoms. She just wants to uphold her duty to her family.

He finishes and, for some reason, he is crying, and she realises she is bleeding down there. She screams, and he slaps her face. She screams louder and he beats her until she stops.

Somewhere, far away, The Sacred Championate is screaming. It's his voice, but it's her terror. The sound is pulling her back and she follows the noise.

Alyse came to. Her hair was wet and her clothes soaked. The Sacred Championate's screaming had been clipped short, like a heavy door slamming shut. She wasn't sure why he'd been screaming; her memories had flitted away. Now, with her sore eyes clearing, she wiped her face and realised her cheeks were wet, too.

At some point, she'd relinquished her grasp of the Sacred Championate's hands and, now, it was he trying to hold her back. Confused, she found herself facing the rest of the room. Her familiars fanned away from her, looks of horror on each face. The room itself was torn apart and, as if the swell of a massive wave had submerged and sullied every surface, the space was saturated and ice cold.

There, slumped on the floor, was the body of the High Inquisitor. Long shards of ice, like broken bones, jutted from his motionless chest. All of him was weeping red.

CHAPTER 26

DEMISE

No one moved. No one spoke. No one had to. They had watched the elf girl and her Championate connect in some queer way. *He* spoke as she read the mind of the High Inquisitor, channelling her words through him as a puppeteer might lever the strings of his puppet. And, then, without warning, her body floated to knee-height off the floor. Her body swirled with the same blue-white energy that burned in her eyes. Her feet hung weightless above pooling water.

The Championate began to scream – yet, it was Alyse's scream that issued from him.

The air in the room became heavy, like walking through a winter rain cloud – then, that moisture turned torrential. Sheets of sleet issued from Alyse in waves. At the very heart of this ice storm, the girl raised her arms free of the Championate and, whatever restraint she once had, vanished. She let herself go.

Jags of ice like crystalline blades issued from her luminous fingertips, propelled in gusts around the room. There was barely time to react. The Championate's screaming, as baffling as it was, was only muted by the howling unearthly rush of etheric winds that ripped through the space, hurtling each of the party backwards.

The girl remained silent throughout.

Yet, as jarringly violently as it had begun, it was over. Tyel, reeling from the experience, watched from behind an upturned lounge as the Championate stopped his wailing and wrenched Alyse back down. Whatever connection they shared was apparently severed.

The High Inquisitor lay in a rapidly expanding pool of his own crimson.

Tyel drew his blade and levelled it at Gehard.

Gehard's pointed toward Alyse.

The Sacred Championate stood between them, and Alyse, breathing hard, eyes wide, crouched and wrapped her arms around herself.

Her head was a mess of disconnected images and sounds. When she closed her eyes, she could feel the sensation of the High Inquisitor on top of her. Of being him, looking out of his eyes. Then of nothing at all – apart from the penetrating gaze of her companions.

"Gehard." Brea started.

"*Shut… your mouth.*" His jaw was tense to the point where the words barely slipped from his lips.

Omanon was slumped against the back wall; his cheek was bleeding. A single shard of ice, rapidly melting, was planted in the wall beside his head.

"The High Inquisitor… What've ye done, girl?" He squinted, wiped his cheek and grunted as he rolled himself forward and onto his feet. He leaned over and pulled at Dusty's outstretched arm.

"I'm sorry. I'm so sorry." Alyse's muted sobs were barely audible above the dripping of water onto the saturated carpets and hardwood floor. The walls ran with rivulets of meltwater.

"Don't hurt her, Gehard." Tyel moved slowly, blade outstretched, towards the space between Alyse and the Luminary. A droplet of water landed on his forehead and it rolled down the side of his nose.

"Boy, I'll cut you in half, I swear it. Stand aside."

"No."

He took another step. "Don't hurt her, Gehard."

"She killed my father, Tyel. He— was my father— the High Inquisitor! He—"

"He *betrayed* us, Gehard. You heard him. He was conspiring with the Necromant. And your mother—"

"Don't you *speak* of my mother!"

Tyel motioned toward Isidyr. The Luminary weakened his posture for the merest instant. The Championate saw his opening and, with shocking swiftness, swept Gehard's leg from beneath him. The Luminary's sword fell from his grasp as his stocky body collapsed onto itself, splashing against the floor.

"Now. Stay there." The Championate held him at sword-point. "Or join your father. Your choice."

Gehard's mouth hung open. His eyebrows raised, face reddening; to Tyel, he looked almost like an abandoned child. He looked lost and broken and pathetic

"Your father was a corrupt and lecherous man. And, as I can attest, a disgusting and violent one. He lived in the light of Sol. But he turned from it long ago."

"He was my father." Gehard's eyes welled. "He's gone."

The Championate lowered his blade. "I knew him when he was a boy. If only he knew the man he would become."

"Your Luminary, there's… something else." Omanon approached the heap of a man, sitting slouched in the puddled slushwater. "I'm… sorry, your Grace, to be the one to tell you this."

Gehard raised his red eyes.

"Your sister, Melodis. She's… passed away. I'm sorry."

Gehard lowered his eyes once more. "Melodis. What happened?"

"She took ill. It's same-such that come up from the waterways – an' the same thing that's happening out in the streets right now." Omanon gestured to the window. "Ta put it lightly, we have an invasion hanging over our heads. 'S why I came – or was summoned at any rate – here. We have a problem needs fixing – an' I can't set about fixin' it by myself. I need capable hands that can hold a blade."

The Luminary appeared to ignore Omanon's plea. "I have nothing left," he whispered.

The dwarf, however, did not. He slicked back his hair with a badly bruised palm. "Would you pull yourself together, Gehard? We're sick of your self-pity. Nothing left? You've just inherited the highest seat of power in Solumbrya, at a time when your people need strong leadership the most."

"I don't want it. I don't want the power. I don't want anything."

That's a change of heart, Tyel mused.

Tyel spoke up. "Fine then. Stay here and mourn. Quartermaster Omanon is right. Every moment we delay is a moment longer the enemy has to spread into the city."

"Aye," Omanon nodded. "But they didn' count on One Eye and his Battleblessed. I've already sent word."

This seemed to garner a flicker of recognition from the Luminary, if no one else. This point did not go unnoticed by the man with one eyeball.

"Wha— you mean to tell me you dinnae know of the Battleblessed?"

Tyel shook his head. Brea folded her arms. "Go on then, old man. Illuminate us."

The Quartermaster tsked his tongue. "You young'ns have so little world-wary learnings these days. I wasn't always the Quartermaster y'know. How'd ye think I lost me eye? Accident with a table knife? No. The Battleblessed are agents of the House of Sol – a bit like the Sacred Championate 'ere – save he works for them faceless lot at the Magisterium."

He looked to Isidyr who said nothing.

"Aye, well – anyhap. The Battleblessed are a secret sect y'see. Trained in complex arms such as my Circuitris 'ere."

"But they're also spellcasters. So am I. An' so, in times of need, I can call on 'em to form up. We have that need now, says I."

"Will it be enough?"

"Better than nothin', not as good as a prepared standing army, lad. We dinnae have that. But we have these." He waved his thumb and forefinger, pinched together and clicked apart smoothly, in front of the golden ring. As before, it flickered into azure and orange flame. With another movement of his hand, it extinguished in a ripple.

"Just as well, then. I'm no brawler." Dusty moved toward Omanon. "But I am something of an alchemical master. Alas, my supplies have fallen victim to the perils of overland travel and reanimated dead. Perhaps I could be of use in other ways, if His Grace's storehouse – assuming he had one – might resupply me?"

Omanon studied the squat man for a moment. Behind cracked lenses, his eyes were wise and sincere. There was something else there too – unease perhaps. He could hardly blame him. Clearly they'd been through a lot in a short amount of time.

"Aye," he replied. "I think we can abide yeh. There's a storehouse beside the infirmary that migh' do the trick. Mind, the beds are full and the care on hand is short righ' now. So best you slip in an' away quickly, no questions asked."

"Agreed and understood, Quartermaster," the dwarf nodded. "Sight unseen."

"And how are you, lad?" He turned to the boy – Tyel. When he left, his head was spinning. Now, a few turns of the Sol had returned a man. He looked thin and tired, but hardened as forged iron.

"Your outfitting kept me alive. But I'd be lying if I said I wasn't well over fighting for my life."

Omanon's gruff laugh warmed him. "Aye, and none would disagree with yeh. And the lot of you – I don' know what you've seen ou' there, but if it's anything like the Capital streets righ' now, it's a wonder you're alive."

He put an encouraging hand on Tyel's shoulder. "We'll soon see if Ser Filip knocked some sense ino ye, lad. I wager he did."

He turned to the rest.

"Now listen well, all of yeh. My Battleblessed are summoned, but I need to return to the yard and command them. Stay if ye wish – I would be grateful for more capable fighters and casters – but I cannae force yeh."

He knew not what to make of the Solsetter, or the elfikin, though surely if the Sacred Championate had stepped in to defend her, then her true worth must be high beyond his understanding.

Then there was the matter of Gehard. What to do about the soft man. He was trained in combat, but until now his involvement in conflicts had been mostly perfunctory. The Luminary was a ceremonial title, after all.

Where he'd lost his fine plate he couldn't begin to guess, but that armour was some of the finest in the realm. Omanon was sure he wouldn't have parted ways with it easily. Speed of transit must've been a factor, he figured.

"I'll fight." Gehard stood up, wiping his face. "If the big man stays, I'll fight." He glanced at the Sacred Championate.

"It's up to Alyse," Isidyr replied. "I serve at her command."

Alyse looked up from the tops of her knees. "I'm no warrior."

Isidyr crouched by her side. "No, lass, you're not. You're something much more powerful. Much more important." With a gentle hand, he lifted her back to her feet. "But I think your time in the Capital may be over now."

Tyel approached her now. "Alyse, we can leave today. Now. My family homestead is southwest of here, in County Keep. It's a fair distance, but we could be there by nightfall if we hurry."

Alyse's luminous eyes turned to him. "I think we might wish to wait for nightfall first, Tyel. It may change your intentions."

"My intentions are to keep us *alive*," Tyel shrugged. "But if that's your wish, I'll stay and fight until you say."

"It is my wish," she spoke softly. "For my fleet approaches with haste."

~ ~ ~

The morning sky was a sickeningly bright azure. From a lounging recline, Vimnir watched the bright gash of Sol light in an elongated arch that mirrored the slit window, creeping slowly down the stone walls of his chamber and onto the floor.

He could have everything, he mused – and was on his way toward that goal. But some sacrifices were inevitable.

Far beneath him, in the subterranean pits of the Atheron caverns, he knew the next birth of dwarven corpus would soon be emerging. Babies and weaklings would be crushed and reforged, recombinant and stronger. Some would become behemoths; others would take wings or additional limbs. All would be beautiful and more purposeful now.

Until today, he'd travelled them south in the fast-flowing waterways that ran beneath the mountain range and down the valleys. The night was their time, but at least the dark waters protected them from the day's cursed immolation.

It wasn't efficient, however. The fishing villages presented no real strategic benefit, aside from disrupting certain trade and stock. He added new and interesting creatures to his repertoire; so much diversity through his dark means. But inland towns and villages still stood – and until they fell, he could not risk an organised uprising.

The Sol's light would need to be dealt with.

He wrapped himself in a crimson cloak of heavy velvet and took to the hallway. At the far end, he rapped thrice on Lyssy's door.

She bade him come. Without delay, he entered. Her shutters were closed, thankfully, and she was sitting upright in her canopied bedspace.

"Lyssy."

"Uncle."

"How are you feeling today?"

"More rested, thank you. Hungry, as well."

He had forgotten that feeling. "Of course. Allow me to conjure something for you. What would you care for?"

"Hen eggs, roasted stone fruit and a large pitcher of clean water."

"Done." He opened his hand and spread his fingers, as if holding an invisible bowl. With one smooth movement, he drew his index finger across the open palm. A ribbon of red seeped from the slit.

Lyssy watched with a mix of fascination and disgust. Vimnir took his index finger and dabbed it in his weeping palm. His mouth moved wordlessly as the fingertip glowed faintly. In the air above, he drew a series of figures.

The blood in his palm coagulated and, within an eye blink, he was holding a silver tray, neatly laid out with a plate of eggs – both hard-boiled and runny-yolked, a bowl of toasted fruit over oats, a carafe of water and of what appeared to Lyssy to be milk.

He set it down gently on the end of her bed.

"Eat. I have matters to attend to today and will be preoccupied. Until then, I ask you please stay on this floor and do not wander. There is a sitting room of scrolls and tomes off the dining room. You may wish to utilise it."

He nodded at her and turned to leave. "Oh. And do take in the view today. It may be some time before we see the light of day again."

Lyssy, dragging the platter toward herself, stopped short, but he was gone before those words fully settled on her. She did hope he was joking – but in her heart, knew most certainly he was not.

Vimnir closed the door behind him.

Now that his niece was attended to, it was time to tend to the needs of his other family.

Down he went into the sub-chamber. The spiral staircase led down many flights, past halls of countless storehouses, cluttered work chambers, dishevelled bed chambers, rooms full of mining equipment, rusting armaments and mountains of books and ledgers. Too many rooms to deal with and none of particular relevance. Once he had cleared the castle of the living, he knew the most important step was done. There was, he knew, a magically fortified vault of great wealth somewhere deep within the mountain – but finding it, let alone opening it, was a task for another time.

Down, toward the bottom-most floors, sat a modest reception hall. It was heavily fortified; no windows, one door at either end. It made for the perfect summoning chamber. He knew, beneath him, thousands of new-ly-formed bodies thrashed and wailed and waited for his summoning. And he would summon them.

He stood in the centre of the hall within a large ring of dried blood. It stood out in streaks of black against the ash-grey slab. Vimnir bent down and ran a bony finger along the stain. Its thick crust cracked at his touch.

So much of his own blood had been spilled to bring him this far. It would be impossible to extend himself much further. He would need to feed. Then, with a great sacrifice, he would be able to perform flawlessly on his dark stage for none to see until he wanted them to.

"*Ge'horoahee*," he murmured. The dark, secret name. At once, a slash of red appeared at his feet, spreading toward the ring. Blackfire lit the space in beauteously wicked oily purple and gold. "Come forth, servant of my blood."

For a moment, he recalled the enormous bald-pate solider he had raised in Dormanstar. The larger subjects tended to make the best hosts. That one in particular was gloriously massive and unflinchingly violent. He felt him pass farther back south, in the raid and razing of the fishing village. A waste. Perhaps this one would fare better. He would form it purely from ritual blood this time.

The blackfire ring flared; the dry and cracked blood liquified once more as oily umber-black liquid began to spread towards his feet from the perimeter.

"Come."

And it did so; slowly pooled and congealed. It took shape, gathering blood and black bile into a mound; bones built themselves in long, thick columns as rotten tissue bound its way around ligaments and between ribs. A behemoth twice as tall as Vimnir, with twice as many faces on its enormous, miserable head.

"Dark one, I command thee now. You are my child and you will listen only to me."

"Mmmurr" It groaned, deep and guttural, like a foul wind rushing from a pitch abyss.

"Join your brethren. Together, you will bring to me six and sixty live captives. A portal will open. Bring them forth through it. Then, a feast we shall enjoy. Oh yes."

If the thing could laugh, a rolling burst would have rumbled out of its three mouths. Instead, only wordless moaning.

Vimnir drew up his gnarled, black staff, raising the crowning crimson gem into the air; it lit up like a candle.

With a vaporous whoosh, a ring of portal light formed in front of the behemoth. Vimnir twisted the staff slightly and the ring expanded dramatically in all directions. Before him, a pit of smoke and molten stone could be seen within. Stray embers caught in the vacuum pulled inward through the portal's barrier and flitted into nothingness. A chorus of screams took flight with them. A sea of dead and dying and pitiful living.

"A waste in life. And yet, in death…" Vimnir smiled. "Go. Bring them to me."

The beast turned slowly on heaving footfalls and passed through the portal's threshold. Vimnir stepped through behind it.

Even with his diminished sensations, the Necromant could feel the pressing heat on his face and exposed forearms. The underprison was a wholly unpleasant place. The cavernous expanse was carved in a time beyond reckoning for channelling natural heat up into the expansive network of dwarven towns, but Vimnir found another use for it.

Hundreds of hairy, unwashed faces were a shifting dune in a sea of strega. The dying lay where they once stood; the living barely stood at all.

Like a boulder splitting a river in two, Vimnir followed his newborn creation as it waded through his other children. The cacophony of inhuman voices subsided slightly, but only now to a slightly less deafening white noise.

Vimnir looked out at the gaunt faces and profusely sweating skin. Most were seated, legs bound by energetic bindings; some were clearly on their way out, laying helplessly in each other's laps or curled against each other. It was a pathetic sight, made worse by the rising stench of waste and filth that seemed to hover in a cloudless vapour just above them.

"These will suffice. Gather the living and bring them back – six and sixty, remember. No fewer."

The behemoth was joined by several others of similar dysmorphic physique and pliable disposition. The screaming began almost immediately. Vimnir turned and made his way up towards the lip of the cavern's upper path. The portal hummed quietly. He stepped back through, sensing but not really feeling the cool change in air temperature and pressure.

He wondered if his master would delight in his application of this ritual; certainly he had never known anything of the sort to be successfully performed. The blood cost was terrifically high, as was the physical sacrifice.

Vimnir opened a second portal; this one smaller. It led through to the entry hall. He would bring Lyssy to observe.

He stepped through, barely feeling the shift, and rapped on her door. She answered, now fully dressed and hair up in a dark knot above her slender face.

"Yes?"

"Come join me downstairs. I'd like you to witness something wonderful."

"Can I dress first? I've barely finished eating."

"No."

Lyssy nodded uneasily and wrapped her nightgown around herself. She was grateful that at least she had a proper meal in her stomach now. Sleep had not come smoothly to her last night, but her thoughts were clearing this morning. She followed him out and, at the threshold of the portal, observed the other side.

"Wait. Where are you taking me?"

Vimnir exhaled, frustrated at the interruption. "To the underkeep. No more questions. I must return and begin. Come."

Lyssy felt the disorientation of instantaneous transit flip her centre of gravity momentarily as she stepped through the threshold. Even after all these years, it never became easier – or felt any less unnatural.

She appeared on the other side. What she saw made her wish she'd never opened the door to her uncle.

At first glance, there had to be at least fifty dwarves – all of them clearly afflicted with illness or approaching death, only a few standing – huddled together in the centre of a large ring of flame as dark as the midnight sky. Men, women, children. Vimnir approached them confidently. On four sides of the ring stood horrific monstrosities of flesh and muscle and bone, nearly as tall as the ceiling. They stood motionless. None made a sound. The very air of the room hung heavy with misery and defeat. With a crackling burst, the portal dissolved behind her. She found that just as off-putting.

"This is not six and sixty," her uncle said flatly and approached one of the behemoths. "Were there no others?"

Vimnir frowned, cupping his narrow chin in his hand. His forehead crumpled like dry bark as he considered.

He tapped his staff twice on the stone slap. With the other hand, he parted his fingers and twisted his wrist. A thick, leather-bound book appeared in his upturned hand, causing his arm to sag with the weight.

He whispered a few words. The book opened on his command and the hand-inscribed sepia pages flipped with invisible swiftness. Scratchings and scrawlings, diagrams and drawings and dashed lines. Abruptly, toward the end of the tome, the flicking stopped.

Outwardly, Vimnir remained calm. He glanced behind him at his niece. She took a small step backwards, such was the force in those eyes.

Inwardly, he was a rolling storm. His master's words lay in front of him, spells so sacred and personal, surely they were unseen by any other eyes in all the history of this world. When he lost his master, he immolated him and took on his power. With that transference came buried knowledge, like a chartist's topography of new ideas. In his mind, he found a secret trove of wisdom that had never been there before. He felt the limits of his own mind expand in all directions and realised how limited, blunted, his thinking had been. No longer.

In those new thoughts, reclaimed memories, he also found a key – or rather, the path that had held this key along the while. It was hidden not in a box or under a stone – but within a chest. Not a chest of wood; a chest of flesh and bone. His master had absorbed it by some means, storing it within his body, and in doing so, left Vimnir a memory and a clue.

Within those glowing pyre ashes, Vimnir retrieved the key he knew he would find. With that key, he found the hidden room within the Necro-mantic palisade. And within that room, he found his future laid out before him. He took his master's staff and cloak of protection. He took the stone of teleportation. And he took the tome. The binding was wiry hair, boiled fat, wax and tanned leather that surely came from the same corpse. It was a dark and powerful weapon and one he knew held yet more secrets. His master's memories were his. He found quickly, so were his righteous desires for his people's supremacy.

Such victory would cost in blood and be repaid through rebirth.

He looked out at his conquered, feeding on their fear. He uttered a word and the tome hung in the air before him. With his hand free, he drew his reclaimed blackened dagger from the leather scabbard at his side and raised it high. With the other hand, he raised his staff. He touched one to the other and began the rite.

At once, the four behemoths started into the ring of captive dwarves, living boulders of pure punishment.

The screaming was immediately deafening. Lyssy's own screams rose in discordant harmony.

She felt her stomach come up as this horrific choir gave way to the wet, sloshing sounds of crushing and mutilation and utter decimation. The floor pooled and coated the legs of the behemoths in a thick wash of crimson, like a wine-maker's mash.

Lyssy found herself on her knees, one hand on the floor – the other clutching her mouth as she heaved. Her fingers touched warm liquid and, eyes closed, she hoped it was her own. She opened them and found her fingers submerged in the lifeblood of the dwarven sacrifices. She willed herself to look up, if only for a moment. The circle was long buried beneath a mangled mound of pulverised bodies, barely distinguishable from each other.

In front, back to her, Vimnir's staff and blade glowed. They seemed to be drawing up some kind of energy from the circle in front of him.

A single bloodshot eyeball lay in a spreading lake of red, looking sightlessly at her.

It was the last thing she would see as she lost consciousness.

Vimnir too was coated in red. It splashed him like warm sea foam with each stamp of his glorious creations. He felt the death energy begin to syphon towards his implements and knew the process was beginning. All other thoughts faded away as the ritual began. The pages of the book, protected by some means, remained unblemished – and Vimnir began to read each tract of the dark language, a derivation of his race's ancient tongue and a mongrel bastardisation of modern Solumbryan.

He began, as he understood it, to draw down the aspects of the Trine in confluence. He knew this was tied to the alignment of the world they lived within – because his master knew this. He knew also that Solum and Lunum were always in opposition in the skies above; the day would always turn to night, and the cycle would continue forever.

There was, of course, a third aspect of the Trine: Nulum – and it was through Nulum that he would upend the balance in his favour. He would draw on the great void that lay out in the vast infinity and pull power from it, redirecting it, redirecting the alignment of the planet.

Vimnir's hands vibrated; he could feel the intense pressure of the constant beam of energy channelling into the staff and dagger.

The next line he spoke more emphatically; the rhythmic cadence of his master's words was carefully constructed prose, designed to raise the energy in the chamber itself. He could sense the air begin to warm, charged with latent magical plasma. So much death! So much potential. It excited him, enticed him – but he needed to remain calm.

The next step was more complicated.

Here, with some effort, he parted the dagger from the staff. The staff's gem was fully imbued now. He took a step forward, and another, until he reached the crush of dead. Toward each of his four beautiful creations, he angled the gem and began their unmaking. He watched his creations moan in surprise and confusion as their legs disintegrated, then their bloated bodies in tow, down into the sludgy black fluid of their birth. Vimnir felt nothing for the dwarves. They were barely worth remarking. But his heart went out to his babies. Each was a small piece of him and they knew now the death he would never know.

Vimnir pointed the dagger toward the pages of the tome. The tip pressed into a carefully inscribed diagram of the Trine in confluence. As he raised it back up off the paper, he drew from it a strand of golden light, as fine as silk, but radiant as the Solum itself. He felt its brilliance scald his hand and redden his face. *I must make this quick.*

With a flick, the beam of pure light darted from the dagger's tip toward the sacrificial crush. At once, the air pressure in the room gave way to a suction of tremendous force. Where the mount of bodies lay, an abyss had formed. The bodies, what few remained intact, were dragged into the black pit. Within, Vimnir could see specks of light. He felt the blood rushing around his feet towards the open vacuum.

Then, something else collided with his legs: his niece.

Lyssy curled around his legs, limply. The distraction threw him; the beam from the dagger wavered. He steeled himself. Her thin body's pressure against him was yet another distraction to contend with, but she would have to wait. He could hold her back with his planted feet for now.

The beam steadied. The Necromant swirled his staff, reading the next line of the tome, just below the diagram. The beam swirled with his movement. Within the abyssal void, the very perspective seemed to shift. What was once a night sky now looked down upon green earth and blue sea.

Such a vantage, he realised. *This, this is what I stand to gain. All of this.*

Wordlessly, the page turned. The final stage was beginning.

The swirling staff exuded another beam now, entwined with that of the golden light of the dagger. This one, however, was cold and severe and silvery as fish scales. The beams twisted like ivy, bending and pulling downward together, over the edge of the void and into the space beyond.

Within, he could see a perfect sphere of his sacrificial chosen's spent lives. An orb of offering, as demanded by the text. He considered that sacrifice – comprising not the six and sixty his master's words and thoughts demanded—a mere thirty or so, and dwarven, not full-blooded elves. He had come this far being resourceful; he would adapt as needed.

Once more, Vimnir read aloud an extract. These words, the darkest of them all, formed the curse of shade. It called upon the Nulum, the void between all things, the swirling mass that sat at the edge of their existence.

The sphere of entrails and blood spun in place, slowly at first, then gradually more rapidly.

Exposed once again, the ritual ring of black fire at the heart of the chamber took flame once more. This time, those indigo tongues joined the strands of gold and silver. Three energies danced as one, down into the open abyss high above the world.

If one were to look up at the sky at the moment, it would appear as though a black star had formed, crowned in purple and gold. It was growing, rapidly. Spreading across the sky in a translucent haze.

Now, Vimnir realised. *Now is my moment.* His sensations were alive – a most unexpected reaction. He was still most assuredly undead, but his body felt somehow different. Potent and sensorial.

To his shock, the pages in front of him began to ignite. A dot of heat spread as those few pages, and those alone, sizzled and charred in a swipe of blue flame and were gone. Vimnir's eyes widened. The rest of his master's writings remained, but the rite had unmade itself.

Vimnir snarled in disbelief. Was this some kind of trick? Had his master intended for that to happen, or did Vimir himself trigger it somehow? There was no time to consider it deeply. He was so close.

He brought together the dagger and staff; he ignored the roar of burning flesh and ice of etheric cold. He wrenched the two beams of Solum and Lunum away as a fisherman might pull their catch from the water's embrace, leaving only the channelling of pure Nulum from the chamber.

And then he felt it. A sting in his side.

Lyssy.

"Monster!" she shrieked.

Distracted, utterly absorbed in the rite, Vimnir had not realised she had regained consciousness.

He recoiled; the beams flickered and broke apart.

"No!" he screamed. "What did you *do?*" He pulled the table knife from between his ribs. The sensation was dull and distant once more. That fleeting, tantalising moment of life had gone.

"You fool! My own blood! Betrayer!"

She withdrew the blade and buried it again before losing her grip. He shoved her backwards with his staff; she slid along the blood-slick floor. With a grunt, he pulled the blade loose from his side and let it fall. It had been quite some time since he had felt such a powerful sensation – but the interruption sent his focus adrift. His vitality was escaping him after so brief a moment.

He jerked his head back around; the abyss remained open. Purple flames funnelled towards the mass on the other side – but something was wrong. The growth had slowed considerably.

More! It's not enough! The words slapped his mind to full focus. The wound was nothing. His betrayer niece was nothing. All that mattered was the rite. And the rite demanded more, he could sense. He must restore it. He hoped it would be enough.

Lyssy.

What she had undone, she would make right. Blood of the elfkin; potent magically and the one thing unquestionably missing from his ritual.

He twisted his arm toward her, the staff's energy pulling her back toward him, lifting her up off the floor. Tears streaked clean lines down her blood-stained cheeks as she thrashed against him, against the endless pull of the open abyss.

He directed her gliding form past him. With his ceremonial dagger out-stretched, Vimnir directed the finely-honed edge to her neck and pushed. He opened her from earlobe to earlobe. Blood streamed out of her in pump-ing gushes as he guided her over the abyss.

Vimnir looked into those quivering saucer-eyes. The eyes of elves; another of their kind lost to the world for all time.

"You were a vessel of the blood of the first elves! I would have ruled this world with you." He shouted. "If only you would have trusted me. If only."

She hung there, a blood-soaked Queen of nothing. In Lyssy's mind, she thought of her babies. Her lips moved; blood gurgled.

"I…*curse y-you.*"

Vimnir roared and broke his hold.

Below, swirling above the curve of the world, Vimnir's creation – his gift – rippled violently in reaction as Lyssy Delcryth Fendrigar passed into the dusklight and was gone.

Chapter 27

INTO THE DUSKLIGHT

High Inquisitor Boff Fendrigar struggled to move under his own weight even when he was alive. Now they discovered a large and inert dead man was no easy thing to shift either. However, even with other pressing matters, it did not seem right to leave the man to decompose in his quarters. Tyel volunteered to help Gehard shift his father downstairs to the cool of the infirmary ahead of what would be a most spectacular burning, Gehard promised. Certainly, a part of Tyel looked forward to his eventual immolation and erasure from this world.

Eventually, they shifted him onto a carpet. With Isidyr, Brea and even Dusty taking a corner of the carpet, Fendrigar's rotund form was pulled, step by awkward step, down into the foyer. Alyse watched wordlessly, a crust of dried blood formed beneath her nose from the magical exertion of the morning.

It was here that guard Tildor Gefrey, sent away to retrieve a trough of soup and a cob of bread, came upon them. "What— *what*—" Out of a sense of duty, if not personal preference, Tildor scrambled for his short sword.

The silver tray tumbled from his hands and joined his High Inquisitor on the floor of the hall.

"His Grace has passed." Omanon gently set down his corner of carpet, now soaked in red. "Who's posted t' House security this day?"

Tildor's jaw hung agape. The young man did not relinquish his grasp of the pommel. At first, he did not respond – his eyes were fixed on the oozing corpse that until so recently had him in a very compromised position.

"Gefrey!" Gehard snapped. "Answer the Quartermaster."

His stammering reply was interrupted by the deep, rounded tolling of a bell and muffled shouting from down in the courtyard.

"That's a general alarm," Omanon grunted. "They've broken through. Gefrey, find three – *four* – able arms. Bring his Grace to the cool cellar to await anointing. Go."

The soldier nodded, slipping slightly in the puddle of spilled broth, before turning and darting back toward the direction of the mess hall.

"As for the rest o' yeh," he continued, "take arms an' join me – or watch as this city's overrun. You, Dusty – you want access to crafting materials and the-like?"

"Aye," The dwarf nodded.

"Follow the soldier, through the staff quarters and down the spiral steps at the end of the hall yon. There y'll find the apothecary's storehouse. Use this key."

Omanon dug around in his trouser pocket and pulled a ring of skeleton keys. He slid them around and retrieved a small silver one. He unclipped it and handed it to the dwarf. "Take what ye' need, and make full use of it."

"Solsetter, I know y'r face. I couldnae place it before, but now…" He shook his head. "You're a thief and killer. I've seen th' bounty."

She scoffed. "You have me confused with someone else – or someone who cares what your one old eye might see, for that matter."

"No. I know who y'are." He levelled a calloused finger at her. "Fight with us today and I'll do what I can to clear y'r name."

She looked at him with cold eyes. "I've done my share of fighting this turn of the Lunum. You have your Championate – and Alyse is a weapon herself. Even Branson can hold his own." She folded her arms and turned. "I make no promises. Alyse, Tyel – look after each other. Don't rely on an agent of the Magisterium to protect you. That's my advice. Do with it what you will."

Alyse exchanged glances with her Championate.

"Be well," the elfkin replied. "And if you're heading south, perhaps we'll cross paths again."

The dwarf nodded in agreement. "Aye. Tyel, keep your wits about you and your shield raised. And Alyse, I hope you, well – I hope your people can bring some order to this broken place."

Brea took a breath, smiled, bowed gracefully. "If fate deems it, the Capital will stand strong. But while the Necromant lives, our mission remains unfulfilled. This is not our battle to fight – so we won't. Or, I won't anyway. Dusty, let's go."

Tyel watched his travelling companions leave. Their footsteps clapped a staccato rhythm on the tiles between the tolling bell.

Omanon dipped his head and looked at the four remaining in the foyer. "Luminary Gehard. With the passing of y'r father and sister, and y'r mother's whereabouts unknown, the mantle of High Inquisitor falls to yeh."

"I'm well aware."

"Aye. Then you'll know that, even without the ceremony, your charge is immediate. This city needs y'r leadership. The people must see yeh on the field of battle—"

"Are you mad? I'm not entering the fray. If I pass, the line of succession ends!"

"W'out leadership, your people will falter," Omanon pleaded. "Y'must see them on the streets. Much longer, and we'll need t' resort to conscription. We don' have the numbers. They don't even have a Knight Commander n'more. You *must* rally your soldiers."

Gehard's expression soured.

"I see. Fine."

"Then my first order of duty? I hereby appoint you, Omanon, Knight Commander of the Anointed Protectorate, beneath the radiant Solum, from this hour to your final."

"Your Grace, I cannot accept this post."

"Oh, hells to that. You *will* – you have long years of experience. The soldiers know you. It is my decree, witnessed, and it is done."

Omanon's one good eye squinted, his lined face tightening. "So be it," he frowned. "Ever I am at the service of the High Inquisitor, your Grace."

"Indeed." Gehard crouched beside his father. "Now go, Knight Commander. Serve the realm. Leave me to mourn."

"At once. Come Tyel, Alyse – and Isidyr, if yeh be true to y'r word, protect the vassal and defend this city. We'll group up with the Battleblessed in th' yard and take back our streets."

~ ~ ~

The bell continued to sound, pulled by anonymous hands from the top of the outpost tower on the perimeter wall.

The Courtyard was afire under the brilliance of the Solum. To Tyel, it reminded him of the morning the vanguard rode out and north. How long ago that seemed to him now. How naively simple he believed their ride would be; astride his beautiful horse, armed and leathered and tense with excitement. His father would surely make him work off the loss of his horse.

His father. His brother. His mother. He felt a twist of guilt at not being there with them now. He wondered if his letter made it – if it even left the Capital at all. He supposed he wouldn't know until he asked them himself. He only hoped they did not fear his death among the rising chaos. He pushed the thought away. He would return home soon – perhaps with Alyse in tow.

"There they be." Omanon crossed the yard in great strides. There, at the gate, stood five figures of varying size and age – two women of elder-age, two men of roughly average build and thinning hair – they might be brothers, Tyel thought – and a figure of indeterminate origin and gender. To Tyel's eyes, it looked for all the world like a figure hewn from quarry stone and stacked by careful hands into human form.

"*These* are the Battleblessed?" Tyel questioned.

"Don' sound so surprised," Omanon replied. "Appearances deceive, y'know."

Tyel couldn't argue with that logic.

Omanon walked to a portly old woman on the left of the gathering. Her garb was simple grey-green cloth of the sort a washerwoman might wear. Her curly greying hair was tied back with a strip of beige material. From how she presented, Tyel would think she was a washerwoman, fresh from the High Inquisitor's keep. In fact, he was almost certain he'd seen her face before.

"One Eye!" She embraced the old man warmly.

"Dot!" He returned her embrace. "Y'look well."

"You look old as dried sheep shit," she barked, but there was affection in her tone – warm and grandmotherly.

"Wait," Tyel leaned forward. "Don't you work in the chambers?"

The woman laughed. "Of course. We all do. Omanon, who is this impetuous young sprout?"

Omanon clapped Tyel on the shoulder. "Tyel Branson, this is Dorothea of The Weir."

Tyel didn't know exactly what that meant, but it certainly sounded significant. He extended his hand. Dot shook it firmly, which surprised him.

"Dot runs the kitchen, aye. But she's also Battleblessed – a veteran manipulator of blessed techniques. So watch y'r tongue."

"Oh, don't give the boy a hard time, One Eye. He meant no offence."

"Nice meet you, Dorothea," Tyel smiled through his bewilderment.

"And these are my companions." Dot nodded to another silver-haired woman. "Librarian Jene Porl—" Tyel extended his hand once again, "This is Blessed Edwain Endicott, Solum Priest and Conjurer, and his brother, Reginald Endicott. Reggie is a Publican." The two ageing men took Tyel's hand.

"Commit your sins at the watering house, then cleanse them at the temple. It's a syndicate," Endicott laughed. "Keeps us both in business."

At last, they came upon the stone man. Dot placed her age-speckled hand upon the motionless chest of her great boulder-born counterpart. "And this is my Construct. It has no name. But it has bloody huge fists."

Omanon laughed heartily. "Aye, plain enough to see. You still have plenty of sting in your barb, Dot."

"Age is as much a construct as the stone man here, and I'm not dead yet," she replied wryly. "We're the Battleblessed; the finest subversive agents alive. That's no exaggeration, lad." She winked at Tyel.

Coyly, Alyse watched this curious interplay. It was amusing watching a man with the composition of boiled leather soften up in front of this woman. She wondered just how intimately they knew each other from years past. She sensed more than simple friendship – not that she needed to read deeply to sense this.

However, there was something else she was sensing – strongly. While the doorway between her mind and the Necromant's was closed firmly, she felt the connection was not cleanly severed. Something – something very far away from them, but unmistakably *powerful* – was happening. She could feel his prying fingers tugging at the energetic fabric around them. A small but persistent pull, like a weight at the hem of her skirt.

"Tyel," she started. "I feel strange."

Dot's lined mouth dropped. "What is it, lass?"

"Alyse?" Tyel approached her. Isidyr stood motionless, watching her expression closely with a look of concern that matched it.

"Something's happening." Alyse's eyes guided their line of sight skyward. "Look."

High up, barely distinguishable at first, a speck was forming in front of the Solum, like a small ship far out on the sea's horizon. But that spec was growing. The light had begun to take on a queer quality. Their short-falling shadows seemed to disperse as the azure sky darkened in a haze of purple-green. High above them, the Solum was becoming noticeably obscured, as if smudged by a painter's brush.

"That's— that's a—," Tyel pointed, squinting. "There's a *portal* up there – something is coming out of it. I can just see it.

"I don' like the look o' that." Omanon's words reflected their shared thoughts.

"It's the Necromant. I know it is." Alyse stared into the rapidly darkening orb in the sky. No one doubted this to be the case.

"By now, you've all come to hear that a Necromant is feeding the constant army of strega," The Sacred Championate spoke, taking his eyes off the sky. The Battleblessed nodded wordlessly, nearly in unison. "It is, of course, true. But so far, their progress has been hampered by Solum. They cannot travel effectively in the light of day."

Alyse finished his thought. "The Necromant means to change this."

"She's right. I've never seen anything quite like it before." The Championate looked once more at the sky. What had begun as a dark sphere, perhaps the size of a green pea held out at arm's length was growing rapidly. "This is dark spellcraft – of the most literal sort. He means to block out the light. This is – well, I've no word for this."

Tyel's heart pounded. "If this happens—"

"It's *already* happening, lad," Librarian Porl replied curtly.

"If he *succeeds*, I mean," Tyel remained transfixed on the darkening sky, "The strega in the Capital will be free to run rampant in the streets. We'll be inundated."

The darkening effect was spreading across the expanse of blue, like an upturned bowl of smoky amethyst. Somewhere, a hound was yelping and yowling. A soft and oddly alluring scent of wood smoke drifted in from beyond the walls. The Championate frowned. His recent immolation had left him with no strong desire to return to the streets of a burning town. Yet, he knew, if the capital was to stand, they could not afford further deliberation.

"Can we discuss the finer points of Necromantic battle strategy as we move, if you please?" Isidyr gestured toward the gate. "People are dying as we stand here making pleasantries."

"The tall man speaks true," Dot nodded.

"He does. Then, let's divide up," Jene agreed. The woman clutched a small, heavily edge-worn book to her chest. "Though, admittedly I am more inclined to cast from the safety of distance."

"Nowhere is safe, Jene. Not now. We'll have to do what we can. The stone man and I will fend north and press back the brunt of the new risers. Jene Porl, why don't you and the brothers Endicott take East Gate? West is mostly industrial – few homesteads, few bodies to protect."

"We'll keep you safe, my dear," Reginald bowed stiffly. "Through Solum's grace or my own."

The publican raised his hand above his head. Within the grasp of his gloved fingers materialised a long, thin blade of blue-green energy. He gave it a little swirling flourish. It transformed into a broadaxe. He lowered it carefully in front of the librarian, and, with a nod, the energetic weapon transformed into a broad, semi-circular shield. Once more, he twisted his hand and the shield disintegrated completely.

Tyel couldn't contain his grin, to Omanon's amusement. He clapped the young man on the shoulder once more. "Yeh like that? That's nothin'."

"And what of these two?" Dot indicated toward Alyse and Tyel.

"Hm. Isidyr, why don' yeh take Alyse and Tyel south, then? The lass made mention of a ship 'parrently inbound. The dockyards are much the same as West Gate, all told."

"But I can fight!" Tyel protested. "I can be of service." He was struck by Omanon's seeming disregard for his ability to hold his own so far. Then, part of him longed to find a space safe enough to rest and recover. His body continued to push itself farther and harder than he had ever expected, but he knew once he stopped to rest, pain would settle in.

"I know yeh can, lad. And that's why I want yeh and the big man to protect her Grace 'ere. If it's true her blood is a-comin' our way, I want her safe as can be."

"Her *Grace*? What did I miss?" Dot blinked.

"Alyse is a princess of House Elsteme. A vassal – but no longer. Now, please – time escapes us rapidly."

Dot smiled at the elfkin. "A princess. I can see it in your face. I know your grandmother, you know. But it's a story for another time. Agreed, big man. Time we move. And what 'bout you, old salt?"

"Front lines. I'll join yeh, Dot."

She smiled. "Course you will. Come on then. North we go. And if we should survive, we will raid my kitchens and drink this great house dry."

~ ~ ~

The void swirled like the eye of a colossal storm, cracking with lilac forks of energy. Vimnir wiped a thin smear of blood from his brow. If his master could see this, would he be pleased? He would never know. He licked the edge of his palm, tasting Lyssy's essence. A curling ripple of anger swirled in him.

All he needed was for the Dusklight spell to hold long enough to bring down Fendrigar's city. Deep inside, he worried that it would fail. He knew he'd bastardised the spell – he only had dwarven blood to sacrifice, and too few from whom to draw it. Lyssy's contribution may have made the difference – such was the potent energy in her lineage.

Why, Lyssy? Why couldn't you see? Her fool husband had made her weak and doubtful and morose. He ran a hand down his side where she had planted the knife. The wound no longer seeped, nor did his side ache, but he took that to mean he'd lost that small and tantalising taste of soul restoration. This was frustrating. It was something to address later. For now, he needed to guide his army with a considered hand.

He withdrew from the portal's edge. His master's spellbook snapped shut in the air before him and, with a wave of his dagger, disincorporated back into the safety of his private stowage.

Blood-streaked and tense, he turned his thoughts to the girl – Alyse of House Elsteme. She had much to answer for. Her self-righteous assertiveness, her meddling against her own kind; another graceless, visionless elf. Her little protectorate rallied behind her, driving a wedge into his plans. Why could they not appreciate the superiority of their kind? Blood spilled in sacrifice was ultimately blood that would be replaced and reborn by generations of elves to come.

Perhaps he could make the girl see. *Yes,* Vimnir considered as he stared at the stone floor where the miasmic void had been. The pavers were slick, but free of dwarven befoulment. *She has a royal bloodline – not immediate to mine-own, but Elsteme nonetheless.* The solution was beginning to solidify in his mind.

Alyse, the vassal. Alyse, the vessel. She manifested his subtle thoughts and actions for a time. With help from the pretentious and profligate Magisterium, she had cast aside this most convenient intrusion – but traces of her remained, like a faint and passing aroma of perfume in the still air.

He needed a more direct means of communication. She was in the capital by now, surely – and that was precisely where he was going now.

A portal would take him to the footsteps of the Capital. He would need escorts, of course, but now with the dusklight, he would have the freedom to walk straight through the gates. From there – well, a show of might, followed by a ruler's mercy, might quell the resistance. Vimnir smiled, drew up his staff and raised a gateway.

~ ~ ~

Dusty and Brea passed without incident through the inner chambers, working across long stretches of finely appointed walls and countless sitting rooms, bedchambers and kitchens. They heard the infirmary before they could see it. Even then, a trail of bile and coppery blood led them down the corridor as the stench met their noses before their eyes saw the carnage.

The infirmary was enormous and full to overflowing. Beneath the vaulted ceilings were scores of beds and platforms – all of them filled with the dead and dying. Most – though not nearly all – were uniformed men. A scant few dedicated and extremely tired-looking medicinal healers darted from point to point, carrying baskets of tinctures, phials of fluids, poultices and wraps. A sole conjurer far at the back was administering some energetic rite, bathing the corner of the room in white radiance.

"If you're not here to help, get out of the way," came a small and anxious voice from behind them. Soft-footed, a young woman of no more than eighteen years pushed past them and into the infirmary. Her arms were crusted in dried blood and she turned her head for a moment, revealing dark lines beneath her auburn eyes. To Brea, she looked vaguely familiar but there seemed no reason for her to be.

Dusty felt a tinge of guilt; he knew the dead and dying in the halls were beyond help.

"Girl." Dusty raised a hand, pulling her aside. "Listen. You cannot help these people. If you wish to survive yourself, do not tarry here."

For a moment, the woman's face, brow dirtied and furled, betrayed a sense of agreement.

"I— I want to help." But she turned and was gone, and with her, the thought. Dusty watched with pity as the young woman worked her way around moaning, outreached hands, grasping at her for want of any kind of respite.

In truth, Dusty thought he might be able to stem the infections, but without time and precision, it would be dangerous – if not hopeless – to attempt.

"Come on, Dusty. There's the storehouse. Far end." Her voice was as low and tense as her posture. A nurse emerged from the simple wooden door. Even at this distance, Brea could see shelves stacked high with supplies.

"I'll take your word for it. I can barely see over the tables."

Brea barked a laugh. "Come on, Shorty."

To their left, they passed a soldier slumped with his back against a wall. He sat bleeding from a deep cut across his forehead and a gouge on his cheek. The thin spun-weave bandage did little to stem the flow. Only in looking back did Dusty see he was missing an ear.

Another and another and another – soldiers in various states of undoing. A young man shared a space next to an old woman. He was holding her round, pudgy face in his lap and weeping.

The sour odour of death saturated the air. Brea held her breath, eyeing an open window along the far-right wall.

"Did it suddenly get darker?" She muttered to the dwarf, stepping over bundles of soiled garments and discarded armour.

Dusty's vision was terribly average, of course, but even in the well-lit infirmary, the outside light took on a strange quality. "Maybe there's a storm building," he suggested, but then, as he said it, the words felt immediately wrong. Something felt off.

They came upon the door and, ignoring the eyes on them, simply opened it and stepped through. The space was lined with two dozen shelves staggered toward the back of the stone-walled room. The only light source came from thin sconces to the right, between the rows.

It *was* getting dark out, he realised. It was midday, with fine weather – yet he could hardly see a thing. He squinted and began to parse the jars and boxes as best he could.

From here, they would make for the South Gate and see if they could find the Necromant once more, then, with luck, finish the job they had begun. Brea leaned, head down and arms folded, against the door, holding it closed behind them. "Hurry up and get what you need. Or – what I need, as is more the case, dwarf."

He nodded, adjusted his lenses, and began to fill his satchel.

~ ~ ~

The stone Construct raised its fist and brought it down like a sledge. The strega dodged with unnatural reactive swiftness – right into the Construct's open fist. It collided with the strega's skull, wrapping a glove of stony fingers around the top of its head. With a squelching crunch, the strega's brain was pressed through a stony grate of digits like a sieve.

Dorothea's outstretched arms extracted the earth in great spikes as thick as tree trunks from the cobblestone street leading toward the great Solum Temple. The North was a mess, she could see. The streets were overrun with blood vermin – the likes of which she had not seen in a great age. The sky was a dark bowl above her, casting hues of a sickly shade of green and umber over all things. Looming down, the crest of the golden circuitris crowned the top of the Temple, in defiance of the Dusklight's gloom.

She wiped a few warm dots of entrail from her face and pressed forward. The streets were chaotic. Omanon had ignited his circuitris to devastating result. The old man surged forward like a ship's prow through choppy seas, using the radiant arc of energy the ring emanated to cut a swath through the skittering, writhing monsters. The strega never knew what hit them, but they certainly felt it. Arms and torsos burst into sacred flame. Skin charred like pork fat as the creatures darted, on hand and foot, for any cover they could secure.

She feared she could not keep this up for long, however. They needed horses and a legion of trained spearmen. Ground combat was proving relentless and only a height advantage and some distance-weapons might press them back.

Dot had, in her younger years, defended the city against a comparatively minor strega outbreak. Those days, under the rule of the late High Inquisitor Ahran Fendrigar, the Battleblessed had been formed to undertake such tasks with precision, in coordination with the Knight Commander and legions of soldiers and conscripts.

But long generations had passed – and with her accumulated years, things were certainly no easier. She felt her energy diminishing more rapidly, though her spells were certainly more potent. Her mastery of bilocation meant raising her Construct had been no major feat, but keeping it functioning and focussed – while doing the same for herself – was exhausting mentally.

As if reading her mental cues, Omanon turned to her. "I can hear our soldiers ahead. Dot, we need t'link up with the front line," Omanon shouted over his shoulder. "But not on foot. The stables are back behind. We need to form up on mounts and press them back at height."

She nodded vigorously and began their retreat. She just hoped they were not already routed by other foes in the side streets and lanes.

~ ~ ~

The portal fizzled shut with a hiss of electrified atmosphere. Vimnir Delcryth pulled his hood back, took a lifeless breath and looked up at the dusklight void filling the sky. It was a decidedly odd sensation of being outdoors in this artificial twilight. His skin could feel little – certainly no warmth – but the minute hairs on his forearm caught in the light breeze.

Before him, the rise of the road, broad and compacted by the wheels of countless carts and bootsoles, led toward what he knew to be the Northern Gate of the Capital.

Either side, farmsteads now stood on land that, only a generation ago, was densely grown woodland and underbrush. The human population crept its wandering fingers across Solumbrya, clawing away at ever more land for harvest and beast. Each new farm was a wasteful blight. The dead had no need for foodstores and harvest, of course. He would see the land recovered in time.

Coursing through the valley to his right, the Marshtide churned and pumped into the Capital, delivering his spawn. His seer-lens had shown him the remarkable progress his legion had made – even under the burning rays of Solum. Now, without that oppressive flame, he would rally them forth and take the throne room for his own.

With a wave of his staff, he sent up a signal; a howling crimson flare of exceeding radiance. It cut through the dusklight's gloom as it sailed high into the sky. He did not need to hone his senses to know any beast under his control would come to his side now.

It would be seen by all and understood by none, he knew – none that breathed, at any rate. It would, however, disrupt the combat for the moment and, to those poor souls fighting against him, it would bring momentary respite.

He could feel his disparate army of strega moving toward him – down streets, up from the river's edge, between the strands of tree trunks.

He took his first few steps forward and up, his staff tapping a rhythm as he walked.

Already, he could hear the delightful fracas – a clashing of blade and dull, distant screaming – indiscriminate as the birds in the trees. He could hear something else now, too: the clop-clop of horse's hooves. He spied the mounted soldiers departing the gateway, beneath an iron portcullis. There was no drawbridge, however. The South Gate, he knew, had such a deterrent.

Twelve men in heavy armour were on him quite immediately, circling him with drawn swords and halberds.

Vimnir raised his bony arms above his head.

"Please. I am but an old man. Please!" His mind's voice was a wailing cackle. Outside, he was elderly and stone-faced.

A grim and dirty face peered at him through a slotted face guard.

"He lies. We seen what yeh done jus' now. Y'r a wizard o' some kind. Throw y'r staff, or I'll have yeh head."

"Let's start with yours," Vimnir replied, tilting the crystalline head of his staff toward the mounted soldier. With a bolt of amber light, faster than any fletched arrow, the soldier's head rolled one way, his body collapsed the other, spilling sideways out of his saddle. He didn't even have time to scream.

"Do not corner a cut serpent. Make no threats against me."

The men reeled around him, steading their shrieking, whinnying horses.

"Kill him!" Another shouted, and a bladed polearm came toward him. The Necromant swished it aside as if it were nothing more than a blowfly.

"Oh, enough." Vimnir spat back. "My patience is thinning."

Another rider came along his side. He removed the horse's legs from beneath it. Four pillars of blood erupted from the muscular stumps as the beast's momentum spilled both it and the soldier onto the ground. The pumping blood coated the hard earth in a fan.

Not one to waste material, Vimnir raised his staff once more and began to collect the vital fluid in a sphere of mottled crimson and ruby and off-white. With his free hand, he pulled at the space above the horse, which now lay twitching pathetically. The soldier's neck twisted violently to the left and, with a sharp snap, he too lay still.

"No more. None here can slow me. Cease and save your pitiable lives." Vimnir's outstretched hand closed in on itself and he raised his balled fist into the air. His eyes were locked on the body of the horse and its departed rider.

He needed one more.

"Wait. Who among you is the strongest?" He looked at the circled horses and wide-eyed soldiers. None spoke. None dared to make another move against him.

"You killed 'im," came a wavering voice. "He was our Squad Leader."

Vimnir smiled. "Shame. And who are you, boy?"

"No one, ser."

"That's right. And do you wish to live?"

"Y-yes ser."

"You are a wise boy. A good and wise one, aren't you?" He took a small step forward, a sphere of blood spinning just above his head.

"Go and ride into town. Find your Knight Commander. Tell him to stand his men down and I will redeem the Capital. Go. Now. Do not look back and do not stop and do not speak to any other."

The young soldier kicked his spurs into the sides of his mount and spun his horse around. He was gone in a flurry of dust plumes bursting from the surface of the road.

Six other soldiers, weapons still drawn, cantered anxiously.

The pool of blood was nearly all coagulated in the Necromant's sphere now. He would need more blood – and more limbs.

"Now, as for the rest of you. Just one more of your rank must die today. I'll leave it to you to decide who."

He strolled smoothly toward the side of the road and began to raise the horse and its rider. The sphere of blood glided silently toward the horse; thin tendrils of the swirling muck began to draw away and into the corpse.

The soldiers eyed each other nervously. Swords, once pointed at the Necromant, slowly levelled toward each other.

Vimnir gesticulated toward them. "You may begin."

CHAPTER 28

INUNDATION

So much had happened, and so quickly. Dilain and his father had set out to find Tyel before becoming waylaid by a conflict that seemed to erupt from all directions, all at once. The letter indicated his brother had been waylaid by the Anointed Protectorate, which was odd in itself – but more than that, the nature of what they were hearing on The Eastern Road out of County Keep was disturbing. Strange stories and pale faces told of monsters rising from the rivers and overrunning villages from the north to the south. Trade was being severed – and now, there was word of massive conscription – Tyel was among the recruits.

"Your brother is no fighter, Dil," Dain spoke softly as the wheels clacked over the sporadic cobbles of the Eastern Road. "He's a Branson. He's tough enough, but he knows nothing of battle. You're both children of peace time. I'd like it much and more if that peace held."

Dil just wanted his best friend back. He'd been gone more than a week and that was long enough. The letter did not reassure them. Now, as stories reached their ears, it was imperative they retrieve him.

They arrived in the Capital late in the evening. Guards greeted them with drawn blades. His father showed the gate guard Tyel's letter, but the young man stationed at the gates couldn't read so well. Dilain was at once grateful for the small amount of education his mother had given him. He was no writer of fanciful manuscripts, but at least he and his brother could read and write in the common language of the Solumbryan lands.

After some convincing, they were allowed to pass. It was full-dark beneath a cloudy sky. Dil's eyes adjusted to the low lamplight. Their glow attracted gold-wing moths which, under ordinary circumstances, made for great collecting, he thought.

Rows of thin terraces led on a gentle incline toward the centre of the city. The streets buzzed with unease. Almost as soon as they made their way to the main square, things began to fall apart. There seemed far too many residents milling around, for a start. He could see families packing possessions into their own small carriages, which, Dilain figured, was likely not a good sign.

Another boy about his age was carting his baby sister into a push-pram. The girl was fussing, teary-eyed. Dil tugged his father's sleeve.

Their packhorse whinnied.

"What's going on?" he asked his father. Dain only shook his head and flicked the reins as their cart wheels clattered down the road. The Capital citadel was a black obelisk rising above the rooftops at the end of the long central street. A great defensive wall was lit with pin-pricks of torchlight as guards hurried here and there.

"Is Tyel in there, Papa?"

"If he is, I'm starting to think he may be safer than out here."

As if tempting fate, his sentence was punctuated with a chilling yelp behind them some distance back.

"Something is very off tonight, lad," Dain turned to his son. "We need to find your brother and plead our need to his Commander. I don't wish to stay in town. We'll make our camp off the Easterling and mayhap Tyel can tell us his tale."

"Okay, Papa," Dilain frowned.

This disappointed him some, as he'd rarely stayed away from home overnight before – and he heard that the Capital had many incredible sights, vendors, playhouses and gardens. He'd been quite looking forward to the morning sun and the chance to play with the local kids. Maybe he'd buy some sweets to take home.

Of course, Dilain knew nothing would happen with his father by his side. Dain was dependable and tough as the ancient white stone wall that surrounded the Capital. Even so, he could see his father's concern plainly enough. Time had made Father a cautious person – particularly after losing his sister. Perhaps he was different when he and his mother were younger.

Dilain was trying to picture his father as a boy, and his mother just a lass, when the attack came.

The very road beneath them gave way as a recessed sewer grate, as large as the spoked wheel of their cart, was pulled downward, ripped from the stone surface. There was no time to react. Their packhorse spilled into the chasm of stone and soil. Dain grasped at his son's chest, holding him in his seat as the cart was wrenched forward and down. The horse connected with something far below in a horrific squeal of pain and surprise – then it went silent. At the same time, his father spilled forward over the toe board. He was saved by the leather straps of the reins. The cart hung, lopsided, front wheels dangling.

"Dil!" His father shouted, desperately trying to pull himself back upward over the front lip of the carriage. Dilain scrambled for his clutch and pulled with as much force as his scrawny arms could muster. Dain's feet found a brief hold against the rim of the wheel – just long enough to push against as it spun.

Dain could see down into the sewer at that moment, but though his eyes could see, his mind did not understand what it was seeing. In the blackness, bodies writhed and piled onto their horse. A tangle of limbs. There were other things, too – enormous, too large to be human. But by then, his father was crawling past him, pulling his arm.

"Go!" He screamed. They did. The timbers of the cart's frame were creaking and snapping under the pull of whatever was down in the sewers.

They spilled over the side, onto hard stone, and together they scrambled toward the sidewalk.

Their cart splintered and split and, in a blink, it was gone into the chasm that had opened.

"Dil! Are you hurt?" HIs father didn't wait for a reply – but spun him around, half embracing, half inspecting.

"I'm okay." His shoulder felt a bit wrenched, but the sensation barely registered.

The sound of sloshing and moaning rose from the pit – as did something else. An enormous forearm. And another. Something huge was trying to climb out.

Behind them, a door swung inward and the pair fell backwards into warmth and firelight.

"Inside!"

An older woman stood by the open door, shooing them into the narrow entry. Dain wriggled backwards, still holding his son tightly. He looked up at her as she slammed the door shut.

"Try anything and I'll kill you both," she flashed a glimpse of a concealed dagger at her side. "I may look old, but I still got it where it counts."

"We don't want trouble," Dain replied, breathily.

"Well, trouble found you instead. Get away from the door."

Dain scrambled to his feet, lifting his son to his. Outside, they could hear the continued destruction of what remained of the road surface and a rising scream.

"I'm Dorothea."

"Dain. And this is Dilain."

The boy nodded but remained by his father's side.

"You fell into the right doorway, Dain."

"How so?" He turned from her and, limping slightly, made for a small slatted window. He parted the wooden slats.

Dot approached him. "You should probably get away from—"

Dain reeled backwards as the front wall of the terrace blew inward, scattering two shelves of books, decorative planters and several oil burners. The air was immediately filled with pulverised stone dust and the sounds of abject carnage and ruin.

Dorothea stood back, both arms raised. At her feet, Dain lay motionless. Dilain rubbed soot from his eyes; the oil burner lay on its side, spilling its contents onto a large brown woven carpet. Within moments, it was lit in tongues of golden flame.

"Pa!" Dilan wailed – but his voice was stifled by the bellowing cry of something enormous being held away by the old woman.

"Stay back!" She cried. From her forearms radiated an arc of luminous purple energy, pulsing in waves outward from her open palms. The oily beast roared; its distorted facial features were illuminated by the spell, revealing twin mouths and six inhuman eyes in a vee up its broad, creased forehead. Dil shrank backwards, his heart near to bursting from his chest.

The beast struck out with one of its four fists, bashing against the magical barrier. Each blow sent a burst of white particles backward toward Dorothea. The woman turned her head for a second and, spotting the growing flames, freed one arm.

With it, she fished around for something in her pocket, drew it up and spoke words that sounded foreign to Dilain's ears.

"Time for you to go, boy!"

She raised the object and pointed it toward Dil. At once, the floor fell away beneath him in a funny sensation of being pulled down into a warm sea; he felt his sense of up and down flip, like hanging upside down from a bench for too long, rolling down a hill, or doing a somersault while underwater. He tried to speak, but found he couldn't – nor could he *breathe*. All around him, the world stretched into strands of soft light in a tunnel that stretched beyond the point his eyes could discern.

Yet as suddenly as the panic of his situation set in, he found himself able to breathe again, gasping and sitting knees up, next to his father's curled body. They were on the carpeted runner in a grand hallway. The old woman was nowhere to be seen. The air still swirled with grey smoke and fine pulver.

"Who— what— Another one?"

A man's voice startled Dilain, who instinctively wriggled backwards towards his father. His small fingers touched far too much warm blood on Dain's exposed chest.

Dain's heart was racing. Time seemed to quicken into a series of rapid but disjointed moments. One minute, they were riding along – the next, nothing made much sense at all.

A young man, face mottled with curly beard growth, and wearing a brown linen tunic and long white robe, rushed to his side and crouched beside him.

"Boy! Where did you come from? Who sent you here? Was your father fighting under his Grace's banner?"

"I— the woman— I mean," Dil's head ached and his stomach churned. My father! He's a blacksmith from County Keep. He's… he's hurt—"

He felt blood rushing in his head. Sounds had become muffled and detached and his face felt simultaneously unbearably hot and frigid cold. Distantly, he felt firm hands beneath his arms, but his eyes closed anyway as he rolled sideways into unconsciousness.

~ ~ ~

Morning came upon him like the crashing of their carriage: violently and with complete disorientation. He awoke next to his father, on a makeshift platform in a long and extremely noisy room. His head ached badly and, as he raised it slowly, he realised his forehead was bandaged.

His father was pale, but his eyes were open.

"Boy." Dain's voice was weak. He raised a hand from his side and drew the blanket upward slightly from his chest. At some point, his shirt had been removed. Dain could see his father's torso was blackened with bruising. "It was a mistake to come here. But now I must ask… you… to…find—" His chest rattled a cough and he winced in agonised, raspy breath.

That was when Dil spotted his wayward brother passing in the hallway, flanked by two others.

"*Tyel!*" Dil rolled from his father's side, letting his papa's hand fall onto the platform limply.

He felt his cheeks redden as his eyes flushed with hot tears, keenly aware of how grateful he was to see Tyel again.

A nurse in a heavily soiled gown rushed by the platform carrying a wooden tray and several bloodied medical implements. The room was a cacophony of moaning. "Slow down, lad!" She scolded him. Dil pushed past her anyway.

Tyel was nearly toppled over by the force of Dilain's embrace. At first, he thought he might be under attack – his heart skipped a beat as he looked at his attacker.

"Dil?" That was all he could manage. A surge of feelings – confusion, delight and apprehension – filled him and he held his little brother for a long moment.

He pulled back, admiring Dil's face – the freckles and pointy chin, the shaggy sand-coloured hair that spilled over his forehead. He had a graze on his chin that looked fresh and powdery dust in his hair. He smelled of woodsmoke and sweat.

"*What are you doing here*, Dil?" He held him by his thin shoulders and bent to look at his face. He saw himself a few years removed in the boy who stared back, eyes teary.

"It's Pa. You need to come now!" Dil withdrew and, with a double-glance, noted the tall elfin girl by Tyel's side, and the large and well-armed man next to her. He'd rarely been in the presence of an elf before – and this one was striking to the point of being intimidating. He found himself staring, then forced himself to look away.

"Where? In there? Dil!" Dil snapped back to the moment and darted back into the makeshift ward. Tyel followed, Alyse in tow.

He spotted Dain immediately and, weaving around injured and dying soldiers and civilians, came to his side. His father lay on his back, eyes closed. His face was beaded with sweat, lips contorted in a grim expression of deep pain. He looked, to Tyel, like a man at the end of his days. His heart began to beat rapidly and, without even realising it, he was seeing his father through blurred and watery eyes.

"Father,' he took a deep breath. Dain's blue eyes opened and his face relaxed slightly, but his gaze remained slightly unfocussed.

"Tyel." He took his eldest son's hand in his own. Tyel bit back tears. He could feel the calluses on Dain's palms; the scar tissue of endless years of burns and cuts and wear. "Don't weep. Before me, I see a… man-grown," he winced. "And I am proud of him."

He doggedly attempted to lift himself up on his elbows, but did not succeed. "Tyel, Dilain. I do not… have long, I fear. Tyel, take Dil home. This battle is not yours to fight."

Tyel wiped his eyes with a dirtied sleeve. "I can't. I swore an oath to serve."

"Oaths are nothing to dead men, Tyel. Please. Look after your family now. Look after each other."

Dain squeezed his hand firmly. "Go home with Dil."

Deep conflict that lay dormant in him began to simmer once more. He looked at his father but his mind reeled at the horrors he had already faced – those strega that now were descending upon them on all sides at the hands of a madman. Now he would be bringing Dil into the fray and abandoning his father on what might be his death-bed. It wasn't right. It didn't feel right.

Tyel.

Alyse's songbird voice filled his mind. He turned at once towards the doorway where the princess and her Championate stood.

He's coming. He's coming for me.

Who? He responded, but his mind filled with the image of the thin, black veil of the Necromant's form. His skin crawled.

There came a great repeated thudding from somewhere deep within the citadel's underground. The foundations of the tower felt as if a great mace were being swung against it. The walls vibrated, dislodging dust; the plaster walls split like baked clay in the heat of the Sol.

The sudden shock of the reverberations was enough to dull the incessant groaning of those bed-bound souls in the infirmary.

"What's happening?" Dil tugged at his brother's sleeve.

"Go. Both of you," Dain urged.

Then, the screaming began — at first, far away, then approaching in the halls.

Tyel! Alyse screamed into his mind. His vision blurred with the intensity and he staggered sideways. HIs father's eyes watched his eldest stumble, unable to comprehend.

He's here!

~ ~ ~

The Capital Citadel was protected from most forms of magical intrusion — translocation and uninvited teleportation chiefly. Vimnir knew it was no use trying to conjure the gateway into the innermost heart of the Citadel.

He sensed, however, that his children had already worked their way into the one undefended, unprotected area of the Citadel: the bathing chambers deep beneath the tower. Here, in the underworks, the cool waters of the Westerling flowed and gathered for the High Inquisitor's personal use.

The waters, of course, were now deeply tainted by his hand, but still the river flowed unabated, spreading his infective liquids into the most important — yet vulnerable — seat in the land.

The High Inquisitor was dead. He could not see him, could not read him, could not feel him. He wanted to know *how* – though that too, felt connected to the Elstemer Princess, Alyse. Both the death of the High Inquisitor and the continued dogged existence of the powerful elf girl presented great opportunities. He intended very much to take advantage of this.

The dusklight illuminated his path ahead. Behind him, a steady stream of strega followed. Some took wing, others shambled and scurried along the ground, but more critically, many more poured through the canals below. All were dutifully obedient and strong – empowered and emboldened. Above ground, they numbered in the hundreds. Below, he needed just a few dozen well-placed and powerful creations.

With his staff and his telepathic command, he moved a contingency beneath the street, channelling them down the water canal as he moved above. Soon they would breach the Citadel's subterranean depths. Then the fun would begin in earnest.

Topside, the streets were lined with hastily blockaded barriers, windows and doors shuttered tight with a ramshackle crisscrossing of planks and crooked iron nails.

Vimnir could feel the life forces behind these thin walls, pinching their breath, cowering pitifully, watching between cracks as he passed them by. He would be their redeemer and their guardian of mercy now.

He stopped short at an intersection with a central market promenade. *This will do for now.*

The Necromant raised his staff high above his head; the casting stone emanated a white-hot glow as his voice was carried, amplified in all directions.

"Citizens of the Capital," he began. "Hear this."

His children circled around him, filling the streets, their claws clicking against cobblestone. Wet muscle slapped and slid against dripping tissue. Bone and cartilage and gristle and tissue. Dead but alive, mindless but manipulable. His beloved playthings.

"I am Overlord Vimnir Delcryth, of House Delcryth. Despite your people's prejudices and purgings against my kind, I will stem my assault for a time. I have harnessed these beasts – something your city guard could not manage. I can control them – a feat not even your finest spellcasters can perform."

With a wave of his staff, a rippling ring of emerald light burst from its tip.

"And I can end this siege completely if you so choose." He tapped the base of his staff on the ground. "I shall demonstrate."

With both hands wrapped around the twisted wood of his staff, he lowered the glowing stone down to the ground in front of him. Immediately, his brood force sat, as best they could, upon broken haunches and limbs, with pestilential innards now extruding outward. At once, his deathly minions ceased to move entirely. A sickening quiet fell across the city.

"All of you – you can live today. Or, if you choose – and it is *your* choice – you can forfeit your simple lives."

Shuttered eaves creaked open on sills that extended slightly over the elevated sidewalks.

"All I ask is that your Anointed Protectorates vacate the Citadel. If they do so, I shall spare your Capital – and your lives – from further torment."

He looked around expectantly, amused at his own generosity.

"Well, that's it. I shall await a reply from your designated representatives."

Vimnir, however, did not sit among his children. Instead, he turned his attention skyward to the swirling green, opaline umbrella of dusklight encapsulating the skyline all the way to the horizon. Something seemed off.

A thin breeze fluttered through his thin hair. Farther up the street, he could hear the wailing cry of an infant. Elsewhere, the rattling cough of an elderly man. All around him, the potent and unmistakable energy traces of fear and misery. Vimnir closed his eyes and reached out for the girl.

Her mental barriers were far stronger now; she had repelled him, much to his dismay, but still there remained an essence of connection linking them. An echo down a corridor; he needed only to call to her and his essence would traverse the plane between.

She pressed back against the thrust of his mind's intrusion.

He did not persist. He had tasted enough of her trace to know she was in the Citadel.

Vimnir relinquished and opened his eyes once more. The dusklight had definitely begun to take on a thinner, hazy quality. He pursed his lips and stood up.

Hooves beating against stone, rapidly approaching from the direction of the Northern Gate.

There would be no truce or negotiation, he assumed. It was, from the outset, a preposterous gesture to even presume discussions might take place at this stage. However, all he needed was a distraction that pulled attention away from the Capital Citadel and he would take it from them quickly and violently. Their preoccupation with city defence would leave them woefully exposed inside.

Here you come, he laughed to himself. *With a word, I will swallow your forces whole, and my family will grow yet larger.*

Overhead, a crackle of white-hot lightning shot across the dusklight's void in a resonant clap and was gone. He knew not what that meant, but it was, oddly, startling.

Perhaps there was a trace of life left in him after all.

~ ~ ~

Omanon and Dorothea's hasty retreat had been strategically perilous, not to mention overtly dangerous. The few dozen foot-soldiers who remained in the morning's wave had hastily fashioned barricades within the lanes and alleys to funnel the flow of the strega into their swords and spears. But with so many winged beasts flapping down upon them, the fight soon spread to rooftops and balconies. Bowmen were coming, Omanon promised, and casters from across the seas, he hoped, but to that he held his tongue.

However, the stables had not yet been breached, and a garrison of soldiers were rapidly outfitted and saddled. These reinforcements were among the last able bodies in the capital barracks.

When they re-emerged, they expected a frontal assault – and were braced for this. What they encountered was, instead, a disturbing stillness in the smoke-tinged air. The strega that had been steadily advancing had all but disappeared. The sky overhead still bore the sickly amethyst and emerald emersion that blanketed outward in waves from the mysterious portal high above.

"Where are they?" Dot looked at the Knight Commander.

"Sers!" A footsoldier approached from behind a heavy wooden barricade. An older man; his face was sooty and beard sodden with foulness. "They jus' stopped. Turned and fled!"

"Hold th' post," Omanon replied. "This in't over. Not nearly." He rode on.

Indeed, the streets were vacant, save for the still, lifeless corpses of both strega and their victims.

Two and thirty mounted soldiers in pairs, two spearmen between each pair of swords. The last mounts in the city stables. Omanon led the brigade, with Dorothea astride a black horse. Her Construct trundled heavily by her side, stone grinding against stone.

Omanon's grip tightened on the rein. "Do noth'n until I command. Do not draw, do not loose, do not attack. Is that clear?"

"Aye," his vanguard replied in unison, but the Knight Commander suspected that cowardice and the atavistic instinct to survive would drown out his commands. *Old men and young men and women and babes and beasts – we all meet the same end,* he knew. Then, a Necromant was all and none of these. Could he bring the sorcerer low? Could he be felled at all? He would soon find out. They all would.

He glanced sideways at Dot. Her lined face wore years much the rings on a tree. She was just as steadfast, too. A wonder of a woman and ability.

"Be ready, Dot."

She smiled and, letting her own rein fall to her lap, cupped her palms together as she had learned so many long years before. She closed her eyes and allowed plasmic energy to pool there, simmering like a pot above flames in preparation.

"I can see the first of them." Omanon fixed his eye on the square at the end of the central street's long and winding course. It would open into the trade square. There, in the open intersection, he saw endless forms crouched and still. Heads in singles, pairs, clusters. Twisted limbs and pale spines and blood-washed bone-forms that had no right place on this plane sat or crouched or lay in waiting.

Omanon pressed forward, but slowed to a canter. Then, he stopped.

"Comp'ny, hold." He raised his hand. He wouldn't risk a deluge descending on his men if he could but speak terms with this invader. "Dot, join me if you would."

She started forward without hesitation. "But my stone man comes with."

"O' course. And for the rest of yeh – if these bastards take flight, so do ye. Until then, *y'hold and watch*."

Not one soldier moved another step. Even their horses sensed the unnatural stillness and dared not jostle or adjust themselves restlessly as they ought.

There, at the heart of the square, on a raised dais like a small island in the formless sea of dead, was Vimnir Delcryth, a Necromant of both boldness and callousness.

The Necromant turned to greet them.

"Ah. At long last, a delegate approaches."

There is a pitsnake's tone in this man's dry voice, Omanon felt. It was amplified by some magical means, carried out across the heads of his blood creations.

Omanon rested his hand on the pommel of his sword. Carefully, he stepped past the first skeletal strega – so close, he could see the cloudy whites of its eyes. Flecks of black blood dotted its teeth, which were deformed and inhuman. Yet, not a single muscle twitched within it. Nor did any other creature. Not even their eyes tracked their slow and careful approach as they weaved between them. All of these death dealers were held in suspense. He hoped it would remain that way until opportunity presented itself.

Dot held a ball of potent energy in front of her. She felt like a child navigating an open field of desert thornbrush. Her senses were sharp but her training kept her steady; her nerves were reactive but her wits were calm.

"Come," Vimnir soothed. "You have naught to fear from me as we speak. My children are most obedient."

"An old man, is it? And an older woman! Practically relics of the Eld!" He clapped his bony hands together and slowly descended to meet them. His children parted swiftly as he raised his staff above him. "No matter. Wisdom comes with age, does it not?"

"I come with reinforcements," Omanon replied. "Make no mistake, death dealer. If anything's t' happen to us, great hells will fall on yeh. Be sure o' that."

Vimnir smiled warmly. "Then let us palaver and hope we can reach agreement. Expel your magical arms, dear woman."

Dot ignored this.

"Fine. As you will." He stepped forward.

"By now you know who I am and you have seen what I can do. Tell me, how is your High Inquisitor?"

"Dead 'n' gone," Omanon uttered.

"No love lost between you, I see."

"Aye, on this we agree." Omanon studied the man before him now. The measure of him. Thin; wire-tight build, in fact. Elf. Indiscernible age, but his eyes were young and full of wit, fire and menace. Arrogant.

"Let us see if we can find another accord, then."

Vimnir's eyes rolled up in their sockets for the briefest moment. "Omanon One-Eye." He peered down at him. Omanon One-Eye appeared nonplussed by this quick feat of mentalism. "And Dorothea of the Weir. Do you know what a weir does, my dear?"

"Holds back flood water."

"Too true." His small teeth flashed as he continued. "It prevents a flood." He took one more step toward them. "And, as you can see, so do I. Another thing we share in common."

"Look around you," he waved a hand in front of his thin torso. "This is the pressing surge I hold back. I too am a weir – and this is an act of mercy. I could, so easily, sweep you along in it. But that is entirely up to you now."

"A *mercy*, is it?" Omanon frowned. "Piss on those words. Your deeds show oth'rwise."

A burst of lightning, overhead, chased by a thunderclap. Then another. All three looked up at the sky.

"This is y'r doing?"

"The dusklight? Of course. A spectacular gift to my babies. A mask to hold back Sol for now and ever more."

Dusklight, Omanon repeated to himself. He'd not heard of such a thing – certainly not of this scale. Did it cover just the sky above the town like an upturned bowl? Or was the effect wider than this?

"I grow tired of your tedious twaddle, Necromant." Dot brushed him aside and, with a flick of her wrist, allowed the sphere of energy to dissipate in a twist of plasmic vapour. "What are your terms, then?"

Vimnir laughed at the old woman's zest. "Fine," he shrugged. "My terms are thus: I claim the Capital as mine, under the banner of House Delcryth. The throne, the citadel, the city streets – above and below – these you will surrender to me, most immediately, and the Anointed Protectorate will lay down their arms."

Vimnir tapped his cane once. The gem glowed softly. Far above, the sky rumbled long and low.

"The time of High Inquisitors and indulgence, of Circuitris and Sol, is ended."

Vimnir's smile broadened. He felt such power in those words, rising effortlessly from the root of him. They resonated in his ears, as if generations before him, a chorus of ancient elfkin, were calling his name in praise.

"And?" Omanon folded his arms.

"And? And *what*?" Vimnir barked. "That's it. Those are my terms. Should you agree to them, I shall see no more harm done to the denizens of this city. If you do not, I will open my weir upon you and wash you all away."

Omanon ran his hand through his beard and turned to Dot.

"What d'yeh think, love?"

"I think this man is crackers. And, I think it's starting to rain."

Vimnir, wrapped in his magnificent cloak, felt the droplets as they impacted heavily on his shoulders. But, there was something else to this. He glanced up. His eyes widened.

"That's not rain," Omanon replied, turning his attention sky-ward. "Look."

The Necromant unleashed a guttural howl. He knew what was happening. He knew why, too. The old man was right.

This was disintegrating plasma, punctured by Sol. The dusklight itself was dripping down upon them; thick, viscous, putrid drops of spent mag-ical energy, peppered by thin cones of light, golden shafts beaming down through the disintegrating shell of dusklight. The sky was a sieve of light bursting through the miasmic haze. The void was rapidly deteriorating.

All at once, there was an eruption of confusion and violence on all sides. Omanon drew his sword as gracefully as a painter might run brush against canvas. Around them, the intersection writhed into motion. Vimnir raised his staff against the incoming blade and repelled Omanon. With another swing, the old man sailed backwards. The stone Construct caught him, though the impact was nearly as painful as landing on the cobblestone street. Omanon felt his breath escape him as his eye bulged with exploding pain. He sucked inward, forcing his lungs to fill, and pushed away from the stone man.

The Construct followed him into the fray, tearing a path toward Dorothea. The caster was already beset by two strega.

Distant horse hooves clapped. "Vanguard," Omanon grunted – and, in the frantic downpour of gelatinous dusklight, he spun to see a sudden shaft of Sol light obliterate three undead forms in a gout of fire from above. Bedlam. His soldiers charged into the square. Shrieks of pain echoed from hollow chests and gaping maws as Vimnir's blood monsters scrambled to avoid pillars of cleansing light.

Horrified, Vimnir withdrew to the dais once more and began hastily drawing up a portal.

The surface street itself seemed to shift like ants pouring from a colony; corpses slick with plasma and blood scrambling over each other, up walls, into the sky, attacking each other, clawing at themselves as Sol turned them, limb and head and tail, into cinder. For the utter havoc and madness of it all, Omanon couldn't help but smile at Vimnir's misfortune.

His one good eye was fixed on that murderous Elf now.

Between Vimnir and Omanon, a dozen of his children stirred. With his free hand, he pointed toward the old man; dozens of dead eyes whipped toward the Knight Commander and set upon him.

Omanon raised his blade and twisted his burly torso, building as much momentum and power as he could. The bluesteel edge connected solidly with the shoulder of a two-headed strega and continued down through the rib cage. He felt each rib bone shatter in a rhythmic crunch. The two-headed strega lolled helplessly sideways, grasping at itself. He retracted his blade and, wincing at the pain in his own chest blowing hot fire down his side, he steadied himself for another attack.

The whooping cries of a rider charged between him and his next target, trampling through his path. The soldier's longsword cut a looping swathe down both sides of his horse, narrowly missing his Commander. Omanon reeled backwards as the steed crushed a strega under its hooves like dry tinder.

As his field of view cleared, wiping gunk from his eye, he saw the portal. "*Dot!*"

She raised her open palm. A rapid stream of stone jags burst, one by one, out of the surface of the road in a line toward the dais. Her construct slammed its forearm into a strega, sending it flailing haplessly backwards. She barely broke focus. The stone spines surged forward, tearing up the surface of the road, fracturing the steps and splintering the dais.

With one step, the Necromant was through and gone as a final spire of grey rock sheared up through the spot where the portal hovered.

Omanon, huffing in pain and exertion, made his way along the row of spikes. The Necromant was away – where to, he could only guess. Perhaps back to his residence in the North, perhaps farther. Or, maybe he was still within the town limits. No matter. The break-down of his twisted dusklight conjuration had clearly not been intended and could not have come at a better moment – or a worse one, from Vimnir's perspective.

Sol light beat down on the intersection. The day remained hazy although the dusklight void had all but shrunk to a dot in the sky. The magical aura was as fractured and dotted across the sky as a thawing lake in early spring. The Sol light was flushing out the strega and immolating them as they ran for cover anywhere it could be found.

Omanon's riders had advanced into the square just in time to flank the mass of blood monsters. Not all of them fared well, however. A horse and rider, caught between an emerging behemoth and two winged strega, found themselves upturned. A spear intended to keep these foul creatures at some distance instead ended up inside the horse. The rider was trampled.

Another rider had been grabbed by a flying beast and lifted clear from his mount high into the sky. Where he ended up, only he knew.

Omanon pinched the fuller of his blade, slicking black blood between his thumb and forefinger as he ran his fingertips down the length of it. Sol glinted in the oily remnants as he sheathed it.

From his back, he retrieved his Circuitris. He spoke the Eld language and the ring ignited. He would cleave anything that came close to him in a short-throw beam of radiance.

The sky continued to dribble in blobs of spent dusklight. Every surface was coated now in a thick film of muck.

"Dot, we lost 'im," Omanon shouted.

"I know it – not happy about it," she replied, magically levitating and repelling a wayward cobblestone with her hands outstretched. It rebounded with a dry crack against the skull of a slow, lumbering behemoth. The monstrosity was bleeding like a boar caught in a trap, groaning – and on fire. The Sol was guttering any kind of resistance far faster than swords, spears and magically-hurtled stones.

Once more, Omanon wiped his reddened face.

"Company! Form up!" He bellowed. The riders, still more than a dozen circling in wide loops, and yet more chasing their targets down lanes and streets, began to return to the intersection.

Omnanon charged toward the mouth of the southron-most street, carving an arc of blue and gold flame, a wall of pure heat and light, in front of him.

Three dwarven creatures – or, what Omanon presumed were dwarves once, ran flailing. *Those poor bastards.* He'd had many dealings with the Atheroni Dwarves, travelling to Yrkanh, the Mountain City, and beyond. In his youth, he'd trained in the frozen wastes of the Northern Sprawl of Havrohd and Minovarh. Never once had his hosts been anything less than utterly gracious and kind to him. With this Necromant rooted in the mountains, he feared they had been taken by surprise – possibly decimated.

He shook his head as the three creatures, all rotting muscle and hair and bloody sinew, ran into the sun and were at once set ablaze.

The battle, such as it was, appeared over for now. His vanguard had returned to the square, sodden and stained and alive. Dot's Construct trundled into the street. It was plastered in a brine of dusklight fluid and the foetid black blood of anything that came too near. On one arm sat Dot, a full body-height above the street, carried along propped against her Construct's shoulder like a sack of stone fruit.

"That was short-lived," she laughed. She commanded her Construct to kneel. Gingerly, she stepped down. Putting weight on her leg, she winced and immediately leaned back onto the support of her stone servant's arm.

"Aye– you okay?"

"Aye," she replied. Clearly though, she wasn't. She was bleeding heavily from somewhere at her waist and it was running down her leg.

"Perhaps best if I make haste back to the keep. I need a sew-up."

Omanon frowned. Like or not, they were both sailing into the sunset of their lives.

"Company," He addressed his gathered soldiers. "Eigh' o' yeh hold the streets. Six, search for injured. Bring 'em back to the Citadel if needs be. The rest o' yeh, divide up and set for the South, East 'n' West Gates. Hold for word. Go."

Dot looked terrible now; her construct lifted her up and began a rapid journey south towards the Citadel, Omanon beside them on a procured horseback. She was half-way up the concourse when her Construct slowed.

Then it stopped.

It set her down.

She lay still.

The Construct began to fall apart.

So did Omanon. He howled and held her close, for that was all he could do.

CHAPTER 29

TRINE

That had not gone entirely to plan.

The portal crackled and dissolved in a waft of lavender haze as Vimnir's eyes adjusted to the scene unfolding around him. He would have to adjust his strategy, and quickly.

Teleportation suppression existed within the confines of the citadel perimeter, he knew, but the waterway feeding into the subchamber bathhouse remained the soft, exposed underbelly at the heart of the city. His most powerful creations had been fed into it; their infective essence had removed the porcine daughter of the late High Inquisitor, which was unforeseen but not unfortunate. But it did serve to prove that the waterway remained overlooked by virtually all.

Fools, all. But then, so am I, evidently. There is so much I yearn to know.

His spell, adapted as it was from his master's instruction, had failed most spectacularly. Despite Lyssy's sacrifice, he had feared the quality of the blood had been low. It had held for a time and, if nothing else, it had proven that the spell might be resurrected later – if he could recall the precise steps and incantations. The page was now little more than the same ash that his children had become in the streets above. This result was not a trifling matter. The disintegration of the dusklight had rained its remains down upon the land. There was no telling what consequences this might cause in the land around the Capital. Within that unknown, there may be further opportunities.

Great change does not come easily. In the din, he clenched his jaw. *Or without high cost.* He would return to that potential later. For now, he had other paths to the same end.

Vimnir stepped through the sewer channel and looked out at the crushed and blown-out remains of the wall that once held an iron grate that fed fresh water into the bathhouse. Beyond, where once a series of arches supported a low, curved and hand-tiled roof, the ceiling had come crashing down.

Hazy illumination from the floors above filled the chamber. His minions had been eager to leave the damp and dark to feast and fester, he knew. Good. Their hunger would fuel their single-minded drive to feed.

He peered up through the gaping hole in the ceiling. Far above, he could hear the sounds of further struggle and destruction. It did not deter him. If anything, he was eager to see this beautiful tribute to excess brought low.

The day had not been a complete loss, then. He had impregnated the Citadel. Now he would come for his throne and take it by force, if that was how it had to be. He still had many and more tricks to employ.

Vimnir took the stairs upward.

~ ~ ~

The wall of ice barely slowed the behemoth's approach. Sword drawn, Tyel watched helplessly as the behemoth burst through Alyse's barricade, a valiant but futile attempt to keep whatever was out there in the halls from entering the infirmary.

The Sacred Championate was on the beast immediately, his Circuitris already aflame. Alyse grabbed Tyel's free hand.

"This will be a massacre. He's here. He's here for me, I know it."

"I'll die before he takes you," Tyel blurted — and, in speaking those words, he felt the tempting fingers of fate wrapping around his heart.

"That's what I fear, Tyel." In her burning gaze, he could feel her deep forlorn.

"You – and your brother – take your father and go. Climb out the window and make for the docks."

"Go, boy!" The Championate shouted back at him. "I'll keep her safe."

He was on the beast now. The monstrosity was easily the height of two men and as wide as four, conjoined unnaturally into rotten stalks of torsos and warped, disfigured limbs. Its ribs burst from its chest like bramble thorns, and, grotesquely, the three heads shared just one broken, split mouth that spouted a guttural blend of groaning and something akin to a baby's babble. Across its forehead, dead eyes sat like almonds of smoky quartz embedded in a demonic diadem of veiny flesh.

Alyse's hands were raised once more; the shattered crystals of ice were already accumulating in front of her.

Dilain was already propping his father's left shoulder up. Tyel sheathed his blade and positioned himself beneath the right. His father struggled to lift his head.

The elfkin let fly with a shard-sphere of ice; this time, as they had in the High Inquisitor's chambers, daggers of ice planted themselves in the exposed flesh of the behemoth. It reeled as its chest was peppered with dozens of shards of crystalline ice.

The Sacred Championate cleaved the curve of the Circuitris downward into one limb, withdrew, and took another swipe. A chunk of burning tissue fell to the floor, followed by the twitching, clutching arm it came from.

At least the building isn't aflame this time, he mused darkly. He would keep a firm grip on the blade too.

It charged at him. He pushed Alyse sideways, sending her towards the side wall as the brunt of its attack knocked him backwards. He could feel the bone spines crushing and splitting against his armour, but even with the weight behind it, it merely repelled him sideways.

Alyse, momentarily stunned by her sworn protector's deflecting blow, staggered to her feet. Her arm was bleeding. She ran a finger along it and the wound turned to crimson frost.

The behemoth raised another twisted, muscular limb and brought it crashing down on the body of a soldier as she lay helpless and unconscious. Again, and again. Another and another. It spun around as the Championate crisscrossed its backside with burning serration. Blind with indiscriminate rage, the blood creature threw punches and blows at anything within its radius now. The room was in disarray. Bodies spilled from tables; crippled figures crawled along the ground toward any sort of cover they could find. The behemoth crushed them under foot like ripe grapes in a press.

Heavy footfalls in the hall and the beating of fists against the wall. Within moments, the plaster and stone gave out completely, showering the room in a rain of white powder.

The Championate's eyes widened. His jaw dropped.

The room was flooded with strega. There, behind them, a figure clad in black.

Strega poured into the room; a flow of reanimated corpses – some wiry and fast, others slow and dumb – all of them strong. They clamoured through the blown-out hole in the wall, climbing across tables, spilling them sideways, occupying themselves on this found-feast of helpless victims. Blood lashed their mouths and hands, spilling and gurgling streams onto the floor.

The Championate came for Alyse, diving on top of her, keeping her from immediate harm. She instinctively curled sideways.

"Tyel!" Dil was stumbling, pulling at their father who had spilled onto the floor now. "He's— too heavy! I can't hold him up!"

"We just… have to make it to the window," Tyel clenched his jaw tight and, with a heave, he dragged his father sideways through broken brick, stone and tumbled, shattered tables. Dain groaned. Blood was spreading across his stomach.

"S—stop," he rasped. "Leave me."

Dilain was openly weeping. His small chest was rising and falling with panic and exertion.

"Girl!"

The death voice. A black tone of miserable quality. Tyel knew it immediately.

"*Cease*, my children," the voice spat.

Immediately, all movement ceased. Somewhere, a metal pan fell to the floor with a reverberant clatter.

The Necromant traipsed into the room as casually as a man on a summer frolic in the meadows. His obedient strega were still as black marble statues.

"Girl! Come out, come out! Spare yourselves more loss."

Tyel watched, barely aware that his forehead had begun to bleed. All sensations seemed so distant now. The air in the room stank of filth and blood and apart from the sounds of the Necromant's voice, all he could hear was the beating of his own heart and the rush of his own blood in his head.

The Sacred Championate held Alyse down, cupping her beneath his large frame, carefully – almost paternally. He looked at her; their faces so close that he could feel her small, panicked breaths on his cheek.

"*Don't*," he murmured. Slowly, he pressed a hand to her chest and held it there for just a moment. Then, with a deep breath, he found his feet and met the Necromant's eyes from across the hell-spun room.

"Necromant." Isidyr took a step forward, raising the Circuitris in front of him.

"Ah. Championate. Dutiful to the end. Ever the puppet of the Magisterium." Vimnir revealed his awful grin. "How many of my kind met their end at your blade?"

"Only those that deserved it, deathspeaker." He took another step forward. "You'll lay with them shortly." He raised the ring above his head, wordlessly mouthing the language of the ancient Trinic Arts.

The ring hummed. A golden arc of light formed around his body, spreading a film of honey-hued luminescence down his waist and legs to his feet.

"But does the girl know your true allegiance?"

The Championate hurtled forward. The Circuitris split the air in a fan of flame.

"*Please*." Vimnir raised his staff and waved it sideways. His staff pulsed with a spiralling jet of purple-black energy. The Championate skidded to a halt, knocking a crouching strega sideways and returning Vimnir's gesture with an arc of Sol light that fanned outward in a rippling wave. The space between them ignited in a crackling vapour of plasmic discharge as their magic collided. Flames of light and dark clashed and repelled, sending a sheet of kaleidoscopic fire outwards.

On the ground, laying low, Tyel held a hand to Dil's mouth. He began to protest, but Tyel shook his head. He shot his eyes down at his father, then back at his brother. The message was clear; Dil lay across his father's chest protectively – or perhaps seeking that protection himself.

He took one last look at his family. He could do this. He could do this one thing, of all things, and end this. He had to try.

The ground was covered in debris. Broken pottery, shards of glass, stone, bloody garments and the pulverised and indiscernible remains of the late residents of the Capital. Around him, strega perched, frozen in place. Their dead eyes watched him as he slowly crawled past, holding his breath and hoping against reason that whatever spell by which they were constrained would hold out.

The air was thick with the stench of wood ash, burning hair and rotting flesh – depressingly, a combination of scents with which he had become all too familiar. There was another element in the miasma as well – as if latent magical discharge was burning the very vapour around it. It emanated distinctly from the mass of flaming plasma that lit the space between the Sacred

Championate and the Necromant.

Vimnir's focus was fixed in front of him, as he stroked one of his terrible creations. Tyel rounded an overturned table, avoiding eye contact with yet another strega.

Slowly, Tyel drew his short blade from its scabbard, feeling every miniscule nick and abrasion as the edge crept across the boiled leather sheath. When this was over, he thought, he would find a whetstone and work the edge until it was honed once more. Then he would stow the weapon for good and leave it for his offspring to ponder one day.

Fully exposed, the weight now felt greater than it ever had before.

A hand. Around his ankle.

Branson suppressed a yelp and whipped his blade towards it. He found an elderly woman, face bloodied, holding him and whimpering.

"Please…" her voice was as worn and pained as the rest of her appearance.

His heart broke for her, but he tried to quiet her down with motions. She just kept pulling at him.

"Shh! Stop!" He waved a hand at her, pleading.

Then a sensation he'd never experienced before came over him. A lightness. He felt himself lifted off the soiled ground, his cut knees leaving the floor behind as his entire body was lifted into the air.

"   B   o   y   .   "

Vimnir was facing him now. With his spare arm extended, he raised Tyel up to eye-level. Suddenly, that outstretched hand, fingers fanned and pointed towards him, clenched into a nobbly ball. With a violent jerk, Tyel was swept towards the Necromant, his toetips dragging slickly through broken detritus.

He could feel invisible hands clenching his waist and neck. Cuffs of frigid energy. Desperately, with his free hand, Tyel grasped at nothing — trying to pry at his throat. Vimnir had cut off his breath. The more he thrashed, the tighter the grip became.

"Did you think I couldn't see you there, boy? And, what, you would strike at me from behind like a coward? Pathetic."

Tyel felt his fingers involuntarily release the short sword. It fell to the floor with a rounded clank.

"Tyel!"

His eyes shot towards the far end of the room. Alyse was on her feet now, just behind the Championate.

"Cease, or I'll end him," Vimnir bellowed. "Know it."

Isidyr grunted. His protective field was diminishing and now the radiant heat of the Necromant's blackfire magic was scalding him. Even without consideration for Tyel's predicament, he could no longer maintain his defence.

He lowered the Circuitris, shifting his stance. Vimnir's energetic cast blew past his frame, narrowly missing Alyse behind him.

The Elfkin began to move towards him. "I know you're here for me. Let him live."

"Why? He is worthless."

"You're wrong." Her eyes were aflame.

"Do you so loathe your own kind, girl?" Vimnir's eyes pierced deeply into her, then wrenched Tyel between them. Tyel's eyes were closed. His head hung limply; his bruised, bleeding face had taken on the hue of a boiled beet.

Vimnir smiled.

"Release him! You're killing him!" Hot tears pricked at the edges of her eyes.

Deep in Alyse's mind, in the tender and vulnerable core of her id, she felt his familiar dark fingers prying at her. Pressing sore spots so private and painful that she felt utterly violated and repulsed. Somehow, he still had a connection with her. She had to fight this.

"I know how you have been exploited, dear one, at the hands of these men. You were a slave here, when you are so far above them all."

With a flex of his fingers, Vimnir let Tyel fall limply to his feet.

"Here. Here is where they belong, Alyse. This is where humans should be." He looked at her pitifully. "Look well. See how they cower and crumple. They are deceitful and weak, and in the end, they will fall at our feet."

Tyel lay still. The Championate circled between them, shifting side-step along the wall. Tyel, for his faults, had the right idea. If Alyse could keep him preoccupied…

"And you, a daughter of the usurper House Elsteme. A ruler you could be, Alyse. A ruler I can make you. Elsteme in the South – and, together, Elsteme-Delcryth in the North."

Vimnir lowered his arms. He could sense something within her beginning to shift, as if she stood upon loose slate at the edge of a vast precipice. All she required was a gentle push. One final manipulation.

"We can unify a broken land, Alyse. Elves were the unquestioned rulers of this world, once. And can be again. *Must* be. These—" He cast a roving look across the faces of his strega spawn. "These are a means to that end. Don't you see? The men and women of these lands are blight far worse than my children."

He twisted his staff and tapped the base against the ground. At once, his strega began to disintegrate before them – flesh sloughing from bone, vile fluid spilling from the ears and eyes and mouths of confused and suddenly too-human faces. They were being unborn – but conscious of this. Alyse exchanged glances with Isidyr, horrified.

"I can make and unmake the creatures at will – but I cannot control the corrupt and corrupting spread of humans."

He lowered his staff – then, after a step, pointed it towards The Championate. He cocked his head. "No further. You. Stay put, now."

The Championate had no intentions of complying. He reached behind his back, feeling for the handle of his dagger. It pulled smoothly.

Alyse's head swam with conflicting thoughts. She pressed him outwards, in the only way she knew how, towards the surface of her mind. He clung to her.

Part of her yearned for this. A small, loathsome element. She knew her name carried power, and that her vassalage had been a grave injustice. The Grand High Inquisitor. His bulbous face littered with broken veins and streaks of sweat. His grunting, awful thrusting. Smothering and pathetic. The disturbing flagellation and tearful remorse. Those thoughts never left her – they remained buried so shallowly, so inadequately. She fought against the rising sensation of nausea and helplessness – unable to speak, unable to fight back; only an innate desire to be far from here and safe among her own people again.

She crept toward him, drawn towards his outstretched hand.

"Alyse Elsteme, join me at my table. You need never be abused again."

The Championate whispered three words, nodding towards Tyel. Curled, Tyel stirred, coughing. He rolled onto his back, clutching his throat, gasping for air.

Alyse's azurine eyes were wide and transfixed, burning and distant.

I have her, Vimnir cooed to himself.

She raised her own hand to meet his.

Her slender fingers clutched Vimnir's, weaving them together. Then, quick as a snake bite, she whipped her other hand around the Necromant's staff. She prayed to herself, to the magical ether, The Trine, the powers behind all things – whatever and whomever would hear her small inner voice – that this would work.

Vimnir reeled, but Alyse held tight.

A void of golden, flaxen brilliance, perfectly round, began to form beneath her feet.

She looked down at Tyel; he lived – he would continue to, she knew.

He reached up for her.

"I'm sorry, Tyel. Thank you."

The void expanded in a crackling flash of honey-golden light as The Championate chose his moment.

The dagger cut the air across the room. Alyse drew in close to Vimnir, refusing to relinquish the staff.

The blade found purchase.

Alyse Elsteme, her mouth open in a gasp of pain and surprise, stumbled forward into Vimnir Delcryth. A shaft of frozen wind pulled them downward into the portal as the floor dropped away beneath them. A small, swirling squall of ice-blasted air erupted outward where they once stood; delicate flakes of pristine snow filled the room, too perfect for the awfulness within it, flitted to the floor, before the golden portal shrank shut and the momentary tempest ended as abruptly as it had begun.

They were gone.

Chapter 30

ARMADA

"**S**he moved."

Isidyr collapsed to his knees in pool of black and crimson decomposition. His face crumpled into his hand, shadowed beneath his long blonde hair.

Tyel, broken and bleeding, felt his world upturn. Through bleary eyes, he saw the portal open and Alyse fall.

"What?" His voice was weak and croakingly rasped from the prolonged strangulation.

Isidyr looked up, shattered. "I had him and she *moved*. She's… gone."

Tyel crawled towards the spot where Alyse and the Necromant had stood only a moment before, running his hand through rapidly melting flakes of snow. It was all a blur. His last recollection was readying to strike Vimnir down, then something – something stopped him. He came to, gasping for air, only to see Alyse embracing Vimnir. A portal. They fell.

"I failed her. I've never failed so dismally as this before in my long life. Not nearly." Isidyr couldn't bring himself to meet Tyel's eyes.

Tyel slowly sat upright.

The Championate said nothing for a moment. He looked down at his lap. "I don't know how she raised that portal. It was unlike any I've seen before – and this space is protected from portal conjurations——-”

"Tyel!" Dilain's thin, weepy voice carried across the room. His face craned from behind a broken table top.

"Dil!" He scrambled to his feet, slipping in the muck and mire. The room looked as if a powerful river of blood and entrails had fed directly into it. Everything was awash in befoulment.

He found Dil still holding their father. He knelt down next to his brother.

"Are you hurt?" Tyel examined him, but Dilain looked down distractedly.

"I tried to keep him awake but he…" Dilain trailed off in a deep, shuddering breath that gave way to tears. Tyel held him there, like that, his father's head resting in Dil's lap, eyes closed gently, pale and serene. He looked, as was said, like a man sleeping, yet the vessel was now clearly empty. "He's gone, Ty."

"I know, Dil. I know. You did so well." And he found himself crying too. Powerful, shuddering sobs racked him. He wept for Ser Filip, he wept for his horse, Mancer. He wept for his sister and now his Father and he wept for Alyse.

Alyse. It was coming back to him now.

She fell forward into Vimnir's arms, but something else happened too.

A dagger. The Sacred Championate had thrown a dagger.

Now he understood what Isidyr meant. Tyel's stomach sank. He assumed Isidyr was upset with himself that he the Necromant had seemingly escaped with Alyse; that Alyse had shifted with him into that strange portal. But now… now there was another horrific possibility. Had he struck her by mistake?

He looked up from his father, pulling away from Dil. The Championate was standing over them. He crouched down.

"Oh Tyel. I'm sorry. Your father – I was able to bring you back, but he… he was too far gone. The light of the Sol God be on him and within him. We will bring him to a ring."

"No. My father held no Trinic beliefs." That was untrue – or, not fully true anyway. But he did not want Dilain to watch their father burn. "We'll lay him to rest back home, if you'll help us." He hoped he would. He also suspected that keeping the Championate close might lead them back to Alyse.

Isidyr considered this for a moment.

"And this young man is your brother?

"Aye. Dilain is his name," Tyel replied, holding his brother's hand.

"Dilain Branson," The Champion raised his chin with his thumb and forefinger. "You did more than anyone could ask to protect your father. You should know that and be proud. I am sure he was. Is. Of both of you."

"*Is.*" Tyel tripped on that word.

Dilain wiped snot from his nose with a sniff and rubbed it against his shirt. He didn't smile, but something about Isidyr's face had captivated him. Once he looked up, he found it hard to withdraw. Tyel thought it kind of him to say those things – though, his wording also puzzled him.

"Come," the man spoke softly. "I shall carry him forth for you."

Tyel stopped him short.

"About Alyse," he began.

"Tyel." The Championate took a breath and looked despondently at him. "I don't know if she lives. But in my actions, I may have done her grievous harm. I thereby broke my oath to her. All I can do is try to redeem myself – and her."

Isidyr placed a hand on his shoulder. "And if she is alive, we will find her."

Tyel nodded. An odd sensation came over him – not one of relief, but of reassurance. They stood up together, Tyel helping Dil to his feet. With one smooth motion, The Sacred Championate lifted their father and cradled him as a parent might a baby.

From out in the hall, a familiar voice interrupted them.

"Ye bleeding gods of Eld! *Look at the state of things!* What did we miss?"

~ ~ ~

After departing the Citadel in search of the Necromant, Brea and Dust-in-His-Eyes watched as a strange effect in the sky had overtaken the city, coating it in eerie green light. The light had dimmed while they were hastily foraging for supplies, but the full scale of the magical aura was not apparent until they made it out to the South Yard. This was clearly the work of the Necromant, Dusty assumed. He suggested the filtered Sol light might be aiding or even empowering his forces.

Given the unrelenting resistance they were facing, she certainly agreed. They did not find Vimnir, but they damned-sure found his progeny.

They were everywhere; the city's residents – those fortunate enough to be inside – barricaded themselves in. Those who dared to stay in the streets quickly found themselves ether mandatorily conscripted – meagre weapons thrust into cagey, nervous hands – or overwhelmed in a sea of blood monsters.

The off-nature light in the sky darkened the alleyways considerably, hiding deadly horrors.

True to her word, Alyse had managed to call down the force of her family's royal armada.

The South dockyards, with their rope-and-plank bridges and well-worn stone concourses were already swarming with House Elsteme soldiers. The dockyards were a short walk across the open trade markets, which, despite the chaos, appeared to still be conducting some business. Shop and stall owners steadfastly refused to leave their wares unattended, nor would they relinquish the day's catch. Those foolhardy enough to operate during this influx might come away with coin in their pockets for their troubles.

The fleet had arrived just in time to reinforce the Anointed Protectorate and the rapidly failing soldiers and conscripts. Those Elven landed forces, numbering six longships of at least two-by-one hundred hands, by her reckoning, had cruised into the bay and, via their long plankwalks, spilled into the sprawling trade yards.

Soon, they would fill the streets South to North, East to West.

She knew they would come for the throne in the absence of the High Inquisitor. There was an opportunity for House Elsteme to claim territory – why would they not? At one time, long ago, it had already been under their banner. She wondered if Elfking Thirandyse himself might not be onboard – or already disembarked.

"Alyse would surely thrill at this sight," Dusty noted. Dusty, a shank of lamb in hand, quickly found that a bellyful of wine and a plate of meat while under threat of death did nothing for one's digestion. After a brief respite beyond the South Gate, watching the Elstemeri soldiers press past them to the North – and those soldiers paying them no mind, the dwarf insisted on a small detour.

On a small barrel in an alleyway, he conjured a profoundly decadent meal and was determined to sup. Brea was achingly hungry, too – but, unlike the dwarf, she was on edge. She hurriedly ate what she could stomach.

As soon as she spied the Elstemeri fleet sailing into the South Gate dockyards, she knew she would be in a very different sort of danger now. Any agent of the ruling House would claim her skull. Her face, if not the precise nature of her dealings and deeds, was well-known. She was no friend to the House Elsteme – which she'd kept to herself, after finding out Alyse's true heritage.

Even with Dusty's reassurance that by now word of her demise would have spread due to the collection of her bounty, she knew better than to make dangerous assumptions. She would have to disguise herself somehow – but, for now, they would make for the Capital Citadel and she would try to line her pockets.

Then, something unexpected happened. The sky had begun to clear – raining thick, oily muck down upon the streets in disgusting mucosal blobs.

As soon as the Sol came flooding down on the streets, the sounds of inhuman shrieking and yelping issued from all directions. The crush of strega had seemingly vanished – suddenly replaced with decaying, malformed and steaming piles of corpus meat amidst the chaos and ruin they had inflicted upon the Capital.

The South Gate guards were, as before, not at their post; the few they had seen earlier had taken to horseback and were, then, trying to fell any undead monstrosity they could find. Brea wondered if that old man, Omanon, had managed to coordinate his soldiers – or if he survived at all.

Fight with us today and I'll do what I can't clear y'r name. He'd made a pledge of a sort, but would he stay true to his word? Or would those words travel to the grave with him?

Soon they were within the Citadel. It was eerily quiet – but surely House Elsteme reinforcements would soon take the Capital. The temptation to fill a sack was overwhelming – but secondary to the need to clear her name – if she could.

Dusty had, at some stage, purged. He looked green from overexertion. She laughed at the site of him, pouring with meat-sweats. He frowned and picked at a stray fleck of meat in his teeth as they peered into empty doorway after empty doorway.

There, down the central hallway, was a long streak of blood. The walls and whole segments of floor and ceiling had given way – or been brought in – by something. Brea leaped over a gaping chasm that plunged at least two flights down into the Citadel underworks. She pulled Dusty over as he sidled around the outskirts of the hole.

Whatever had happened here, they had just missed it.

"That's Branson," Dusty jabbed at Brea. "Listen."

It was a reunion of extraordinary mixed emotions among the carnage.

The Championate, holding the body of Dain Branson, related the outcome of their encounter to stony faces. Tyel stood holding his brother.

"Can you sense her, Tyel? I know you were close."

"No. Nothing."

Brea's entire demeanour had changed in the span of a few moments. Something about her was deeply wounded in knowing Alyse was effectively missing – and, wherever she was, she was with Vimnir, which made things infinitely worse.

~ ~ ~

Omanon carried Dot himself, though his arms shook and his legs trembled and he felt as though his exhaustion might just do him in there and then. In some ways, he wouldn't have minded so much.

He let the horse go; it would find its own way back to the stables. But this was something he felt he had to do himself.

"Oh, Dorothea," he murmured. Her face in death was as kindly and beautiful as in life. He would take her to the infirmary and ensure she was returned to ash. He'd never told her how fond he was of her. He wished he had. He hoped the other Battleblessed had fared better, but it was a distant thought now.

Omanon found himself among his remaining regimen in the North Gateyard at the foot of the Citadel.

At the sight of him, his soldiers rushed to his aid. With some hesitation, he allowed them to assist in transporting Dot up into the Citadel.

What he found beyond the threshold was a decimated interior – and he knew even before being told that the Necromant had made his way inside.

He must have come from below.

There, in the open reception that led to the main hallways, a very different sight lifted his spirits somewhat.

"Branson."

The boy, Branson – nay, man – and his vagabond crew. He was uneasy on his feet, but he hobbled toward them. The Elfkin girl, he noted, was not among them. In the arms of the Sacred Championate, however, was a face he was sad to recognise. Another casualty.

"Oh, my word." He came to Branson's side, looking down at Dil and connecting the relationship immediately. "Dain." He shook his head banefully. "I'm sorry for yeh loss, my lad. He was a tremendous man, Dain was."

"I'm sorry for yours." Tyel nodded towards Dot.

"Aye. Dot. Silly ol' bat, but I loved her. Believe it."

"She knew," the Championate replied.

Omanon betrayed a sad little smile. "From yer mouth to her ears, then. And what of Alyse Elsteme? And the Necromant?"

The Championate shook his head.

"He took her – or, rather, they somehow drew up a portal and they left. To where, we're not clear."

Tyel nodded. "But we'll find her."

"I trust yeh will, Tyel, for she's special beyon' words," the old man replied. Omanon frowned, his one eye closing for a moment as he pondered this new development. "But I think yeh know that. Tell her when yeh see her, won't yeh?"

Clearing his head, he coughed, puffed his chest and ambled toward Brea. "Ah. Th' sellsword lives, I see. And her dwarf."

"I do."

"*Her* dwarf? Excuse me. She's *my* sellsword."

"*Spell*sword." She fought the urge to roll her eyes.

"And I s'pose you'll be wantin' me to clear your name, then."

"If it so pleases you." Brea allowed herself an eyeroll.

"Well, aye. It does at that. Thank yeh both for staying and fighting. I'll sign the papers and send them far and wide. On m' word. I'll do it t'day."

Brea looked visibly relieved, which Dusty found highly amusing. "For a woman of ill repute and stony disposition, you're blushing."

She crossed her arms and turned away. "Best you crack on and do it, as Alyse's family are on our shores and they're not too happy with me. What's more, they may well be taking back this seat before Solset. If so, you might find yourself deposed."

The group turned to her, sharing a look of surprise.

"What? Did I fail to mention that? Well excuse me."

"If that's true—' Omanon started.

"It is," Brea insisted.

"Then they're none-too-likely to be happy that their Princess is missing. Nor that yeh let the Necromant escape wi' her, be that the case or not."

"It's not like that," Tyel protested.

"Course not. But I would leave now, all the same. If they came in through the South Docklands, I'd leave North. I'll go and greet their emissary. Per'aps the Elfking 'imself."

"*After* you clear my name!" Brea blurted.

"Mind your brass," Omanon squinted at her. "And don' make me change my mind, Solsetter."

Brea sniffed and waved him off.

Tyel turned to his companions. "We need to lay our father to rest. Isidyr, come with us to County Keep, near Feldstone Inlet. All of you are welcome there. Stay with us for now. We'll do what needs to be done after that."

Dusty smiled. "Will there be food?"

"You *just* ate, you pig. *He just ate!*" Brea threw a hand in the air in disgust and turned to walk away.

"Of course," Tyel replied. "Unless Dil emptied the storehouse while I was gone."

Dil, who until now, had been shying away from view, kicked him in the shin and followed after the Solsetter. She clapped him on the backside as he stomped past.

"Come then," Brea called back. "Let's go if we're going. I'd prefer to keep my head attached to my neck. House Elsteme may not agree."

Omanon smiled, warmly this time. He looked tired, but buoyed. "I'm proud 'o' yeh, lad. I know Dain would be too." He took Tyel around the shoulders and gave him a hug.

"There's a fine man in 'ere, Tyel. I see why she likes you."

"Now," Omanon started away, toward the South Hall. He gave one last look over his shoulder. "Go find your elf."

EPILOGUE

The Sacred Championate, without the slightest grumble or stumble, carried Dain Branson all the way to the North Gate as promised. The walk was long, but not without curiosities. Dilain, nearly as exhausted as his brother – in his mind, anyway, trundled on. To his great delight, they passed an upturned trolley of boiled sweets and jam rolls. Dil filled his knapsack without the slightest hesitation.

The city streets were already filling with residents emerging from their homes, stories on their lips of fearsome encounters and dark skies. The dusk-light's disintegration had left a pungent residue across most roofs – which, in addition to the incredible accumulation of dead and decomposing strega, meant the clean-up effort would be a monumental task.

Many other towns had been decimated, and by now, word had spread in the wake of the downflow of infected Westerling river system.

Tyel figured the city would need to find alternate means of procuring water – but, then, House Elsteme were desert-faring waterspinners. Their magic, which flowed through Alyse, allowed her to conjure drinking water. He had seen it – and much more. Water was their element. He suspected they might hold a solution.

It was a problem for another time and place. Tyel was glad to be leaving it all behind for now.

Beyond the city limits, along the Northern Road, Isidyr summoned a portal. One by one, they entered. At last, the Sacred Championate stepped through, bearing Dain, on behalf of his children, on one last journey home.

~ ~ ~

The cool afternoon breeze kept Tyel refreshed as he and his brother dug at the soft, loamy earth beneath the sweetapple tree on the hill near their home. The shovels bore the Branson-"B". Their father's work in life was now at an end. It seemed fitting his fine implements would carry him into the next.

The view to Feldstone Inlet and beyond was glistening and glorious as it ever was, in protest to the melancholic occasion. His mother watched her two sons bury their father wordlessly, but her thoughts were of her late daughter, as they ever were. She turned and left them there, as they had left her behind in her sorrow.

Isidyr laid Dain gently in the plot, a few feet down. Tyel rested a shovel down with him.

He stood there for a moment. The shovel seemed an inadequate offering.

Dust-in-His-Eyes, watching closely, felt a subtle urge. He walked up the hill, leaving Brea at the base, and joined Tyel and Dilain.

At his side, he flipped open his now heavily-stained apothecary satchel and reached inside.

"Here."

He took Tyel's hand, faced the palm upward, and deposited two small fangs.

"Remember these?" He looked up at Tyel through his cracked lenses.

He would never forget, for as long as he lived. He held one up, looking at it closely.

"How it started."

Slowly, Tyel walked to the edge of his father's resting place and tipped his hand over, letting the two cream-coloured strega teeth fall into the grave.

"Let this be the end."

~ ~ ~

Tyel's brow was coated in blood – mostly, but not entirely, his own. He examined his reflection thoughtfully in the still pool of water in the weathered barrel by the downpipe around the back of the workshop. The face that stared back looked as worn down as the barrel's surface. Another face arose, reflected next to his own.

"What are you looking at?"

"Nothing. Myself."

He scooped up a handful of the cool liquid and tipped it against his forehead. It ran down his face, feeling the crust of blood slough off into the basin, and the sting of a slowly healing cut somewhere in his hairline.

Dilain peered in beside his brother. All he saw was greywater. He shrugged and made for the kitchen, where Dusty had already taken up residence.

He peered down once more, just to be sure.

"Alyse," he whispered.

ACKNOWLEDGEMENTS

Much like *Dusklight Falling*, the path ahead is rarely straightforward – and even when you think you can see the lay of the land, life is full of surprise detours. It's always better to go on these kinds of trips with people you love and trust.

To Mathew Weiss, who started Melbourne Interactive Studios with the lofty goal of birthing games and worlds that he wanted to see realized. He took on a plucky writer to tend to one of those concepts: a horror-survival video game that drew on Eastern European vampire lore and dystopian ruined villages – and then set that writer loose. What started as blog entries turned into a novella, then into a novel – and eventually grew into this deformed, three-headed behemoth you are reading. Thank you, Mat, for paying me to write a book, reading it with me week by week throughout the process, providing insightful feedback and logic and criticism – all the elements that transform a bloody mess into neatly sutured order. You are a brave, generous person and this book is here because of you. I hope it gives life to that original vision, does it some form of justice and extends far beyond it as well.

To the team at MIS, thank you for the passion in which you took on this project during pre-production and keeping us focused on the core pillars of grit, horror and survival. Big thanks to the sensational cover art by Lachlan Page, for capturing the mood so perfectly and giving our Sacred Championate his moment.

To my friend, colleague and fellow movie devourer, Anthony O'Connor – your support and advice on how to navigate the murky waters of book publishing was invaluable. Please check out his novels, *Straya* and *Emma After*, which are naturally far superior to mine.

To my father, Rick, for providing me with the first full edit, along with comprehensive notes, long phone calls and the kind of encouragement that can only come from a parent who genuinely cares about their kid's dream. You are very much woven into the pages here for all-time. Thanks for keeping our childhoods full of pulpy fantasy, science fiction and horror. I saw my future when I was six and that was it. Thank you. I love you.

To Catherine, my mother, for raising two nerdy boys with love and encouragement and only minimal bafflement at how both of us could make a living with video games and words. Yet, you always let us follow our passions to whatever end – and here we are, doing our things with video games and words. I hope you like the book! Either way, it's also partially your fault it exists. Thank you. I love you.

To Mikaela, my best friend and partner, creative collaborator and soulmate. I dragged you through years of creative ups and downs, long-dark-nights-of-the-soul, belt-cinching poverty that comes with working on passion projects at the expense of money-making ones, many moments of self-doubt, disillusion, exhaustion, elation and eventually indifference. But you insisted I had something here, and now it's out there for all to see. I owe you most of all, because you kept me on the rails, found my sore spots and protected them. Your encouragement means everything. Thank you. I love you.

And finally, to you, the reader. Thank you for letting me take you on a journey.

See you for the next one.

PK

ABOUT THE AUTHOR

Patch Kolan is a celebrated author, screenwriter, film critic and journalist currently based in Australia. Over the past 20 years of his career, he has built an international reputation as a storyteller across a diverse range of mediums. His work has appeared on IGN.com, Rotten Tomatoes and in video games from PlaySide Studios and others.